"This is Captain James Kirk of the *U.S.S. Sacagawea*.

"If you do not cease this unprovoked attack, we will be forced to destroy you. Please respond so we can discuss this like honorable men."

That did it. A snarling Klingon face, eyes flashing fiercely beneath bony forehead ridges, appeared on the viewer. *"I am Grnar, commander of the* Vrot. *You speak of honor, boy? Then do not begin with the lie of claiming manhood. I see the intelligence reports are true—Starfleet has assigned a mere child to guard its border."*

Kirk smiled. "The human warlord Alexander of Macedon had built an empire across three continents by my age. Maybe Klingons are just late bloomers."

"Then show me your empire, boy. You are but a whelp! Starfleet has lost so many of its best captains to my valiant brothers that they must now give their ships to babies still wet with the blood of their mothers' wombs."

Kirk stepped forward alongside Khorasani's station to look the Klingon in the eye. "I did not . . . just hear you talk about my mother."

What Grnar went on to say about Kirk's mother was unrepeatable. What Kirk said in return about Grnar's mother was inadvisable. The upshot was that the *Sacagawea* was under heavy fire moments later and Khorasani was firing back with full phasers.

Lieutenant Commander Egdor sidled up to Kirk as the latter studied the enemy ship's trajectory on the viewscreen. "It was unwise to make him angry, Captain."

Kirk stared. *"Make* him angry? Isn't that a Klingon's default state?"

STAR TREK®

THE ORIGINAL SERIES

THE CAPTAIN'S OATH

Christopher L. Bennett

Based on *Star Trek*
created by Gene Roddenberry

G

GALLERY BOOKS

New York London Toronto Sydney New Delhi Orpheus City

G

Gallery Books
An Imprint of Simon & Schuster, Inc.
1230 Avenue of the Americas
New York, NY 10020

First Gallery Books trade paperback edition May 2019

GALLERY BOOKS and colophon are trademarks of Simon & Schuster, Inc.

For information about special discounts for bulk purchases, please contact Simon & Schuster Special Sales at 1-866-506-1949 or business@simonandschuster.com.

The Simon & Schuster Speakers Bureau can bring authors to your live event. For more information or to book an event, contact the Simon & Schuster Speakers Bureau at 1-866-248-3049 or visit our website at www.simonspeakers.com.

Manufactured in the United States of America

10   9   8   7   6   5   4   3   2   1

Library of Congress Cataloging-in-Publication Data

Names: Bennett, Christopher L., author.
Title: Star Trek: the original series : The captain's oath / Christopher L. Bennett.
Other titles: Captain's oath
Description: First Gallery Books trade paperback edition. | New York : Gallery Books, 2019. | "Based on Star Trek created by Gene Roddenberry." | Identifiers: LCCN 2018055862 (print) | LCCN 2018059210 (ebook) | ISBN 9781982113308 (ebook) | ISBN 9781982113292 | ISBN 9781982113292 (trade paperback) | ISBN 9781982113308 (ebook)
Subjects: LCSH: Interplanetary voyages—Fiction. | Extraterrestrial beings— Fiction. | Space warfare—Fiction. | Star Trek fiction.
Classification: LCC PS3602.E66447 (ebook) | LCC PS3602.E66447 C37 2019 (print) | DDC 813/.6—dc23
LC record available at https://lccn.loc.gov/2018055862

ISBN 978-1-9821-1329-2
ISBN 978-1-9821-1330-8 (ebook)

To Clarence,
for help when I needed it.

I, [name], having been appointed an officer in the United Federation of Planets as indicated in the grade of captain, do solemnly swear to uphold the regulations of the United Federation Starfleet as well as the laws of the United Federation of Planets: to represent the highest ideals for which they stand, to become an ambassador of peace and goodwill, to protect the security of the Federation and its member worlds, and to offer aid to any and all beings that request it.

—Starfleet Oath of Service

ENTERPRISE
2265

Prologue

U.S.S. *Enterprise* NCC-1701

And all I ask is a tall ship and a star to steer her by . . .

The words of John Masefield's poem resonated in James Kirk's mind as he reached out to touch the *Enterprise*'s command chair. He stared at it for a while, drinking it in. It wasn't that different from his chair aboard the *Sacagawea*, nor was its view of the bridge at whose center it sat. But this chair came with much greater power and responsibility. The power of a *Constitution*-class vessel, one of Starfleet's capital ships—the mightiest and most advanced ships of the line. The responsibility for the lives of the 430 people aboard her, and for the security and prestige of the entire United Federation of Planets as he represented it on the vanguard of Starfleet's exploration of the final frontier.

Yet in this moment, those concerns receded in his mind. As he gazed at the command chair, all he could think of was the ship. He had developed a deep appreciation for the *Constitution* class years ago when he had cut his teeth aboard the *Farragut*, and many of his formative experiences as a junior officer had been aboard other ships of the class. He had always seen great beauty in their clean, elegant proportions. Where others saw nothing but functional straight lines and circles, Kirk saw Pegasus in flight—the skin gleaming white, the dorsal connector evoking the neck of a horse with head held high, the nacelle struts angled like wings poised for a forceful downstroke. But there was something special about the *Enterprise*, something that made her even more beautiful to behold, more compelling to contemplate. Perhaps it was the fact that she had been one of the first vessels of the class, with greater character than her more standardized successors. Perhaps it was the history of her achievements under captains of the caliber of Robert April and Christopher Pike.

Or perhaps it was simply that the *Enterprise* was *his* now. It had been several hours since he and Chris Pike had stood before the assembled crew in the hangar deck, where Pike had raised his data slate and recited his official orders: "*From Starfleet Headquarters, Office of the Admiralty, to Captain Christopher Pike, commanding officer U.S.S.* Enterprise, *Stardate 1278.4. You are hereby requested and required to relinquish command of your vessel to Captain James Kirk, commanding officer U.S.S.* Sacagawea, *as of this date. Signed, Admiral Robert L. Comsol, Starfleet Command.*'" At which point Kirk had received the ship's computer command codes from Pike and delivered his brief response: *"I relieve you, sir."* With those four small words, he had become captain of the *Enterprise*, and he knew his life had changed in ways he had not yet begun to discover.

Pike had disembarked promptly at Starbase 11, saying he didn't want to get in Kirk's way on his first day. He had already said what he needed to say to Kirk during their tour of the ship before the ceremony. That tour had included the bridge, of course, but Kirk had not presumed to take the command chair while it still belonged to Pike. In the hours since, Kirk had been too busy familiarizing himself with his new ship and crew and readying the vessel for departure. It wasn't until now, in the lull before setting out for space, that he had the luxury to contemplate the command chair for a moment before finally taking his seat astride Pegasus.

No, Kirk told himself. *Don't be pretentious. You're an officer, not a poet. Just do the job Starfleet has assigned you.* It had been his drive and discipline, he reminded himself, that had gotten him to this point. By taking his work seriously, by committing himself passionately to his duties and goals, by setting aside the distractions of a personal life, he had become the youngest person ever to earn a starship command when he had taken over the *Sacagawea* nearly four years ago. Now he was the youngest person ever to command a *Constitution*-class starship, and one of a very few to earn one as his second command. He hadn't accomplished that by indulging his romantic side. He was no mythic hero—just a man with a duty.

"Is there something wrong with your chair, Captain Kirk?"

Startled from his reverie, Kirk looked up at Lieutenant Commander Spock, who studied him curiously from his seat at the library computer station at starboard aft. Kirk blushed under the cool scrutiny of the half-Vulcan, half-human science officer, who doubled as his first officer. "Uh, no, Mister Spock. I was just . . . contemplating the moment."

Spock quirked one of his sharply slanted eyebrows and examined Kirk like a lab specimen. "I see. The perennial human need to ascribe emotional significance to arbitrary points of transition such as promotions, birthdates, anniversaries, and so forth. Perhaps if you thought of it simply as the mechanical act of lowering your body into a chair—"

"Thank you, Mister Spock. I think I've got it from here." Having a Vulcan second-in-command was definitely going to take some getting used to.

Still, Spock had a point—*no pun intended*, Kirk thought as he glanced at the first officer's gracefully tapered ears. It was high time to stop milking the moment and just get on with it. With a decisive casualness, Kirk turned, took hold of the command chair's wide, boxy arms, and sat down. It was almost too comfortable, somehow, and it felt strange compared to his old chair aboard the *Sacagawea*, but maybe he just needed time to break it in—

Never mind. The chair was simply a station from which to do his job. Time to get to work.

He looked around the circle of the bridge, taking in the crew at their stations: Spock at sciences, Lieutenant Philip Alden at communications, Ensign Sarah Lopez at bridge engineering. Lieutenant Lee Kelso manned the portside helm station of the freestanding pilots' console, while Lieutenant Nyota Uhura, a junior communications officer, filled in at navigation thanks to her cross-training. It was a mild annoyance to Kirk that his command crew was incomplete. His chief engineer, Montgomery Scott, had been diverted to Starbase 10 at the last minute to assist in an emergency, and thus would be several days late to take his post. His chief navigator and second officer, Gary Mitchell—who had served the same role for Kirk aboard the *Sacagawea*—was late for a less constructive reason; he had been on an extended shore leave binge on Wrigley's Pleasure Planet when Kirk's transfer orders to the *Enterprise* had come through, and Mitchell's transport to Starbase 11, the *Nehru*, had been delayed by an ion storm. As for his chief medical officer, Dr. Mark Piper had put in for retirement on the day Captain Pike had accepted promotion to fleet captain, and had only grudgingly agreed to postpone his departure until Kirk could secure a permanent CMO—a task he was still working on, since he had someone specific in mind.

Well, it'll do for now, he thought. Settling into his chair, he took a breath, stabbed at the intercom button, and missed. Clearly the chair wasn't exactly like his old one. Clearing his throat, he said, "Lieutenant Alden, address intercraft."

Alden worked the control. "Intercraft open, sir."

Another breath. He'd already made his introductory speech to the crew after the change-of-command ceremony, so now it was time to get down to business—a milk run to deliver medical supplies to the Draxis II colony, but a good opportunity for Kirk to familiarize himself with his new ship and crew. "All hands, this is Captain Kirk. Ready all stations and prepare for departure." He thought for a moment. "I look forward to serving with you in the weeks and months ahead. Kirk out."

After several moments of overlapping comm chatter from the decks below, Spock stood. "All stations report ready, Captain."

Kirk nodded and faced forward. "Lieutenant Uhura, set course for Draxis II."

Elegant hands worked the navigation controls, and the lieutenant spoke in a melodious voice. "Course computed and on the board, sir."

"Mister Kelso, take us out of orbit, full impulse."

The blond helmsman seemed slightly slow to react, but after a split second, he engaged the helm controls. "Full impulse, aye."

The deck rumbled beneath Kirk's feet as the impulse engines at the rear of the saucer engaged. Kirk's fingers tightened around his chair arms. The engines were tangibly more powerful than the *Sacagawea*'s, necessary to propel a mass twice as great. He couldn't wait to feel the ship go to warp.

Still, he felt a moment's regret that he had no friends by his side as he experienced these firsts. At least the *Nehru* would rendezvous with them en route, delivering Gary Mitchell at last. But there was still one more old friend Kirk was hoping to bring aboard.

"*I don't know, Jim,*" Leonard McCoy said over the display in Kirk's quarters. "*I've had my fill of starship duty.*"

"As a junior medical officer, or CMO aboard a scout ship," Kirk countered. "This is a major step up. A front-line capital ship, Bones, and you'd run the whole medical department."

"*Jim, do you think I want to look at four hundred people's tonsils?*" the craggy-faced physician fired back. "*You know me—I'm just a country doctor.*"

"That's what you said when you left the *Sacagawea* for that relief program of yours. And I just know you've spent the whole time complaining about the lack of decent climate control and mint juleps."

McCoy had spent the past year on assignment to Starfleet Medical, providing care and health education to preindustrial civilizations that were already aware of alien life—usually because they had been contacted before the Prime Directive was established, or by some other civilization that had no Prime Directive. That put them in a gray area where noninterference was concerned, and the heads of the program at Starfleet Medical had convinced Command that offering them humanitarian aid and health assistance was not only a moral duty, but a pragmatic choice to avoid earning the resentment of cultures who knew of the Federation's advancement and would wonder why it did nothing to help their people. After all, many of those species had been contacted first by the Klingons or other hostiles, powers that would wish to take advantage of any bad blood that might develop between them and the Federation. So it was strategically as well as ethically appropriate to stay in those societies' good graces.

Not that any of that mattered to Leonard McCoy, of course. All he cared about was the good of his patients. *"It's been very rewarding work. We're helping a lot of people out here."* McCoy fidgeted. *"Still . . . it can be frustrating dealing with the local attitudes sometimes. My last stint was on Capella IV—a fine people in their way, proud and honorable, but incredibly stubborn when it came to accepting even the most basic medical care. We spent months butting heads with them, helping where we could, until we finally decided it was a lost cause and just left."*

"Then it sounds like you could use a change of pace. Take the job, Bones. Gary's here too—it'll be like old times."

"Not entirely," McCoy replied. *"Not since Rhen retired."*

"She had to retire. You're still a long way from that."

"You never know. A starship on the frontier isn't exactly the safest place."

"Which is exactly why I need a doctor I know is an expert in treating the kinds of injuries and illnesses my crew might sustain. And . . . why I need a friend I can rely on when things get tough out here." He leaned forward. "Bones—I need you."

The doctor's frown intensified, but Kirk could tell he was softening. *"Well . . . I'll think it over. But it's not like you're in any rush, is it?"*

". . . No. Doctor Piper's agreed to stay on for a few more months."

"Then I'll consider it. And if you haven't found a better candidate by then . . . well, I'll consider it."

"There's no one else I trust the same way."

McCoy grunted. *"You know how I feel about flattery, Jim."*

"You eat it up."

"From an attractive young lady, sure. From you? I know better."

"Come on, Bones, this is the big time. This is what Gary and I have been working toward our whole career. I want you to be a part of that too, my friend."

The doctor studied him. *"Well, you sure aren't lacking for confidence. I guess that's what comes of having a ship that big given to you at your age."* He shook his head. *"Quite a change from the man I met three years ago . . ."*

VEGA COLONY
2262

One

The only greater mystery than why the ancient Vegans destroyed themselves in a war so mighty that it shattered entire dwarf planets is why they decided in the first place to terraform worlds around a star as young, hot, and inhospitable as Alpha Lyrae. But perhaps both are manifestations of the same blend of great power and stubborn ambition, a determination to bend worlds to their will instead of learning to compromise with reality. Let this be an object lesson to humanity as we contend with new worlds and new cosmic neighbors.

—Zhi Nu Palmer

Starfleet Medical Research Hospital, Orpheus City, Vega IX
"Don't you ever go home?"

The gruff voice startled Jim Kirk back to full wakefulness. He realized he must have dozed off in his chair at Elena Yu's bedside. He'd been visiting the young lieutenant, telling her about his day's work overseeing the Starfleet archaeological station in Eagle's Landing, supervising its researchers' efforts to tease out the secrets of the long-extinct Vegan civilization. As exciting as that hidden history was, the work of uncovering it was slow and tedious, and he must have bored himself to sleep while narrating it to his former science officer. Perhaps it wasn't the wisest choice of subjects for keeping a coma patient's mind stimulated.

He turned toward the speaker, wincing at the stiffness in his neck—a new pain to provide companionship for the headache he'd been nursing all day. "I'm sorry, Doctor, ah, McCoy." It took him a moment to place the sour-faced, blue-eyed Earthman; he had tried to get to know all the doctors who were caring for the wounded from the *Sacagawea*, but there were just so many of them. "Is it past visiting hours again?"

Leonard McCoy harrumphed. "The operative word being 'again,' Captain Kirk. You're in here so often that the staff sometimes forgets you're not a fixture of the place. And look what it's doing to you. You look exhausted, overstressed. You're in here every evening after work, talking to the patients, worrying over people you can't help, like Elena here, when you should be at home getting some sleep—or out on the town having some fun. With a name like Orpheus, you better believe this city has a fine music scene. I know some good cabarets I could recommend."

A noisy club was the last thing that would help Kirk's headache right now. "Maybe some other time, Doctor. I appreciate your concern, but surely you can understand my own concern for my crew."

"Except they aren't your crew anymore. Your crew, as I understand it, is the archaeology team over in Eagle's Landing. Your responsibility to these men and women ended when you left the *Sacajawea*."

"The *Sacagawea* will be repaired," Kirk replied, implicitly correcting McCoy's pronunciation by stressing the second syllable and the hard *g*. "I'm hoping that I and many of my crew will be back aboard her once she's ready."

McCoy looked him over skeptically. "So that's the only reason you took a ground post instead of accepting another starship command? So you could be with your crew while they recovered?"

"Is there a better reason?"

The doctor narrowed his eyes. "Maybe not, but I can think of a few worse ones. The *Sack—Sacagawea* was your first starship command. You're the youngest person ever to achieve that posting in Starfleet history. And less than a year later, your ship is crippled and more than half its crew is either hospitalized or—"

"I don't appreciate what you're insinuating, Doctor."

McCoy raised his hands. "Not insinuating—just wondering if you're trying to punish yourself for something nobody's blaming you for."

Kirk's irritation with this man was worsening. "Are you a surgeon or a psychiatrist?"

"I'm whatever my patients need me to be, sir."

"Well, I'm not one of your patients. And frankly, I'm not impressed with your care for the people who are your patients. This is supposed to be the finest, most cutting-edge medical facility in Starfleet. Elena Yu has serious brain damage that needs attention. There are implants, regeneration techniques you could be trying. Instead you just put her in an induced coma and let her waste away in this bed."

"Before we can do any of that, we need to ease the metabolic demands on her brain so it can bring down the inflammation on its own." The doctor attempted an appeasing smile. "If there's one thing I've learned over the years, it's that you should never underestimate the body's power to heal itself. Even with all this high-tech, cutting-edge science and gadgetry, often the best healing techniques are still time, rest, and patience."

"Listen, McCoy, I'm getting tired of your 'old country doctor' routine. You're a Starfleet-trained medical officer working in the most advanced hospital in the Federation, not some . . . some frontier-town sawbones!"

"No, *you* listen. I—" McCoy broke off and stared at Kirk. "Sawbones?" He started laughing. "Did you actually just say 'sawbones'? Where did you pull that from?" He laughed harder—and a moment later, Kirk joined in.

The shared moment lasted only briefly, for as Kirk threw his head back in laughter, the painful stiffness in his neck worsened and he cried out. McCoy instantly grew serious and peered more closely at him. "What is it?" he asked after a moment. "Pain, rigidity in your neck? Trouble turning your head?"

Kirk rubbed the back of his neck. "Must be stiff from staring at reports all day. Sitting at a desk . . . my arms and legs are sore. And this headache . . ."

"Top or back of the head? Behind the eyes?"

"Both, on and off."

"Worse when you move your head?" McCoy put his hand on Kirk's forehead.

The captain pulled back. "What are you—are you taking my temperature? Ever heard of a tricorder?"

The doctor glowered. "I don't need mechanical help to tell me the obvious. Headache, limb pain, nuchal rigidity, early signs of fever—I've seen these symptoms a dozen times since I came to Vega. Captain Kirk, you're suffering from the first stage of Vegan choriomeningitis."

Kirk laughed. "You're kidding. That's extremely rare."

"Yes, and you'd probably never get it just walking around a Vegan city. But instead, you choose to spend all your off hours hanging around a top-notch hospital, exactly the place where the largest number of choriomeningitis sufferers are concentrated. And with a weakened immune system from all the stress and sleep deprivation you subject yourself to by worrying over people who are officially no longer your responsibility."

Kirk grimaced at his tone. "Did anyone ever tell you your bedside manner is terrible?"

"All the time. But I come by it honestly. In your case, I'd say your heightened irritability and mood swings are the first symptoms of delirium, which is why I'm not taking them personally. Now, come with me and I'll get you checked in. Hopefully we've caught it early enough."

"To a room? You expect me to stay the night?"

"Why not? You practically live here anyway."

Kirk tried to brush away McCoy's arms as the doctor guided him toward the door. "Can't you just give me something and send me to my quarters? No—my home. I mean send me home."

McCoy's voice grew even sharper. "Captain Kirk. Vegan choriomeningitis is always fatal if not treated in twenty-four hours—and it often takes nearly that long for the symptoms to start showing, which is why the disease is so deadly. At the rate your symptoms are developing, we're already cutting it close. You're lucky I noticed them before you left, because if you'd gone home tonight, you might never have woken up again."

"No. My crew . . . my ship . . . Can't leave . . . my ship. I'm in command, Doctor. They need me. I'm in command . . ."

He barely knew where he was anymore, but he sensed somehow that he could trust the man guiding him through the corridor. "It's all right, Captain. Just come with me and we'll get you all patched up. You'll be back on the bridge before you know it."

Qixi, Vega IX

Kirk's symptoms flared up quickly, and for a while, it was unclear if Dr. McCoy had administered the antibiotic regimen in time. The young captain had to endure two days of intense fever, delirium, and convulsions before the infection was finally purged. McCoy's was the first face he saw upon returning to his senses, and he felt immense gratitude to the doctor for saving his life. "The best way to thank me," McCoy replied, "is to stay the hell away from this hospital once you're released. Do your job, live your life. Leave your crew to us. We know what we're doing." After what Kirk had just endured, he had a greater appreciation of the truth of that statement.

McCoy also recommended that Kirk take several days off work to recuperate after his release. Though Kirk chafed at the inactivity, he reassured himself that the research station would be in good hands without him. His executive officer, Rhenas Sherev, had managed things smoothly during his unplanned hospital stay, so surely he could trust her to continue doing so for a few more days.

Or so he thought until he got a call from the authorities in the growing Vegan city of Qixi, informing him that they had arrested Commander Sherev for vandalism.

When Kirk entered the interview room at the Qixi police station, Rhenas Sherev smiled up at him. She was a small but strongly built Andorian *shen*, her skin an atypically dark shade of blue. Her eggshell-white hair was coiffed in a short, wavy style that was currently fashionable on Vega but could have used some maintenance at the moment. "It's good to see you, Captain," she said in a confident, casual tone belying their surroundings, "but shouldn't you be recuperating back home?"

He glared back, not without affection. "I *would* be, but your actions made that impossible. What were you thinking? Ordering a civilian construction crew to halt work? Beaming their equipment away when they refused?"

"I had to. They might've destroyed a vital archaeological site."

"The Vegan Archaeology Council cleared that site as free of ancient ruins."

"That's because they didn't know what to look for. You know we figured out a way to scan for the ceramic composite identified in the ruins of Fragment B32."

"Your assignment was to scan for it in the debris disk, not on Vega IX." The ancient Vegans' final war had been so cataclysmic that it had not only wiped out all large fauna on Vega IX but shattered several dwarf planets and created an extensive disk of debris around the star. Most of the archaeological evidence on the planet had been wiped out by erosion and geologic forces over the subsequent millennia, so the spaceborne rubble from those wrecked worlds was, paradoxically, a more likely place to find at least partially intact ruins.

Though Sherev apparently believed otherwise. "We finished the scan in the disk. The *Caliban* was back in orbit here anyway, so I figured, what the hell?" She leaned forward excitedly. "And it paid off. We picked up signatures of the ceramic in deeper strata than we ever expected. Jim, this means the ancient Vegans terraformed this planet thousands of years earlier than we believed. Their civilization may have endured peacefully for nearly twice as long as we thought before the war destroyed them. There's no telling how that could transform our understanding of their history!"

"That may be, Rhen, but you have to learn to respect other people's boundaries. Civilian archaeologists have been studying this system's ruins since before Starfleet even existed. They let us take the lead in studying the debris disk because we're better qualified to do research in space, but when it comes to the ruins here—"

"I know, Captain, I know. But there wasn't time to go through bureaucratic channels. Vital evidence might have been destroyed because some petty-minded construction boss wouldn't listen to reason!"

"If so, that would've been their responsibility, not yours." Kirk sighed and went on in a softer tone. "You were right to inform the construction officials of your concerns, Rhen, but you crossed the line when you took matters into your own hands. There are limits to a commander's responsibility—to our ability to get the results we want. We have to respect other leaders' authority as well, even when we think they're making a mistake."

Sherev looked unconvinced. "With all due respect, Jim, you're too married to the rule book. Sometimes you have to bend the rules when there's a higher principle at stake. As for respecting authority, I've always felt that respect needs to be earned. I'd respect a leader who gave full and fair consideration to opposing arguments, like you do. That construction chief only cared about her schedule and wouldn't even hear me out."

"Rhen . . ." Kirk paused, then gave her a cockeyed smile. "Only you would treat the study of a long-dead civilization as an urgent, now-or-never affair. You're the most impatient archaeologist I've ever met."

"When a new discovery is hours away from being destroyed, hell, yes, I am."

"You said yourself that your scan picked up several new sites on the planet. Do you know for a fact that losing this one would've cost us knowledge we couldn't get from the others?"

"I don't know that it wouldn't. And I wasn't about to take the chance."

Kirk studied the intense, vivacious Andorian for a moment longer, then shook his head. "Your passion for your work makes you an admirable science officer, Rhen, but your command judgment leaves something to be desired."

She cocked her antennae in the equivalent of a shrug. "Just as well I'm not interested in command. I joined Starfleet to do science. I leave the leadership in more capable hands. Which is why I'll be glad to turn the big desk back over to you."

He narrowed his eyes. "Are you trying to flatter me so I'll go easy on you?"

"I find it works pretty well on humans."

"Well, I'm not the human you have to worry about. You still have to smooth things over with the Qixi police and the Archaeology Council."

Sherev gave him a skeptical look. "Seriously. You expect *me* to be diplomatic and appeasing?"

"I expect you to make an effort to learn how."

She fidgeted like an adolescent faced with a term paper. "Your faith in me is overwhelming, Captain."

"That's the spirit. Now, let's get you out of here . . ."

Orpheus City
In the weeks that followed, Kirk stayed in contact with Leonard McCoy—not merely to keep abreast of his former crew's recov-

ery (including that of Elena Yu, who'd finally come out of her coma, though whether she would regain full cognitive function was not yet clear), but to take the doctor up on his offer to show Kirk the night life of Orpheus City. The captain had come to appreciate the doctor's plain-talking, brutally honest manner—as well as the deep reservoir of compassion and integrity that drove it—and had realized that, if he were to take McCoy's advice to get out more and establish a social life, he could think of far worse choices for a friend than McCoy himself. Indeed, the doctor proved a charming and stalwart companion—a conversationalist of an affably cynical bent, a good judge of music and food, and an even better connoisseur of potable intoxicants, with a seemingly inexhaustible stash of high-grade Saurian brandy. All in all, the companionship of "Sawbones" McCoy—as Kirk had inevitably nicknamed him as an inside joke—effectively filled the void left in Kirk's life when Gary Mitchell had been reassigned after the crippling of the *Sacagawea*, even though the two men could hardly be more different.

The drawback to McCoy's forthrightness was his recurring tendency to try to get Kirk to talk about what had happened to his ship. Of course, the doctor knew the tale from his patients and from Starfleet records, but he insisted that it would help Kirk work through any lingering sense of guilt or responsibility if he opened up about it. What McCoy didn't understand was that Kirk had no desire to get past that sense of responsibility. It was the thing that drove him to keep trying harder to protect his people—just as it had been since five years earlier, when his brief moment of hesitation at the *Farragut*'s phaser station had allowed a cloudlike entity to penetrate the starship and kill nearly half its crew, including his mentor Captain Garrovick. He couldn't blame the doctor for wanting to ease his pain, but this was a pain Kirk needed to keep him focused.

The doctor was also a pretty good poker player, though for this they required a larger group. As it happened, Rhenas Sherev was a mean player herself, and she and McCoy between them were able to bring in other friends of theirs to fill out the table. (In Sherev's case, remarkably, this included the vice chairman of the Vegan Archaeology Council, with whom she'd somehow managed to make peace after all, though she had no qualms about repeatedly cleaning him out at the poker table.) Sherev proved as aggressive and impulsive a gambler as she was an archaeologist, yet she somehow managed to make it a winning strategy in both areas. The one and only time that another player—a radiologist colleague of McCoy's—accused Sherev of cheating by using her antennae to distinguish the cards by the electric fields of their ink patterns, she sent him away whimpering by challenging him to an *Ushaan* duel to avenge her honor . . . after which she fell back laughing. "Believe me, I *wish* my antennae had that kind of resolution. I'd cheat you all blind."

Sherev also joined Kirk and McCoy in their visits to Orpheus's cabarets, and she shared their appreciation for the dancing girls, though she'd previously shown an equal appreciation for the male physique. "Male, female—you two-sex species have it easy," she chuckled one evening while on her third brandy. "Try having to find *three* bondmates compatible with you *and* with one another. Then try juggling the needs and hang-ups of four adults and two young children, with a third on the way." She shook her head. "I'm lucky I just had to fertilize and not actually *carry* our kids. I don't know how my *zh'yi* handles it." A laugh. "Especially since the little ones have my genes, which means they're headstrong and hard to corral. As you know too well, Jim."

Across the cozy table, McCoy quirked a brow at her. "Is that why you joined Starfleet? To get away from the chaos at home?"

She stared at him, her antennae rearing back in surprise. "Get away? Why would I want that? I love a challenge. And I love my bondmates and my kids. They're all unbearable in the most wonderful ways—just like me," she finished with a wink. After a sip of her brandy, she grew more serious. "No, knowing that they're waiting for me at home, that they'll be there for the long haul no matter what, because they're part of me . . . that's what anchors me when I'm out here, what keeps me sane and gives me the incentive to do my best. I'd be nothing without them." The fact that she was raptly watching the stripper onstage while she spoke somehow failed to detract from her declaration of devotion to her family.

"Well, I don't know how you pull it off," McCoy said. "I couldn't even balance *one* wife and daughter with my career. I came out to this godforsaken frontier because I had nothing left back home after the divorce. Serves me right, though. I brought it on myself . . ." He trailed off.

Sherev reached over and pulled his drink away before he could take another sip. "Cut it out, Sawbones. You're a maudlin drunk, you know that? Oh, you humans and your liquor. There was this engineer stationed here last year—he hated the local food, but the way he drank . . . Oh, what was his name? Montgomery . . . something. I remember his surname was the same as his nationality, which confused me no end . . ."

Kirk barely noticed her rambling, for he was still preoccupied with the earlier conversation. How *did* she manage to balance family and career so well? It was an ability he envied deeply. His own attempts to establish a lasting relationship that could survive the pressures of his career had never ended well. In the end, his duty had always come first.

SACAGAWEA
2261

Two

Jim Kirk was many things, but he was never a Boy Scout.
                                                    —Dr. Carol Marcus

U.S.S. *Sacagawea* NCC-598
"This is Captain James Tiberius Kirk of the *U.S.S. Sacagawea*, Federation Border Patrol."

Kirk's voice hitched on the "Tiberius," and he hoped no one else noticed. He'd thought his full name would make him sound more intimidating, but once he heard it out loud, it felt pretentious. What were the odds that the name of a Roman emperor would have any meaning to the Xarantine smugglers he addressed? Was he really saying it for their benefit, or to sound more impressive to his bridge crew? Did it come off as overcompensation for the fact that he was younger and less experienced than several of the officers around him?

His sense of discipline reasserted itself, shoving aside his fleeting moment of doubt. Kirk may have been the youngest captain in Starfleet, but he had worked hard for eleven years, excelling at Starfleet Academy and working his way up the ranks from the *Republic* to the *Farragut* to the *Constitution* to the *Eagle*, in order to earn that rank. He wasn't going to forget that accumulated learning now.

"You have entered Federation space illegally," Kirk went on. "Stand down and prepare to be boarded." As the silence continued, he couldn't help adding, "You're not fooling anyone, you know. Certainly not at this range."

The freighter on the *Sacagawea* bridge's forward viewscreen was mostly hidden from view, dwarfed by the dozen or so massive ice boulders that had been lashed against its hull. It was not the first time smugglers had used this trick, hiding their ships inside chunks of cometary ice and rock and coasting across the border to fool long-range sensors. But that was why Gary Mitchell and Elena Yu, respectively the *Sacagawea*'s navigator and science officer, had worked together over the past few weeks to compile a detailed catalog of cometary and asteroidal bodies in the region of interstellar space that the midsized vessel patrolled. Anything whose motion didn't match the tables was flagged for further investigation—which led to many false alarms and newly cataloged minor objects, but occasionally produced positive hits.

The Xarantines finally reacted to Kirk's demand. "Their impulse engines are warming up," Lieutenant Yu reported. "I think they're going to try to make a break for it."

"They know they can't outrun us," answered Lieutenant Commander Mehran Egdor. The Rigelian first officer frowned, wrinkling the dark vertical lines tattooed on his pale, craggy forehead and cheeks. "But they'll probably try to find an opening to jettison or destroy their cargo before we can search them. They'll probably—"

"Release the ice to give themselves cover," Kirk finished for him, trying to keep the irritation out of his voice. Egdor was eight years older than Kirk but two steps below him in rank, and he never seemed able to forget it. Kirk was glad to have a first officer whose experience he could draw on and learn from, but Egdor's manner consistently made him feel more lectured to than mentored. The commander insisted on offering his advice even when Kirk did not seek it, as if he doubted Kirk's ability to figure things out for himself.

But that was a matter to sort out later. "Khorasani," Kirk told the statuesque lieutenant at the helm, "lock phasers on the ice boulders. Stand by to fire at full power, wide dispersal on my command."

"Yes, sir," Azadeh Khorasani replied, her brow furrowing in confusion. But she programmed the target lock efficiently, her bionic left hand working the targeting scope controls as easily as living fingers would, if not more so.

On the viewscreen, explosive bolts flashed and the lashed-on ice boulders flew free from the Xarantine ship. "Standing by, sir," Khorasani said.

But the Xarantines beat her to it. Their particle cannon banks opened up on the ice boulders, beginning to blow them apart. "As I thought, they're trying to blind our sensors," Egdor cautioned. "I recomm—"

But Kirk was already raising his hand. "Khorasani, fire!"

The *Sacagawea*'s powerful phasers lashed out, having a far more potent and immediate effect on the comet chunks than the Xarantines' weaker particle cannons. In seconds, the masses of dirty ice had been largely sublimated to vapor, with the remainder blown well out of range by the explosive force of the expanding gases.

Egdor blinked, staring at the screen. "You . . . dispersed the debris cloud before they could use it for cover," he said.

"Plus he gave them a pretty good warning shot in the process, Commander," Mitchell added with a grin. "They're powering down, Captain. Looks like they're surrendering."

Kirk rose from the command chair. "Then let's go see what they were so determined to hide from us. Lieutenant Mitchell, Ensign Khorasani, with me."

Egdor took a step forward to delay him. "I'm curious, Captain. How did you know they'd attempt that maneuver?"

Kirk shrugged. "It's what I would've done."

Xarantine freighter

Even after their captain surrendered, the Xarantine crew resisted opening their cargo hold to the Starfleet boarding party. "Please, Captain Kirk," the hairless, yellow-skinned merchant insisted, "our cargo facilities are shielded for purposes of security. Not only must we honor our clients' confidences, but to expose the cargo to the radiations of space in uncontrolled conditions could damage sensitive data . . ."

But that was why Kirk had brought Azadeh Khorasani. The Klingon raid that had cost the lieutenant her left arm on her first cadet training cruise had also damaged her ribs and spine; the resulting prosthetic replacements had the necessary anchoring to exert more than twice human strength without damaging the rest of her body. Khorasani took pride in her artificial limb, refusing to sheathe it in synthetic skin. And at times like this, Kirk could see why. Her bionic hand made short work of the cargo hold's locking mechanism.

What lay within the hold was stunning in more ways than one. They were Orions—nearly two dozen, some three-quarters of them female, and all mostly or completely nude. After a long moment, Kirk forced himself to look away. His gaze fell on the Xarantine captain, who quailed from its intensity.

"Please, Captain," the portly merchant attempted, "this is not what it appears. These are refugees, fleeing enslavement in Orion space. As you can see, they lacked the means to immigrate legally, and sometimes one must place mercy and decency over the strict letter of—"

Kirk seized the trafficker by the front of his ornate robes. "Is that the best lie you can come up with? You know Federation law doesn't restrict immigration. Everyone is welcome!" He shoved the Xarantine away. "Although I'd make an exception for you."

He wiped his hands of the imagined slime and turned back toward the open hold. The slaves' accommodations were reasonably clean and sanitary, and a protein resequencer and lavatory facilities were in evidence; no doubt they would bring their sellers less profit if they were malnourished or unclean. Still, they were packed closely together, given barely enough light to see by. They gazed up at him languidly, appearing sedated, probably by something in their food or water. Even so, he could see the hopelessness in their eyes. A comfortable cage was still a cage.

"Get them all to sickbay right away," he ordered the security team. "Notify Commander Egdor to prepare guest accommodations. And get them some clothes."

Gary Mitchell was still staring. "Can we skip that part?" the navigator whispered. "I mean, my God. Even the men look amazing."

"Gary!" Kirk yanked his friend away from the door. "Get a hold of yourself. They're slaves!"

Mitchell shrugged, spreading his hands. "Not anymore!"

"They don't know that yet. Show some consideration." He threw a glance toward Khorasani and the security team. "Don't forget, I specifically requested you as my navigator. Your actions and attitude reflect on me."

The other man visibly shook himself. "Right. Sorry. I do appreciate it, Jim. And the last thing I want is to screw up your first command." He sighed, looking over his shoulder. "It's just . . . I've never seen so much gorgeous green skin in one place before. I tell you, Jim, you're the most disciplined man I know. I'm amazed you can resist all that beauty."

Kirk didn't let on how hard he was struggling to do just that. A captain couldn't show weakness to his crew, even when one was his best friend. So he shrugged it off. "My duty comes first, Gary, you know that." He smirked. "Besides, I've got a girl back at the starbase."

Mitchell nodded. "Ah, yes, the charming Doctor Miller." He chuckled. "I gotta say, Jim . . . you've always had a type, I know, but if you think another blond lady scientist can take Carol's place—"

Kirk stiffened. "That's enough, mister."

Mitchell winced at the sharpness of his tone, but snapped to attention. "Aye, aye, sir. Understood. Sorry, Captain. I guess my brain's still addled from the Orion pheromones, but it's no excuse."

After a moment, Kirk softened. "I didn't mean to bite your head off. It's just . . ." He looked around, thinking about the weeks that the Orion captives must have spent in these cramped conditions while the ship coasted past the border at sublight. Thinking about the ways the freighter captain might have destroyed the "evidence" if he hadn't acted quickly enough. "They were being smuggled *in*, Gary. Slaves. Being taken to customers somewhere in Federation space." He fumed in silence, not trusting himself to say more.

"I hear you, Jim. But that's the frontier for you. We draw a plane in space, call it a border, and pretend we control what's inside it, but a lot of it's still the Wild West."

"Then what are we defending?"

Mitchell smiled. "We're giving the colonies room to grow. Keeping them safe so someday they'll be as nice and civilized as the core worlds."

"And then the border will move farther out, and the cycle will start all over." Kirk sighed. "I want to be part of expanding those borders, Gary. I want to improve our knowledge and understanding of our neighbors, bring us closer, not just maintain the barriers that make it easier to exploit or fear outsiders. The *Sacagawea* was designed as a scout, not a patrol ship. She doesn't deserve to be stuck here on the border any more than we do."

"Everybody's gotta start somewhere, Jim. And you scored a big win today. Be glad of that. And be glad you're based at a starbase so you can go back and celebrate with your lovely doctor friend."

Starbase 24

Jim Kirk had been waiting in the Moonbeam Club for over twenty minutes by the time Janet Miller finally showed up. He was embarrassed to realize he'd barely noticed the passage of time, for his table afforded a clear view of the *Sacagawea* at her docking port. Even after nearly two months in command of the *Hermes*-class starship, he still couldn't help staring at the sleek lines of her saucer and single nacelle and feeling a sense of awe that she and the 195 people aboard her were his to command.

Even so, he felt an equal thrill at the sight of Janet's girl-next-door features and her apologetic smile as she hurried up to the table and kissed him on the cheek. "I'm so sorry I'm late, Jim."

"It's all right, Jan."

"I just lost track of time again," the pale-haired biophysicist said as she lowered her lean figure into the seat across from his. "I've been having the most fascinating correspondence with Doctor Theodore Wallace of the Aldebaran III colony. He's a truly brilliant man, Jim. He's discovered a spatial anomaly connecting with a four-dimensional subspace domain, and he thinks he's found evidence of organic molecules within it. We've been collaborating on a simulation of how protein folding and translation would occur in a higher-dimensional space. I mean, we've had higher-dimensional protein folding models for centuries, but as abstract computational aids, not as something with real physical existence, with the binding forces between particles going as inverse cubes instead of inverse squares . . ." She trailed off. "I'm sorry, I don't mean to babble."

Kirk smiled. "Not at all, Jan. I love your enthusiasm about your work. It's something we both have in common."

"Yes, but we only have a few more days before I have to leave for that terraforming conference on Minori IV. I want to make the most of them."

Minori IV? It took Kirk a moment to place the name. Her impending conference had completely slipped his mind. Smiling in an attempt to cover for it, he slid his arm around her shoulders. "Well, in that case, maybe we could just skip dinner."

Janet chuckled. "Jim, not that I don't appreciate how insatiable you've been since you got that whiff of Orion pheromones last week . . . but I would appreciate the chance just to sit and talk more. To have a nice, quiet, friendly dinner conversation before we get back to the *really* friendly stuff."

Kirk nodded, taking her point. He and Janet were both committed professionals, and they recognized the limitations that placed on their relationship. Kirk was determined not to repeat the mistakes that had driven Carol Marcus away—that had made her forbid him from seeing David, the son he'd only recently discovered he had. He still struggled with his ambivalent feelings about fatherhood, but he refused to hurt Jan or insult her intelligence by making the same kind of false promises he'd impulsively offered Carol about his readiness for a commitment. If there was a way to make a relationship with a dedicated career woman work, perhaps it was to keep things comfortably loose and casual—to approach it more as an intimate, abiding friendship than a grand, poignant romance. That way, the necessity of frequent separation would be easier to cope with, and perhaps they could find a stable balance allowing the relationship to last indefinitely, without the need for painful choices between conflicting commitments. (Being more careful with contraception this time was a good idea as well.)

Unfortunately, their friendly dinner conversation had barely gotten started when a gray-haired, craggy-faced man in a captain's uniform approached the table. "Bob, hi!" Janet said. "Good to see you. I hope you're here to grace us with some jazz."

"Not tonight, Jan," Robert Wesley said, throwing a wistful

glance at the Moonbeam Club's piano. "I'm afraid I have to take Jim away from you."

"Oh, no, Bob."

But Kirk was already rising from the table, shifting back into officer mode. Robert Wesley was the senior captain of Starbase 24's border task force, a forty-five-year-old Earthman who'd commanded the *U.S.S. Beowulf* for nearly a decade. In the two months they'd served together, Kirk had learned a great deal from the older man, whom he saw as a natural leader. If Captain Wesley needed him, he was there. "What is it, sir?"

"The Klingons again, Jim. A raiding party's been detected crossing the border. Looks like a big one this time. We're going to need all hands."

Kirk turned back to Janet. "I'm sorry, Jan."

She took it with calm resignation. "Like you said—we have this in common." She rose, put her arms around his neck, and kissed him. "In case you don't get back before my trip. And for luck."

U.S.S. *Sacagawea*

Starbase 24 was one of the closest Federation bases to the Klingon border, proximate to the sector containing the Klingons' primary prison planet, Rura Penthe. The high security around the planet known far and wide as "the Aliens' Graveyard," as well as the Empire's heavy demand for the dilithium mined there, made for a large and active Klingon military presence along that portion of the border. As such, Starbase 24 maintained a fair-sized border patrol fleet, led by Captain Wesley's *Beowulf*. That ship currently led three others in defense of the human colony on Shinohara's World: James Kirk's *Sacagawea*, the *Sau Lan Wu* under Captain Vishakha Gupta, and the *Hannibal* under Captain Jaulas nd'Omeshef.

Shinohara's World was a small, unremarkable colony on the

fourth planet of UFC 620, a tiny M dwarf whose six planets were packed so tightly around it that their "years" were measured in days or weeks. It had no great strategic or astropolitical importance in itself. But Klingon raiders often targeted such young, remote colonies because they were relatively undefended, and although the Klingon High Council nominally abided by the tenuous peace between the two powers, it tacitly encouraged such raids in the hope of deterring further Federation expansion into territories the Empire hoped to claim.

None of that mattered to James Kirk at the moment, for none of it would matter to the few hundred families who had made Shinohara's World their home. He had seen the impact of violence and loss on a small frontier community during his youth on Tarsus IV, when Kodos the Executioner had slaughtered half the population in the name of his deranged theories of eugenics. Ever since that dark day, Kirk had resolved never to stand by and let sentient lives be discarded by those who dismissed them as mere collateral damage in the pursuit of some abstract strategy or cause. In the years since, he had often had occasion to see how fundamentally the Klingon Empire's guiding philosophy toward life and death conflicted with his own. He had lost friends in battles against the Klingons during his time on the *Farragut*. Later on, he had led a Starfleet contingent defending the planet Shad's world government against an insurrection backed and armed by the Klingons, and had seen firsthand the brutality the Empire encouraged in others. As second officer of the *Constitution*, he had spent weeks assisting in the detoxification and reconstruction of a Federation colony devastated by a Klingon attack; even two years after the fact, there had still been remains that needed to be exhumed from the rubble, identified, and delivered home to their families in hopes of bringing them some closure. Kirk was determined to make sure the same would not happen here.

He let that determination fill his voice as he hailed his rival commander to give challenge. The Klingon raiders had broken up, following multiple courses through UFC 620's close-packed planetary system and forcing the Starfleet squadron to split up as well. Mitchell and Khorasani had managed to intercept their designated ship, positioning the *Sacagawea* to block its approach to the colony world. While the ships themselves were dust motes on the scale of even this compact system, their weapons ranges were considerably larger, making the *Sacagawea*'s sphere of influence an effective obstacle to the Klingon ship's progress.

"Attention, Klingon vessel," Kirk intoned to underline that fact. "This is Captain James Kirk of the *U.S.S. Sacagawea*. If you do not cease this unprovoked attack, we will be forced to destroy you. Please respond so we can discuss this like honorable men."

That did it. A snarling Klingon face, eyes flashing fiercely beneath bony forehead ridges, appeared on the viewer. *"I am Grnar, commander of the* Vrot. *You speak of honor, boy? Then do not begin with the lie of claiming manhood. I see the intelligence reports are true—Starfleet has assigned a mere child to guard its border."*

Kirk smiled. "The human warlord Alexander of Macedon had built an empire across three continents by my age. Maybe Klingons are just late bloomers."

"Then show me your empire, boy. You are but a whelp! Starfleet has lost so many of its best captains to my valiant brothers that they must now give their ships to babies still wet with the blood of their mothers' wombs."

Kirk stepped forward alongside Khorasani's station to look the Klingon in the eye. "I did not . . . just hear you talk about my mother."

What Grnar went on to say about Kirk's mother was unrepeatable. What Kirk said in return about Grnar's mother was inadvisable. The upshot was that the *Sacagawea* was under heavy fire moments later and Khorasani was firing back with full phasers.

Lieutenant Commander Egdor sidled up to Kirk as the latter studied the enemy ship's trajectory on the viewscreen. "It was unwise to make him angry, Captain."

Kirk stared. "*Make* him angry? Isn't that a Klingon's default state?"

"Even so, it's a bad idea to make it worse."

The first officer's continued condescension troubled Kirk. If he didn't find a way to establish mutual trust with Egdor, then something would have to be done.

For now, though, he kept his calm. The real battle was still outside. "I don't know about that, Commander. There's nothing like a predictable enemy."

He stepped forward, placing a hand on Mitchell's shoulder. "Keep pressing the attack. Meet their aggression in kind, no backing down."

The bridge trembled under the *Vrot*'s fire and its console lights flickered. "Sure, Captain, if you don't mind a bloody nose," Mitchell replied.

"Under the circumstances, no, I don't." He leaned forward, gesturing at the navigation display. "There. Vector to 109 mark 27. Drive them toward the fifth planet."

"The fifth . . . Oh!" Mitchell grinned up at Kirk. "Got it, sir."

The deck convulsed under Kirk's feet, and he almost fell. As Kirk returned to the command chair, Egdor clung to its back and leaned closer. "Taking such an aggressive tack is exposing us to a lot of damage, Captain. In my opinion, this is a reckless move."

Kirk smiled confidently. "Let's hope Grnar shares that opinion."

Soon, the two ships drew near enough to the fifth planet that its gravity began to affect their courses. Nonetheless, Kirk had his crew continue their head-on attack with no adjustment of their strategy. Egdor furrowed his pale, craggy brow, but this time he kept his counsel even as the *Vrot* dove nearer the planet and used its lower pseudo-orbit to pull ahead of the *Sacagawea*. Once it had gained enough of a lead, it would no doubt thrust on a tangent, raising its orbit until it had the high-ground advantage in a head-on approach. Khorasani looked back at Kirk, concern in her eyes. "Sir? Your orders?"

"Wait for it," he said.

Moments later, the *Vrot* began its tangential thrust toward a higher orbit.

Moments after that, it was struck by a phaser barrage from a new direction. The *Beowulf* swept into view around the curve of the planet, keeping the Klingon cruiser in its field of fire and pressing the attack. "Resume fire," Kirk ordered. "Pincer maneuver."

Mitchell and Khorasani followed through on the order, and in moments the combined assault had overwhelmed the *Vrot*'s shields. Split-second conflagrations of escaping atmosphere bloomed from multiple hull breaches before dissipating in the vacuum, and the ship began to tumble.

Egdor's eyes widened in realization. "You kept track of the other ships. You knew Wesley would be there."

"It was just a matter of luring Grnar there without him noticing," Kirk replied.

"That's why you made it personal. You let him think you were angry, that you were as monomaniacally fixated on avenging an insult as a Klingon would be."

"And since he didn't think I was paying attention to anything but him, he forgot to pay attention to anything but me."

Now Wesley's voice came over the comms in a general hail. *"This is Captain Robert Wesley to the Klingon vessel. We are prepared to beam your survivors over for medical—"*

"Captain!" Elena Yu spoke up. "They've initiated a warp core overload."

"Khorasani, veer off!" Kirk barked. "Aft shields to maximum! Kirk to Captain Wesley—"

The blinding flash was gone in an eyeblink, the reaction so powerful that it devoured or dispersed all the matter and antimatter within the *Vrot* with ravenous speed. But the radiation burst and the subspace shock wave both struck the *Sacagawea* with enough intensity to rock the ship and overload consoles. Kirk barely stayed in his command chair as the lights went out—and he hoped that power was all that had been lost.

Shinohara's World

Kirk stood by Robert Wesley's side, gazing out at the swath of wreckage that had been carved through the colony's industrial district. "Despite our best efforts," Wesley said, "one ship got through. Before the *Hannibal* caught up and drove them away, they managed to pillage half the colony's most valuable materiel and equipment, devastate the rest, and kill thirty-four people. It looks like they may have abducted up to two dozen more, no doubt as slave labor."

Kirk clenched his fists, letting himself feel the burden of every loss. "With respect, sir . . . if we let that happen, then this *wasn't* our best effort."

Wesley met his gaze sternly. "No, Jim, it wasn't. And I'm afraid that's largely on you."

In other circumstances, Kirk might have taken umbrage. But he already felt too guilty to question the senior captain's judgment. It was a familiar feeling—one he had been living with ever since the *Farragut* disaster four years before. In the wake of that incident, First Officer Cheng had refused to hold Kirk accountable, instead calling him "a fine young officer who performed with uncommon bravery." But Cheng hadn't been there in the moment, peering through the sights at the mysterious attacker. He hadn't felt Kirk's doubt and disbelief that a mere cloud of vapor could pose a mortal threat to a mighty starship. What his superiors had forgiven as a young officer's understandable hesitation in the face of the unknown, Kirk knew to be the result of his arrogance and overconfidence. That arrogance had gotten Captain Garrovick and two hundred others killed. And now, despite Kirk's best efforts to outgrow it or at least tame it, his arrogance had claimed even more lives.

"What should I have done differently, sir?" he asked with humility.

Wesley sighed. "It was a good plan as far as it went. Looking three moves ahead, luring the *Vrot* to where you and I could take it out together. Unfortunately, Klingons have their own version of chess, and whoever commanded that fleet was planning *five* moves ahead.

"Jim, you counted on a Klingon believing that you'd act just like them—that you'd place personal honor and retribution for an insult above the mission. And maybe the late Captain Grnar fell for it. But smart Klingon leaders, those who've fought us and studied us before, know that Starfleet doesn't train its captains to act that way. They know we're trained to place the defense of others above all else. They may find that contemptible, but they understand it's how we operate. When the fleet commander saw you acting out of character, he must've deduced the trap you were setting for Grnar, and he positioned his other ships to take advantage of the opening your maneuver created. He may have ordered Grnar to sacrifice himself so that we'd be too damaged to come to the colony's aid in time, with the *Hannibal* and the *Sau Lan Wu* not being enough to stop them."

Wesley's mien grew more solemn. "Once I saw what you were trying to do, Jim, I also saw the opening it gave the Klingons. But you left me no choice but to come to your rescue. You gambled the safety of your ship to move the *Vrot* into position, and you forced me to gamble the safety of the colony to make sure your gamble succeeded. As a result, I lost my bet." He turned back to face the devastation. "And the colonists paid for it."

Kirk absorbed Wesley's words for a long, painful moment.

Finally he spoke. "Captain . . . I'm sorry I put you in that position. It was unfair."

Wesley shook his head. "It was necessary. Against a lesser commander, your plan probably would've worked. But you won't always have other captains to rely on, Jim. If you hope to command an explorer ship one day, you'll have to be able to solve any problem you encounter with only your own ship and crew. You won't be able to rely on anyone else's help.

"Being a starship captain is the most coveted job in Starfleet," Wesley finished. "But it's also the loneliest."

U.S.S. *Sacagawea*

"We need to be better," Kirk said to Mehran Egdor.

"'We,' sir?" The Rigelian stood alongside the desk in the small ready room that this class of ship had just off its bridge. Kirk paced the room's tight confines; he had never felt comfortable behind a desk.

"I thought I had every variable calculated," the captain went on. "And so I didn't give enough consideration to your cautions, Commander. That was my mistake, and I apologize."

Egdor blinked, surprised by what he heard. He cleared his throat. "I . . . appreciate that, Captain. But . . . if I'm being honest, sir . . . I underestimated you. I didn't even see the variables you recognized."

"Even so, it's your job to challenge me, to make me think twice. If I had listened, I might have taken a closer look at my assumptions and seen what I was missing." Kirk noted a hint of a grimace that Egdor quickly suppressed. "Something troubles you, Commander?"

"It's nothing, sir."

"Whatever it is, Mister Egdor, it's been interfering with our professional relationship for two months now. You have my permission to speak freely."

The Rigelian sighed. "I just find it typical of human arrogance that you assume you can always master every problem, triumph over every adversary, if you try hard enough."

Kirk stared, finding the suggestion bewildering. "I've never seen the advantage in thinking otherwise. If you assume ahead of time that you're facing a no-win scenario—"

"I don't mean ahead of time. I mean how you react after a defeat. You humans always act as though you're entitled to victory by default, and you take it as an affront whenever someone else comes out ahead. The fact is, you're intrinsically no better or more capable than the rest of us. You don't always get to be the winners."

"It's not about *humans* winning, Commander. Not to me, certainly. My only interest is the success of Starfleet, of the Federation. That's as much about Rigelians, Vulcans, Andorians . . ."

"Is it really, Captain?" Egdor asked. "Look around you, at your fellow Starfleet officers. Oh, yes, it's a diverse lot, with several dozen species represented. But look at the captains and most of them are human. Look at the admirals and it's even more so. Can you deny that?"

Kirk thought it over. He couldn't deny that of the current task force, only one captain out of four was nonhuman, and the ratio for the starbase's overall ship complement was little better. "I admit, I can't. But—"

"Yes, I've heard the usual rationalization. That space exploration is simply more central to humanity's historical role in the Federation, to its sense of identity and heritage, than it is to most other member races. That humans are simply drawn to Starfleet service in larger numbers as a result. But Rigelians have a long history with exploration as well, with contact and cooperation with the sister worlds in our own star system. It was my people, the Jelna, who first made contact with the Zami and Chelon peoples and built the interplanetary accord and trading network that would one day make us an interstellar power."

Egdor took a step closer to Kirk. "Yet here I am, still a lieutenant commander after nearly two decades in the service, while you have made captain in less than one." He caught himself, stepping back. "I don't mean to imply you don't deserve it. I know your reputation, the things you achieved as first officer of the *Eagle*, the discoveries you made on the Vulcanian Expedition. I'm aware that the entire Baezian civilization would be extinct now if you hadn't stayed behind to defuse that doomsday weapon. You've achieved a great deal in a remarkably short time, easily enough to earn a starship command. However . . ."

Kirk tilted his head. "However, you think it's possible that my path to command was smoother than yours by virtue of the privilege I was born with. That I may have been given more opportunities for achievement than you have."

"That is a fair way of putting it," Egdor said, holding his gaze unwaveringly.

Kirk was silent for a long moment. "I can't deny that possibility," he finally said, surprising Egdor. "I don't want to believe that Starfleet is governed by such unfair attitudes, and I don't believe anyone consciously intends it to be . . . but those who are born to privilege often fail to recognize the imbalances it creates. There are certainly enough examples of that in the history of my own nation on Earth. It takes a conscious effort to recognize those imbalances, and not *meaning* to be part of a problem doesn't entitle us to deny that it exists. So I'm not going to reject your concern out of hand. We don't become better people by patting ourselves on the back at how enlightened we are. We do it by remaining aware of our own potential to make mistakes, since that's the only way to do better in the future." He closed his eyes, still seeing the image of the devastated colony below—and the image of more than two hundred coffins lined up in the *Farragut*'s hangar bay.

"I . . . genuinely appreciate that, Captain," Egdor said. "I was wrong to call you arrogant. And . . . I've been wrong to resent your captaincy. You are worthy of it—by your judgment, and by your leadership."

Kirk shook his head. "I'm still learning. I'm still capable of mistakes—and of oversights. That's why I need a first officer I can trust to be a backstop on my judgment. To see the things I don't see, and to say the things I need to hear. If you promise to continue doing that, then I promise I'll do my best to listen."

He extended his hand to Egdor. The older man clasped it warmly.

Three

A sharp knife is nothing without a sharp eye.
—Koloth, Son of Lasshar

Starbase 24, Moonbeam Club

Janet Miller laughed breathlessly as she and Jim Kirk sat back down at their table, tired from an extended and acrobatic stint on the Moonbeam Club's dance floor. "Oh, Jim. This really has been the perfect evening."

"Only because you've put everything you could into making it perfect," Kirk replied. He clasped Janet's hands. "And I think it's time you let me in on whatever it is you've been trying to get me in the right mood to hear."

She sighed. "I should've known I couldn't get anything past you."

He gave a small shrug. "That is essentially my job."

Janet chuckled nervously, then said, "You know I've been working with Doctor Wallace on Aldebaran."

"You hardly talk about anything else lately." He smiled to soften it.

"Well . . . we've reached a point where subspace correspondence is no longer enough. He needs me there on the scene, working with him directly."

Kirk nodded, more to himself than to her. "And you've accepted."

"Jim, it's a career-making opportunity. Not just to study the extradimensional life, but to work with a man like Theodore Wallace . . . I could learn so much as his protégée. He's the most brilliant man I've ever met."

Kirk suppressed a twinge of jealousy. He'd be a fool to mistake her professional admiration of a much older man for something romantic. Still, he couldn't shake the feeling that she'd chosen Wallace over him. For all his determination to keep their romance casual and friendly, the prospect of losing her stung. It had always been his way to fall hard and fast for a woman, and now that he was about to lose Jan, he realized he'd been fooling himself into thinking he'd succeeded at resisting that tendency this time.

So he put his cards on the table. "Jan . . . I don't want to lose you. What we have . . . it's important to me. I can't just . . . turn it off."

"Oh, Jim. I can't either. This was a hard decision, one I've been struggling with for days while you were out on patrol. I'm sorry it has to be so much more abrupt for you. Hurting you is the last thing I want. But this is my *work*, Jim. This is a chance for me to make a real difference in my field."

"I know your career is important, Jan, but there has to be some way we can work it out."

"How? Would *you* be willing to give up starship command and take a desk job on Aldebaran Colony?"

He lowered his gaze, knowing she was right. "No. You know I wouldn't."

"Of course not. Work is an overriding passion for us both." She gave a wistful sigh. "And I'm afraid it doesn't leave us much room for anything more."

He gazed into her eyes, appreciating her honesty and wisdom more than ever. "If only one of us weren't quite so dedicated."

"Then the other wouldn't have cared as deeply. Being so much alike is what made this work—but it's also what made it brief by necessity."

Kirk rose from his seat and took her hand, guiding her to her feet. "Then I suggest we go to my quarters and make the most of the time we have left."

Jan's smile was as brilliant and beautiful as he'd ever seen it. "Once again, dear friend, we think alike."

Starbase 24, Commander's Office

"Captain Kirk? Have you been listening?"

Commodore Lam's sharp question broke Kirk out of his momentary reverie. He turned back to face the mature, gray-haired woman across the desk, embarrassed that he was still brooding like a schoolboy over Jan's departure nearly two weeks before. Luckily, his mind had better discipline than his heart. "Yes, Commodore. The Klingons are arming several of Acamar III's largest clans to intensify their blood feuds with their hereditary enemies."

Hong Ngoc Lam nodded, reassured that Kirk had been paying attention. "And thereby scuttle the peace process that many of the Acamarian clans are attempting to push forward. After millennia of senseless violence, the Acamarians are finally growing weary of the cycle of revenge and searching for a better way forward. They've even requested Federation assistance to mediate the peace talks. But the Klingons benefit if that process fails and Acamar continues to be ruled by the sword."

"A sword provided by the Klingons," Kirk extrapolated, "in exchange for which the Acamarians grant them an alliance and a strategic foothold on our border. It's the same thing they attempted on Shad and Mobita."

"But it only works if the peace talks break down. That's the outcome the Klingons are trying to engineer—and it's what you need to prevent."

Kirk furrowed his brow. "If I may ask, Commodore . . . why send the *Sacagawea*? Surely Captain Wesley—"

"Recommended that I send you."

He blinked. "Commodore, I'm a soldier, not a diplomat."

"You're a Starfleet captain, which means you're both of those when you need to be—preferably the latter whenever possible."

"Of course, Commodore. I just meant that my experience—"

"Your past experience confronting Klingon infiltration is part of the reason for this assignment, Captain. The other reason is that a starship captain needs to *gain* experience at more than just patrolling a border. That's the baseline of what we do here, not the limit of it. Just because you've reached the center seat, that doesn't mean your learning process is over. On the contrary—it means it's just begun."

Zemrok City, Acamar III

"I keep telling ya, Jim, you dodged a phaser beam."

Kirk glared at Gary Mitchell, who strolled alongside him and Azadeh Khorasani through a street bazaar in the central district of Zemrok City, capital of the politically prominent Liu Region and host to the ongoing peace talks between Acamar III's rival clans. Those talks were what Kirk needed to concentrate on right now, and Gary's well-meaning romantic advice didn't help. "I said I didn't want to talk about it."

Mitchell took a bite out of the *cralluck* wrap he'd picked up from one of the vendors, a concoction of seasoned avian meat and root vegetables wrapped in the leaves of something called *shemras*. "I'm just saying," he went on with his mouth full, "there's no point in brooding over Jan. I saw right away that it was never going to work, that you were just repeating the same mistake you made with—"

"Gary, I mean it."

"But the past is the past. That's my point. Now you're free to look to the future. Broaden your horizons. Experiment, play the field. Keep your options open and have some fun. You want to be an explorer, so explore the endlessly varied wonders of the female half of humanity. They aren't *all* blond scientists, you know."

Kirk rolled his eyes, despairing of ever getting his friend off this topic. Gary Mitchell's interest in women was parsecs wide and a centimeter deep—the opposite of Kirk's proclivity to fall deeply and devotedly for one woman at a time. Granted, in the wake of losing Carol and Jan, the idea of pursuing a few more casual, safely inconsequential love affairs had its appeal. But Kirk doubted he could ever be a superficial womanizer like Gary.

Khorasani had been doing her best to ignore the men's conversation, chewing on her own vegetarian *parthas* wrap and checking out the vendor booths the trio passed. "Hey, what's this?" she called out with interest, plowing through the crowd of Acamarian pedestrians (who parted readily at the approach of the statuesque, uniformed woman with the gleaming bionic arm) to reach a kiosk where a bulbous-browed K'normian trader was hawking a variety of knives and bladed weapons.

Moving closer in Khorasani's wake, Kirk recognized several of the blades—*d'k tahg, mevak, tajtik, mek'leth.* "Klingon weapons," he said.

"Yes, sir," Khorasani said, hefting a particularly nasty-looking *qutluch* with appreciation. "Authentic ones, too."

"Imported directly from the Empire itself," the vendor boasted. "All tested in actual combat, all guaranteed to give you an edge—ha-ha—in whatever blood feud you wish to pursue."

"Oh, I've got nothing against anyone in particular," Khorasani said. "I just admire fine craftsmanship."

"Of course, of course. They also make excellent display pieces, gifts . . ."

Kirk looked over the deadly collection with distaste. He shared his helm officer's admiration for weapons as collector's pieces, but he couldn't forget the source of these particular weapons, or ignore the fact that they were being openly hawked as tools for clan warfare. "Were you in the Empire recently?" he probed. "Who supplied you with these weapons?"

The K'normian quailed at Kirk's suspicious tone, paying greater attention to the uniforms the three officers were wearing. "I assure you, sir, my sources are legitimate. Weapons are not exactly hard to come by in Klingon space—and we are not in Federation space, so there are no restrictions on their import."

Khorasani, however, noted her captain's disapproval. After one more longing look at the knife, she handed it back to the trader. "Sorry. Not my color."

"Well, if you're not in the market for blades, perhaps I can make it up to you by offering you some of my more . . . special wares?" He gave her a suggestive smile. "I have recently received a new shipment from a . . . discreet but reliable source. The finest Klingon erotica in the sector."

Kirk exchanged a stunned look with Mitchell. "Klingon erotica?" the captain asked.

"I don't want to know," Mitchell said, emphatically shaking his head. "I just do not want to know."

But Khorasani looked intrigued. "Well, in the interests of scientific curiosity . . . promoting interspecies understanding . . ."

"Azadeh, there are some things humans were not meant to understand."

"Come on," Kirk told them both. "We'll be late for the first session if we dawdle any longer."

He drew them away. Mitchell came willingly, but Khorasani threw a wistful look back at the kiosk. "Sometimes you amaze me, Azadeh," Mitchell went on.

She smirked. "Only sometimes?"

"I mean, I would've thought you'd hate everything about the Klingons."

"Why should I?" she answered, brandishing her prosthetic.

"It's thanks to them that I have this gorgeous arm. If anything, I owe them my gratitude."

"For almost killing you?" Kirk asked, bewildered.

"I've killed more than a few of them," she said after a moment, her light tone faltering. "Probably maimed some as well. In my mind, I had no choice. They probably felt the same way. So who am I to blame them?"

"I doubt the noncombatants they've slaughtered and enslaved would feel the same."

"I wouldn't expect them to. And it's not like I approve of the things the Klingons do to innocent people. But they're hardly the only species prone to violence. The Acamarians are just as bloodthirsty, and we're trying to help them. Because we know we're the same way."

"We *used to be* the same way," Kirk countered.

Khorasani shook her head. "Fundamentally, biologically, we're still the same as we ever were, no matter what social veneer we try to put on. We're still killers by nature, even if we choose not to kill today." Kirk studied her, intrigued by her words. Maybe the Acamarians could stand to hear them.

Mitchell noticed his frown. "What's on your mind, Jim? You seemed awfully bothered by that vendor having Klingon goods."

"*Authentic* Klingon goods. And right when the Klingons are trying to infiltrate this planet." He shook his head. "I've seen Klingon attempts to gain footholds on unaligned worlds before. They send military advisors, energy weapons, explosives. When they don't just send in shock troops and bombers." He gestured back at the kiosk. "That back there . . . selling their blades as collectibles, marketing their—literature . . . That's more like propaganda. Trying to win hearts and minds. That's subtler than the Klingons I know."

He reflected on his misstep at Shinohara's World, how he'd been outplayed by an opponent who saw more moves ahead than he did. "I have a feeling there's nothing more dangerous than a subtle Klingon."

The venue for the peace talks was the Council Hall, a heavily fortified edifice in the heart of Zemrok City, and the historic meeting place of the Council of Clans. The Council was one of the ways the Acamarians attempted to maintain some kind of order and cooperation among their fractious, feud-prone clans, a place for the clan leaders to gather and negotiate trade deals and alliances, reconcile disputes, and address shared, planet-wide problems such as the resource shortages and environmental crises that were caused or exacerbated by the ongoing clan wars. But according to the Starfleet briefings Kirk had studied, the Council was often a token institution at best, for the clans remained politically independent and were rarely unified in opinion or policy even within themselves, except where matters of clan rivalries and blood vendettas were concerned.

The current peace talks had been organized by the largest, most successful alliance of clans, built through generations of intermarriage and trading partnerships so lucrative that they created a strong disincentive for blood feuds, or at least encouraged the member clans to limit blood vengeance for murders to the actual murderers instead of their entire families. The Inter-clan Alliance was pushing for a strengthening of the Council, giving it the clout to regulate and limit blood feuds or even enforce less violent alternative means of redressing grievances. Apparently a large segment of the Acamarian populace was sick of the endless violence and suffering resulting from their clan leaders' prideful vendettas, and there was a growing movement to establish a strong Ruling Council that could outlaw blood feuds altogether. A recent, particularly brazen attack on an Alliance hospital, killing dozens of innocents uninvolved in the feuds, had intensified the demands for change and convinced several resistant factions to attend the talks. Yet this movement was opposed by traditionalist voices insisting that abandoning blood vengeance for attacks on one's clan would mean abandoning the very essence of Acamarian identity. This, naturally, was the side that the Klingon Empire's representative was here to advocate.

Kirk was surprised upon his first meeting with the imperial envoy. The man wore the uniform of a Klingon battleship captain, but he looked unlike any Klingon Kirk had faced before. It wasn't because he belonged to the subtype of Klingon that looked almost human, for Kirk had encountered some of those in the past. No—what made this Klingon so different was the way he carried himself. The goateed, widow's-peaked captain approached Kirk's party without the usual aggressive, threatening swagger of a Klingon warrior. He strode with confidence, to be sure, but it was a relaxed, almost debonair self-assurance. He even offered Kirk a charming smile, clicking his heels together and offering a slight bow as if they were Victorian gentlemen running into each other at the opera. "Ahh, you must be the young Captain Kirk I've been hearing so much about. A pleasure, sir. I am Koloth, son of Lasshar, at your service." He extended a hand.

Kirk only let himself be nonplussed for a moment. If this Koloth wanted to play at being charming and debonair, he would find that he'd more than met his match. Smiling, Kirk returned the handshake with firmness and warmth. "My *dear* Captain Koloth. The pleasure is surely mine. How refreshing to meet a Klingon versed in diplomacy rather than combat."

Koloth's eyes flashed, but he maintained his genteel façade, merely a bit more stiffly. "I assure you, Captain, I am equally well versed in both. As I believe you may have learned last month at—what did you call it—Shinohara's World?" His smile widened, growing more smug. "I do hope for your sake that your own diplomatic skills are more polished than your battle strategies. But we shall see inside, shall we not?" He offered Kirk one more bow. "Good day, Captain," he said before striding off toward the debate hall.

"Damn." Gary Mitchell sidled up to Kirk, shaking his head. "I see what you mean about subtle Klingons."

Khorasani scoffed. "Only you would think that act of his was subtle. What a slimeball."

Kirk controlled his reaction. Koloth was clearly the sort who relished playing mind games with his adversaries. He could have been falsely taking credit for Shinohara's World to dishearten Kirk. But if he were capable of a ploy like that, he might just as easily have been the genuine strategist behind the Klingons' victory there. Best, then, not to make the same mistake of overconfidence.

"The greatest lie on Acamar is that vengeance balances the scales."

Surima, chieftain of the clan Kayok, paced the debate floor before the assembled Council of Clans, her melodious but powerful voice resonating through the hall. The middle-aged chieftain was a slight, dark-haired woman, appearing almost human to Kirk's eyes save for the vertical crease bisecting her forehead and the clan markings tattooed across her left cheek.

"Everyone can see this is a lie," Surima went on. "When one of us is wronged even slightly, the clan is compelled to retaliate with even greater force, to warn all rivals of the dreadful cost of crossing them. And yet all rivals feel the same way, of course. So when they are attacked with greater force, they must strike back even more violently. Far from bringing balance, the cycle of revenge quickly escalates.

"There was a time when such feuds, brutal though they were, nonetheless could be carried out with limited effect. Our clans held less territory or were migratory. A vendetta could drive one clan away from another's lands for good, so the enmity would endure but the bloodshed would burn out. If close neighbors warred on each other, at worst they would wipe each other out with minimal impact on other clans, so the feud would not spread farther.

"Yet now we live in a modern world," Surima went on, her voice rising. "Our population is far larger, our space to roam diminished, our lands and peoples far more interconnected. Clans depend on their alliances with one another to thrive, and a crime against one clan must be avenged by all its allies, spreading the violence still further. At the same time, our weapons have grown deadlier, far more likely to take the lives of bystanders and draw even more clans into the feud. Rather than burning out, our vendettas now routinely grow out of control, engulfing whole regions, even whole continents. Blood feuds only end when one clan is too devastated to fight anymore, or is exterminated altogether."

Surima's delivery had continued to grow sharper, her initial soft-spoken manner now replaced by a compelling intensity. Kirk had seen other noteworthy leaders use much the same rhetorical style to capture the attention of their listeners, and he had tried to emulate their example. "Every clan knows this will happen," she went on in the tone of an accuser. "Every clan knows that by following the ancient traditions of vengeance, they only bring further destruction on themselves and their neighbors. Every clan knows that the economic cost of such a feud will require them to slash spending on economic growth, medical care, worker salaries, infrastructure repair, and countless other necessities of life. Every clan knows the loss of lives and the destruction of property will weaken them even further.

"And yet we still retaliate. We still escalate. We still perpetuate the mindless reflexes of our ancestors, knowing the material cost, because we are more afraid of the intangible cost of losing pride, of appearing disloyal to our clans and our traditions. We place our hate for our rivals above our love for our own, and we feel any damage we bring down upon ourselves and our clanmates is worth it so long as we can convince ourselves we've hurt our enemies more.

"But there is another way. The Interclan Alliance has proven it. We have built bonds of trust between clans through intermarriage, diplomacy, and trade. We have instituted a system of laws that designates specific penalties for transgressions—penalties directed only against the individuals who transgressed, and accepted by their clans when guilt is proven, so no further retaliation is sought."

The chieftain of the Lornak clan, a burly, long-haired man named Zylnas, rose to his feet and protested, "And by so doing, you make yourselves weak and expose yourselves to attack! We have seen this in the recent massacre at Naraga Hospital. Not merely an attack on your territory, but a slaughter of helpless children, the infirm, the elderly. This atrocity is an outrage to all Acamarians, Alliance or not. If you do not find the culprits and retaliate against their clan in greater force, you merely embolden them to massacre other innocents!"

"We shall identify the culprits," Surima countered, her more delicate voice nonetheless overpowering his with its calm strength. "But we shall punish them according to the same laws we apply within the Alliance. Because those laws are the source of our strength, not our weakness. They show others that we will deal with them fairly, that they may unite with us in trust and be stronger together than apart. By extending the same treatment to all, without as well as within the Alliance, we shall grow the Alliance further—perhaps, one day, to all of Acamar, once we finally set aside our ancient addiction to vengeance and are ready to join the galaxy as a united, peaceful people."

"What a revealing choice of words."

Having drawn the crowd's attention with his acerbic interjection, Koloth rose and offered a slight bow. "Forgive the interruption, but I could remain silent no longer," the Klingon envoy said. "Esteemed councillors, if I may . . . what Chieftain Surima clearly means is that she wishes to suppress Acamar's long-standing traditions of clan loyalty and honor in order to appease the squeamish values of the Federation. She hopes to reduce your proud people to a tamed and neutered client state of the Earthers."

Kirk laughed out loud. It was only partly a ploy, but it succeeded in getting the attention of the room. "Captain Koloth is one to talk," Kirk spoke out, rising to his feet. "The Acamarians have dealt with the Klingons before. Surely you are all aware that they are the ones who wish to tame and possess your world, as they have possessed and enslaved many others."

Koloth's eyes flashed, but he still retained his cool. "The esteemed Captain Kirk is correct that the clans of Acamar know the ways of the Klingons. They know we, too, value the honor of our families and clans, our Great Houses. That we do not hesitate to fight for their honor when they are injured. That we value the blood of our kinsmen above all else, and therefore will always repay its spilling in kind, swiftly and decisively.

"It is because of this that we understand the Acamarian people. We honor your ways and we admire your warrior spirit. We wish to nurture your martial traditions, not muzzle them as the Federation and their toadies seek to do."

"What the Klingons want," Kirk countered, "is to use your internal conflicts against you. To arm one side and help it conquer all others, after which they will be puppet rulers doing the Empire's bidding. I've seen them do it before." His eyes locked on Koloth's. "I've stopped them from doing it before."

"Captain Kirk is right," Surima intoned. "It is our division that makes us vulnerable. We pit our strengths against one another, and thus any outsider who co-opts one faction can use it to weaken all the others. It is only by recognizing that our common bond as Acamarians outweighs our differences that we can survive in this contentious galaxy."

"But which outsider is really trying to weaken us?" Zylnas boomed. "You say, Surima, that you will punish the culprits in the Naraga massacre. Well, we can identify them!"

While Surima quelled the resulting outburst from the crowd, Zylnas called in an aide carrying a long, narrow case. Once the noise had diminished sufficiently, he and the aide stepped forward to face Surima on the debate floor, the aide laying the case on one of the low tables that flanked it. "As I said, this assault was an outrage to all Acamarians, so the Lornak clan offered its assistance in the investigation. Our search divers found this weapon and two others like it dumped in Naraga Bay." At his gesture, the aide opened the case.

Inside it was the unmistakable, triple-barreled shape of a Starfleet phaser rifle.

This time, it took more of an effort for Surima to quiet the crowd. Koloth crossed his arms and directed a smug smile Kirk's way. Kirk merely kept his own counsel, thinking.

"Our scientists have tested the weapons," Zylnas went on. "We will freely make our data available to all. The tests confirm that these are phased nadion rifles of Starfleet manufacture . . . and that their energy signatures match the blast damage at the hospital!"

It took even longer for the next outburst to subside, but Kirk let the noise and fury flow past him. Finally, Surima gave him the chance to respond. "Captain Kirk, do you wish to comment on this allegation?"

Grateful that the uproar had given him time to think through his response, Kirk spoke calmly. "I have no doubt that the Lornak scientists did their work diligently and in good faith. However, I can add one thing to their findings: That rifle is of a model that Starfleet discontinued nearly two years ago. It was, however, in use during several of our past conflicts with the Klingon Empire. They captured many of our armaments during those conflicts, as we did theirs.

"And if we had committed an atrocity on your soil and sought to destroy the evidence, we would simply have beamed the weapons away or set them to self-destruct, not simply dumped them where you could find them."

"If your troops had committed the massacre themselves, no," Koloth countered. "But you yourself just accused us of providing arms to local factions. You might well have done the same—in which case you would surely have given them obsolete models that you no longer needed."

"But what would we gain by it? We are not the ones who would profit from greater conflict between Acamar's clans."

"Yet this was a crime that all of Acamar's clans are united in condemning," the dapper Klingon continued, pacing the debate floor and addressing the assembled crowd. "It has brought them closer to agreement than they have been in a long time. The Interclan Alliance capitalized on that sympathy to organize this peace conference that you so proudly endorse." Koloth ended up facing Kirk. "Convenient for the Federation, is it not?"

The mood of the room was clearly beginning to turn against the Starfleet party now. Khorasani rose and began to step closer to Kirk, but he held her back with a gesture. Even Surima looked unsure. "Captain Kirk," she said, "do you wish to request a recess so that you may review the evidence and prepare a response?"

Kirk took a few moments to consider her words. "Thank you, Chieftain . . . but no. That will not be necessary."

The spectators reacted with surprise and Koloth with a smug look of triumph, but Kirk disregarded them, stepping forward confidently onto the debate floor. "I could attempt to prove to you what I know—that this is a ploy by the Klingon Empire to discredit the Federation. I could ask you to put your peace negotiations on hold so that I could defend Starfleet's integrity and honor. But I won't—because that would merely be a distraction.

"Ultimately, this debate is not about what the Federation did or did not do. It's not about what the Klingons did or didn't do in the past, or what they might do in the future. It's about the Acamarians and what *you* will do. It's about whether you remain bound by your ancient tradition of blood feuds . . . or find a new path, a better path of your own choosing.

"With this charge against us, you're being offered a temptation—an excuse to fall back on the easy, familiar path you've followed for so long, to act on the old, comfortable reflexes of rage and revenge, and in so doing, abandon the more difficult, challenging, courageous effort to build a new way of living. It's always easy to give in to that temptation, which is why it must be looked on with skepticism when it's offered.

"Captain Koloth wants to make this debate about us, about the Federation and the Klingon Empire—because that is what serves his agenda, never mind what serves the Acamarians. In his mind, you are nothing but pawns in the ongoing game between the Empire and the Federation. But I will not play that game here. I will not ask you to set aside this conference's rightful focus on the people of Acamar, and on the future you wish to create. I and my crew are here to support *your* initiative and *your* courage . . . and we will respect the decisions that you make."

The mood in the room was uneasy after Kirk finished. The clan leaders murmured to one another for several moments, and at last Surima spoke. "In any case, Captains, you have both left us much to think about. As your continued presence might be . . . disruptive, we request that you both withdraw while we debate the matter among ourselves."

As Kirk led his party from the room, he wondered if he had made a serious mistake by refusing to counter the charges. It had felt like the right play, an expression of trust in the Acamarians' better natures to inspire them to live up to the same. But what if their need for revenge against any perceived slight was too great? What if, by offering no defense, he had ceded the victory to Koloth?

U.S.S. *Sacagawea*

"Acamar owes you a debt of gratitude, Captain Kirk."

Chieftain Surima smiled at Kirk over the bridge viewscreen. *"Ignoring the accusation against you was a bold move, and a successful one. By showing that you did not take the charge seriously, you made it easier for me to convince the independent clans that it was false. Had you been guilty, you would have tried much harder to persuade us of your innocence. Much as Koloth is still attempting to persuade us of his, though mainly by casting further aspersions upon Starfleet."*

Kirk smiled back, standing before his command chair as a gesture of respect. "I did what seemed right in the moment, Chieftain, but I'm certain I have your own persuasive skills to thank as well."

"Don't undervalue yourself, Captain. Your gesture had another, even more striking impact. You declined to fight in defense of your people's honor . . . and you made it a victory to do so. That was a potent advertisement for the principles the Alliance represents."

The captain thought for a moment. "A great philosopher on our world, a champion of peace and nonviolence, once said, 'If anyone slaps you on the right cheek, turn to him the other also.' To many people over the ages, this has sounded like mere surrender, an invitation to further abuse. But in the culture that ruled over his people, a backhand strike with the right hand was used to assert dominance over an inferior, while a forehand slap was used between equals."

Surima nodded in understanding. *"So by turning the left cheek toward them, you denied them the ability to treat you as an inferior. You resisted and defied them without aggression. This is very deft. I take it you are a follower of this philosopher?"*

"Let's just say that I respect many of his teachings, and those of others like him throughout history. We have found that truth comes from many teachers."

"I shall remember that. Again, my thanks, Captain Kirk. You have helped to keep this peace conference alive. It may be many years yet before we finally unite and end the violence, but I am surer than ever that it will one day happen. And on that day, I hope you and I are both present to witness it."

Once Surima said her farewells and the screen went dark, Gary Mitchell gave Kirk a skeptical look. "I know you love your books, Captain, but I doubt you were thinking of the Sermon on the Mount when you pulled that little gambit on Koloth down there."

"No, I wasn't." Kirk sat down in the center seat and crossed his legs. "If anything, I was thinking more of Polonius."

Mitchell stared. "The guy Hamlet stabbed behind a curtain?"

Kirk nodded. "'This above all: to thine own self be true.' The last time I faced the Klingons, at Shinohara's World, I tried to beat them at their own game, to out-Klingon them, and that just gave them the edge. So this time, I tried to be true to my own principles. My own belief in peace, and in the Acamarians' right to self-determination." He shrugged. "And that let me go somewhere that Koloth, for all his pretentions of tact and diplomacy, didn't know how to follow." Commodore Lam had been right—thinking like a soldier wasn't always the answer. Or rather, a true soldier used every available means to protect the peace, and force was not always the appropriate tool.

Mehran Egdor smiled at Kirk. "You were right to trust your instincts, Captain," the first officer said. "Even if your inspirations were merely human."

Kirk smiled back. "We've been known to get it right every once in a while."

"Captain," Elena Yu reported from the science station, "I've detected a transporter signal from the surface to the Klingon cruiser, and the cruiser is now thrusting to break orbit."

"Hmm," Egdor said. "I'd say Captain Koloth is no longer welcome on Acamar III."

"That's fine with me, sir," Azadeh Khorasani said. "If I never see that Koloth again, it'll be too soon."

Mitchell stared at her. "I thought you had nothing against Klingons."

"Not as a race. That doesn't mean I have to like them all as individuals. I can respect a Klingon who's making a forthright, honest attempt to kill me. But that guy's all smarm and insincerity. He sets my teeth on edge. So good riddance to him."

Though Kirk kept it to himself, he found he couldn't agree with Khorasani's words. He'd rather enjoyed his battle of wits with Koloth. It was a refreshing change of pace from his previous, more visceral conflicts with the Klingons.

Maybe someday, he thought, *we'll have a rematch.*

ENTERPRISE
2265

Four

[A] starship also runs on loyalty to one man.

—Spock

U.S.S. *Enterprise*

One perquisite of commanding a ship as large as the *Enterprise* was that Kirk was now assigned his own personal yeoman to handle much of his everyday business such as filing and organizing logs, reviewing department reports, and so forth. His yeoman, a young enlisted man named Aaron Maynard, also served as a personal valet of sorts, taking care of the captain's meals, readying his uniforms, and otherwise managing his everyday concerns. Kirk was ambivalent about this; while he appreciated being freed from the distractions of such quotidian matters so that he could focus fully on his command responsibilities, his parents had raised him to be self-reliant and hard-working, to give to others rather than take from them. It was difficult to adjust to letting someone else tend to his personal needs.

Another consequence of having a yeoman to handle the paperwork was that the *Enterprise* had no ready room adjoining the bridge. Essentially, the bridge itself was the captain's office, while Yeoman Maynard had his own workstation on deck five, adjacent to Kirk's quarters. This arrangement sat better with Kirk, who had made little use of his ready room aboard the *Sacagawea*, except when the need for private conversations arose. On the *Enterprise*, Kirk supposed he could use his quarters or any of the ship's briefing rooms for such a purpose. Even a turbolift would do in a pinch.

For now, the last thing Kirk wanted was a private space in which to retreat from the rest of the ship. He preferred being out among the crew, getting to know them and the vessel they operated, forming a bond with the people he would be leading over the years to come. Naturally, that meant forming a bond with his first officer, a captain's main point of contact with his crew. Though Kirk had initially hoped to promote Gary Mitchell to the post, he was grateful to have an executive officer like Lieutenant Commander Spock, who had spent eleven years aboard the *Enterprise* and knew the vessel intimately. As a young captain finding his way aboard the *Sacagawea*, Kirk had benefited greatly from the seasoning and experience of both his first officers. He hoped he could learn just as much from Mister Spock. He knew the man was only a few years older than himself and had been an upperclassman when Kirk had entered the Academy, but Spock had already accumulated achievements well beyond his years. Kirk hoped that would give them common ground to build on.

"But most of your achievements have been aboard this ship," Kirk said to Spock as the latter led the former on a familiarization tour of the *Enterprise*'s engineering section, filling the new captain in on the vessel's unique modifications and idiosyncrasies. Normally the chief engineer would have handled this, but Commander Scott was still en route from his last assignment, and Spock had been aboard long enough to have an intimate knowledge of every system—particularly the engineering control computers they were currently surveying, multiple large mainframe units arrayed in parallel rows in this portion of the engineering hull's cavernous lower levels. "Eleven years is a long time to spend in one place. With your record, you could have easily put in for promotion to your own command. I appreciate that you chose to remain aboard and show me the ropes."

Spock raised a brow. "'Ropes,' Captain? A vessel of this advancement requires no such primitive mechanisms for its operation."

Kirk stared at him. "Pardon me, Mister Spock, but is that some form of Vulcan humor? Surely after serving with a mostly human crew for so long, you've heard people using antique nautical metaphors before."

"I am aware of the human fondness for deliberate imprecision, Captain Kirk," the other man replied stiffly. "I do not, however, choose to participate in it. My responsibility as science officer is to strive for accuracy at all times."

And Gary says I'm stiff and humorless, Kirk thought. *But who knows? It might be refreshing not to be the most serious one in the room.*

Spock led Kirk into the adjacent main energizer monitor section, housing the circuits that channeled power from the warp engines into the starship's systems. "In response to your observation, Captain," the first officer went on, "I have no interest in pursuing a command position. I am a scientist first. That is the role for which my skills are best suited. As for why I remained aboard the *Enterprise*, it was Captain Pike's preference that I do so. It is a logical choice, for as you say, I have more experience with this vessel than any remaining member of its complement. And the passage of time does not concern me. I do not seek change for the sake of change. I am suited for my current position, as it is for me. Additionally, as a Vulcan, I have a significantly greater life expectancy than a human. Eleven years is thus proportionately a less significant interval of my projected lifespan."

Kirk blinked. "I see. So it's basically irrelevant to you who's actually commanding the ship."

"That is essentially correct, sir, as long as said commanding

officer performs competently. And an officer lacking in compe-
tence would be unlikely to be given command of a vessel such as
the *Enterprise.*"

As Spock led him into the dilithium crystal recharging section, Kirk reminded himself not to take the Vulcan's cold response personally. He may have been accustomed to a warmer
relationship with his exec, but different individuals had their
own ways of doing things, especially across the divide of species
and culture. Starfleet was about respecting diversity, after all.
Spock was excellent at his job; it shouldn't matter that he and
Kirk were unlikely to become friends. Kirk would have Mitchell
for that, and hopefully McCoy soon enough.

Still, it wasn't Kirk's way to give up easily. There had to be
some way to make a connection through Spock's icy reserve.
Remembering a bit of advice Captain Pike had offered before
the change-of-command ceremony, Kirk smiled at his new first
officer. "Mister Spock. When the inspection's done, would you
be interested in a game of chess . . . ?"

Lee Kelso entered the deck eight gymnasium to the sound of
clashing metal. A crowd of spectators making impressed noises
blocked his view of the source, but as Kelso moved around
them, he saw a man and a woman engaged in a lively fencing match. Their masks obscured their faces, but the woman's
muscular frame left no doubt in Kelso's mind that it was Sarah
Lopez, the assistant engineer who spent most of her off-duty
time lifting weights. Surprisingly, her leaner male opponent was
beating her handily, matching her athleticism and countering
her strength with speed and agility. Once he scored the final
point and the match was called in his favor, the man whipped
off his mask to reveal a brightly grinning face under a mop of
shaggy black hair. Kelso realized this must be the new astro-
physicist everyone had been talking about for the past few days,

the one who'd already charmed everyone with his cheerful, gregarious manner and eclectic range of hobbies.

The young man spent a few moments accepting the congratulations of his opponent and the accolades of the spectators, then laughed raucously as Nyota Uhura improvised a teasing and slightly ribald song about his prowess with a blade. Kelso just stood back to enjoy the show, but after a while, the physicist spotted him, brightened, and came over to greet him. "Lieutenant Kelso! I've been looking forward to meeting you!" They shook hands. "Hi. I'm Hikaru Sulu."

"Pleased to meet you, Sulu. I've heard a lot about you. They say you're an ace helmsman."

Sulu laughed at the praise, but didn't refute it. "That's my primary field, yes. I was a helm officer on the *Arjuna* and the *Jemison*."

"So why the move to sciences?"

"You mind if we go to the locker room? I need a shower after that match."

"And I need to change *into* my gym clothes, so sure."

"So as for the move to sciences," Sulu said as the two men headed for the locker room, "that's pretty much your fault." At Kelso's stare, Sulu laughed. "Just kidding. I applied for a transfer to the *Enterprise* as soon as I heard Captain Kirk was expected to take her over, but there weren't any helm posts open. Luckily, I minored in astrophysics, and there was a slot available there."

Kelso frowned. "You wanted to serve with Kirk that much?"

"Is that surprising?" Sulu asked as he started to strip off his fencing gear. "I've wanted to serve with him ever since I heard what he achieved at Regulus. And the things he's done before then—the Vulcanian Expedition, Baez IV, Acamar, Chenar . . ." He chuckled. "I just have a feeling that serving under Captain Kirk is going to be quite an adventure."

"Well, maybe," Kelso replied sourly as he pulled off his own tunic. "You know the saying—adventure is what happens when things go wrong."

Sulu's bright mood faltered for the first time, but not fully. "Come on, Kelso. I know you've had your share of adventures under Captain Pike."

"Sure, sometimes it's unavoidable. But Captain Pike is a seasoned veteran, tempered and responsible. When I transferred here from the *Asimov*, I was honored to serve under him, to learn from his years of experience." He grimaced. "And then just a few months later, he gets bumped upstairs and we get a new captain who's barely older than I am."

"I'm sorry you feel that way. But I bet if you give Captain Kirk a chance, he'll win you over. The man's clearly no amateur."

"Oh, I know his reputation," Kelso said. "Disciplined, serious, driven, mature beyond his years."

"You sound unconvinced."

"I was a couple of years behind him at the Academy," Kelso said. "The buzz was, he cheated on the *Kobayashi Maru*. He didn't earn his graduation fairly."

Sulu's smile disappeared, as though Kelso had touched on a sore spot. "The *Kobayashi Maru* is just a psych test," he said. "It's not as big a deal as people make it out to be."

Kelso realized that Sulu must have been unhappy with his own performance on the infamous no-win scenario. Recognizing that it was a sensitive subject, he shifted his tack. "Anyway, the point is, you can't always trust someone's reputation. Some people get where they are through hard work; others take shortcuts and get by on charm. I knew a guy just like that on the *Asimov*. Acted like the whole galaxy revolved around him."

"And you think Captain Kirk's in the latter category."

"Just look at who he brought with him. Don't get me wrong, Gary Mitchell's a good navigator and a really friendly guy. I like him, and having him sitting next to me at the helm keeps things entertaining. But I don't think a class clown like him would ever have become second officer on a capital ship if his best friend Captain Kirk hadn't been showing him favoritism for years."

Sulu grinned as he moved toward the showers. "Tell you what, Kelso. If you're that unhappy working on the bridge, you could always transfer to astrophysics. I'd be happy to take your place at the helm."

"Yeah, you wish." They both knew it didn't work that way. "Don't worry, Sulu, I'll stick it out. We don't always get to serve under people we like."

"Give Kirk a chance," Sulu said over the sound of the water. "It's only been a few days. I bet that once you see him in action, you'll change your mind."

Kelso sighed. "Maybe you're right. Maybe I'm just disappointed that Pike left so soon and I'm taking it out on the new guy."

"That's the spirit!"

But as Kelso returned to the gym and began his workout, his doubts lingered more in his mind than Sulu's assurances. Kirk had gained quite a reputation with a few flashy accomplishments in a relatively brief span of time, sure, but that was just what made Kelso wary. Commanding a *Constitution*-class ship was a unique responsibility, one that demanded broad and deep experience and keen judgment. Was it right to let someone jump the queue past more seasoned officers because of a few big victories?

After all, Kirk's record on the *Sacagawea* hadn't consisted solely of victories. He'd had some major losses too. At least once, he'd come within a hair's breadth of losing his entire ship and crew. How much of his success came down to sheer luck?

And what if the *Enterprise* was where his luck ran out?

———

"You think you're ready for your first real assignment, Jim?"

Kirk sat forward in his command chair, his body language

alone answering José Mendez's question. "More than ready, sir. Commander Scott has joined us, so we're fully staffed at last."

"*Excellent. Because this is the kind of mission where we want to put our best foot forward. The kind a ship like the* Enterprise *is made for—to be the face of the Federation in dealing with an alien culture, in a situation where a show of strength is as important as diplomacy.*"

Kirk took that in, noting as the rest of the bridge crew turned forward to focus on what Mendez said next. "You have our attention, Commodore."

"*Have you heard of the Aulacri?*"

"I can't say I have." Time to give his science officer a try. "Mister Spock?"

The Vulcan answered without even consulting his station. "Aulacri. A minor starfaring power whose territory abuts the Federation. First formally contacted four years ago; recommended as candidates for Federation membership last year, following cultural survey and assessment. The surveyors spoke highly of their peaceful, cooperative society, with little history of warfare for thousands of years. Their government and populace are currently evaluating their response to the Federation's invitation." His brows rose as his head took on a curious tilt. "If I recall correctly, they are one of the few known humanoid species to possess tails." That remark evoked a grin from Gary Mitchell, who was no doubt wondering what their women looked like.

"*That's all correct, Mister Spock,*" said Mendez. "*What you left out was that the Aulacri are planning to terraform a dead planet in their territory, Karabos II by name.*"

"I am familiar with the name Karabos II," Spock pointed out, as if to defend himself against the charge of incompleteness. "I gather that an Andorian archaeological team has been surveying the ruins of an extinct civilization on that planet."

"*And that's the crux of the problem, Captain Kirk. The Aulacri*" *are a week away from bombarding the planet with multiple large comets, in order to replenish its water."*

Kirk's eyes widened. "They sound like a very ambitious people. No wonder the Federation wants them."

"A patient people as well," Spock added. "A terraforming operation of that sort could take centuries to complete."

"The archaeologists would disagree with you about the Aulacri's patience, Commander," said Mendez. *"They insist there are still undiscovered ruins on the planet, that bombarding it with comets could destroy the knowledge and legacy of a lost civilization. And their team leader is refusing to evacuate. She insists the ruins on Karabos II are too important to abandon."*

"So . . . which side are we being sent to convince?" Kirk asked.

"Your job, ideally, is to negotiate a compromise or alternative that will give everyone what they want. Naturally the potential for scientific discovery is important—but studying the Aulacri's terraforming techniques could potentially be of greater benefit than studying another set of ancient alien ruins. And there's the additional consideration of the Aulacri's potential membership. If you can convince them to choose an alternate site or at least postpone the bombardment long enough for the archaeologists to complete their survey, that's fine. But tread carefully, Captain. Our goal is to keep Federation citizens alive and safe, of course—but also to do so without offending the Aulacri. The planet is in their territory, so if they say our people need to go, we have no business disagreeing."

Kirk absorbed that. "So when you said 'a show of strength,' you meant it might be Federation scientists we need to strong-arm."

"I'm hoping it won't come to that, Jim. After all, the team leader is one of our own. Ex-Starfleet."

The captain blinked, then traded a look with Gary Mitchell. A female-identifying Andorian archaeologist, ex-Starfleet and stubborn as hell? Kirk began to realize why he had been given this assignment.

"I see you've anticipated me," Mendez said. *"The team leader is your old crewmate Rhenas Sherev. I'm hoping that if she won't listen to the Diplomatic Corps or the Aulacri, maybe she'll listen to an old friend."*

Kirk sighed. "I'll do my best to convince her, sir. But Rhenas Sherev is not someone who backs down easily."

VEGA COLONY

2262

Five

I don't believe in a no-win scenario.

—James T. Kirk

Fragment A57, Vega debris disk

Commander Sherev's antennae twitched within her helmet, bumping nervously against its interior padding. She was tempted to rip the confining helmet off so she would be free to express her excitement properly, but she supposed that having air to breathe was slightly more important. She just wished the *Caliban* had a wider variety of EVA suit designs available. That was the drawback of such a small ship.

Then again, a larger ship would present a larger target for the particles of dust and rock that were unusually densely packed in this portion of the debris disk, with a greater probability of being struck. Of course, that was what deflector shields were for, but the *Caliban's* compact size meant it could nestle in the lee of this 1,800-meter-wide chunk of dwarf planet crust and leave its shields down, making it easier for its six crew members to move between the sleek *Titania*-class surveyor and the Vegan ruins buried within the dwarf fragment. If more personnel were needed for the excavation, then Captain Kirk and the base at Eagle's Landing were just a subspace call away.

For the moment, though, Sherev was glad to have the ruins all to herself and her immediate team. The human colonists on

Vega IX had spent the past century and a half excavating the planet surface and sifting through the debris disk to recover artifacts of the ancient civilization that had terraformed the planet nearly a million standard years ago, but they had rarely found a facility as relatively intact as this one. What the *Caliban* had discovered was the remains of an underground base or bunker buried hundreds of meters beneath the surface of what, judging by the fragment's curvature and spectroscopic readings, had been the largest of the dwarf planets whose destruction had created the debris disk around the star. The depth of the facility must have protected it from the bombardments that had destroyed the Vegans' civilization, leaving little in the way of identifiable technology or organic remains. Not fully protected, of course; the final planetbuster bombardment that had cracked apart the dwarf planet had split the bunker's corridors and vented it to space, probably sucking any occupants out along with the air, moisture, loose equipment and documents, and so forth.

However, by the grace of Uzaveh, this fragment did contain the bunker's central reactor, as well as several workstations with power connections leading to it. As they had been surrounded by planetary crust, the reactor and the workstations had been shielded from all but the highest-velocity micrometeoroid impacts, and thus many of them remained intact enough that there might actually be a chance of reactivating them. Sherev had insisted on hooking up the portable generator from the *Caliban* herself, hoping that if she could power up one of the workstations, and if by some miracle it held a visual log or security recording, she might become the first archaeologist to see and hear a record of a living Vegan. What a story that would be to tell her bondmates and kids the next time she came home! Sure, the eternal academic fame and glory wouldn't hurt, but getting to share her enthusiasm for discovery with her children was the real prize.

Maybe, assuming the universal translator lived up to its name, she could even gain some insight into the causes of the devastating war between the inhabitants of Vega IX and those who had chosen to remain on the dwarf planets. To all indications, the ancient species had settled the dwarfs first and overseen the terraforming of Vega IX from them; yet when the planet was finally habitable generations later, a segment of the population had chosen to remain in space. Over time, the two civilizations had grown further apart, going through cycles of conflict and reconciliation, yet eventually having a falling-out so extreme that it had led to their mutual annihilation. If Sherev could discover the reasons why, it might enable future civilizations to avoid similar cataclysms of their own. Even today, there were still some Andorians who resented having to share the Federation with Vulcans and Tellarites, and no doubt members of those species who reciprocated. The laws and social standards of the Federation had kept the peace among its members (though not always with outsiders) for a hundred years now—but there had been far longer periods of peace between the branches of Vegan civilization. Was peace always doomed to fail eventually? Or could the failure be prevented if its causes could be anticipated?

"*Okay,*" Sawa Isurugi announced over the comm channel, startling Sherev out of her reverie. "*The last power circuit is patched now. You can try jump-starting the reactor at your convenience, Commander.*"

Sherev sighed. "Finally."

Arhanla's deep, gentle voice sounded next. "*Are we certain we want to do this?*" the Deltan lieutenant asked. "*I feel there's still too much uncertainty in our models of the reactor's power output and stability. We barely understand its mechanism for power generation.*"

"The thing about most kinds of high-energy power sources besides antimatter," Sherev told him, "is that it's hard to make them react in the first place. So if the process doesn't work right, you're more likely to get no power at all than a runaway reaction. At worst, this will just fizzle and we'll have to find some way to power the workstations ourselves." The stations were designed to draw on the reactor's exotic power and thus couldn't be energized by the portable generator. Using a charge from the generator to trigger the reactor itself was simpler than inventing some way to convert the power directly.

"Is there a reason we can't just wait to do that?" Arhanla replied.

"We've waited long enough," Sherev countered. "We've run multiple simulations showing we can make this work. The few percentage points of uncertainty we could shave off aren't worth the delay. We are in a debris disk, after all. There's always a chance, however small, that an impact could damage these systems and cost us valuable knowledge. The sooner we learn all this ruin has to teach us, the better."

"Besides, I'm transferring to Mars in three weeks," Isurugi said. *"I don't want to miss the big moment when it comes."*

"You don't have to, Sawa," Sherev told her. "Because here we go. Power activation in five . . . four . . . three . . . two . . . one . . . Now!"

Her antennae were drumming audibly against the helmet padding as she hit the activation switch. The readouts on the generator showed that power was being delivered, so they simply had to wait for the reactor deep below to react to the spark and build up its own energy. It was only a matter of time now before the workstation before her lit up with alien symbols.

Only a matter of time . . .

"Oh, come on," she said two minutes later. "What's taking so long?" Jim Kirk's voice echoed in her memory: *You're the most impatient archaeologist I've ever met.*

"The reactor is receiving power," Isurugi reported. *"Something is happening in there . . . Energy is building up, but it's not being*

sent out through the conduits. Maybe we underestimated how eroded they were."

"I suppose you were right, Commander," Arhanla said with a sigh. "The worst that will happen is that nothing happens."

"Oh no. No!"

"Sawa? Report!" Any thoughts on the irony of the young engineer's outburst would have to wait.

"Shimatta . . . The power is surging! It's going to blow!"

No, not when we're so close! "Is there any way to stop it?"

"We have no time! Move, everyone! Hayaku, hayaku!"

Clenching her teeth to suppress a shriek of frustration, Sherev spun around and fired her suit thrusters, propelling herself through the fragment's near-weightless corridors toward the surface of the fragment. She prayed to Uzaveh that she could get far enough from the blast that the intervening rock would shield her. She prayed even harder that the same would be true for Isurugi and Arhanla. Then she remembered the three others on the ship nearby. "Sherev to *Caliban*. Fall back, gain some distance from—"

The walls around her convulsed, heaved, and fractured. A massive piece of them collided with her suit from behind, and in the instant before she blacked out, she prayed that she would see her children again.

U.S.S. *Somerville* NCC-S471

"Kirk to Sherev, come in! Come in, please!"

Kirk leaned forward urgently in the *Somerville*'s command chair, hoping for a reply. It brought him no pleasure to be back in a starship's center seat, for it was not his to command. The midsized *Capella*-class ship was a workhorse vessel shared among the various Starfleet research, defense, and operations units active in the Vega system, and it had happened to be attached to the archaeological station when the *Caliban*'s distress call had come in. Normally Sherev would have occupied this command chair for whatever mission the ship needed to carry out. But she had considered the much smaller *Caliban* a better choice for her mission to the dwarf planet fragment—a decision that had seemed reasonable until her attempt to revive the fragment's ancient reactor had somehow triggered it to explode.

According to the distress call, the explosion had shattered the fragment and sent the three EV-suited personnel aboard her flying out into space. The *Caliban* itself had suffered engine, shield, and transporter damage in the explosion and was unable to rescue them; it had been forced to limp out of the debris belt and head for home, leaving the *Somerville* to handle the rescue effort. With the usual commander being the one in need of rescue, Kirk had taken her place on the bridge.

After what seemed an eternity, Sherev's voice came through the static. "*—here. Are you—ding me?*"

Kirk clutched the arms of the chair. "We're here, Rhen. The *Somerville* is on its way. Status?"

"*Not good. The explosion . . . I and the other two were thrusting in opposite directions when it blew, at high speed. The blast dazed all of us, but our suits must have kept accelerating. By the time we recovered, we were already hundreds of kilometers apart and out of thruster fuel. We must be thousands apart by now, and moving fast. Captain, if a debris fragment were to hit one of us at this speed . . .*"

Kirk nodded. Her account matched what the *Caliban*'s remaining three personnel had reported. "Just hang tight. We're coming to beam you to safety. Another twenty, thirty minutes."

A deep male voice interposed. "*Ah. Arhanla here, Captain. I fear that's cutting it quite close for me. I sustained an oxygen leak. It's patched, but my supply is dwindling. I'm . . . meditating to minimize my respiration, but swift rescue would be appreciated, sir.*"

"Captain?" Ensign Hussein at the science station gave Kirk a worried look. "I'm getting suit telemetry from all three, sir. I confirm, Arhanla's oxygen is dangerously depleted. A human might've already passed out."

"The others?" Kirk asked him.

"Isurugi has no more than forty minutes' air remaining, sir. Commander Sherev . . . It'd be right down to the wire, sir."

"Once we get in range, can we beam all three at once?"

Hussein shook his head. "The subspace radiation from the explosion is creating interference. Transporter range will be no more than six hundred kilometers, three hundred on the safe side."

Lieutenant Corot at the navigation station frowned, brushing back a strand of her honey-brown hair. "Sir, that means we'll have to enter the debris disk, right within the new-formed field of debris from the explosion. It increases the navigation hazard considerably. We'll have to proceed slowly."

Sherev's voice over the comm was heavy. "Sounds like you can't save all of us, Jim. Go get Arhanla and Isurugi. Obvious choice."

"I don't accept that," Kirk barked. "There has to be another option, a way to save all three of you."

"I'm not worth it! Listen to me. I caused this. I was reckless, I didn't listen to Arhanla's cautions. I won't be responsible for getting him killed!"

"And I won't be responsible for letting you die! Think of your family, Rhen."

"I am. How could I face my kids if I let someone else die to save myself?"

"That doesn't have to happen. I refuse to believe in a scenario where it's impossible to win."

She laughed. "Then it's true what they say. You cheated on the Kobayashi Maru."

"It wasn't a valid test to begin with. It was designed to force defeat no matter what you did. In real life, there's always a way. Just give us time to find it."

He stepped forward to study the astrogation display. "Plot their positions, and ours," he told the navigator. With that done, he studied the field of battle and considered his options.

He turned to Hussein a moment later. "Ensign. If we channel all shield power to forward deflectors, how much would that improve our maximum safe speed through the debris field?"

Ajay Hussein's eyes widened in concern, but he applied himself to the problem. "Ah, by about a hundred ninety percent, Captain. But it would leave us vulnerable to lateral strikes . . ."

"Which are less likely if we move fast enough. And we wouldn't have to drop shields to transport, saving us further time. It could work. We make a shallow dive through the debris field on the shortest possible course that gets us in transporter range of all three of our people. We beam one party up *en passant*, then continue without slowing down to get the other."

"But, sir," Justine Corot put in, "from our current position, Commander Sherev is closer. We'd be beaming up Mister Arhanla last." The young woman flushed. Clearly she was susceptible to the Deltan man's potent allure.

"*No, Jim,*" Sherev said forcefully. "*Don't gamble like I did. Get . . . Arhanla first.*" She already sounded short of breath.

"This way, we can save all of you," Kirk insisted. "I won't knowingly sacrifice one of my people when there's another option."

"*Damn . . . fool!*"

Ignoring her, Kirk took the center seat again. "All power to forward deflectors. Set fastest intercept course and engage, best available speed. Hussein, coordinate with transporter room. Get a lock on all three people and keep that lock! Beam up as soon as we're in range. Corot, scan for potential impactors along our course. Coordinate with phaser crew for point defense. Communications, inform sickbay to have a medical team standing by in the transporter room."

The crew acknowledged his orders one by one, and at his

command, the *Somerville* surged forward. Within minutes, they had entered the debris disk. At first, there was no visible sign of any change; in the vast emptiness of space, even a "dense" field of debris had its particles millions of kilometers apart. But the longer the ship remained within the disk, the higher the odds of impact—and at these velocities, the kinetic energy of a pebble's impact could rival a hit from a Klingon disruptor bank.

Soon, a pinpoint burst of light flared on the viewscreen and the ship rocked from the impact against its skintight deflector screens. The hit was comparatively mild, no more than a grain of sand. Minutes later, another micrometeoroid exploded against the screens, then another soon after that. The debris was getting denser. The crew around Kirk was growing nervous, but he remained focused on his goal. "Steady as she goes, helm."

"Entering maximum transporter range for Commander Sherev, sir," Hussein reported. "Locking on now." A tense moment passed. "Transporter room reports . . . Sherev aboard and safe, sir!"

Kirk felt a surge of relief, but there was no time to celebrate. "Hold course, helm. Best speed to the others."

"Eighty seconds to intercept," reported the Caitian at the helm, whose name Kirk couldn't recall.

"Status on the others, Hussein?"

"Arhanla's air is nearing critical, sir. We're cutting it close."

"Please hurry, sir," Arhanla called. *"Don't . . . don't let me die alone. No one to share my essence with . . . Everything lost . . ."*

"We won't let you down, Ensign," Kirk assured him. "We're almost there."

An alarm sounded from Corot's console. "Incoming debris, bearing thirty-two mark eight! Locking phasers—"

But it was too late. The ship rocked under a heavy impact, and the lights and console displays flickered. "Damage report!" Kirk barked as soon as he steadied himself.

"Deflectors down to sixty percent, sir. We can't keep up this speed!" Corot blinked tears from her eyes as she said it.

But Kirk knew he couldn't hesitate. He had to weigh two people against the entire crew. "Slow to revised best speed. Hold intercept course. Engineer, divert all possible power to boost transporter range!"

"Sir . . ." Hussein's voice was bleak. "Starboard transporter emitters are down. We're rerouting power around the damage, but it cuts our maximum range in half."

Kirk felt a hollow void open up in his gut. "Do your best, Ensign. We have to try."

In the end, it took another three minutes to reach transporter range and beam Isurugi and Arhanla aboard. The report from the transporter room was grim. "*Sir . . . Arhanla didn't make it.*"

Corot let out a sob and was unable to stop herself from hurling an accusing look at Kirk. But at this moment, Kirk could hardly blame her.

Eagle's Landing, Vega IX
For the next few days, Sherev refused to speak to Kirk outside of the line of duty. They both tried to comport themselves with dignity during Arhanla's memorial service, for the sake of his grieving family, but the tension between them was palpable nonetheless.

Leonard McCoy was still there to offer Kirk support, though. The young captain was surprised by how quickly he'd grown to rely on the older doctor's friendship. Or maybe it was just the Saurian brandy. "Sherev is convinced there was no way to save them all," Kirk told McCoy as he sat in his living room and nursed his third drink of the evening. "That I was wrong to try. I just can't accept that, Bones." He was too weary to bother with the full nickname, but McCoy took the elision in stride. "It *could* have worked, if not for that freak impact at just the wrong time. It was a risk, but a calculated one."

"But she isn't wrong, Jim," the doctor said. "Try as you might, you can't save everyone. That's a lesson all doctors have to learn. Sometimes . . . sometimes you just have to accept the losses when they happen, and let them motivate you to keep on fighting to save those you can." A haunted look passed behind his eyes, and Kirk sensed he was speaking from experience. But whatever loss preoccupied him seemed very personal, and Kirk was reluctant to pry.

"That's exactly what I try to do," Kirk said. "To keep fighting. The problem with teaching us to prepare for no-win scenarios is that it gives us an excuse to stop trying. To lose our will." His thoughts again went back to the *Farragut*, as they did every time he lost someone he was responsible for. To the time that people had died because he had not tried hard enough. But he kept those thoughts to himself. He was already leaning heavily enough on McCoy's shoulder without adding that burden.

After a moment's quiet, he shook his head. "I can live with trying to save someone and failing. I have no choice but to live with it, any more than you do. But what I will not accept is failing to try. I wasn't about to write off Rhen's life without even making the attempt. Because if I could do that once . . . how many more lives might I decide were expendable in the future?"

McCoy refilled both their glasses. "It's a terrible trick the universe plays on us. If we want to do jobs that let us save lives . . . we have to accept sometimes being responsible for people's deaths. In the long run, we just have to hope the good we do is worth the cost to our own souls."

———

As both men had work the next day—and since McCoy was starting to become a maudlin drunk—Kirk soon called a cab for the doctor and sent him on his way. The next morning at the research station, the captain was not exactly bright-eyed and bushy-tailed, but at least he was functional. He concentrated on the work, since it still had to be done.

Yet it wasn't long before Rhenas Sherev showed up at his office door, surprising him. "Can I have a moment, Captain?"

"Of course." Kirk gestured her to a seat and sat patiently, not knowing what to expect.

The commander sighed, her antennae fidgeting. "I'm sorry, Jim. For blaming you. The fact is, I was blaming myself. I felt responsible for causing the explosion, for getting Arhanla killed, and I was angry at you for not letting me pay for my sins."

He leaned toward her. "Rhen . . . I got the report—"

She held up a hand. "I got it too. The radiation signature from the blast . . . it proved it wasn't a reactor overload. It was a disruptor bomb. The spacegoing faction, they must've booby-trapped their base in the event of enemy capture. Just one more unexploded bomb, like so many wars leave lying around long afterward. We didn't detect it, didn't know what to look for, couldn't have known it was there. My plan *should* have worked, if not for one random factor I couldn't have anticipated." A pause. "Just like your plan."

Kirk looked down at his hands. "I appreciate you saying that. Honestly, I've been second-guessing myself for days, wondering if there was a possibility I missed. It helps to hear that from . . . someone whose judgment I respect so much."

She smiled, but it was tinged with pain. "You know, Jim . . . I was this close to opening my helmet and forcing the issue. Taking myself out of the equation so you'd have to go save the others." He stared at her, shocked. "But I warred with myself over the decision long enough for the transporter to catch me. I suppose . . . I respected *your* judgment too much. I knew, on some level, that if you believed the plan could work, I should give you the chance. It's because of my faith in you as a captain that I'm still alive."

Kirk was touched, but he resisted accepting the praise. "I wish Arhanla were here to say the same."

She nodded, her antennae sagging. "Dealing with loss is part of command—which is why I'm not interested in it. But you showed me that the time for that is after it happens, not before. I admire your refusal to quit when there's even the slightest glimmer of hope. That persistence won't always pay off, but it's important not to give up on it. To take our failures as learning experiences, use them to goad us to keep moving, keep striving."

He sat a moment, absorbing. "Those are wise words. Worth keeping in mind going forward."

Her head tilted. "Forward, sir?"

He sighed. "I received new orders today. The *Sacagawea* is about to be relaunched—and Starfleet wants me to finish what I started. I've been ordered to report back as her captain in three weeks."

Sherev beamed. "That's great news, Jim!"

"It is. Especially since the new assignment is for an exploration tour. No more border patrol for me."

"Even better." She peered at him. "Then why do you sound ambivalent?"

"Not ambivalent, just . . . keenly aware of the burden that comes with it. When I think about going back to that bridge after what happened last time . . ."

Sherev rose and crossed her arms. "What have we just been talking about?" she demanded. "I mean, Uzaveh, if a stubborn cuss like me can admit she was wrong to blame herself, then it shouldn't be so hard for you to do the same. You still saved more lives than you lost that day. And if Starfleet had any doubts that you did the best you could, they wouldn't have given you the ship back."

He smiled. "I guess what I'm saying is . . . I appreciate your moral support at times like these. And there probably will be more such times ahead, for all our best efforts to prevent them." He paused. "Most of the crew has been reassigned. I'm going to need a science officer. I'd like it to be you, Rhen."

Her antennae jerked backward in surprise. After a moment,

though, she gave a wistful smile. "I'm touched by the offer, Jim. And frankly, recent events have soured me on Vegan archaeology. I could use a different challenge. And . . . I could use your moral support too."

They clasped hands, and Kirk felt deep gratitude for her friendship. He hoped that the new memories that he and Sherev would form together on the *Sacagawea* would help him lay to rest the memory of what had happened the last time he was aboard that ship.

SACAGAWEA

EARLY 2262

Six

I hereby declare victory in the Battle of Qalras. The invading fleet has been repelled, but at a heavy cost. We destroyed one of their vessels and severely damaged two more, but the crews of two battle cruisers and three birds-of-prey won their places in Sto-Vo-Kor in the process. These creatures' armor and weapons are unlike anything in Klingon experience.

. . . The enemy towed their damaged ships away into warp, leaving us no prizes to claim. But from what we were able to scan of the interior of the destroyed ship, it is better that way. Based on my science officer's report, I could easily believe these foes were demons from the depths of Gre'thor *itself. But based on their departure course, they now go to bedevil the Federation. So some good may come of this yet.*

—Kang, son of K'naiah
Battle Report to Klingon High Command

U.S.S. *Beowulf* **NCC-1605**
"This border incursion had better not be another false alarm," Captain Vishakha Gupta grumbled as she flopped down into a seat near the head of the *Beowulf's* briefing room table. "The *Sau Lan Wu's* been out for three weeks, she's overdue for maintenance, and I'm overdue for getting smashed at the Moonbeam Club and talking at least two young ladies into carrying me to bed."

Across from her, the captain of the *Leonov* directed a scathing raised eyebrow her way. "Captain Wesley would not have scrambled four additional ships on such short notice for an unconfirmed threat," Captain T'Saren said. "And surely the colonists on Adelphous IV would consider it preferable if it *were* a false alarm."

"Well, pardon me for not having a Vulcan's endless stamina or sterile social life."

"If you consider seducing random strangers under the influence of alcohol to be a social life, no wonder your stamina is so poor."

Jim Kirk watched the two mature women uneasily as he took his own seat farther down the table. Next to him, Daniel Baek of the *Oshosi* leaned over and murmured, "Don't worry about them. They've been bickering like that for fifteen years. It's not serious."

"I didn't think Vulcans were known for their sense of humor," Kirk whispered back, aware that Vulcans *were* known for their keen hearing.

"That's what they want us to think. Lets them poke fun at us more efficiently." Baek sighed, stroking his angular jawline. "Although I don't think Gupta's entirely joking. My crew's restless too, overdue for shore leave. And I'll be glad to get back to my son on the starbase. He's had to put up with my wife's cooking for too long." The two men shared a laugh. "How about you, Jim? You seem pretty untroubled by the delay."

Kirk shrugged. "I guess I'm married to my ship. My crew's all the companionship I need right now."

Baek threw him a skeptical look, but mercifully didn't pursue it further. The older captain was surely up on the starbase gossip, so he had no doubt heard about it when Janet Miller had announced her marriage to Dr. Theodore Wallace, a man nearly twice her age, mere months after leaving the starbase. It had given the lie to her comforting insistence that she had left Kirk purely for the sake of her career, and that her fascination had been with Wallace's brilliant research rather than with the man himself. Perhaps it had been unfair for Kirk to feel betrayed, for the two of them had never made any serious commitment. Yet he had been hurt nonetheless, and had refused to acknowledge her letters or send even token congratulations.

Instead, Kirk had thrown himself into his work patrolling the border, settling into a comfortable routine aboard the *Sacagawea*. He'd occupied his downtime on the starbase with reading, chess, sparring in the gym, and occasional amiable but casual dalliances with various women, such as the sweetly lovely paramedic Monika Tatsumi, the passionate and spiritual geologist Tina Sanchez, and the *Hannibal*'s second officer, a tall, dark, and stunning Makusian lieutenant commander named Nijen Danehl. Contrary to Gary Mitchell's gibes, there had been only one blonde in the bunch, a JAG lieutenant named Areel Shaw—and she had been the one to pursue him, not the other way around. He'd been hesitant at first, but the ambitious attorney had proven highly effective at arguing her case.

"Thank you all for coming." Captain Wesley's voice broke Kirk out of his momentary reverie. The *Beowulf*'s captain took his seat at the head of the table. "As you're all aware, we're responding to a border incursion by a fleet of ships on course for the Adelphous system, which houses a Federation colony of over two million inhabitants on its fourth planet. Long-range scans have not provided an identification of the incoming ships, but we know there are nine of them and they're quite large."

"But we're heading for the Klingon border," Gupta said. "We sure they aren't some new kind of Klingon ship?"

"Their energy signatures and profiles don't match any known variant of Klingon starship technology," Wesley answered. "What's more, I was just briefed by Starfleet Intelligence. Their long-range scans and signal intercepts, backtracking along the intruders' course, show evidence of a battle between these ships and Klingon forces on the outskirts of the Qalras system, an imperial mining colony some two parsecs from the border. It looks like the Klingons repelled them from entering the system, but at considerable cost. A transmission fragment we managed to decrypt called them 'demons.' They may not have managed to defeat the Klingons, but they certainly spooked them."

"And now these 'demons' have picked Adelphous as their Plan B," Baek conjectured.

"Possibly," Wesley replied. "We don't yet know their motives, but we know their capabilities, and we know they've ignored warnings from our border marker buoys. We must treat this as a hostile incursion, until and unless we manage to achieve communication with the intruders and determine otherwise."

"Could this be some Klingon trick?" Kirk mused. "Maybe we were supposed to see evidence of a battle, to give the Klingons deniability for breaking the truce. Even if these are some other species, they may be doing the Klingons' bidding. We've seen before that at least some Klingons are capable of that kind of deviousness."

"Up to a point, perhaps," Captain T'Saren replied. "But one of the key doctrines of Klingon philosophy is 'Always face your enemy.' Even when employing a deceptive stratagem, Klingons prefer to do so themselves rather than hide, as they would perceive it, behind a proxy. When Klingons have attempted espionage in Federation space, they have employed Klingon agents surgically altered to appear human, rather than co-opting Federation citizens as intelligence assets."

Wesley raised a hand. "We can sort out their goals and agendas later. Right now, we need to devise a plan for our initial confrontation. We'll be heavily outnumbered and outpowered. Starbase 24 is sending an additional three ships as reinforcements, led by the *Potemkin*. But they'll be two hours behind us.

We have those two hours to either establish peaceful contact . . . or do what we can to hold the line and stop them from reaching Adelphous IV."

U.S.S. *Sacagawea*

First contact missions had always given Jim Kirk a special thrill. The opportunity for new discovery, the chance to learn about a species and culture previously unknown to the Federation, fulfilled the dreams of the explorer in him—even as the potential risk and the prospect of hostility fired the caution of the soldier in him. Of all the missions Starfleet undertook, none was so fraught with possibility and peril, so potentially important to the future of entire civilizations.

In his years of Starfleet service, Kirk had been involved in his share of first contacts, particularly during the Vulcanian Expedition—the vernacular nickname that the press and public had somehow adopted for an eight-month joint survey of deep space by the Vulcan Expeditionary Group and Starfleet, in which Kirk had participated as first officer of the *Eagle*. The first contacts he had been involved with during that probe—both clandestine ones with pre-warp civilizations like the Xarakans and the Habardians and overt ones with starfaring peoples like the Alraki and the Escherites—were among the most cherished highlights of his career so far. But the impending encounter with the fleet of mystery ships would be Kirk's first such mission as a captain. He regretted that it might turn out to be a hostile one.

Of course, it was Robert Wesley who was in overall command of the mission, and even though the older captain had risen through the ranks as a tactical officer and distinguished himself in battles from Donatu V to Omega Leonis, Kirk was confident that he would do everything possible to find a peaceful resolution before resorting to combat. Indeed, as the Starfleet task force drew closer to the oncoming alien fleet, Wesley transmitted a general hail, which was heard on the *Sacagawea*'s bridge through the open channel among all five ships.

"*Attention, unidentified vessels. This is Captain Robert Wesley of the U.S.S.* Beowulf, *speaking on behalf of the United Federation of Planets. You have been notified that the space you have recently entered is the territory of the Federation. The star system toward which you are heading, which we call Adelphous, is home to a Federation colony. We ask that you identify yourselves and explain your purpose in approaching the Adelphous system.*"

Silence. After a few moments, Kirk looked over his shoulder toward the communications officer. "Ensign Moravec, any reaction?"

The young man shook his head. "Nothing, Captain."

After the silence from the alien fleet had dragged on for a sufficient time, Wesley's voice resumed. "*Once again: You have intruded on Federation territory. If you do not identify yourselves and explain your purpose in approaching the Adelphous system, we will be forced to conclude that your intentions are hostile, in which case we will react accordingly. We do not wish to engage in conflict if it can be avoided. Our purpose is to protect the lives of the Federation's citizens. But if you do not halt your approach and explain your presence in our territory, you will leave us no choice but to take defensive action.*"

The ships continued to ignore Wesley's hails. "*All vessels, raise shields,*" the senior captain ordered. "*Weapons on standby. Once in range, the* Beowulf *will attempt a warning shot. Stand ready to maneuver.*"

Per proper chain of command, Kirk repeated the instructions to his bridge crew. "Shields up, phasers on standby. Lieutenant Yu, can you show us what we're facing?"

"Coming into sensor range now, Captain," Elena Yu reported. "One moment." She finessed the science station's controls for a few more seconds, then sent an image to the main viewer.

The nine oncoming ships were massive cylinders, nearly as wide as they were long. They appeared to have hollow cores running clear through them, inside which were delicate-looking lattices supporting piercingly bright energy sources of some kind. Their exterior surfaces were covered in hexagonal plates of a dark yellow-brown material. The ships came in at least three different sizes, with the largest one in the lead.

"Ships range in size from roughly one to one-point-six kilometers," Yu reported. "Hull composition is largely tritanium alloys and high-performance crystalline ceramics. The heat signatures suggest considerable power output. I can't get any clear readings on interior conditions or biosigns through the shielding."

"No warp nacelles," Mehran Egdor observed from his place by the command chair. "Is that central lattice some kind of warp assembly?"

"Stand by." Yu worked her controls to redirect her scans. "I am picking up intense gravimetric distortions from those central energy sources." She shook her head in bewilderment. "The spectral readings I'm getting off those things . . . they're consistent with the radiation emitted by matter falling into a microsingularity."

Mitchell turned to stare at Yu in disbelief. "A miniature black hole? We've detected, what, a handful of those in centuries of looking? And they have nine of them?"

"Eighteen. Each ship has two of equal mass, one fore and one aft. The consistency . . . they couldn't have just harvested them. They must have manufactured them, or at least regulated their growth."

"What kind of weapons could a thing like that power?" Azadeh Khorasani mused from the helm.

Mitchell reacted to an alarm. "Sir, they're neutralizing warp!"

Khorasani sighed. "I had to ask. Something tells me they aren't surrendering."

As usual, her tactical instincts proved sound. Immediately after the *Beowulf* fired its warning shot at the lead cylinder ship, the alien fleet split off into four groups of two or three, veering onto multiple different trajectories. *"They're trying to make an end run around us,"* Wesley announced. *"Break formation and intercept before they can return to warp.* Sacagawea, *stick with* Leonov.*"*

That last order made sense; the *Hermes*-class scout and the *Miranda*-class frigate were two of the smallest ships in the task force. Kirk was grateful for the backup, though he wasn't sure a Vulcan like T'Saren was the best partner to have in a combat situation.

"Interesting that they had to break warp to change course," Egdor observed. "Vulcan ringships tend to have limited maneuverability at warp, and these ships have a similar configuration. That could be an advantage for us."

"Unless they stay at impulse," Kirk reminded him. "Which is what we've been ordered to ensure."

In moments, the two ships had placed themselves in the path of their chosen pair of cylinder ships. Kirk followed T'Saren's lead in dropping out of warp and firing another pair of warning shots across the much larger vessels' prows. The reaction was unexpected. For a moment, it looked like debris was flying outward from the ships in all directions. "Did we . . . hit them somehow?" Mitchell wondered.

"No, it's too uniform," Khorasani said.

"It's the armor plating," Kirk realized, even as the pieces began to slow. "It's . . . expanding."

While Kirk was reminded of a blowfish inflating itself in response to a threat, the reality was not quite the same. The armor plates retained their size, but increased their separation from one another. They stopped about a hundred meters out from each ship's hull, settling into an ovoid configuration fully surrounding each vessel, and began to rotate. "They're suspended in a powerful electromagnetic field," Elena Yu reported. "Flux-pinned in place like a maglev train above its superconducting track."

"It's like an ablative deflector shield," Egdor realized. "The plates absorb hits and the ship is insulated from the damage. Remarkable."

"I could get a shot in through the gaps, no problem," Khorasani said. "Just give me a few more moments to correct for the pattern."

"The field is surging," Yu announced. "Something's cha—whoa, incoming!"

A moment later, the ship rocked under a massive hit. Kirk clutched the arms of his command chair as the lights flickered and the shield circuits audibly strained. "What hit us?" the captain cried once the noise subsided.

Yu turned to face him, alarm in her youthful eyes. "One of the armor plates, sir. It's massive, dense, and the field accelerated it so sharply I could barely detect its approach."

"Shields are down eighteen percent, Jim," Mitchell reported. "From just one hit."

"The *Leonov* is taking fire too," Ensign Moravec reported. "If . . . you can call it fire."

"Close enough," Kirk said. "They're lobbing cannonballs at us."

Egdor shook his head. "It seems almost primitive—but also very sophisticated."

"Kinetic energy's as deadly as any other kind," Khorasani observed. "Just ask the dinosaurs."

"Another incoming!" Mitchell cried, and Kirk braced himself. After the thunder and the rocking, Mitchell cursed under his breath. "Shields at seventy-one percent."

Kirk had had enough. "Khorasani, fire at will on the attacker."

"My pleasure, Captain!" Bionic fingers caressed her targeting scope as she unleashed her counterattack.

"Yu, see if you can identify any external field emitters she can target," Egdor said.

"Aye, sir."

"Damn it!" Khorasani cried. "The rotation pattern keeps changing. Only one shot got through, and only for a second before a plate intercepted it. Not enough to do more than scratch the paint."

The ship rocked from another blow. "Missed that one," Mitchell growled. "It came in from the side. With their field control, they can throw them at us on arced courses."

Kirk furrowed his brow. "Yu, what happens to the plates that hit us?"

"They partially disintegrate at the striking edge, but otherwise they seem largely intact. About what you'd expect if you dropped a paving tile on its corner. They then rejoin the shielding array."

"And how much damage are they taking from the phaser hits?"

Once Khorasani had let off a few more shots, the science officer had an answer. "Comparable. A few hits or maybe ten seconds' sustained fire could destroy one of the plates."

"So we could wear them down," Mitchell said. "But not if they break our shields down first. We're at sixty-three percent." Another blow nearly knocked the navigator out of his seat.

Egdor was clutching the side rail to stay on his feet. "Our shields are designed with energy weapons and radiation in mind. This is more like being hit by meteoroids."

Kirk stared at him. "That's it! The navigational deflector. It's designed for deflecting solid matter coming in at relativistic speeds."

"From ahead, yes. Can the dish pivot fast enough to intercept them?"

"I suggest you take that up with Engineer Desai," Kirk told him. Nodding, Egdor stepped over to the engineering station to consult with the chief engineer below.

Captain T'Saren's voice came over the dedicated command-channel speaker on Kirk's chair arm. *"Captain Kirk, I have been monitoring your situation. Fall back while you assess the deflector dish option. As the* Miranda *class has no dish system, our shields and tractor emitters are already configured for meteoroid deflection and are better able to cope with these attacks."*

Kirk observed the *Leonov* on the viewscreen for a few moments. "It looks like you're still taking heavy fire from both ships," he said.

"And returning it. We are also more heavily armed than you." Indeed, phaser beams and torpedoes were flying out of the *Leonov*'s weapons pod, slowly but systematically eroding the cylinder ships' whirling armor arrays. *"You will not aid us effectively if you fail to optimize your own safety in the process."*

Kirk's pride rebelled, but his reason and discipline were stronger. "Acknowledged, Captain. Khorasani, pull us back out of their attack range."

A general hail came in as the *Sacagawea* fell back. *"Wesley to all ships. Be advised the hostiles can fire intense, focused plasma beams from their singularity drives. We lost a phaser array and a whole weapons crew to it, and that was a glancing blow. It blew through our portside shields like they were crepe paper. Whatever you do, don't let them bring their prows to bear on you. Stay away from the central axis."*

"Acknowledged, Beowulf," came Captain Baek's voice. *"Those support frames for the singularities look like a weak spot, though. Any luck targeting them?"*

"We'd have to put ourselves in the line of fire. It's too risky."

"What about transporters?" Captain Gupta asked from the *Sau Lan Wu. "They don't have conventional shields. If we could identify their bridges, send in boarding parties . . ."*

T'Saren replied, *"Their hull composition resists sensors,* Sau Lan Wu. *We have failed to refine our scans sufficiently to allow a target lock or even determine interior environmental conditions.*

No doubt a transporter beam would be similarly refracted and scattered."

"Then beam away pieces of the singularity frames," Gupta countered. *"Shut them down, or blow them up."*

Kirk and his bridge crew looked up at that in surprise. Few starfarers ever acknowledged the fact that a transporter beam was essentially a highly efficient disintegration beam, potentially a devastating weapon if one simply omitted the rematerialization phase. Or if one selectively beamed away the shielding on an enemy's engine core, or merely beamed their crew into space. That avoidance wasn't just because deflector shields negated the risk, since shields could fall in battle. Rather, the weaponization of transporters was an almost universal taboo, much as with chemical or biological weapons. The technique was at once too dangerous and too cruel, a line that no one wanted to cross because of the floodgates it would open. Transporters had too many beneficial uses for anyone to risk getting them outlawed. So for a Starfleet captain to suggest crossing that line was startling.

"We aren't there yet, Vishakha," Wesley replied firmly.

"Besides," T'Saren countered, *"the singularity radiation and gravimetric distortion would prohibit a transporter lock in any case."*

"Okay, okay," Gupta said. *"Sorry I brought it up. I've taken casualties too. I just want to make them pay."*

"Understood, Captain," said Wesley. *"But let's settle for making them stop."*

Over the next few minutes, while Kirk watched the *Leonov* continue the battle, Egdor and Desai worked out a way to step up the power and speed of the rotational actuator on the deflector dish, though they couldn't guarantee it would last for long before burning out. Meanwhile, the *Beowulf* and the *Sau Lan Wu* continued to hold their own, chipping away at the enemy's shields, but it was slow going. *"We just dodged another plasma beam,"* Wesley announced. *"It looks like they need about five minutes to recharge. That's a small mercy."*

"Captain Wesley, what's the range on those plasma beams?" Kirk called.

"Unknown, but much greater than the plate projectiles."

"Oh, no," Mitchell said. "I've been too busy watching the battle with the *Leonov* . . . one of the hostiles almost has its bow to bear on us!"

"Evasive action!" Kirk cried.

Khorasani worked her controls. "Thrusters are sluggish!" she called. "They need more power."

Egdor cursed. "The dish is demanding too much power. Rerouting back to thrusters!"

But it was too late. On the screen, the nearer cylinder ship was now a perfect circle around a blazing point of light. The light burst out and filled the screen, dazzlingly bright . . .

"Captain! Jim, wake up!"

As Kirk revived, he recognized that Egdor was shaking him, calling to him. The first officer's pale, craggy face was burned and bleeding, and it felt to Kirk like he was in similar condition. "Sta . . . status." He looked around. The bridge was dark and filled with smoke. The constant electronic chirp and chatter of the computers and sensors was nearly silenced.

"We're in bad shape. It was a severe hit. Main power is out . . . I'm not even sure the nacelle's still attached. But the battle seems to have stopped, so there's that. Maybe the others drove them away."

Kirk sighed. *Or the others are destroyed and the "demon" fleet is on its way to Adelphous.*

He looked around. The first person he saw was Azadeh Khorasani. Her bionic arm spasmed from random power surges . . . but it was clearly the only part of her that would ever move again. He wondered if she would still be forgiving of the enemy that had killed her.

"Moravec's gone too," Egdor reported. "Yu . . . she's breathing, but we need medics, fast." He knelt by the science officer, tried to do what he could.

For a moment, Kirk was afraid to check on Gary Mitchell. But then he heard a familiar groan. He turned in time to see his old friend staring at Khorasani's body with a look of resigned sorrow. "Oh, damn," Mitchell grated as Kirk moved to his side. "I really thought she was indestructible."

Kirk reminded himself to focus on those who could still be helped. "Are you hurt?"

Mitchell shook himself, finally looking away from Khorasani. "Nothing serious, I think. God, you look worse than I feel."

Kirk reached out and hit the nearest comm switch. "Kirk to sickbay. Medical assistance to the bridge. Any emergency medical teams, please respond." But there was no signal. He looked toward the turbolift doors; they were burned and crumpled, the lift behind them wrecked. There was no way in or out of the dead bridge.

As if to correct his thought, the sound of a transporter beam filled the air. Robert Wesley materialized along with his CMO and a paramedic team. "Jim, Mehran, thank God. We were afraid we'd lost you."

Kirk stared at Khorasani and Moravec. "We were the lucky ones. Status of the fleet?"

Wesley sighed. "We held out long enough for the reinforcements to arrive. With the help of the *Potemkin* and the others, we managed to drive the aliens into retreat. They've left Federation space. But it came at a high price. Jim, we lost the *Leonov* with all hands."

Kirk winced, lowering his head. Hundreds of people lost, many of whom he had known personally. Guilt tore through him. "We were supposed to back them up."

"You backed each other up. That's how this works. After you were hit, T'Saren made a choice to shield you. She and her crew fought them with everything they had, held the line just long enough to keep you alive until reinforcements came." Wesley clasped his shoulder. "Jim, you made a difference. Your deflector dish insight helped us hold our own against them. The mission was a success . . . though the cost was great."

"The rest of the fleet?"

"We survived, but not without loss." The elder captain sighed. "Including Captain Baek and his bridge crew."

Kirk looked around at the ruined bridge—the ruined crew. "Why, Bob? Who were they? What did they want? Why did they attack? There has to be some reason for all this. It has to mean something."

Wesley put a hand on his shoulder as the paramedics prepared Elena Yu for transport. "I know how you feel, Jim. But honestly, I'll be willing to live without an answer if it means we never see those demon ships again."

Starbase 24

The *Sacagawea* had needed to be towed back to the starbase. Her warp drive was crippled, her hull ruptured, her spaceframe damaged. The starbase engineers remained unsure if the vessel would even be salvageable. Kirk felt guilty that he cared almost as much about that as about the eighty-seven dead and thirty-nine badly wounded members of his crew.

"It doesn't make you a bad person," Bob Wesley had assured him when he confessed to it at the wake in the Moonbeam Club. "Or a bad captain. We all grow attached to our ships. They aren't just meaningless hunks of metal and composite. They keep us alive. They take us to places we never dreamed possible. We value the ships *because* of what they do for the crew, not in spite of the crew. So don't be guilty that you care for the body of the ship as much as the people inside it. Just transfer that care, that love and devotion, to whatever ship you serve on next. And the one after that, and the one after that."

Kirk had stared into his drink, unable to meet the senior captain's eyes. "Do you really think they'll let me have another ship after this?"

"Jim, you did nothing wrong. I know how it feels now, but that feeling is a burden shared by every captain in Starfleet, myself included. It doesn't mean you've failed. It means you're really one of us now. And you'll learn from it and try harder next time, same as we all do."

The JAG office's routine inquiry a few days later came to the same conclusion—that neither Kirk nor any other captain in the task force had been in any way derelict in their duty. The finding had brought Kirk only limited comfort, but the chance to see Areel Shaw again provided a temporary distraction on the night after the inquiry.

While Kirk's career may have been secure, he no longer had a ship to command. Even if the *Sacagawea* could be repaired, it would take months in dry dock. In the meantime, the surviving crew would be reassigned. As for the injured, the most severe cases had already been shipped out to the Starfleet Medical facility on Vega Colony—a long trip, but worth it for the specialized care they could receive there. When Kirk learned that the Starfleet archaeological post in the Vega system was in need of a new commander, he immediately applied for the position.

"A ground assignment?" Commodore Lam asked when he made the request. "It seems a waste of your talents, Jim."

"With respect, Commodore, you told me yourself that I should keep learning and broadening my horizons."

"I did, didn't I? But are you really committed to the work? Or are you just going there to stick close to your injured crew—and mark time until the *Sacagawea*'s fixed? It's not good to get too attached to a single ship, you know."

"Permission to speak freely?"

"As a rule, yes."

"Border patrol wasn't my preferred assignment either, Commodore. I joined Starfleet to be an explorer. But did I ever commit myself less than fully to my duties here?"

"No. You're one of the most dedicated officers I've ever served with. I just don't want to see you languish where you aren't making full use of your potential."

Nonetheless, Lam agreed to endorse Kirk's transfer request, and before long, the orders came through. All that remained was to say his farewells to the remainder of his crew. *"I guess you'll have to go on without me from here,"* Gary Mitchell told him over subspace. The navigator had already departed for his recuperative leave, which he had chosen to take on Argelius. *"However will you survive?"*

Kirk smiled at his old friend. "You really think you'd be happy doing archaeology, digging through dead ruins?"

"I guess not. That kind of brain work is much more your sort of thing."

"It won't be forever. It's a low-priority post, so they might rotate me back to the *Sacagawea* once she's repaired. Whatever ship I get, though, I'll try to request you for it."

"Don't hold your breath. I've already gotten orders to report to the Anggitay *next month."*

Kirk searched his memory. "That's a *Centaurus*-class scout, right? Pretty small."

"But fast and good with maneuvers. Just like me." Mitchell chuckled. *"Which reminds me, you gotta get out here to Argelius sometime. There's this café I know where the women are so—"*

"Tell me later, Gary. You're supposed to be there for rest, remember?"

"Jim, no one comes to Argelius to rest."

That left only Mehran Egdor, who came to see Kirk while he was packing up the meager belongings in his starbase quarters.

"I understand you recommended me for promotion to captain," the Rigelian said. "I wanted to thank you for that attempt."

Kirk frowned. "'Attempt'?"

Egdor held out the data slate with the orders. "First officer of the *Kongo*, under Captain Chandra."

The human's eyes widened. "A *Constitution*-class ship. That's a major step upward, Mehran."

"But not the one I wanted."

Kirk clasped his shoulder. "You've made it to where I was until a year ago. I have no doubt you'll catch up before long."

Egdor studied him. "But now you're taking a ground post. I trust you intend to remain in the race, Jim."

A pause. "I go where I'm needed. That's the job."

"It's more than duty for us, Jim. It's a calling. Don't forget that. Don't stop striving for greater heights."

Egdor left, and Kirk was alone with his memories. Packing up the last of his sparse belongings, he looked around his now-barren quarters, reflecting on his time on Starbase 24 and the *Sacagawea*.

Mere seconds later, he strode to the door and left. There was nothing here for him anymore.

ENTERPRISE
2265

Seven

A great terraformer needs the green thumb of a gardener, the eye of a painter, and the soul of a poet. And of course it doesn't hurt to be a raging egomaniac.

—Gideon Seyetik

Aulacri terraforming command ship

Upon the *Enterprise*'s arrival in orbit of Karabos II, the head of the Aulacri terraformers, Director Skovir, had invited Kirk to bring a delegation aboard her ship to discuss the situation. Kirk brought Spock and Mitchell with him, leaving Chief Engineer Scott in command of the ship. He knew he would need to learn to work with his new first officer, but he had come to rely on Gary Mitchell as a gadfly, reminding him not to become too rigid and bound by the rules. Kirk doubted that the highly regimented Spock could counterbalance him in the same way.

The Aulacri were small but fierce-looking, with gray-brown skin, sharp teeth, pronounced cheekbones, and narrow eyes under heavy brows that tapered to the bridges of their upturned noses, giving them a part-feline, part-simian aspect that was amplified by their long, prehensile tails. Despite their somewhat predatory appearance, they welcomed their Starfleet visitors with cheerful enthusiasm and warmth. Skovir insisted on treating the party to a meal before they got down to business, and even presented them with live entertainment, as several of her junior terraformers put on an impromptu acrobatic performance for them, tumbling, jumping, and spinning in a way that seemed to come naturally to their people. It seemed they had retained more from their distant brachiating ancestors than most humanoids had. It also seemed that Skovir's group really wanted to make a good impression on the Federation.

This continued once Skovir showed the trio of officers a presentation of her terraforming plan for Karabos II, projecting a holographic simulation over her copper-haired head as she spoke. "The current climate of the planet is too hot and dry to support M-Class life," she explained. "The ancient natives devastated their world with antimatter bombs, heating it sufficiently that its oceans evaporated and their hydrogen escaped into space through photodissociation." A shudder of revulsion went through her lithe frame. "Fortunately, the Karabos system has an extensive cometary belt relatively near its star, giving us an abundance of water ice, nitrogen, and organic compounds to replenish the planet's lost supply."

"The people of my world, Earth," Kirk said, "have spent the past century employing a similar method to terraform our neighbor planet Mars. But our efforts were directed mainly at bombarding its ice caps to melt the water and carbon dioxide trapped within them, in order to warm the planet with the greenhouse effect. It seems you have the opposite problem here."

"Yes, our bombardment has a different goal," Skovir said. "The four largest impactors are partially depleted comets with a high proportion of rock and metal in their composition—dense and massive enough to survive atmospheric entry and strike the surface. The impacts should propel enough dust and ash into the upper atmosphere to induce global cooling, allowing the cometary water vapor to precipitate into new oceans and waterways."

"You would need to calculate the impacts very precisely," Spock replied. "Too powerful an impact would propel much of the cometary volatiles beyond the atmosphere altogether, as well as ejecting some of the existing atmosphere into space. You would lose more than you gained."

"Quite so, Mister Spock!" Skovir replied with a sharp-toothed grin. "This is why the rest of the comets will make a shallower entry, vaporizing slowly as they descend into the atmosphere."

"Then would that not be sufficient to allow the terraforming to proceed without endangering the archaeological sites on the surface?"

Skovir's pleasure in the discussion dimmed at the question. "It would be nice if it were that simple, wouldn't it? But as you say, Captain Kirk, your Earth people also chose direct bombardment of the surface. Why did they do that, if I may ask?"

Kirk considered his words. "As I understand it, to accelerate the process by releasing Mars's own volatiles."

Skovir nodded. "To accelerate the process. Terraforming is slow, the work of generations. Those who begin it know we will not live to see the completion of our work. But that does not mean we are free from time pressures. Our worlds teem with people, people who need new places to live and start families. The sooner we can make a new world livable, the better." She shrugged. "With all due respect to your archaeologists on the surface, Captain, I care more about what those future lives will build than about the ruins left over by people long dead.

"Especially a people as savage as the Karabosi," she added with some heat. "A people so brutal and violent that they bombed their own civilization out of existence. Drove not only themselves but their whole biosphere extinct through their cruelty toward each other, their irresponsibility toward their world. Frankly, I don't believe a people such as that have anything useful to teach us."

Kirk pursed his lips. "I remember Doctor Sherev saying that

investigating civilizations that destroyed themselves through war could help us learn how to avoid the same fate."

"We avoid that fate by learning to care for our worlds' ecosystems," Skovir said, "to nurture and create rather than exploit and destroy. And we avoid it by settling other worlds, so that a cataclysm on one world, natural or otherwise, will not wipe out our entire species."

Mitchell leaned forward in his seat. "There are a lot of planets in the galaxy, though. This can't be the only world you could terraform."

"It's the best one, certainly, of the worlds in Aulacri space. As you know, our territory is fairly limited, which is why we need to add to our tally of livable worlds. And Karabos II is the world that comes closest to fitting our needs already. Its gravity, rotation rate, and orbital parameters are nearly ideal for Aulacri habitation. Besides, it *was* habitable in the past, and merely needs to be restored to its former state—a simpler operation than transforming a world that was never habitable."

"So why the rush? This is the work of lifetimes, like you said. Can't you just give Sherev and her team enough time to finish their work?"

Skovir's fierce-looking features took on a wistful mien. "I assure you, Commander Mitchell, we've already given Doctor Sherev and her team as much time to conduct their survey as we could spare. But the timing of our operation is dictated by orbital mechanics. As a starship flight officer, you surely understand the complexities of orbital dynamics." Mitchell nodded. "Objects massive enough to survive atmospheric entry, and to deliver the necessary quantities of water, nitrogen, and organics, are difficult to redirect. And we do not have the powerful tractors and verteron beams that the Federation employs; we must instead rely on thruster units installed upon the comets themselves. So we had to find comets that were already on trajectories close to what we need, so that they could be gently nudged onto new courses without risking fragmentation. We've already waited more than twenty years for the optimal orbital configuration. If we missed this one, the next suitable one wouldn't be for thirty-six more years."

She turned to Kirk. "This operation needs to happen now, and it's already underway. The impactors are on course to hit Karabos II within sixty hours. You must convince Doctor Sherev and her team to evacuate while they still can." Skovir sighed. "I only hope that you can. She seems irrationally determined to remain. She even refused to join us for this meeting, for fear it was some sort of ploy to remove her team."

Kirk and Mitchell traded a knowing look. It sounded as if, without Starfleet discipline to temper it, Sherev's stubbornness had reached new heights. Still, Kirk didn't want to make any promises until he'd heard both sides. "Rest assured, Director Skovir—we will do everything in our power to find the best possible resolution for this dispute."

Karabos II

Rhenas Sherev looked different than Kirk remembered her. She'd let her hair grow out since leaving Starfleet, wearing it in a white braid that dangled halfway down her back, with shaggy bangs across her dark blue forehead. She was dressed for warm weather, in a tank top, shorts, and low boots, and Kirk could see that an intricate metallic support frame hugged the skin of her left leg. Her left hand clutched the tip of an ornate antique cane.

However, as soon as she spotted Kirk and Mitchell, she laughed out loud and ran toward them, the cane clutched loosely in her fingers. Her gait was a bit slow and uneven, but she seemed untroubled by it as she loped across the sere, rocky surface of the local landscape, a barren desert at the foot of a craggy mountain range. The low oxygen level of the air, like that of a mountain peak on Earth, did not seem to faze her either.

Kirk and Mitchell had needed tri-ox injections from Dr. Piper before beaming down, but Sherev had been here long enough to acclimate.

"Jim! Gary!" She threw her arms around them one by one. "It is so wonderful to see you both again." She noticed them eyeing her cane, whose grip Kirk could now see was styled after the head of an *atlirith*, an Andorian eagle. "Oh, this? A gift from my eldest *zhei*. It's mainly just for show. Makes me look distinguished and professorial. Sure, I'm a little slower than I used to be, but I still get around.

"And so do you, Jim! I couldn't believe it when I heard your voice calling from the *Enterprise*! You finally traded up, and to a *Constitution*, no less. I'm so proud of you!"

Kirk chuckled, grateful but puzzled. "You mean this is the first you've heard of it?"

"I'm sorry, I've just been so caught up in this survey. It takes up just about all my attention."

"So we hear," Mitchell said. "You also seem to have overlooked that there are several huge chunks of rock and ice on the way to hit this planet in two and a half days."

Sherev grimaced, her antennae rearing back in disgust. "Believe me, I'm aware. But now that you're here, Jim, you can convince Skovir and her people to give me more time."

Kirk touched her shoulder, noting that her upper body was significantly more muscular than he remembered. "We've already spoken to Director Skovir, Rhen. She's firmly committed to her timetable."

"Then you have to *un*-commit her. What we're on the verge of discovering here is too important."

Mitchell looked around the barren, empty landscape. "Here? All I see is a whole lot of nothing."

"Well, for a navigator, you were never very good at seeing what was right under your nose, Gary," Sherev teased. "Come on, boys, I'll show you what we've found."

She led them toward the large geodesic dome that served as her team's base. Mitchell stared at Kirk and mouthed, *"Boys?"* Kirk shrugged. She was a civilian now; she could call them what she pleased.

Entering the dome was a breath of fresh air, quite literally. It was a welcome relief from the stiflingly hot, thin atmosphere outside. Sherev took a few moments to introduce Kirk and Mitchell to the three Andorians, two humans, and one towering Makusian who made up the rest of her team, but didn't let them linger to get acquainted, instead leading them over to a work-table on which she called up images of her team's discoveries.

"The first clue we had was a low-level radiation signature over three hundred kilometers southwest of here," she said, indicating another portion of the same large continent where they now stood.

"Left over from the ancient war?" Mitchell asked.

"What? Use your head, Gary. You know antimatter weapons are clean, no fallout."

"Oh, right, antimatter. I forgot. You mean like photon torpe-does."

"Yeah, only bigger. It's why we haven't found much in the way of ruins on the surface, or even underground. Most of the cities were cratered in the final war. It's almost as bad as the Vega cataclysm."

Kirk studied her. "Is that why you're so invested in this one, Rhen? The hope that you can achieve here what you couldn't at Vega?"

She patted him on the back. "Don't try to psychoanalyze me, Jim, I've been to experts. I'm here because my experience studying a similar cataclysm makes me useful here. I know what to look for."

He nodded. "Understood. I apologize."

But Sherev had already moved on. "For instance, this." She called up an image of a massive stone slab at the bottom of a large excavation. Judging from the archaeologists standing next to it, it was some two meters high and wide and four times that in length, tapering from one end to the other. "It's mostly concrete encased in sapphire, highly resistant to erosion. But it contains enough thorium-232 to give off a low-level radiation signature that our sensors were able to detect through several meters of rock. Clearly it was meant to get someone's attention. And to remain noticeable for millions of years if necessary. That isotope has a very long half-life."

Kirk stared in wonder. "They knew their world was dying. So they buried a message for posterity, in case aliens ever came here."

"And we came a lot sooner than they anticipated—only about four thousand years."

Mitchell peered closer at the image. "I don't see any writing on it."

"How could they expect aliens to read their language?" Sherev asked him. "No, the slab *is* the message."

Kirk examined the way it tapered. "A directional marker?"

She grinned at him, her antennae perking up. "Bright boy! Go to the head of the class." She worked a control, and more lights appeared on the map of the continent. "We found a total of five of these markers buried around this continental plate . . . all of them pointing inward to the location where we're standing. Whatever they wanted us to find is here." She zoomed in on the area. "It's nonvolcanic, far from a fault line, about as geologically stable a site as you can find on this planet. And our scans detect a void several hundred meters inside the mountain. It's shielded by walls denser than the surrounding rock, so it's hard to get a clear sense of its interior layout, but we can tell it's there.

"Jim, they left this for us. Whatever's in there, it was important enough to them to preserve for posterity, to invite alien visitors to find. It's the legacy of their civilization, the only surviving part of a dead people. Could *you* just up and walk away from that?"

Kirk was moved by her urgency, her empathy for a long-extinct people crying out to be remembered. "Not if I had a choice, no. But to paraphrase an Earth poet, just because they said to the universe that they existed, that doesn't mean the universe has any obligation to let them be heard."

"It's not the universe trying to silence them, it's the Aulacri."

"Whose plans are dictated by the universe. This world is their best candidate for terraforming, and the current orbital configuration is the best they'll have for decades."

Sherev narrowed her eyes. "Is that what Skovir told you? She's lying, Jim."

"That's a strong accusation."

"Well, call it being selective in her presentation of the data. There's at least one other world in Aulacri space that would be almost as good for them to colonize; it'd just take a little more work to terraform and it'd be a little less ideal. And, hell, there are at least two good candidate worlds in the adjacent Federation sectors. If they really want to join us, they could apply with the Bureau of Colonization for one of those worlds once they're members. I already offered that option to Skovir, and she rejected it out of hand."

"Rhen, look at it from their perspective. They may be interested in joining us, yes, but we're still new to them. They need more time to evaluate whether it's in their best interests. We can't expect them to take it for granted that we'd give them what they need."

"There's more to it than that, Jim. Skovir wouldn't even consider it. She's hell-bent on smashing the crap out of this particular planet."

"It's been her life's work for twenty years, Rhen. Surely you of all people can understand being stubborn about completing a project."

She accepted the characterization without complaint. "Yeah, so I know what it looks like. I even tried to engage with her on those grounds, to show I was sympathetic, but no luck. Jim, I'm telling you, there's something deeper driving her. It was when I told her about the information the Karabosi left for us to find that she got more resistant. It's like she doesn't *want* us to discover it for some reason."

"She was pretty clear about her reason," Mitchell said. "She was really mad at them for killing off the rest of the planet's life along with themselves. Makes sense for a terraformer."

"No, I'm sure it's more than that," she insisted. "It's like she's afraid of what we might discover here. Like she's trying to cover something up." Her antennae twisted tighter, like clenching fists. "And she'll probably succeed. As comparatively stable as this region is, the quakes resulting from the comet impacts will probably bring down the mountains on top of the underground complex. Whatever's in there would be crushed."

Kirk thought it over. "There are fifty-eight hours left. Is there any chance you could penetrate the complex within the next day or two? Soon enough to gather at least some data from the facility before you have to evacuate?"

Sherev brightened, clutching his arms. "Oh, I was hoping you'd ask! Yes, with phaser bores and an additional science team from the *Enterprise*, we could probably pull it off."

"I think that could be arranged."

The archaeologist sobered. "But there's only so much we could learn from a quick look. Whatever we find in there, we'd need to learn more about the planet as a whole to put it in meaningful context. It could take months, years of work to get real answers. You've got to keep trying to convince Skovir to divert the comets."

"I'll do what I can, Rhen. But you need to be ready to leave with time to spare if it comes to that. I'm getting a little tired of having to rescue you."

Sherev smiled. "But you haven't let me down yet, Jim. And I don't expect you to start now."

U.S.S. *Enterprise*

". . . So we need to penetrate that underground site within the next day, if possible," Kirk told the officers assembled in the main briefing room, "and retrieve what information we can before it becomes necessary to leave."

Next to Kirk, Gary Mitchell took in the reactions of the gathered officers. Spock was unreadable, as always; the man was so stiff he made Kirk seem like, well, like Mitchell. Chief Engineer Scott and Lieutenant Sulu had listened with fascination as Kirk had relayed Sherev's discoveries, and both men looked eager to get involved. But Lee Kelso sat brooding by Spock's side, looking unhappy about something. Mitchell was still unsure what to make of the man. He seemed amiable enough most of the time, but whenever Kirk was around, he closed off and grew far more serious. Mitchell wondered if he was trying to emulate a captain with a reputation for seriousness. If so, he was overdoing it. Mitchell would probably have to talk with him about it before he serioused himself into a heart attack, or at least a sore jaw from all that teeth-clenching.

"Mister Spock," the captain went on, "I want you to assemble a party to assist Doctor Sherev, favoring personnel with experience in archaeology and underground excavation. Engineer Scott, you'll assist with the phaser bores."

The burly, squarish-featured Scotsman gave Kirk a brisk nod. "Aye, sir. I've been hopin' to give the latest model a try."

"Pardon me, Captain," Spock put in, "but Commodore Mendez's orders were to prioritize the safety of Federation citizens along with the territorial demands of the Aulacri. Assisting the researchers in furthering their excavations seems counterproductive to both."

"Mendez also said we were free to convince the Aulacri to choose an alternative. That will be your job, Mister Sulu. Work with Commander Mitchell to survey the system's cometary belt. Perhaps our navigational computers can find an alternate cometary configuration that they could use to bombard the planet at a later date, but still in the reasonably near future. We just need enough extra time to excavate the mountain site."

"Yes, sir!" Sulu answered.

"Oh, goody," Mitchell said with a sigh. "Plotting the courses of space rocks. That brings back memories. Dull ones." Sulu grinned, his enthusiasm undimmed.

"In the meantime," Kirk finished, "I intend to invite Director Skovir aboard and inform her of our efforts. If we return the Aulacri's hospitality, maybe they'll be more receptive to considering a compromise. Mister Kelso, since Commanders Spock and Mitchell have their own tasks, I'd like you to join me in greeting our guests and showing them the ship."

"Permission to speak freely, sir?" Kelso asked.

Kirk blinked in surprise, but said, "Go ahead."

"With all due respect, sir," the helmsman went on, "what if they don't appreciate your efforts to change their minds? We're guests in their space. They're within their rights to ask our scientists to leave, and they've done so already. I'm afraid that what we're doing will look to them like an act of defiance—showing them we don't respect their territory or their wishes. What will that do for their membership prospects?"

The captain pondered for a moment, then replied quietly, "Those are valid concerns, Mister Kelso. That's why it's important to present our case as diplomatically as possible. Remember, the discoveries we could make on Karabos II would benefit the Aulacri as well as the Federation. It is, as you say, one of their own worlds."

Kelso let out a breath through his nostrils. "Understood, Captain."

But Mitchell could tell the man was unhappy with Kirk's orders. Once the captain dismissed them and exited with the others, Mitchell held Kelso back for a moment. "Okay, Lee, are you gonna tell me what's bugging you? I thought you were trying to impress the captain with how serious you could be, but I finally figured out you've got something against the guy."

The blond helmsman fidgeted. "I'd rather not talk about it, Commander. I know you and the captain are old friends."

"Forget that. I know how to keep a secret. And if there's an issue between you and Captain Kirk, that's for you and Captain Kirk to hash out. Trust me, if I finally figured out you have a problem with him, you better damn well believe he figured it out a week ago. I'd just like to hear your side of it, maybe help you find a way to get over it before the captain has to deal with it himself."

After a moment's thought, Kelso spoke. "Look. I've been trying to give the man a fair shake. I admit, I've been feeling a little cheated that I hardly got a chance to learn from Captain Pike before he got replaced by a guy barely older than me. I've been trying not to hold that against him, figuring Starfleet had their reasons, that Kirk must know what he's doing if they gave him a ship like the *Enterprise*."

"But?"

"But then we get our first mission and . . ." He trailed off.

"Hey, don't lose your nerve now, Lee."

"Well, frankly, Commander, it feels like Kirk's playing favorites. Like he's putting his loyalty to an old friend above the good of the mission. And . . . with all due respect, maybe you can't see it because you're close to them both yourself."

Mitchell chuckled. "First of all, Lee, the amount of respect due to the likes of me is hardly worth worrying about. Second of all, you don't have to worry about Jim's objectivity. He'll fight for his friends, sure, but he knows his duty."

"Are you really sure of that, Gary? I mean . . . well, I saw Doctor Sherev in those images from the site. She's a damned attractive woman. Is it possible the captain is more attached to her than he should be?"

The navigator stared at Kelso for a moment, then laughed long and hard. "Jim Kirk? Putting romance ahead of his career?" He needed a moment to catch his breath. "Oh, man, are you ever reading from the wrong data card!" He broke up again, then struggled to get it under control. "Trust me, Lee, you're way off base. I mean, the man enjoys a good shore-leave fling like the rest of us, but on the job, he's the most focused, disciplined man I've ever met. His career's always come first, and he decided long ago not to let anything else get in its way.

"Oh—and Sherev, for your information, is happily married to *three* other people. Jim respects that too much to even consider what you're suggesting."

"Well . . . all right," Kelso conceded.

Mitchell peered at him. "Somehow you sound *less* reassured than before."

"Like you said, his career is what drives him. Drives him so hard that he got a front-line starship command faster than anyone ever has. Maybe he feels he has to prove he deserves it.

"And if that's so," Kelso finished, "maybe he doesn't."

Realizing he wasn't going to get through to Kelso today, Mitchell dismissed him. He'd leave it to Jim to sort things out with the man, if it came to that. Kelso only saw the relative shortness of Kirk's command record, the fact that he only had one prior starship command under his belt. Maybe if he'd been there aboard the *Sacagawea*, as Mitchell had been, he'd understand how that one command had tested and tempered Jim Kirk, and how his decisions and achievements had proved him ready for still greater things.

SACAGAWEA

2263

Eight

When interacting with the populace of a precontact planet, an officer of Starfleet shall make no identification of self or mission; no attempt at interference with the social development of said planet; no reference to space, to other worlds, or to advanced civilizations . . .

—Starfleet General Order One

U.S.S. Sacagawea

Gary Mitchell bounded down off the transporter pad the instant the beam released him. "Jim!" he crowed, and seemed about to throw his arms around Kirk until he saw the other officers standing by Kirk's side and remembered his Starfleet discipline. "I mean, Captain," he said, extending his hand, which Kirk clasped warmly. "It's great to see you again. And great to be back aboard the *Sac*." He looked around the transporter room. "She's looking good. New paint and everything. I can't wait to see what they've done with the bridge."

"Well, it certainly hasn't been the same without you," Kirk said. "Speaking of which . . ." He gestured to the tall, gray-haired, leathery-featured man by his side. "Lieutenant Commander Gary Mitchell, this is Commander Eshu Adebayo, my first officer."

Adebayo shook Mitchell's hand firmly and spoke in a booming voice with a Nigerian accent. "Welcome aboard, Mister

Mitchell. The captain has spoken highly of your navigation skills—and your proclivity for fun. We should do just fine so long as you remember to practice them both at the appropriate times." He softened it with a smile and a wink.

"I'll try my best, sir," Mitchell said, returning the smile.

"You'd better try harder than you did aboard the *Anggitay*, Gary," Kirk said. "Captain Sabatini sounded downright glad to send you back to me. He seemed to think I was the only one who could keep you under control. Seriously, Gary, the Betazoid ambassador's sister?"

Mitchell shrugged, though he blushed a bit at the same time. "What can I say? We just clicked. I tried to tell Sabatini, she was the one who made the moves. I tell you, Jim, it was like she could read my mind. Knew exactly what I wanted and was happy to take me up on it."

Next to Kirk, Commander Sherev chuckled. "Go easy on him, Jim. I've met a few Betazoids myself. Let's just say they're a very . . . open-minded people." She extended a hand. "Welcome aboard. Rhenas Sherev, science officer and second officer."

"It's a pleasure," Mitchell told her. "The captain's had nothing but praise for you in his letters. Sounds like you helped him through some rough times. Glad you were there for him when I couldn't be."

"Well, I wouldn't say I was the only one." Sherev smiled up at the other new arrival, who was only belatedly stepping down from the transporter pad. "Don't be shy, Sawbones, come say hello!"

Leonard McCoy flashed her a quick smile, but he still seemed nervous. "Don't mean to be rude, Commander. I just needed a moment to make sure all my molecules were still attached. I hate traveling in these blasted contraptions."

Adebayo laughed. "Oh, I think I'm going to like having you aboard, Doctor. Half my age and you're already a more crotchety old coot than I'll ever be. Takes the burden off me to act *my* age."

McCoy shook his hand. "Always glad to see a seasoned veteran like yourself on one of these things. It gives me hope that I'll actually survive this mission and make it to my own golden years." He turned to Kirk. "I swear, Jim, I still can't believe you finally talked me into coming back aboard a starship. All this gallivanting around the galaxy, poking uninvited into other species' business . . . I still say it sounds like nothing but trouble."

Kirk chuckled, aware that McCoy was hardly a novice at starship duty and was just putting up his usual grouchy front. "Then why'd you agree?"

"Damned if I know. Maybe I just missed playin' poker with you and Rhen."

Mitchell's eyes lit up. "Poker? I wouldn't mind getting in on that action." He leaned over to McCoy and muttered, "I love playing against Andorians. They don't even notice what their antennae are giving away."

Sherev cleared her throat. "Unless that's just what we *want* you flat-headed races to think." That shut him up quite effectively.

As Kirk led the party out into the corridor to show them the refitted ship, he felt a great sense of contentment. It had been satisfying to get the *Sacagawea* back, but she had felt empty with most of her former crew gone. The most senior officer who remained from the ship's tenure at Starbase 24 was the chief engineer, Kiran Desai, but he and Kirk had never established more than a professional relationship. Sherev's friendship had helped fill the void over the past six months, and Eshu Adebayo had proven a stalwart ally as first officer. Unlike many Kirk had served with, Adebayo had no reluctance to be subordinate to a younger man; on the contrary, he was happy to pass on the lessons of his half-century in Starfleet to a new generation. "Young minds, fresh ideas," he was fond of saying.

Still, having Gary Mitchell back aboard already made the ship feel more like home again, and having both Sherev and McCoy along as well brought him even greater satisfaction. He looked forward to what they would achieve together in the months and hopefully years ahead.

Captain's Log, Stardate 1148.2.

The Sacagawea *has entered orbit over planet II of star system UFC 5179, which we have confirmed as the source of the weak radio emissions that science officer Sherev detected three solar days ago. This world, named Nacmor by its dominant culture, hosts a humanoid civilization at an estimated level F on the industrial scale, corresponding to the early twentieth century on Earth. In addition to radio broadcast capability, our atmospheric scans confirm the presence of fossil fuel–powered industry and transportation, as well as radiation signatures consistent with crude nuclear power and weaponry. As a precaution, we are maintaining extended orbit with deflectors configured to prevent radar detection. This should permit us to observe and assess the Nacmorian civilization without risk of interference.*

"All of us at this remembrance gathering are being murdered one by one," announced the sharp, methodical voice on the bridge speakers. "That means the killer can only be one of you four."

"Surely not I, Investigator Kalamul! It was I who invited you, remember."

"True, Councilwoman, but while I know I am not the killer, I cannot be sure I am not one of the intended victims!"

A dramatic sting of music followed this proclamation, after which an announcer intoned, "Kalamul's investigation will continue in a moment. The investigator may be trapped within the estate during the curfew, but you won't have to feel trapped in a

Gernilod brand family shelter. Gernilod shelters are so roomy and well-ventilated, you'll feel like you're still aboveground!"

"Wow," said Gary Mitchell. "I know this will probably all make sense once the anthropologists get a handle on their culture, but right now this is one of the most confusing things I've ever heard. I mean, I counted. There are six people in the estate besides Kalamul."

"But two of them are servants," Kirk reminded him.

"What, the Nacmorians never heard of 'The butler did it'?"

"Maybe there's some social taboo we aren't aware of," Rhenas Sherev suggested. "Or maybe the writers of the mystery show don't want to put any ideas in the servant class's heads by portraying them as potential killers. We could be dealing with some pretty rigid social stratification."

Mitchell tilted his head. "Or maybe it's just lousy writing."

Eshu Adebayo had been pacing the front of the bridge as the crew listened. Now the aging first officer rested his hands on the front of the helm console. "I think we may learn more from the advertisements than the main programs. These shelters suggest a fear of nuclear war."

Sherev nodded. "A pretty normalized fear, if they're promoting them so casually."

Kirk chimed in. "And a curfew so rigid that even a police detective is bound to obey it. It's a lot to unpack."

The radio drama soon resumed, and the bridge crew listened raptly as Investigator Kalamul dodged a murder attempt, failed to save another victim, and ultimately nabbed the murderer, though his explanation bewildered the crew. *"I realized it had to be your forehusband, Councilwoman, when I remembered that the day he claimed to have traveled to Hormag Island fell on an even multiple of eighth-day feasts after your hindwife's induction."* The councilwoman and the other surviving guests gasped in shock. *"Yes, that's right. His transport would never have been approved! Therefore he must have been the extra figure whose pres-*

ence tainted her induction and led to her suicide! The guilt of that compelled him to reduce the number at this remembrance to one, in order to balance the scales."

The bridge crew spent some time spinning hypotheses to try to explain what they'd just heard, though Mitchell stuck to his opinion: "No, I still say the writers are just hacks and it wouldn't make sense even to a Nacmorian." He sighed. "This is fun up to a point, but are we really just going to sit here in orbit this whole time, watching from a safe distance? Or do archaeology in uninhabited parts of the planet?"

Sherev quirked her antennae at him. "It's a lot harder to do archaeology in an inhabited part."

"Not the point. There's only so much you can learn about people if you don't get up close and personal. You know, walk among them, get a feel for their lives. These folks are pretty humanoid; it wouldn't be hard for Doc McCoy to whip up some prosthetics for a landing party."

Kirk shook his head. "The risk of cultural contamination is too great. It's not worth it for a preliminary survey like this. Once Starfleet gets our report, it's up to them to decide whether to chance a more in-depth follow-up mission."

Mitchell gave him a long-suffering look. "Still the stickler for rules and regulations. I guess we're stuck with the radio, then. Hey, Chalan, can you pick up any sports on that thing?"

"Sorry, sir," the communications officer replied. "Not for another couple of hours, sounds like."

Instead, the next program appeared to be an espionage-themed adventure show, whose announcer introduced it with a bombastic appeal to the listeners' nationalist pride and the defense of what made their nation great. "This could be interesting," Adebayo said. "We might learn something about the political conflicts between their nations."

The spy adventure proved easier to comprehend than the mystery drama, as its plot points were based on straightforward action and physical conflict rather than the nuances of Nac-morian cultural traditions or class and gender roles. Contrary to the first officer's musings, the antagonists seemed to be a nongovernmental rogue faction, a subversive group seeking to undermine the peaceful global order that the drama's protago-nists were fighting to preserve—fighting quite ruthlessly, with very loud and frequent firearm sound effects, and showing no quarter or mercy to the villains, whose deaths were depicted as an unambiguous good.

"It's strange, isn't it?" Ensign Kamisha Diaz asked during another advertising break, this time for some sort of furniture wax. The slim, dark junior science officer was leaning against the communications console, using her skills in cultural anthro-pology and linguistics to assist Ensign Chalan in refining the computer's translation algorithms for the radio transmissions as they came in.

Chalan looked up at her, blinking his huge, catlike eyes. "What's strange?" the Cygnian asked.

"How analogous all this is to Earth just a couple hundred years ago. It's remarkable how many civilizations there are in the galaxy that are within just a few centuries of each other techno-logically," Diaz went on. "Think about it. Human civilization's some eight to ten thousand years old. We've been an industrial-ized society for about five hundred years, spacegoing for barely two hundred. But the galaxy is thirteen *billion* years old. Even assuming it took billions of years for the galactic radiation en-vironment to subside enough to be habitable, we're still talking at least five or six billion years for life to evolve in. So, statisti-cally, what are the odds that your civilization and mine, for instance—let alone so many others, the Vulcans, the Andorians, the Rigelians—all began their space ages within one or two mil-lennia of each other? And that we keep running across worlds like Nacmor that are just a few hundred years behind?"

"It's a big galaxy, flush with life," Eshu Adebayo reminded her.

"In just the first seven months of our mission, how many worlds have we charted with Stone Age societies, or with only primitive, subsentient life? And in my time, I've walked on dozens of worlds with ruins from civilizations that died out hundreds of millennia ago—and caught glimpses of alien races so far beyond our level that they might as well have been gods."

Rhenas Sherev chimed in from the main science station. "Still, Diaz has a point. Even with the sheer number of species we encounter, the percentage that are close to the same technological level—including most of the Federation's members—is disproportionate. It's an enigma in galactic archaeology."

Kirk, who had been quietly following their conversation, noted something familiar in Sherev's tone. "Something tells me you have a theory to offer, Commander."

"There isn't one firm theory, just a number of speculations. Some past galactic cataclysm hundreds of millennia ago that either wiped out life or served as a stressor to drive new evolution on multiple planets, so they were all reset to a similar starting point at the same time. Some ancient race that manipulated different species' biological or technological evolution around the same time. Some universal telepathic field that causes different species to resonate with each other and innovate the same ideas around the same times. None of them really holds up that well, but the paradox keeps us looking."

Diaz flashed her senior science officer a blinding smile. "Nice to know I'm not the first to notice."

"But perhaps you'll be the one to find the answer," Kirk told her. Diaz beamed even brighter at his words, but he wasn't offering idle praise. Kamisha Diaz had an energy and drive that Kirk found very familiar, much like himself when he'd started out aboard the *Farragut*. It was his hope that he could cultivate the young Regulus native's potential, much as Captain Garrovick had done for him.

"Sir!" Ensign Chalan interrupted, adjusting the receiver in his ear. "I'm picking up a new transmission now. It's interrupting normal programming on every band." He paused the translated playback of the spy drama, worked with Diaz for a moment to check the computer translation of the new broadcast, then played it for the bridge crew.

"We interrupt now for an urgent warning. A massive fire has broken out in the Vinorga residential district of Minerith City. The fire is spreading rapidly due to the closely packed and decrepit condition of the structures in the area, one of the oldest in the city, and the overcrowded conditions make it difficult for rescue forces to minimize the death and injury toll. The fire has not yet spread beyond Vinorga, and emergency crews are doing all they can to contain it there. Whether this fire is the latest attack from the sky is not yet known, but all citizens in the vicinity of Minerith City are advised to remain in their homes or move toward the nearest shelter in an orderly manner. Watch for government responders and follow their instructions to the letter. They are your best protection."

"'Attack from the sky'?" Kirk repeated. "Sherev, sensor report."

The Andorian was already taking the scan and studying the readouts. "I can detect the fire, sir. It's raging across seven or eight city blocks. But none of the aircraft I'm scanning in the vicinity appear consistent with a military bomber, and none have a course and speed consistent with having recently passed over the area of the blaze."

"Exhaust trails from missiles?" Adebayo suggested.

"I don't register any. In fact, I'm not reading any indications of energy or chemical residues consistent with explosives. This could be a spontaneous fire. The area's construction does fit the description of slum-like conditions, so if a fire did begin accidentally, it would likely spread rapidly."

"And yet," Kirk said, "the announcement made it clear that there have been earlier attacks, even if this isn't one of them."

"Sir," Chalan said, then put another update on speakers:

"*Our brave watchers of the skies have issued a report. They confirm that classified military detectors have tracked four craft moving too swiftly and flying too high for the naked eye to see. These craft descended into detector range only moments before the fire broke out, and they are now retreating toward outer space. Military aircraft are in pursuit, but the intruders are swiftly outpacing them. Authorities advise us to remain sheltered until the all-clear is given, but it looks like our air defenses have scared off the enemy from beyond once more.*"

Kirk traded a stunned look with Sherev and Adebayo. "An alien attack? Sherev, you looked for aircraft. Any sign of spacecraft?"

The science officer bent to her console, her antennae twisting in deep confusion. "Sir, I'm picking up no sign of any vehicular activity in the upper atmosphere, and nothing else in orbit. The city's in our line of sight—nothing could be hidden behind the planet."

"I confirm," Mitchell said. "Nothing on my screen either. No engine signatures, no ion trails besides ours."

Kamisha Diaz had stepped over to assist Sherev at the science station. "They said the craft couldn't be seen. What if they have some kind of stealth ability, like the Xyrillians?"

"They also said their military trackers were able to pick them up," Sherev reminded her. "These people have nothing but primitive radar. If they can see them, we should see them."

Kirk rose to his feet. "Still—if there's even a chance that someone out here is attacking these people, then we have to investigate."

"Investigate how?" Sherev asked. "You were just reminding us of the Prime Directive."

"General Order One obliges us to shield the Nacmorians from *all* interference," he told her, "not just our own. Knowingly leaving them at someone else's mercy would be as bad as attacking them ourselves." He threw his navigator a look. "Seems you'll get to wear one of those disguises after all, Mister Mitchell. Chalan, contact sickbay and let McCoy know we're on our way."

"You're going yourself, Jim?" Sherev asked.

Kirk hesitated. "Given the short notice, Rhen, it'd take some doing for Bones to hide your antennae."

"I could wear a hat. Do they wear hats?"

Diaz shook her head. "Judging from our optical surveillance, Commander, only Nacmorian males cover their heads in public, at least in the dominant culture."

"Then I'll start a fashion trend."

"The last thing we want is to call attention to ourselves," Kirk told her. "We don't want them discovering us and mistaking us for their attackers."

Sherev nodded, her antennae sagging. "Understood, sir."

Diaz stepped forward. "Permission to join the landing party, sir?"

The captain smiled at her. "I was just about to give the order. You know the Nacmorians as well as any of us." The young science officer struggled to contain her excitement.

Kirk had to admit that he felt a similar thrill at getting back out in the field. He knew that captains should ideally stay on the bridge and rely on their crews, but he preferred to emulate the example of more hands-on commanders like Garth, Pike, and Wesley. It didn't sit right with him to order others into dangers he wouldn't face himself. Especially in a case like this, with the double dangers of the Nacmorians' unknown cultural pitfalls and the unseen attackers from space.

As the three officers entered the turbolift, Gary Mitchell gave Kirk a look acknowledging the uncertainty he must have seen on his friend's face. "I know what you're thinking," Mitchell said. "Where's Investigator Kalamul when we need him?"

Minerith City, Nacmor
It was fortunate for the landing party that Nacmorian males commonly wore cowls in public, since said males were totally

bald, save for thick, bushy bronze eyebrows. The cowls saved Kirk, Mitchell, and security chief Joshua Hauraki from needing to shave their heads, though McCoy still needed to apply prosthetic pieces to simulate the Nacmorian males' bulbous foreheads, which apparently housed some sort of pheromonal glands. Kamisha Diaz, the lone woman on the team, had it comparatively easy, for Nacmorian women were closer to the humanoid norm; she only needed to have her tight curls straightened and dyed bronze, and her skin tinted golden-green along with the men's. The final touch for all four was a pair of uncomfortable scleral contact lenses to match the Nacmorians' wide, bright gold irises with horizontal slit pupils.

The four disguised humans beamed down into a vacant alley not far from the military cordon now surrounding the burned-out slum area. They moved out into pedestrian traffic and wended their way indirectly toward the edge of the burned zone, trying to appear no more than idly curious, like passersby momentarily distracted from their business. Kirk noted that the streets, sidewalks, buildings, and storefronts looked not too different from an Earth city of the early twentieth century, allowing for alien writing and architectural nuances, although the smell was more reminiscent of the nineteenth. While the Nacmorians did have internal combustion engines, it appeared that their use was restricted to government and military vehicles; the general citizenry still relied on wagons and carriages pulled by large draft animals resembling a green-feathered hybrid of camel and ostrich. And where an Earth city might have subway entrances spaced along its street corners, instead there were prominently marked bomb shelters—heavy steel domes with open doors leading into dark stairways and guarded by soldiers who nodded respectfully at the passing citizenry.

As the group made its way around the outskirts of the slum, Kamisha Diaz took what opportunities she could to sneak tricorder scans of the burned-out area, while the three men shielded her hands from the view of the crowd and the military cordon. "Nothing," she said after a dozen blocks' worth of this. "I'm reading no chemical, metallurgical, or radiation signatures inconsistent with Nacmorian materials. Some residue consistent with combustion accelerants, but that could easily be fuel for the crude heaters they use."

"We need to find out more from the people who've been through these attacks," Kirk said. "It's risky, but maybe we can question some of the citizenry, if we're subtle about it."

Soon they found a crowd of Nacmorians huddled around a newsstand where a large radio, the glow of its vacuum tubes visible through a ventilation grille, was delivering a news update on the aftermath of the apparent alien attack. Though the announcer offered reassurances that the government was on the case and advisories to remain vigilant, his report provided little in the way of specifics.

As the report ended and several of the passersby dispersed, a stout, gray-haired woman remained to peruse the newsstand's wares, shaking her head and tut-tutting. "Terrible," she said. "Just terrible."

Ensign Diaz sidled up to her. "It is, isn't it? It's all just so hard to understand. I mean, what do I tell my little brother when he asks me why the people from the sky are attacking us?"

Kirk traded an impressed look with Mitchell. *She's a natural at this.*

Unfortunately, her gambit bore little fruit. "I know, dear. How frustrating not to have any answers for them. Who can know the minds of creatures from another world? Maybe the government has a theory by now, but they tell us what they choose in their own time."

"They want what we have," the news vendor countered. "Our riches, our food, our energy. We've cracked the atom, conquered the world. We took it all from the weaker kind. Now somebody bigger has come to take it from us. It's the way of things."

The old woman threw him a sour look, not seeming pleased by his words. "That's the real shame. I'd hoped that now the wars were won, we'd at least be able to relax our guard. Go back to the way things were before."

"Like what, ma'am?" Diaz asked.

"Oh, before your time, dear. But there was a day before all the rationing, the compulsory donations, the curfews, the checkpoints. A time when we could live our lives in—" She broke off, reacting to the motor sound of a military vehicle that had just rounded the corner. "Forgive me—I've said more than I should. The hazards of aging, I'm afraid." She hurried off without buying anything.

Further attempts turned up little more information—just more of the same mix of reactions from a populace chafing under the government's restrictions and regulations but grateful for the defense the state provided against a terrifying and unknowable foe. But the nature of that alien foe and its agenda remained elusive.

Finally, Kirk's communicator beeped, and he led the party into another alley to answer. *"Radio intercepts say another alien attack is underway,"* Sherev reported from the ship. *"In Derostur City, four hundred kilometers southwest of you."*

"Beam us to that location at once, Sherev," Kirk said. "We need to see this for ourselves."

Derostur City, Nacmor

When the party arrived in the new city, they heard the blaring of air raid sirens and civil defense announcements advising evacuation to the shelters. From the emptiness of the streets, it seemed most of the citizenry had already acted on the warnings. *"The government transmissions say a flight of ships has been detected incoming,"* Sherev reported from the ship, *"but we're still reading nothing on sensors. No ships, no power signatures, no exhaust trails, no atmospheric disturbances."*

This section of Derostur appeared somewhat more prosperous than the Minerith slum district, but the architectural styles were distinctly different and most of the signage was in a different script. "It seems to be an immigrant enclave," Diaz observed. "Like Little Andoria in San Francisco. I think the language is from the country called Vekudi, on the southern continent."

They reached an intersection with what appeared to be the main thoroughfare of the enclave, which had several military vehicles and teams patrolling it. Staying in the shadow of a shop awning, they observed as the soldiers proceeded up the street toward them, stopping to enter the vacant storefronts or apartment buildings on either side of the street. "Are they taking something into those buildings?" Kirk asked.

Diaz's tricorder warbled. "Sir—the bundles read as high explosives!"

Mitchell gasped. "Holy— No wonder we couldn't detect any ships. There aren't any aliens—the whole thing is a hoax! *By* the government!"

Kirk nodded. "It looks that way. They get everyone into the shelters so they can plant bombs unobserved, then claim the destruction was caused by alien attackers that they then fought off."

"But why?" a bewildered Diaz asked.

"We'll figure that out later," Kirk said. "Right now we need to withdraw."

"Hey!" A group of soldiers had spotted them. Five burly men and one woman, dressed in blue-gray military fatigues and black helmets, quickly surrounded them. "You're not supposed to be here, citizens," the man in the lead said. "You were ordered to report to shelters."

"We're sorry, sir," Kirk said, keeping his tone conciliatory. "We were unavoidably detained. We were just on our way—"

"Hold on," the squad leader said. "You're not Vekudi. Your accent is northern. What are you doing in Derostur? Where are your papers?"

"We . . . left them in our hotel, I'm afraid. We weren't expecting to travel far, but then in the confusion we got turned around, the sirens and all . . ."

"Go out on the streets without your papers? No decent citizen would do that. But the resistance would!"

Kirk saw the squad leader reach for his firearm. He reacted instinctively, grabbing the support pole of the awning with both hands and kicking the soldier in the chest, knocking down both him and the woman behind him. He knew the landing party's disguises would not hold up to more than cursory inspection, so escape was the only option.

Lieutenant Hauraki followed his captain's lead and took a third soldier down with a karate chop, and Mitchell decked another with a roundhouse punch. It created enough of an opening for the foursome to break through the encirclement and run. But as soon as they rounded the corner, a second squad confronted them, and the first squad quickly recovered and came in pursuit. Kirk and the others tried to dodge them, but Diaz was grabbed. She fought against the considerably larger woman who held her, but got a hard slap across the face for her trouble. When Kirk tried to run to her rescue, the first squad leader stepped in front of him and felled him with a blow to the chin.

As the soldiers dragged Kirk to his feet, he noted with alarm that an edge of his forehead prosthetic was hanging loose into his field of view. Looking at the others, all just as firmly restrained now, he saw that Mitchell's cowl had come loose, exposing a portion of his hair behind his forehead appliance—and Diaz had lost a contact lens from the slap.

The squad leader was staring at them in disbelief. Hesitantly, he reached out and yanked the cowl from Kirk's head, recoiling in shock at the nearly full head of hair thus exposed. Examining the forehead piece, the soldier soon recognized that it was artificial, emboldening him to tear it free. A pair of the soldiers behind him gasped at the pale pinkish flesh thus exposed.

"Incredible," the big woman said. "Did we find . . . *actual* aliens from outer space?"

"Or something close enough," the squad leader said. He gave Kirk a self-satisfied smile. "Count yourself lucky, whatever you are. We were going to kill you and leave your bodies to be found in the wreckage. Now I think you may be of much more use to us alive—for now."

Nine

The government has learned that the enemy from outer space has the ability to alter the minds of Nacmorian beings, explaining the rash of insurrectionist activity among formerly respectable professors at Nilostig University. If you see hints of subversive thought or behavior expressed by your neighbors, co-workers, or family, then they may have been infected by alien signals and should be promptly reported to the authorities for their own safety.

—Nacmorian government broadcast

U.S.S. Sacagawea

"We're still reading their communicator signals inside the government bunker," Rhenas Sherev reported, leaning forward with her hands on the railing in front of her science station. "But they haven't moved in over two hours. Given the power readings in the chamber they're in, I'm guessing it's some sort of electronics lab. Most likely the equipment has been taken away for study, and the bunker's too deep for us to differentiate human from Nacmorian life signs in there." Her nails dug into the railing as she squeezed it angrily. "I still say we should've beamed them up at the first sign of trouble."

Eshu Adebayo, by contrast, sat calmly in the command chair, which he'd swiveled to face her. "You know what the captain would say. Revealing transporter technology to the Nacmorians would be a massive violation of the Prime Directive."

"And revealing alien life wouldn't? If we leave them there to be examined, dissected—"

"Starfleet explorers have faced situations like this before, going back to Jonathan Archer," the first officer said in a calming tone. "I was in a spot like this myself some, hmm, thirty-two years ago. We were undercover on a planet of Iron Age humanoids—my XO, myself, three others—but we were found out and captured by a local monarch. We hadn't realized that a percentage of their females were telepathic. They saw right through us, read our alienness in our own thoughts. Our knowledge of physics, technology, weapons—if they'd used it, their empire could've conquered the world." He chuckled. "But Commander Shao was able to convince them that she was schizophrenic and had telepathically infected the rest of us with her delusions. They hastened to quarantine us—piled us into a wagon and gave its draft animals a mental command to take us to some sort of leper colony for dangerous telepaths. Once we were alone, we could beam away unobserved. And since they dismissed what they'd read in our minds as delusions, they never attempted to follow up on our scientific knowledge."

"Entertaining as always, Eshu, but this is different. They're medically advanced enough to prove our team is alien. They can study our equipment and learn from it. Beaming the team out right away would've just left them with a mystery they couldn't solve. Now they have all the evidence they need to figure it out. Evidence including our team's bodies. You've heard the broadcasts. These people have little regard for the lives of their enemies."

"I thought the situation was just as helpless back then, Rhenas, but my commanding officer found an option I hadn't considered. You know Jim better than I do. Do you have any reason to doubt he can find a way out of this?"

Adebayo's warm, dark eyes held hers, and the calm within them helped cool her own fires. She sighed. "He's always been more disciplined than I am. I guess I should try to learn from his example."

"Yes. Instead of arguing for an option no longer available, try to predict what the captain might do, so that we can be ready to assist when the chance arises."

"'When,' Commander? You have a lot of faith in such a young captain."

"He wouldn't be a captain at his age if he weren't something special. And sooner or later, all of us old hands need to admit that it's time for fresher, more flexible minds to take the lead." He smiled. "Which includes yours as well, Rhen. So get thinking."

Nacmorian government bunker, outside Derostur

The first few hours of the landing party's captivity were the most unpleasant. The Nacmorians stripped them naked, sprayed them with hoses, and scrubbed them down until their golden-green skin dye wore off, then subjected them to invasive medical examinations and took enough x-ray images that they might need hyronalin treatment if and when they returned to the ship. Interrogators asked them a litany of questions that only Kamisha Diaz could understand even partially, since their communicators and tricorders had been taken away along with their hand phasers, and thus they had no translation capability beyond the junior science officer's linguistic talents.

In time, though, the four humans were given back their Nacmorian clothing (minus the men's cowls, apparently deemed redundant for males with scalp hair) and escorted to a sizable dining hall with a well-appointed table. At the head of the table sat an aged, jowly, bareheaded Nacmorian male dressed in a pseudomilitary suit adorned with ornate epaulets and piping. He lifted his bulky frame from his seat with some effort, and

Kirk noted that he wore one of the landing party's communicators on a chain around his neck. The unit's lid was shut, but the status lights visible through its grille indicated that the translation function was active.

"Ah, greetings, greetings," the man said. "I am Ultimate Premier Ribaul, the leader of Nacmor. I apologize for the way you have been treated, but it was necessary to confirm that you were what you appeared to be. Now that we are certain, however, it changes everything." He gestured to the seats around the table. "Please, be seated and enjoy our hospitality. You are honored guests to our world."

Kirk affected a bewildered look. He turned to the others, mugging in shock, and they quickly caught on and followed his lead. "I'm sorry," he told Ribaul. "'To our world'? What exactly do you think we are?"

"Oh, there's no need to pretend, my friends. You are the answer to our prayers. You have come to us from outer space, just when we need you the most."

After another moment's shocked staring, Kirk broke out laughing, and the others followed suit. Mitchell, always a poor actor, laughed a little too loudly until Diaz nudged his shin with her foot.

"From outer space?" Kirk echoed in a disbelieving tone. "Oh, I'm afraid there's been a misunderstanding, Premier. I can understand how you might think we were the ones responsible for these horrible attacks, but I assure you we're nothing of the kind." He glanced toward the seat he'd been offered, and at Ribaul's nod, he tentatively took it; again, the other three followed suit.

"You see," Kirk went on, glancing down at the table, "we . . . our family . . . have a rare genetic condition. Our land is very remote and isolated, so you've probably never heard of it. When we must travel beyond our tribe, we wear prosthetics to hide our . . . our deformity." He avoided meeting the premier's eyes.

Ribaul looked unconvinced. "Even if that explained you, it would not explain your equipment." He gestured at the communicator. "This radio alone—its capability to instantly translate any language is extraordinary. Its signal range and the compactness and life of its power systems are far beyond anything we have."

Diaz leaned forward. "They're prototypes. Gifts from an organization that wished to facilitate our travels to search for a treatment for our condition." She gave him an apologetic smile. "It's proprietary, I'm afraid. We couldn't sell it to you even if we understood it ourselves."

"That's hardly necessary," Ribaul said, "for under the ongoing state of emergency, the government can nationalize any resources or technologies it wishes." The premier narrowed his lips impatiently. "But I assure you, there is no need for this pretense. You are under no threat from us. We know you are not of this world. I implore you to speak plainly with me."

Kirk shrugged. "We can't control what you believe about us. But neither can we confirm it."

The jowly premier gave a knowing nod. "I see. This is a negotiation. And I have not yet explained what we of Nacmor can offer you in return for your candor—and your aid."

"Even if we were aliens," Mitchell said, "what would you need us for? You've been pulling off an alien invasion well enough without us."

Ribaul sighed. "I suppose the deception must seem bizarre to you, perhaps even comical."

"The loss of life is never comical to us," Kirk said firmly.

"Of course, of course. It is a grave matter, to be sure. Do not doubt that." Clearing his throat, Ribaul folded his chubby hands before him and rested his elbows on the table. "What you must understand is that, not very long ago, our world was torn apart by war after war. This nation's enemies attacked it and plotted against it relentlessly. When we developed nuclear weapons as a deterrent, they stole the technology in the name of conquest and terror. We were forced to break those enemies, to take control of their governments and resources for the greater good, so that we could institute and direct a global order to keep all Nacmorians safe.

"During the wars, you see, our people came to recognize the value of a firm hand. Of obedience to higher authority, with no selfish bleating about individual freedom undermining the security of the whole. They saw—the people did—that a nation, a world, needed to be like a family, with a loving but strict parent ensuring that his children obeyed the rules, and disciplining them firmly when they strayed." His hands parted and clenched into fists. Kirk controlled his reaction tightly.

Ribaul spread his hands in a sort of shrug. "But now we have peace. Our enemies have been crushed, or have recognized the futility of defiance and consented to join the world order. This is an undeniable good. Yet as the peace has continued, it has made the people . . . complacent. Lazy. Self-absorbed. They have begun to lose sight of the urgency of obedience to the state. Groups among them have begun agitating for a relaxation of the laws that keep us safe. For a tolerance toward the . . . aberrations of belief and behavior that led to conflict and hatred in the past. For an elevation of selfish individual interest above the protective hand of the regime." He shook his head. "You can see my fear, surely. Such loss of discipline threatens to plunge our world back into war and chaos once again."

Kirk folded his own hands before him. "So you create a new enemy. A larger, more powerful enemy for the entire world. And you frighten the people into continued obedience."

"Call it . . . an allegory. A reminder that safety is never guaranteed, that we cannot grow weak or undisciplined."

"And if it lets you burn down a slum so you can move in the upscale mansions and businesses," Mitchell put in, "or blow up an immigrant neighborhood so maybe they have to go back where they came from, well, at least you're not killing anyone who actually *matters*, am I right?"

Ribaul looked wounded. "Oh, that's a very harsh way of looking at it. As the parent to my people, I value them all equally. I wish to protect them all equally." His froggish face took on a tragic mien. "But there are those whose weakness or laziness makes them unable to prosper, you see, and many of them are inclined to blame the system for their failure. And in those communities who cling to their old ways, who refuse to assimilate fully into modern culture, well, many fail to understand the reasons why things must be the way they are.

"As a result, dissidents and rebels often arise in those communities. If we wish to quell rebellion, we could simply charge in and arrest or slaughter the lot of them, but that would make them see the state as their enemy and create worse resistance."

"I get it," Diaz said, barely controlling her disgust. "So if they think they're under attack by aliens, it makes them feel they're on the same side as you, that they have to stand with you against the 'invaders.'"

"Exactly!" Ribaul beamed, untroubled by her disapproval. "The problem is, our . . . simulations . . . can only remain convincing for so long. People are already starting to ask questions. Why has no one outside the government seen the invaders from space? Why have we yet to shoot down any of their ships, capture any of their personnel?" Chuckling, he gestured toward the four humans. "As I said, you could not have arrived at a more fortuitous time."

Kirk frowned. "If your intent is to show us off as captive aliens, I've told you—"

"Oh, my friend, you show a lack of vision. Surprising from one whose people have the imagination needed to cross the gulfs between the stars.

"Think on what I have said," Ribaul went on, his eyes gleaming. "The appearance of a threat from outside serves the interests of the state. You and we should be allies, however much we may seem to be adversaries on the surface. All you would need to do is reveal yourselves publicly. Use your spaceships and weapons to stage an open attack or two—in a manner consistent with the established pattern, of course. Issue a proclamation declaring your intent to conquer us, to destroy us, to steal our water, to take our women as mates—whatever will sow the most fear.

"Then, once you've had your fun, you permit us to achieve a staged victory over you, drive you away and thereby demonstrate our strength . . . while making it clear that more of you are out there and will continue to pose a threat."

Ribaul looked them over, his expression showing that he was not as oblivious to their reactions of distaste as he had pretended before. "If my proposal troubles you, consider that this would actually save lives. We are forced to resort to large-scale attacks to convince the populace that the threat is real. In the absence of visible, confirmed aliens, we must create fear through the sheer shock and magnitude of the destruction. But if the people could actually see rocketships descend from the stratosphere and blast our factories with disintegrator rays . . . if dozens of hairy, circle-eyed, pink- and brown-skinned soldiers in spacesuits marched down our streets seizing captives . . . all of that would drive home the reality of the enemy from space with a considerably more measured loss of life and property.

"And our loss would be your gain, keep in mind. What you seize in your raids would be yours to keep, as payment. Our gold, our petroleum, our uranium. Or perhaps you would benefit from slave laborers. If you require scientists or engineers to service your technologies—or if you really do want to take our women—we could direct you toward the most troublesome, rebellious ones, and the transaction would benefit us both. If it's territory you want, we could permit you to establish a base on one of our moons, or on another planet of our sun. Then the people could see the threat you posed on a continuing basis, and they would continue to accept their dependence on us for their protection. There is no need for us to be adversaries, for we can benefit the most as partners."

"In other words," Kirk said, "you'd be uniting with an enemy power against your own people."

Ribaul laughed. "But not a true enemy, of course. A fellow . . . performer, shaping the narrative that guides the people in their submission."

Kirk was growing sick of this. "Whether we're aliens or not, our answer would be the same. Your proposal is obscene. You're a petty tyrant who sees your days are numbered and is desperately trying to stave off the inevitable rebellion. But we can do nothing to slow the arrival of that day—nor do we wish to."

The premier hardened his gaze, abandoning the pretense of hospitality. "Very well. I attempted to appeal to your reason, but there are other options. Your cooperation would have made things easier for us both, but our needs will still be served by the display of four captured alien spies. Perhaps we will even film your vivisection and run it in the theaters. It will be educational, so there will be no reason to turn away the children."

The guards moved in on them, but Mitchell remained defiant. "Don't you think our fellow aliens out in space will have an objection to that? Maybe launch an attack for real, and not according to your script?"

Ribaul narrowed his eyes with reptilian smugness. "Your leader's words have told me what I need to know. 'We can do nothing.' You refuse my offer for the same reason you refuse to admit your identity—because you have some law or inhibition that forbids you from interfering in our affairs. That means you cannot stop me. Even if we expose you to the world, it will be an enhancement of the plan I and my government have already been carrying out on our own. If anything, it would be greater interference if you did stop me."

He rose and gestured the guards forward, ordering them to take the prisoners back to their cell. First, however, he removed the communicator from around his neck and handed it to Kirk. "Here. A gesture of good faith, so you may relay requests to the guards and understand their orders. I am aware it will let you speak to your spaceship as well. Discuss my offer with the rest of your people—perhaps you have a superior who will better understand the responsibilities of a leader. But make sure they are aware that you are hostages for their good behavior. You will be closely watched, and if they attempt to mount a rescue, you will be killed one by one until they desist—beginning with your female." He smirked. "This bunker will be closely watched as well, by government film crews as well as the military. Should your compatriots come in force to break it open and free you, it will give me exactly what I want from you anyway. Either way . . . I win."

U.S.S. *Sacagawea*

"*This is Kirk*," came the captain's voice over the comm channel from the surface. He went on before Adebayo or the others on the bridge could respond. "*I'm just checking in to let you know we're all right. We've been taken in by government troops, but they haven't harmed us. They're just detaining us—watching our every move.*" He chuckled. "*They have this crazy idea that we're people from outer space. They've been staging the attacks they've blamed on offworlders, using them to maintain their grip on the populace, and they want us to help them by launching a real alien attack. As if we were capable of such a thing. They let us have our radio back so we could discuss it with you, but obviously there's nothing to discuss.*"

Sherev exchanged a concerned look with Adebayo and McCoy, who had been hovering on the bridge awaiting news of the landing party. The doctor took a breath, but Adebayo touched his arm, keeping him quiet. Sherev could see that the first officer had taken Kirk's hint to mind his words. "That's . . . quite a mess you're in, Jim. Is there anything we can do to help?"

"For the moment, I don't think so. Even if you could get us out, they've taken the rest of our belongings. I'm worried they might cause some damage if they tinker with them. Hopefully the four of us can figure out a way to talk them out of it. For now, just stand by. We'll be in touch if we need you. Kirk out."

"Well, there it is," said Adebayo, looking up at Sherev again. "We can't just beam them up, because it would be witnessed, and because the Nacmorians would still have their phasers and tricorders. And a more overt raid would surely bring exposure."

"And apparently play into the government's hands," Sherev said.

"Unbelievable," said McCoy. "A government attacking its own people and blaming it on imaginary aliens. It's monstrous!"

The elderly human made a noise in his throat. "Sadly, all too believable, Leonard. The powerful have always found it easy to use outsiders as scapegoats for their own abuses of the less powerful. Although making up imaginary outsiders is a twist."

"Still, it makes a kind of sense," Ensign Chalan said from the communications station.

McCoy stared at the young Cygnian. "How in the name of all that's holy does this make sense to you, Ensign?"

Chalan kept his cool. "Not to me, Doctor, to them. Judging from the news and dramas we've heard, the government takes pride in having unified the planet under its rule, crushed all dissidence and rebellion. Saying this new threat is from within would be admitting weakness."

Sherev nodded. "And since they're in the early decades of radio technology, they've no doubt begun detecting pulsars and other astronomical radio signals, and they've probably speculated that they might be from alien civilizations. So the idea would have been seeded in the popular consciousness by now, available for the government to exploit."

"And now we've given them actual aliens to exploit," Adebayo said. "How long before they discover how to activate one of our hand phasers? Imagine the attacks they could stage with those."

"Well, for God's sake, man," McCoy urged, "don't just stand there talking about it. We've got to do something!"

Clenching the back of the command chair, Sherev leaned closer. "We should beam down a team now. Stun everyone, seize our equipment, break out the captain's party, beam away before anyone knows what happened."

"Sounds good to me," McCoy put in.

"If the captain thought that was a good idea, he would have ordered it," Adebayo told them, retaining his calm. "Think it through, both of you. We can track the communicators, but not the phasers. They may have been separated already. And we couldn't beam in directly, not that deep. We'd have to fight our way down from above, which would give them time to kill our people."

"Right." She sighed. "Damn facts, always getting in the way."

"So what the hell can we do instead?" McCoy demanded.

Adebayo smiled at him. "What Starfleet officers are trained to do: trust our captain."

Nacmorian government bunker

Despite Kirk's instructions to his first officer, he had little luck thinking of a way to escape Ribaul's clutches without compromising the Prime Directive. He had racked his brain for precedents, but none of the established procedures quite fit this situation. On the one hand, the head of Nacmor's global government had learned of the Starfleet personnel's existence and nature and invited them to enter open dialogue, so technically, this might qualify as a legitimate first contact. On the other hand, that government head planned to use their existence to advance his own agenda at the expense of rival factions, and the noninterference rule prohibited Starfleet from taking sides in the internal political and military conflicts of any non-Federation world, even a post-contact one. Besides, Kirk questioned whether a world united by force under a single conquering power would really meet the Federation's definition of a unified global polity.

The Directive could be suspended when the safety of a starship was jeopardized or when vital to larger Federation interests, but neither of those applied here. There were cases where it could be justified for Starfleet personnel to reveal themselves to a small number of people if the knowledge was unlikely to become public. Eight years ago, on his first planetary survey mission among the Iron Age tribes of Neural, Kirk had found it necessary to confide the truth to the tribesman Tyree, who had sworn to keep his secret. But here, admitting the truth to Ribaul would only guarantee that he would reveal it to the rest of Nacmor.

The problem was, *not* admitting the truth would lead to the same outcome. Within a day, the captives were harried out of their cell, informed that they were to be escorted to the site of a press conference where the four of them would be revealed to the world—the story being that they were surviving crew members of a rocketship Ribaul's government had shot down after its heinous attack on the Vekudi district of Derostur City. The group was allowed to keep the communicator so as to understand the guards' instructions, but Kirk expected it to be confiscated before the conference, so that the offworlders would be unable to refute Ribaul's account.

As they were led into the bunker's garage and toward a waiting convoy of motorized ground vehicles, Kirk whispered to Ensign Diaz under the cover of the engine noise, "Is there any chance you could remove the translator and speaker components from the communicator, rig them to work independently? They should be small enough to hide in our clothes."

Diaz thought it over. "Maybe if I had half an hour with the right tools. Under the circumstances, that seems unlikely."

Kirk feared it would be a moot point anyway. Being moved outside the secure bunker could be the best opportunity they would get to escape, but it would also increase the risk that they would be seen by the Nacmorian public. Perhaps that was why they were driven out of the bunker in a transport vehicle with large windows in the rear compartment, allowing Kirk to see that they were being driven through populated areas of Derostur, with curious passersby gathered along the walkways to watch the convoy go by. Sightings of escaped aliens among the populace would serve Ribaul's plans almost as well as the press conference—in some ways, perhaps even better. Kirk leaned back from the window and gestured to the others to do the same. The guards sitting by the rear doors of the compartment smirked at their reticence, aware that they would not be allowed to remain hidden much longer.

Soon, though, after the convoy had turned onto a narrower, less busy street, Kirk heard the galloping and groaning of one of the camel-ostrich draft animals. The vehicle lurched to a halt, almost knocking the humans over. A series of bangs sounded close by, and clouds of dense gas or smoke billowed outside the windows. The yells of the soldiers outside quickly gave way to choking and gasping.

Kirk and the others traded a look, recognizing that the confusion of this apparent attack would be their best chance to slip away unseen. As one, Kirk and Lieutenant Hauraki lunged at the distracted guards, clasping their manacled hands to use as clubs aimed at the Nacmorians' carotid arteries. But their balance was imperfect, so neither succeeded in taking out his guard with one blow. Kirk grappled with his guard as the man tried to bring up his weapon. He managed to swing the guard around, allowing Mitchell to strike him between the shoulder blades, dazing the guard enough for Kirk to pull his gun away and whack him in the jaw with it. The guard slumped, and Kirk glanced over his shoulder to see that Hauraki had taken care of his guard single-handedly. Kirk tried not to be envious; this was the man's job, after all.

Diaz knelt over the first guard and felt in his pockets for the keys. "Next time, leave one for me, okay?" she quipped, even though the guards were half again her size.

"Careful what you wish for," Kirk told her. "We still don't know who's out there."

As if in answer, the rear lock was blown off and the doors flung open. The humans braced themselves. A tall, lean Nacmorian woman with short, shaggy bronze hair leaped into the back of the truck, armed with a truncheon and ready for battle. She was dressed in the local equivalent of a tank top and fatigues and wearing goggles and a bandana to protect her from the gas. But on seeing that the prisoners had taken out their guards, she immediately relaxed.

"It's all right," she told them, pulling down the bandana and lifting the goggles to reveal a youthful, strikingly lovely green-gold face. "We're here to liberate you." Gasping at the sight of Kirk, she reached out and gingerly touched his flat, pink fore-head, stroked his hair. "Oh, you poor people. What have these monsters done to you?"

"Daramoy, come on!" a male voice called from outside.

The young woman shook herself. "We can discuss it later. Now, if you desire your freedom, please come with us!"

Ten

Remember, kids! The state depends on all of you—not just your daddies and mommies, but also you young people— to do your part to fight off the invaders from space. Every meal you go without—kills a spaceman. Every dukor your parents take out of your allowance—kills a spaceman. Every piece of gold or scrap metal your parents turn in to the state—kills a spaceman. And Ultimate Premier Ribaul thanks you all for your sacrifice and your courage as we stand together against the enemy from the stars.

—Nacmorian propaganda broadcast

Derostur City

"Astonishing." The rebel leader, Daramoy, peered closely at the eyes and foreheads of Kirk and Mitchell as they sat in a dimly lit cellar in Derostur's run-down industrial district. Her lieutenant, a cowled male named Seljuron, subjected Diaz and Hauraki to similar scrutiny. "This is truly horrific," Daramoy went on.

"Hey, we don't look that bad!" Mitchell protested.

The young woman instantly grew sympathetic. "Oh, I'm sorry. I don't mean to be insensitive. It's not your fault that this was done to you." She shook her head. "I knew Ribaul would stop at nothing to sell his fantasy of an invasion from outer space—murder civilians, burn and bomb our own cities—but subjecting innocent people to surgical mutilation? It's obscene!"

"Remarkably sophisticated work, though," Seljuron observed. "I can't even see the scars. And the eyes are extraordinary—the circular pupils even contract in response to light. I had no idea Ribaul's surgeons were capable of this. I shudder to think what else they might do with these techniques." He peered closer at Diaz. "Odd that they altered you so much less than the others, miss. If they removed the men's frontal glands, they might also have attempted to amputate your—"

"Yes, I get the picture," Diaz interrupted. "Maybe . . . they thought we would look more alien if both sexes had similar facial traits, but were otherwise distinct."

"Hmm, yes, quite possible."

"We don't really know what their thinking was," Kirk said, throwing Diaz a cautioning look, "so it's probably best that we don't speculate." The young science officer nodded, getting the point. It might be expedient to let these Nacmorians invent their own explanation for the humans' appearance, but attempting to elaborate on it too much could inadvertently make things worse. Kirk reflected on the time that Jonathan Archer and Malcolm Reed of the original Earth starship *Enterprise* had dealt with a similar situation by claiming they were genetically augmented supersoldiers created by the captors' enemy nation, a claim that had backfired by exacerbating the planet's military tensions. Historians still debated the degree to which Archer and Reed had triggered or escalated that world's subsequent wars. Kirk had no desire to go down in history the same way.

All things considered, it was best to invent as little as possible and discourage the rebels from asking too many questions. "It was . . . a traumatic experience," he went on to Daramoy. "We'd really just prefer to move past it."

Daramoy placed a kindly hand on Kirk's arm, the other on Mitchell's. "I understand. But when you feel ready, we'll do everything we can to get you treatment, to undo what was done to you."

"We appreciate that," Kirk said.

"Yeah," Mitchell added, putting his hand atop hers and smiling. "Your kind companionship is a great comfort in my time of need, Daramoy."

The Nacmorian gingerly extricated her hand from his and stepped back. "Yes, well. Unfortunately, there is more at stake here than only the four of you." She paced before them, her tone growing cooler, more commanding. "The fact is, you could be of enormous help to the resistance. I regret the need to ask, but you know what's at stake. As long as the people believe Ribaul's atrocities are the work of enemies from space, they will continue to submit to his ever-tightening grip on our freedoms, on our very lives. They must be made aware that *he* is the true enemy."

The turn this conversation had taken made Kirk uneasy. "We'd really prefer not to get involved, if you don't mind."

"But you are the only ones who can give us what we need!" she insisted, moving closer. "You have been inside the government bunker. You can give us valuable intelligence about its layout and procedures. We have partial information thanks to our inside source—the one who tipped us off to your existence and enabled us to free you," she added pointedly. "We know the layout of their research floor, where we can find the proof we need to expose the hoax. But our source knows little about the security floors, the guard postings—the obstacles we'd need to surmount to reach the research level and get out alive. Your knowledge of the bunker interior could help us complete our picture."

Daramoy moved closer to Kirk, holding his gaze urgently. "Please, Kirk. Please, all of you. I know you come from a distant land. Our people have done horrible things to you, and you have no reason to trust us. But my people are immigrants here too. We were welcome here for generations, but then Ribaul came to power on his rhetoric of hate and fear, of conquest of outsiders and overwhelming force as the only way to ensure security and order. Now it is those like us, the outsiders, who are disproportionately targeted. He uses the false space war to murder our activists, to destroy our businesses, to leave us impoverished and helpless, yet win our allegiance by convincing us we share a common enemy that only he can protect us against."

She clutched his arm. "We truly do share a common enemy, Kirk, and you know it is Ribaul. That is why I plead with you to help us, for the good of all Nacmorians. We must expose the government's conspiracy and tell the people the truth: that aliens are *not* among us!"

Daramoy's plea gave Kirk pause, though not for the reasons she hoped. "If I could have a moment to speak with my people," Kirk said.

"Of course. Take all the time you need."

Kirk led the others into a side room, turning off the communicator's translation function for good measure. "You hear that?" Mitchell asked. "They want us to break them into the research floors. That's got to be where our phasers and gear are."

"I know," Kirk told him. "That's the only reason I'm even considering this."

"What's to consider? We can't leave that stuff there. How long before they find the right setting on a hand phaser and blow out a wall?"

"I agree, sir," Hauraki said. "It could be our only chance to retrieve our equipment."

"But we're being asked to help one faction in an internal dispute gain an advantage over another," Kirk told them. "If Daramoy gets her proof, it could bring down Ribaul's government, and we'd be partially responsible for that."

"Sounds good to me," Mitchell said. "Ribaul is a mass murderer. He needs to go down." Hauraki nodded.

"It's not up to us to decide that for them! They have to achieve their own change from within, or it'll never last."

"And they will, Jim. The rebels will lead the attack. They'll publicize what they learn. We're secondary to that."

"You heard Daramoy. They can't get in without our help."

Diaz spoke up tentatively. "On the other hand, sir . . . The information they're requesting is nothing alien to Nacmor. It's just specifics about the interior of a building. Without us, they might still get that information some other way, at a later time. All we'd be doing is moving the timetable up a bit so that we can get our equipment out."

Kirk nodded at her. "Thank you, Ensign. Your opinion is noted."

He moved to a corner of the room, contemplating. After a few moments, Mitchell came up beside him. "I know you like to consider all the angles, Jim, but is this really that hard a decision? It's just bending the Prime Directive a little to prevent breaking it outright."

The captain glared at him. "You can never 'just' bend the Prime Directive. Compromise it a little and it makes it easier to compromise it more the next time."

"Sometimes you still have to."

"But is this one of those times?"

"What's the alternative? Even if we could beam into the bunker, we wouldn't know where to go, and we'd probably get shot before we found our gear. Daramoy's people are our only real chance of getting in there. And to get their help, we have to give our own."

Kirk cradled the communicator in his hand. "If only we were in range to consult Starfleet Command."

Mitchell put a hand on his shoulder. "The reason Starfleet Command put you in the big chair is because they trust you to figure these things out for yourself. So don't worry so much about rules and regulations. Just trust your instincts. Be the captain I know you can be."

Kirk held Mitchell's eyes for a long moment . . . then made his choice. He flipped open the communicator. "Kirk to *Sacagawea*."

"Adebayo here, Captain! We've been waiting for you. We read you apart from the Nacmorians now. Do you want us to beam you up?"

"No, Commander," Kirk said. "We've been liberated by a resistance group, but we still need to retrieve our equipment from the government bunker, and the rebels are our means to do so. What I need is for you to scan the bunker as thoroughly as possible. Give me detailed information on its internal layout, guard movements, anything you can find."

"Aye, sir. We'll get right on it and contact you again."

"Very good. Kirk out."

Mitchell stared at him, shaking his head. "Wow. When you decide to bend, you really bend. So much for not giving them anything they couldn't find themselves."

"Technically, we're still only giving them information indigenous to Nacmor, as Diaz said. They don't need to know how we got it." He turned to take in all three of the others. "But if we're going to do this, I want to give us the best possible chance for success. We must not allow ourselves to be captured again.

"Ribaul will just have to invent his own aliens from now on."

———

As the landing party worked with the rebels to plan the assault on the bunker, Kirk could not help but be struck by Daramoy's natural leadership, her intelligence, her passion for her work, and her empathy for the Nacmorians in whose name she fought. Her physical beauty, as impressive as it was, felt incidental in comparison. And he could tell the attraction was reciprocated, despite how strange he must appear to Nacmorian eyes. As they planned together, the two leaders meshed easily, their thoughts slipping smoothly into sync, their strategies resonating with and improving each other.

She sat across from Kirk when they ate, examining his features without the pity or revulsion he saw in the other Nacmorians' eyes. "It's not an unattractive appearance, if you consider it the right way," she told him, as if attempting to cheer him up about his "mutilation" at Ribaul's hands. "It's somewhat . . . well, feminine, but that's not a bad thing, is it?"

Kirk granted her a smile. "I've never believed so, no."

Still, he resisted the urge to return her flirtation. He was a Starfleet captain on a sensitive mission; she was a rebel leader fighting to free a world. Both of them had obligations to their people first and foremost—and the Prime Directive formed an impenetrable shield between them. Gary mocked him for his seriousness and self-discipline, but they were needed in a situation like this. So he forced himself to maintain an objective detachment toward Daramoy.

The rebels' plan to penetrate the bunker relied, in a way, on the government's contempt for the cultural heritage of its subjects. In building the bunker, the regime had thoughtlessly dug into and demolished an archaeological ruin, a series of underground aqueducts and sewers serving the ancient city that had preceded Derostur. Kirk was grateful that Sherev was not here; such callous destruction of a historical site would have enraged her. But through their lack of interest in their planet's history, the builders of the bunker had failed to learn of another, lower level of tunnels passing directly underneath the facility. Daramoy's resistance had already managed to dig up to the cement floor of one of the bunker's steam tunnels; breaching it would get them into the facility undetected. The problem was getting through the intervening levels to the research floors without being captured or killed, and that was where the landing party's knowledge of the bunker layout (augmented by the *Sacagawea*'s sensor scans) would prove critical.

Daramoy's four-person team and the four members of the landing party entered the base wearing replica guard uniforms. It was an overly large group for an infiltration, but Kirk had convinced Daramoy that they would need to split up, with his foursome retrieving valuable property that Ribaul's people had taken from them while her group gathered the proof of the government's staged attacks. The humans wore Nacmorian-green makeup once again, with the men cowled to hide their hair; it wouldn't convince anyone up close, but Daramoy and Seljuron hoped that it would let them pass from a distance, or at least keep the base personnel off their guard long enough for the interlopers to overpower them if necessary. The Starfleet team's information let them choose the route likely to bring them into contact with the fewest guards as they made their way up to the research level.

Indeed, as they emerged from the maintenance tunnels on the detention level and made their way to the fire stairs, they were spotted by a soldier passing through a nearby intersection, but the man merely spared them a cursory glance and nod before going on his way, preoccupied with the clipboard he carried. Kirk and Daramoy watched the intersection warily while Seljuron worked to disable the door alarm, but the rebel scientist avoided making noises that would draw the receding soldier's attention. They made it into the stairwell without incident.

Unfortunately, the fire stairs did not go all the way up to the research level; rather, for security reasons, both the lower and upper levels' stairwells connected separately to the main administrative level, which contained the only exits from the bunker (until now). The team would have to make their way through a portion of the main level to reach the upper stairwells. As they crept through the corridors, pausing at intersections to peer around corners, Kirk felt a moment's gratitude that the Nacmorians had not yet invented surveillance cameras.

Finally their luck ran out, and the infiltrators were spotted by a pair of soldiers who rounded the corner ahead of them. "You there," the taller of the two cowled men said, striding toward them. "I don't recognize you. Show me your identification."

Hanging behind the Nacmorians, Kirk saw Daramoy and one

of her fighters reach for their knives. Trading a look with Hauraki, Kirk lunged forward at the soldiers, the security chief right behind him. A few quick, efficient, Starfleet-trained blows later, both men had knocked out the soldiers, whom they began dragging toward a maintenance closet Kirk had spotted near the corner.

"What was that?" Daramoy asked Kirk as they dragged the soldiers into the closet and began to bind them.

"I'd rather not have anyone die because of us, if it can be avoided," Kirk said.

"Admirable, but we don't always have that luxury. They may not kill the four of you if they retake you, since you're still of value to them. The rest of us may not be so lucky."

Kirk kept his eyes on the soldiers' wrists as he secured their bonds. "I'm sorry," he told her. "But we have our own rules to follow."

Once they finished binding and gagging the guards, they made it through the rest of the level without discovery. Once they made it up the stairs to the research level, Daramoy paused at the exit. "Given your principles, Kirk, are you sure you want your group and mine to split up completely? You might be safer if one of us goes with you."

"No." Kirk shook his head. "Your priority needs to be your own mission. What happens to us isn't as important. As long as we retrieve our possessions, that's all that matters to us. You should carry out the rest of your mission as if we were never a part of it. And that means that if you can't find us when you're done, just get out—don't stop to look for us. We'll make our own way home."

Daramoy grimaced. "You're a strange man, Kirk, but there's an honor to you. Whatever happens, I'll count you in my remembrances." After another moment of uncertainty, she kissed him, briefly but intensely, then moved to the door.

"Damn, Jim," Gary Mitchell whispered, shaking his head in envy. Kirk ignored him.

The two teams split up in the corridor, and Kirk strove to put Daramoy out of his mind as he led his own party toward the lab where Sherev's scans showed that their communicators—and hopefully their phasers and tricorders as well—were being stored. At the final intersection, he and Hauraki peered around the corner to see two male guards posted outside the lab. Falling back, Kirk turned to Diaz. "Ensign, you're the one most likely to pass for Nacmorian from this distance. Think you can create a distraction?"

The science officer quirked a small smile. "Certainly, sir. I've found that men are usually absurdly easy to distract." She moved out into the corridor, and Kirk frowned after her, unsure whether he'd just been teased. If so, he realized, he might well have deserved it.

"Excuse me!" Diaz called to the guards. "Could you help me out? The differential analyzer in my lab blew a vacuum tube, and I dropped the replacement tube behind it. I need help moving it away from the wall. Would you mind?"

A pause, then footsteps. "Sorry, what lab was that? What department are you with?"

"It's right around here—it'll just take a moment. Please, I'd be so grateful." She stepped back around the corner, retreating out of the guard's sight. Hauraki was ready when the guard rounded the corner, and the cowled man was quickly rendered unconscious.

The scuffle made enough noise to draw the other guard's attention; Kirk heard him cry out in concern. Nodding to Mitchell to follow him, Kirk leaped out into the other corridor and saw the guard running toward them. At the sight of them, the man's eyes widened in shock; he reversed course and ran for an alarm trigger on the wall. Kirk and Mitchell tackled him and knocked him out before he could raise an alert.

Soon the other two humans joined them outside the main lab. "Differential analyzer?" Mitchell asked Diaz. "Vacuum tube? Where'd you get all that?"

Diaz grinned at him. "You should've paid more attention to the radio shows, sir. Very educational."

Kirk led the party into the lab, where two Nacmorian scientists, a male and a female, were working. The woman, her hair tied back in a bun, was adjusting the intensity dial atop one of the landing party's small, concealable phaser 1 units. Its emitter nozzle was aimed at a cage in which her male colleague was securing a bronze-furred laboratory animal resembling a cross between a hamster and a monkey. "What do you think setting four will do to it?" the man asked.

"Well," the woman replied, "we've gone from nonlethal neural disruption to lethal neural disruption. I suppose this one will . . . kill it more?"

The man laughed. "Maybe it kills it and its whole family."

He moved out of the way—and Kirk saw that a rack of pressurized gas canisters rested against the far wall beyond him and the animal, right in the path of the disintegration-level beam they were about to fire.

"I wouldn't do that if I were you," Kirk announced.

The scientists looked up, then jerked back in shock. "The aliens!" the man gasped.

"If . . . if you were . . . me?" the woman asked, paralyzed with fear. "What—what does that mean? Do you have some power to . . . enter my mind?"

It wasn't the reaction Kirk had expected, but he could work with it. "If you don't want to find out, then kindly step away from our property. We're here to take it back." He stepped forward and picked up the compact phaser. "For your information, I probably just saved both your lives. You're tampering with something too dangerous for you to handle. For your own safety, I recommend you return all our equipment to us at once." He extended the phaser forward. "Unless you want a firsthand demonstration of what the next setting can really do." It was a bluff; he'd already returned it to the stun setting.

Both scientists were quick to cooperate in returning their other phasers, then showing them to the adjoining lab where their communicators and tricorders were being studied. Luckily, the study of those devices was deemed a lower priority than weapons research, so the team working in the second lab had already gone home for the night.

While the team recovered their equipment, the female scientist's curiosity finally outweighed her fear. "P-please . . . if I could just ask you a few questions about these devices' composition, their power sources. The radios seem to work on wavelengths we can't even detect. Please—you could help us so much."

"Look at the man giving you your orders," Kirk told her. "If he had the knowledge you seek . . . do you really think it would help anyone?"

The scientist sighed and lowered her head. "No. No, it wouldn't."

"But if your devices can do what you imply," the male scientist added, "then you could end that problem for us."

"No," Kirk told him. "That kind of thinking *is* the problem." He set the phaser to heavy stun. "Frankly, you might not even remember this conversation. I'm sorry." He fired at the scientist, then at his colleague. Both of them slumped to the floor.

"Scan for records," Kirk told Diaz. "Find any photographs, recordings, notes, anything about us, and destroy them. We have to leave no proof that we were ever here."

While the others carried out this task, Kirk contacted the *Sacagawea* and advised them to lock on and stand by for beam-out. Soon, the party had gathered all the evidence they could carry with them and phasered the rest into ash—including, disturbingly, the autopsied corpses of two lab animals.

But before Kirk could give the beam-out order, an alarm sounded. Hauraki and Mitchell ran to the door and cracked it open. The sounds of yelling, pounding feet, and gunfire echoed from a far hallway, and Kirk heard cries from the guards:

"It's the rebels!" "Halt or we'll fire!" "Stop them, they can't get away!"

"Daramoy," Mitchell breathed. "Jim, we can't just leave them. They could be killed!"

Kirk felt the same way Mitchell did. His impulse was to rush to Daramoy's rescue, to use his superior weaponry to keep her safe and help her free her world. But his sense of duty clamped down on his emotions. He had sworn an oath to uphold the Prime Directive, no matter the temptation. Daramoy's fate was her own, and he had no right to become involved with it. He reminded himself that tough calls like this were the very reason a captain needed to maintain emotional detachment.

"You know the rules, mister," he told Gary. "We have no choice." He opened his communicator. "Kirk to *Sacagawea*. Beam us up now."

Mitchell stared furiously at his captain. "Screw the rules," he said. Just as the shimmering chime of the transporter beam began to sound, the navigator tossed his communicator aside and ran out after the rebels—carrying his phaser. Kirk tried to call to him, but he was already locked in the beam, his vision dissolving into sparkles. Mitchell was on his own.

U.S.S. Sacagawea

Mitchell's communicator had been beamed up with the other three, so it took several hours for Diaz to track the navigator down by the energy signature of his phaser's power cell. Kirk had Hauraki lead a security team to bring him back. By that time, though, Daramoy's resistance network had already hijacked the radio waves and announced the truth that Ribaul's forces had attacked their own people and blamed it on alien invaders, and that documents and films obtained from the government bunker would prove it beyond a doubt. Voices of protest were emboldened, and some even dared to say on the air

that if the allegations proved true, it should lead to Ribaul's resignation. In hours, Daramoy had gone from enemy of the state
to planetary hero.

And Kirk had to face Gary Mitchell and tell him he had been
wrong to help her do it.

"I assume the rebels owe their escape to your skills with a
phaser," Kirk said to Mitchell across the table in an otherwise
empty briefing room.

His friend fidgeted under his gaze. "No more than I could
help," Mitchell said. "I stunned a few guards when nobody was
looking. Melted a lock behind us to stop the soldiers from coming after us. I let them save themselves as much as possible. Hell,
even if Daramoy realized what I was doing, she was too devoted
to her 'aliens are a hoax' belief to put it together.

"Still," he finished defiantly, "they wouldn't have gotten out of
there alive without my help."

"That's exactly the problem, Gary! They *need* to be able to do
things on their own. That's why the Prime Directive exists, to
stop us from solving other people's problems and making them
dependent on us."

"I know the theory, Jim! But it wasn't a theory down there.
It was the lives of people we knew. People who helped us. They
saved us, Jim. We'd probably be getting dissected in a lab now if
not for Daramoy and the others. Deciding not to help them in
return—regs or not, that's a shitty move, Jim. And you're better
than that."

Kirk was silent for a long moment, thinking. Finally, he
sighed. "I know. She trusted me, and I abandoned her. I can't
help wondering if that's who I really want to be. Is that what
being a captain means, having to make choices like that?"

Mitchell leaned forward. "No, Jim. Because that choice was
what the book told you to do. Being captain means it's *your*
call, not the damn book's. You're the man on the scene, so for
God's sake, stop second-guessing yourself! Just make your

own choices and deal with what comes. That's what I did down there."

Another long pause. "And I'm grateful for it," Kirk said at last. "If you hadn't defied my orders, Daramoy and the others would've been captured, tortured, probably executed. I would've had to live with that on my conscience." He held Mitchell's eyes long enough to be sure his gratitude registered—then sharpened his tone. "But that has to be my decision, Gary. Not yours. You said it yourself—it's the captain's call. And *only* the captain's. Remember that in the future, or you'll be in for worse than a reprimand."

"Understood, Captain," Mitchell said, lowering his eyes contritely. Yet he seemed to say "Captain" with new appreciation.

"Now, let's get back to the bridge," Kirk said, rising from the table. "I understand Daramoy's expected to give an address within the hour."

Gary followed suit. "Finally, something worth listening to on the radio." He sighed as they headed out the door. "What really kills me is, I did all that for Daramoy, and I *still* didn't get a kiss."

Kirk rolled his eyes. He doubted his friend would ever change.

Eleven

*Among the Agni's other advantages, their singularity technol-
ogy gave them superior long-range sensor capability through
the use of subspace gravity lensing. This enabled them to
scan star systems throughout Federation space and identify
the worlds that best suited their objectives. With no inkling
of the Agni's real nature and priorities, Starfleet could never
have anticipated where they would make their next move.*

—Dr. Monali Bhasin
Ministers of Sacrifice, 2289

U.S.S. *Kongo* NCC-1710
Mehran Egdor sat uneasily in the *Kongo*'s command chair.
Being in this seat was what he had aspired to for many years, but
not like this.

He had held the conn frequently over the past sixteen
months, of course, when Captain Chandra had been off shift or
away from the ship. In his tenure as the *Kongo*'s first officer, the
Rigelian had never felt that his human crewmates considered
him unwelcome or unworthy to command the bridge. Their casual acceptance had given Egdor hope that there truly was room
for nonhumans to increase their presence in Starfleet command
positions. Even the most well-intentioned of people could fall
prey to unconscious biases, but they were also the ones who
could most easily overcome them.

But then the call had come from Starfleet Command, ordering them to the Bardeezi system. The Bardeezans were an
independent species within Federation-controlled space, trading the rich mineral wealth of their star system to Federation
worlds in exchange for protectorate status. Recently, they had
detected an incursion on the fringes of their planetary space by
a large cylindrical starship identical to the "demon" ships that
had crippled the *Sacagawea* and killed dozens of Egdor's crewmates in their attempted invasion of Adelphous. Fearing that
the vessel was a scout for a second invasion attempt—and concerned that it had somehow slipped past the Federation border
undetected—Starfleet Command had sent the *Kongo* to assist
the Bardeezans in defending the multiple populated worlds and
mining stations throughout their planetary system—not only
because of the *Constitution*-class vessel's proximity, but because
of Mehran Egdor's firsthand experience with these invaders.
Egdor had relished the opportunity to bring his knowledge to
bear in countering them once again.

So it had been a shock when Captain Chandra had insisted
on beaming down personally to Bardeezi Prime to coordinate
with the system's prime and defense ministers, while sending
Egdor and the *Kongo* off on a mere errand to confirm the readiness of the system's extraplanetary defense stations. Chandra's
decision to leave Egdor out of the discussion was a bewildering
affront. He had followed his commanding officer's orders, of
course, but the implication that there were limits to the older
human's faith in his Rigelian first officer had been gnawing at
Egdor ever since.

But then science officer Aaltonen detected five cylinder ships
emerging from warp within the system's main cometary belt,
and everything changed. *"I'll remain here to coordinate with the
Bardeezans,"* said Captain Chandra from the main viewscreen
once Egdor touched base with him. Behind the gray-haired,
tan-skinned human captain, several rotund, large-eyed bipeds

with slate-gray hides and hornlike protrusions on their heads moved through the defense control center as frenetically as their bulky bodies permitted, an activity no doubt paralleled by the full mobilization of their defense forces in space. *"It would take you too long to retrieve me anyway. Instead, proceed to the outer system to engage the hostiles. The Bardeezan Defense Fleet will support you, but they will defer to your command."*

"Me, sir?" Egdor asked, taken by surprise.

"Of course, Mehran. Why do you think I left you on the ship? In case an attack came while I was down here handling the bureaucracy, I wanted you up there where you could do the most good."

The affirmation of Chandra's faith in him was a weight off Egdor's mind, and he led the *Kongo*'s crew into action with renewed confidence. He believed that confidence was warranted, for he and others in Starfleet had spent the past seventeen months studying the first conflict with the cylinder ships and devising defense strategies. Egdor worked with Chansuo Huang, the *Kongo*'s helmsman and security chief, to reconfigure the vessel's main deflector dish to defend against the intruders' deadly armor-plate projectiles, while Huang and Aaltonen coordinated sensor and phaser protocols to allow the hex plates to be targeted as soon as their acceleration was detected. En route to the intercept coordinates, Egdor instructed the Bardeezan defense ship commanders to set up similar protocols as best they could. The Bardeezan ships were smaller and much less powerful than a *Constitution*-class heavy cruiser, but they were specialized for in-system defense at sublight, and they had potent tractor beams for deflecting the small asteroids and comets that occasionally threatened the Bardeezans' mining stations.

Defense against the intruders' singularity-powered beam weapons was another matter. "If we cannot persuade them to stand down and talk to us," Egdor told his crew and the listening Bardeezan commanders, "our main strategy will be to attempt to target our shots between their shield plates and disable their vessels. Our previous encounter, along with our intelligence from their encounter with the Klingons, showed that they retreat upon sustaining too much damage. Their use of their shield plates as projectiles is a potential weakness; if we can destroy enough of their plates, or eject them far enough from the battle that the intruders can no longer control them, then we can erode their protection and leave them vulnerable. But don't risk taking avoidable hits in order to chip away at a few plates; it's not worth the severe damage we'd sustain to inflict relatively minor damage on their defensive ability."

"It's a strange sort of defense system, don't you think?" Henrikka Aaltonen asked once Egdor had concluded his address. "Sacrificing pieces of your own shields to use them as weapons."

"No stranger than reducing available shield energy to power phasers," Huang countered. "Or having to stand up from cover in order to aim your hand phaser. It's a common trade-off in battle—you have to risk something of your own to get the other guy." He shrugged. "Seems fairer that way."

"Your attitude reminds me of another helm officer I once knew," Egdor said. "She was philosophical about her own injuries from battle, and held no grudges against her foes."

Huang nodded approvingly. "She sounds like a clear-headed sort."

"She was. She was also killed by the very foes we now face. So I don't want you to concern yourself with playing fair, Lieutenant. I want you to play to win."

"Yes, Commander," Huang replied, humbled.

Once the *Kongo* had rendezvoused with three of the Bardeezans' largest defense ships—no larger in volume or crew complement than the *Sacagawea*, though more compact and ovoid in shape—they proceeded to intercept the incoming cylinder ships. Egdor hailed the intruders as required and made the standard offer to engage in peaceful dialogue, along with the standard warning that they would be met with force if they failed to stand down. The aliens were predictably unresponsive, merely continuing to barrel forward. "Are we sure they're even detecting our hails?" Egdor asked Ensign Goldanskii at communications.

"I am reading some subspace signal activity among the hostile ships, sir," the ensign replied. "It seems to be data exchange rather than audio, though, so there's nothing I can interpret."

"Maybe they can't interpret *our* language," Aaltonen suggested.

"They should be able to interpret someone standing in their path and firing warning shots," Egdor said. "Their response last time was to attempt to go around us, then to fire on us when we wouldn't let them. I'd say that was a fairly clear mutual communication."

"More than that," Huang said. "They've not only ignored our borders twice now—they've apparently devised some way to evade detection by border sensors and patrols. They're actively working to circumvent our defenses."

"Still, they don't strike first," Aaltonen pointed out. "They try evasion first, and only fight when that doesn't work."

"Either way, the message is the same," Egdor told her. "They want something of ours—territory, resources, whatever—and they intend to take it, with utter disregard for our opinion in the matter. We are merely obstacles to them."

"They're deploying their armor plates," Huang announced. Mikhail Goldanskii magnified the viewscreen image to show the scale armor of yellow-brown hexagonal plates expanding outward from the ships' hulls and beginning to rotate.

"Phaser and deflector dish teams to high alert," Egdor ordered. "Stand by for point defense."

"Point defense teams report ready, sir," Huang answered a moment later.

"Arm photon torpedoes and stand by."

"Torpedoes armed, sir."

"Aaltonen, try to get an internal scan. They don't have conventional deflectors, but we couldn't get a good enough sensor lock to send a boarding party over. Maybe a year and a half worth of sensor upgrades will make a difference."

The science officer worked her controls. "No luck, sir. Their hulls are just too dense and refractory. They may not have deflectors, but they have something almost as good."

"But a lot more massive," Huang pointed out. "It could slow them down in a fight." An alert sounded from his panel. "Incoming plate! Deploying deflector!"

The vessel shook under the first impact, a sharp, sudden shock that Egdor remembered, different from an energy weapon impact or even a torpedo hit. "Shields?" he asked.

"Holding," Huang replied. "The retuning was effective. Clean miss on deflection."

"Get better, fast."

"Aye, sir."

To Huang's credit and that of his teams below, they managed to carry out Egdor's admittedly vague order. The next few plates lobbed at the *Kongo* were either shattered by her phasers or batted away by her deflector beam. The Bardeezans had less success at deflection, sustaining several damaging hits, but they had the limited advantage of being smaller targets.

With the *Kongo*'s defenses holding, Egdor focused on eroding the intruders' defenses, using torpedoes to chip away at the lead ship's whirling bubble of armor plates and attempt to create a large enough opening to slip a torpedo through. He and Huang had discussed this strategy before the battle. The late Captain Baek had suggested that the support frames for the quantum singularities within the cylinder ships' hollow cores could be their weak spots, and Starfleet Tactical had agreed; but there was no way to get a phaser lock on them without coming directly into their plasma beams' line of fire, and that was deemed far too dangerous to risk. But if a torpedo were fired from the side, it could use its thrusters to curve in and damage the support framework, hopefully disrupting the ship's power supply.

Soon, Huang smiled up at Egdor, who stood watching over his shoulder. "There's a gap in the shield pattern."

Egdor knew they would only have moments before the plates evened out their distribution. "Fire torpedo!"

Unfortunately, the plates did more than he expected. They reacted almost immediately to the incoming torpedo, shifting to take a direct hit and destroy it before it could penetrate the perimeter. The vessel had to sacrifice two plates for this, but the remaining distribution evened out quickly.

"Still, this may give us an option," Huang said once the Bardeezans reported the same result from their own attempted missile barrage. "To concentrate for point defense on one side, the plates have to thin out on the opposite side. If we bracket a ship from both directions, attack on one side—"

"It might give the opposing ship a clear shot at the singularity framework," Egdor finished for him. "It's worth a try."

Egdor had Goldanskii hail the lead Bardeezan ship on an encrypted channel, and between them they swiftly worked out the strategy. The *Kongo* closed on a cylinder ship obliquely from the front, firing torpedoes to force it to concentrate its shield plates to fore, while still staying clear of the direct line of fire of its plasma beam. Once the plates were sufficiently thinned out to aft, a Bardeezan ship flew past and fired a missile through the gap. "A hit!" Huang announced. "There's damage to its aft support frame. Power fluctuations . . . Sir, its shield plates are scattering! It's changing course . . . Sir, it's in retreat."

"Let it go," Egdor said, returning to the command chair. "Stay focused on the active threats."

The crew's sense of satisfaction at defeating one of the attacking ships was short-lived. Something unexpected happened when one of the remaining four cylinder ships flew into the field of abandoned shield plates from the fleeing one. "It's drawing the plates in around it," Aaltonen reported. She magnified the viewer image, and Egdor watched in fascination as the salvaged plates began spinning in a second shield layer above the ship's own. "That's a handy way to restore a depleted supply."

"But why keep them in a separate layer?" Egdor asked.

"What worries me more," Huang said, "is that that isn't the most badly depleted ship. But it's heading toward the one that is."

He projected a tactical plot on the helm console's astrogator, directing Egdor's attention toward another cylinder ship whose shield plates had been badly eroded by the combined attack of two Bardeezan defense ships. Even as they watched, one of the ships dodged a burst from its plasma beam. Egdor knew from the first battle that the beams took time to recharge, and the Bardeezans clearly remembered it too, bombarding the shield plate envelope more assertively now that they had several minutes without needing to worry about the beam weapon.

"Maybe it just picked up the plates because it was closer," Aaltonen suggested, "and plans to transfer them."

Two more cylinder ships were closing on the *Kongo* now, preventing it from going to the Bardeezans' aid. Egdor and Huang focused on maintaining their phaser and deflector beams' point defense and evading the enemy's attempts to bring their prows to bear.

But soon Aaltonen called their attention back to the other segment of the battle. The bridge crew watched in shock as the ship with the double layer of shield plates suddenly expelled the outer layer—whose plates shot through space and wrapped around the lead Bardeezan ship like a net fired from a riot-control gun. The egg-shaped defense ship's shield envelope flickered and flared as the heavy hexagonal plates clamped tightly against it.

"*The plates' tractor field is drawing them toward each other!*" the Bardeezan captain reported on an open channel. "*They're compressing our shield envelope. Pressure's increasing . . . circuits overloading . . . We need help! Target the plates, destroy them before—"*

But it was already too late. The defense ship's shields gave one last flare before giving way, and the hex plates snapped together almost instantly, crushing the ship between them. An instant later, it blew apart, sending the plates flying.

"*Bozhe moi*," Goldanskii murmured.

Egdor clung to his discipline, following James Kirk's example. "Stay focused on our own attackers."

His warning was timely, for one of the two cylinder ships had taken advantage of the distraction to bring its bow to bear on the *Kongo*. The viewscreen automatically switched to focus on this urgent threat, showing a ringlike shape whose center was already starting to flare with light. "Evasive action!" he called, and Huang started to swing the ship away.

The ship rocked, and Egdor clung to the chair arms, fearing the worst. But then the *Kongo* stabilized. "Glancing blow to our shields," Aaltonen reported. "But it knocked them down to forty-three percent."

Another, sharper impact came, one Egdor knew all too well. "More plates."

"With our weakened shields . . ."

Egdor nodded. They would have to rely on the main deflector dish. "Keep our bow to the attacker," he ordered Huang, but the helmsman was already doing so.

The deflector beam flung away the next few plate attacks, but Aaltonen stepped forward. "Sir, the second ship still hasn't fired its beam weapon. If we're stuck keeping our bow to the first one—"

"I know. They're making it harder for us to dodge the beam. Do whatever you can to reinforce our shields."

"It won't be enough, sir."

He spun the chair and skewered the slender, pale-haired lieutenant with his gaze. "Never let yourself believe that. Never stop striving."

Eyes wide, the science officer bit her lip and nodded. "Aye, Commander. Thank you."

He watched her turn back resolutely to her station, realizing she was little more than a girl. *How do these officers keep getting so much younger?*

But Egdor knew his order had been more for Aaltonen's morale than anything else. The first cylinder ship's aggressive barrage was pinning the *Kongo* down from the front, and the second ship was already swinging around to bring its beam weapon to bear. Unless somebody on this bridge had a brilliant idea within the next twenty seconds, they might not be here in thirty. And Egdor feared his well of ideas had run dry.

Just then, an alert sounded. "Another ship is coming out of warp!" called the navigator, Ensign zh'Nesierel.

"Sir, it's hailing!" Goldanskii cried.

Just then, a barrage of phaser beams and torpedoes struck at the second cylinder ship's halo of shield plates. The ship altered its rotation, attempting to bring its prow to bear on the new attacker, and Egdor felt a great surge of relief.

Goldanskii smiled and opened the channel. A strong, commanding voice came over the speakers. *"This is Captain Christopher Pike of the* U.S.S. Enterprise, *calling the* Kongo. *Sorry we couldn't get here sooner. This attack took Starfleet by surprise."*

"This is Commander Mehran Egdor, commanding the *Kongo* while Captain Chandra is on Bardeezi Prime. Believe me, Captain Pike, your timing was perfect."

"Well, I've been doing this for a while now. Maybe I'm finally getting the hang of it. But you're the one who knows these attackers, so I'll follow your lead. Fill me in, Commander."

"Thank you, Captain," Egdor said, gratified by the man's ready acceptance. "Since you have that ship's attention, concentrate torpedo fire on its prow while we go in to aft and target its power systems. It's worked once before."

"Understood, Kongo."

Once the maneuver was underway, Aaltonen asked, "Are we sure it'll work a second time, sir? They'll know what we're trying."

"I know. Be ready for surprises."

Nonetheless, the pincer strategy went off much as before. While her fellow *Constitution*-class vessel bombarded the cylinder's forward plate halo with torpedoes—while simultaneously using its phasers to fend off plate bombardment from the other cylinder ship—the *Kongo* swept around to its rear and put one of its last torpedoes through the thinnest point in the halo. A plasma beam lashed out to aft—*so they fire both ways*, Egdor noted—but the narrow, intense beam missed the torpedo and the *Kongo* alike, and the aft support frame took a palpable hit. The damaged cylinder ship thrust away to a safe distance, jettisoned its shield plates, and fled into warp.

"Captain Pike, concentrate fire on the other cylinder ship. Don't let it retrieve the discarded armor plates—trust me on this."

"We're taking enough of a beating from the plates this ship is throwing at us already," Pike replied, *"even with the shields retuned. You sure there's no talking to these people?"*

"They've shown no interest in listening. They're determined to get what they want, whatever it takes."

"I know the type."

Egdor turned to Aaltonen. "Status of the other two intruder ships?"

"The Bardeezans are keeping them busy, sir. One made an attempt to maneuver in this direction, but three defense ships are blockading it pretty relentlessly. After what happened to their friends, they're not going to let it get anywhere near those loose plates."

"It may not need to," Pike warned. *"My science officer's been keeping an eye on the discards. Take a look for yourselves."*

Aaltonen double-checked. "They've drawn themselves together into a loose sphere. We thought they needed a mothership to direct them, but . . ."

"*This is Lieutenant Commander Spock of the* Enterprise. *The gathered mass of armor plates is moving toward our target ship. This may be an emergency protocol to bring it in range of a mothership's control.*"

"Break off, *Enterprise!*" Egdor called. "They plan to encircle and compress your shield envelope. This is a critical threat!"

But it was too late. Before the *Enterprise* could move very far, the sphere of armor plates came under the control of the cylinder ship and flew after it at high speed. Moments later, the *Enterprise* was engulfed by the heavy hex plates, its deflector envelope iridescing under the strain.

"*Phasers!*" Pike called. "*Try to pick some off if you can.*"

"Huang," said Egdor, "try to do the same from outside."

But it was to little avail. The ablative plates wore away slowly even under point-blank phasers, and the *Enterprise* couldn't risk setting off torpedoes right against its own hull. "*Shield strain increasing,*" announced Spock's raised and urgent voice. "*At this rate of depletion, we will be destroyed in eighty-seven seconds.*"

"Kongo, *it's up to you,*" Pike called.

Egdor moved up to Huang's side. "Our only chance is to knock out that controlling ship."

"It still has too many shield plates to penetrate," the tactical officer said. "And we can't do the pincer maneuver with one ship."

The first officer firmed his resolve. "Maybe we can. If we use our last torpedoes to blow a hole in the shield aura, we can hit their power framework with full phasers."

Huang stared up at him. "Sir, that would take a sustained burst. We'd have to put ourselves right in their beam's line of fire, and they've had time to recharge!"

"It's a risk we have to take, Lieutenant. We're the *Enterprise's* only chance."

The human set his jaw and spoke quietly, heavily. "Yes, sir."

Egdor returned to the command chair as the viewscreen image swung away from the ailing *Enterprise* and centered on the cylinder ship, circling around until it had foreshortened nearly to a thick O. "Fire when ready," he ordered.

"Torpedoes away," Huang announced. The dancing lights of three torpedoes' thrusters converged on the whirling array of plates that rushed to meet them. When the flash of antimatter annihilation cleared, the *Kongo*'s vantage was now directly in line with the enemy ship's axis, and the fragile-looking framework supporting its singularity drive was in clear view. "Firing phasers," Huang reported, matching the action to the words. The beams struck out, and Huang sustained the fire as the ship flew toward its target.

"Beam weapon powering up!" Aaltonen warned.

"Maintain fire!" Egdor cried.

"*It's working!*" Pike called. "*They've dropped control of the plates to focus on you. We're shaking free of the last of them. Now get out of there!*"

"Helm, hard to—"

The screen filled with blinding light. Egdor had enough time to reflect that, even if he never made it to captain's rank, he had already commanded the most important mission of his life.

U.S.S. *Enterprise*

Christopher Pike stared sadly at the viewscreen, soaking in the cost of his ship's survival. The two remaining intact cylinder ships had fled into warp with the damaged third in tow, having apparently decided to cut their losses. But they had struck a mortal blow before departing. The *Kongo* drifted in space, the dorsal hull of its saucer section bisected by a deep gouge, carved through it by the beam that had also blown off the aft end of its starboard nacelle.

Nothing remained of its bridge.

Spock stepped down beside Pike and handed him a data slate. "Final survivor census from the *Kongo*'s acting commander, sir. Forty-one dead, including the entire bridge crew. One hundred thirty-seven injured from impact shock, decompression trauma, radiation exposure, and other blast effects." He raised a brow. "Captain Chandra is fortunate to have been off the ship when its bridge was destroyed."

"Believe me, Mister Spock," Pike answered, "he won't see it that way."

"An illogical sentiment, even from the standpoint of human emotion. The *Kongo* crew has suffered a significant loss, but the fact that their captain remains to lead them should facilitate their adjustment."

Even after nearly a decade, Spock's often self-conscious adherence to Vulcan detachment in the face of human emotion still bewildered Pike sometimes. The young science officer would make it easier on himself if he at least kept his opinions private. "Try not to be so dismissive of the importance of a first officer," Pike answered sharply. "You may have the position permanently someday." Spock had been filling the post quite efficiently while Pike's regular first officer was on leave, his keen intellect and discipline allowing him to juggle the duties of both executive and science officer without compromising either. Pike expected he would make some captain a superb second-in-command before much longer.

"It was not my intention to dismiss the loss of Commander Egdor or his bridge crew, sir. I simply meant to point out that there are positives to the situation. Do humans not appreciate being 'cheered up' in times of emotional distress?"

"There's a time and a place for that, Spock. You need to work on figuring out when."

"Aye, sir." He hesitated. "I do, however, have additional news that could be construed as positive. Do you wish to hear it?"

Pike sighed. "Report."

"During the battle, two of the intruder vessels sustained enough hull damage to suffer minor atmosphere breaches. I was able to gather some sensor data on their atmospheric composition and shipboard conditions before they retreated. The results were most . . . unusual."

"In what way?"

"The composition of their shipboard atmosphere is over ninety-five percent carbon dioxide, sir, followed by four percent nitrogen, with the remaining fraction of a percent consisting primarily of sulfur dioxide, argon, and vaporized water and sulfuric acid. The internal temperature of the vessels is over six hundred Kelvin, with an atmospheric pressure of nearly ninety bars. The conditions are analogous to those of a Class-N planet."

Pike stared in amazement. "You're telling me those aliens are from a Venus-type environment?"

"Correct, sir. Even if our transporters could have penetrated their hulls, it would have been unfeasible to send boarding parties. We would have needed to fabricate a sufficient number of heavy-duty environment suits, and those would slow the wearers' movements too much to be effective in combat—besides which, even a minor suit breach would be instantly fatal. We do not even know if phasers would be effective on Class-N lifeforms."

The captain shook his head. "No wonder the Klingons called them demons. Do we even *know* of any kind of life that can survive in those conditions?"

"Only hypothetically, sir. However, the concentration of sulfuric acid and trace quantities of covalent carbon-carbon bonds are consistent with theoretical models. Under Class-N conditions somewhat cooler than the surface of Venus, sulfuric acid could remain liquid and serve as a solvent for exotic biochemistry, with carbon-carbon bonds filling the equivalent function of the carbon-oxygen bond in Class-M biology. A sulfuric acid solvent could also theoretically sustain a silicon-based biology, but that is less likely, and I detected no evidence of such compounds." He tilted his head. "However, the composition of the vessels' hulls is consistent with a Class-N origin. Tritanium is one of the few metals resistant to dissolution by sulfuric acid, along with lead and tungsten. The particular tritanium alloys used in the intruders' hulls are high in silicon, chromium, and molybdenum, like known acid-resistant alloys. The crystalline ceramics used in their hulls are also resistant to acid, as are other compounds I have detected in scans of the debris they left behind, such as quartz, alumina, fluoropolymers, and polyvinyl fluoride."

"All right," Pike said. "So we know something about where they come from. Does it tell us what they want?"

"Possibly, sir. Both of the systems they have intruded upon, Adelphous and Bardeezi, do contain N-Class planets with surface temperatures and pressures that permit liquid sulfuric acid to exist. Long-range astrometric scans also register an N-Class planet in the Qalras system in Klingon space, the intruders' first known target." Spock moved back to his station and worked the controls to put up a trajectory chart on the screen above it, while Pike rose to follow. "Also, the most probable destination of the incoming fleet here at Bardeezi was the system's N-Class world. The Bardeezans and Captain Chandra did not recognize this because Bardeezi Prime, Bardeezi IV, and several major asteroid mining stations were also within the cone of its potential destinations, and it did not occur to them that the intruders might not be from a Class-M environment."

Pike paced along the railing before the science station. "All right . . . so they want to reach a Class-N world. Either to mine it for resources . . . or maybe to colonize."

Spock leaned forward in his seat, steepling his fingers before him. "If that is all they wish, Captain, then perhaps there is no need for conflict. There are many N-Class worlds in Federation space, yet we have little or no use for them. If these intruders are seeking territory or resources, it would cost us nothing to provide them."

"Then why didn't they just ask for them?" Pike countered. "They'd have no use for our worlds either, but still they barge in and fight with us, kill our people without so much as a word of acknowledgment. Maybe they don't even see us as people, because we're not their kind of people."

"Bigotry is quite common," Spock agreed. "But it can also be reciprocal. The intruders did not fire until they were threatened."

"But they still fired. They ignored our warnings and forced a fight, instead of stopping to talk or to ask. We gave them a fair chance to talk to us. We didn't judge them ahead of time—we didn't even know how different they were until now!" Pike shook his head. "No—we judged them by their actions, and their actions are ruthless and violent."

"Conceded," Spock said after a moment's thought.

"But now that we know what they want," Pike added, "or at least where they want to go, we can do something about it. We know they're going after systems with N-Class planets. That lets us concentrate our defenses there, be ready when they come."

"Not necessarily," Spock told him. "We still have not determined how this fleet evaded detection at our border, or between it and the Bardeezi system. If they have some form of stealth technology, we may be taken by surprise yet again."

"True," Pike said. "And what worries me is that this attack force was just over half the size of the first one. Maybe that means they suffered more damage than we thought in the first attack, or maybe they engaged someone besides us and the Klingons in the interim. But maybe it means they've split their forces."

He turned to face the viewscreen, on which the Bardeezan ships were locking tractors on the hulk of the *Kongo* and preparing to tow it into dry dock. "We may be in for an attack on another front," Pike finished, "and soon."

Capital arena, Kalea

Leonard McCoy winced as Jim Kirk took yet another punch from his massive Kalean opponent, twisting his head around and sending blood flying, adding several more splotches to the already wet and reddened arena floor. Kirk staggered but held his ground, managing to block the follow-up punch, but that just left him open for the Kalean to knee him in the gut, doubling him over. Kirk gasped for breath and struggled to rise again, but the sight of the opponent who towered over him—a two-meter quasihumanoid with facial features reminding McCoy of a cross between a gorilla, an opossum, and a horned lizard, covered in sherbet-orange fur everywhere except his face and his muscle-bound chest and abdomen—drove home to the doctor how badly outmatched his friend was.

Mercifully, the horn sounded at that moment, signaling the end of the round and giving Kirk some two and a half minutes' respite before his pummeling resumed. McCoy ran out across the loose clay to the captain's side, sparing an angry glare at Prime Rector Zonetox, who laughed at the bloody spectacle from her throne atop the forward corner of the fan-shaped arena. Kneeling by the crouching Kirk, he administered a shot of tri-ox and an iron supplement to help with the blood loss, plus an analgesic for the pain. He handed Kirk a water pack as well, still the simplest and most essential of remedies.

"How much longer are you going to keep up this farce?" McCoy demanded as Kirk drank, wincing as the nozzle touched his swollen lip. "This is no kind of 'negotiation'! Zonetox just wants to humiliate you. Get her jollies at the expense of the lowly human. Just walk away, Jim. The Federation doesn't need allies this bloodthirsty."

Kirk coughed and spat out a mix of water and blood. "Better allies than enemies, Bones. We have enough of those already. I just have to prove humanity is strong enough to warrant their respect."

"It's the damn twenty-third century! We both have spaceships and computers! What difference does brute physical strength matter to either of us anymore?"

The captain chuckled, then winced again. "Listen to yourself. You're the one who's always saying we should rely on our basic strengths instead of technology."

McCoy fidgeted. "I never say that. Not exactly."

Kirk started to rise again, and McCoy helped him, holding on until he was sure the captain could stand on his own. "Diplomacy by combat is their custom, Bones. We don't have to agree with it. And if I have to stand here and take a beating to win this treaty . . . well, I can handle it. I've been through worse."

"Maybe," McCoy grumbled. "But did you have to agree to do it stark naked?"

Kirk grinned. "That's part of the custom too. Don't worry, you're a doctor."

He strode forward unsteadily, but not without a touch of swagger. He smiled up at Zonetox as she stared down at him covetously. "Show-off," McCoy muttered. What worried him wasn't whether Kirk could handle the beating—it was that this was the kind of challenge a young, virile human male might enjoy a bit too much for his own good.

When the horn sounded again, Kirk came out swinging, getting in a couple of solid blows to his opponent's abdomen, but it made little impact on the Kalean's rock-hard musculature. The gladiator batted Kirk aside with a careless arm sweep, barely giving him time to raise his own arms to protect his head. The captain managed to roll to his feet, but his opponent merely stood there waiting for him. Kirk gathered his energies and charged forward, launching a flying kick at the Kalean's midriff.

It knocked the towering fighter back a few steps, but left Kirk flat on his bare behind. The captain was slow to rise, and that gave the gladiator an opening to grab him by the hair on his head and punch him repeatedly in the face. Kirk fell to the clay and struggled to rise again. Once more, the horn spared him from summary defeat.

Moments later, McCoy was at his side, tending him again. "Your nose is broken," he said. "Hairline fracture of the right ulna. And you still have cracked ribs from before. Jim, you have to stop before you get yourself killed!"

"Just . . . get me back on my feet. The Federation . . . needs this treaty."

"Not this badly! Not so much that they'd want to see you tortured over it! This isn't about the Federation, Jim. It's about you. You still feel you failed when those 'demon' aliens attacked Adelphous, killed so many of your crew. Now they're back and they killed your old first officer, and you feel you let him down somehow too, even though you were hundreds of light-years away. So you're overcompensating. You're so afraid to feel like a failure that you don't know when to stop!"

"That's enough, McCoy! Get me back on my feet. That's an order!"

"The hell with that. I can override your orders where your health is concerned."

The horn sounded. "Resume!" Zonetox called.

"No!" McCoy cried, rising to face the prime rector. "Can't you see he's had enough? Surely you've proven your point by now! What's to be gained by beating him even more?"

The rector glared down at him. "Your captain came here, little man, to try to prove *your* strength to us. Now stand aside and let him—or my gladiator—prove who is the stronger."

"You think caving someone's skull in is an act of strength? A falling rock can do that. Slipping in the damn shower can do that! It's not that impressive! You want us to show you real power? Then let me take my captain to a hospital and watch me heal his injuries. Putting things back together again is much harder work than breaking them."

The gladiator loomed over McCoy. "You heard my rector, tiny human. Stand aside or I will knock you aside to get to my opponent!"

"Fine!" McCoy countered, holding his ground. "Beat me up too if you must. Prove how tough you are by punching someone who won't punch back. But that man is my patient, my captain, and my friend, and I will *not* stand by and let you break any more of his bones for no good goddamn reason!" He took a step closer, arching an eyebrow and continuing in his most scathing tones. "And for your information, sir, the proper form of address in these situations is '*puny* human.'"

The gladiator looked nonplussed, as though trying to decide whether or not to cave McCoy's skull in and unaccustomed to the mental effort it required. After another moment, though, Zonetox laughed and rose from her throne. "Stand down, my champion," she ordered as she descended the steps. "The Rectorate concedes the contest to the champion—the *champions*—from the Federation."

She came to a halt before McCoy, gazing down at him with an intrigued look. "You have demonstrated your people's strength to me, physician, and in a way I never anticipated. Such fearlessness, such passion and rage—all in the name of healing. You are a fighter, but in the name of compassion. This is what your Federation claims to be, but I did not understand what it meant until now. Perhaps what your captain said to us before was true—that your people's real power lies not in what you conquer, but in what you build. Both your technology and your alliances."

"I believe that's true of us on our best days," McCoy said. But he afforded a glance of exasperated concern toward Kirk, who stared up at him speechlessly, seeming content to yield the floor.

"But sometimes even we need to be reminded of it. Maybe that's why we keep trying to build new alliances with people like you."

"And you have done so now," Zonetox said. "Come—we will take you up on your offer. Bring your captain to our champions' hospital, and show us how you heal. And then . . . we will have much to discuss."

U.S.S. Sacagawea

"Chalan's transmitting the signed treaty to the Diplomatic Corps as we speak," Eshu Adebayo told Kirk as the latter rested in a sickbay bed. "Admiral Komack was quite pleased to hear of our success. He's putting you in for a commendation, Jim."

Kirk shook his head. "I wasn't the one who pulled it off. Doctor McCoy's the one who deserves the commendation." He turned to the doctor. "And I intend to see that you get one."

"I'll see to it myself," Adebayo said, smiling at both men. "Great work, both of you."

The first officer left them alone in the ward. McCoy scowled as he fiddled with his medical scanner, but Kirk saw a trace of a proud smile slip through. "I don't care about any of that non-sense," the doctor said. "I'm just getting tired of patching you up all the time. I was tryin' to make my job easier."

"Well, say what you like, Bones. But you single-handedly pulled off a diplomatic coup just by being your usual ornery self." He lowered his head. "And doing what I couldn't."

"You could, Jim," the doctor countered. "You just forgot you could for a while there."

"You were right, you know. Losing Commander Egdor . . . and to the same aliens who cost me so much before . . ." He sighed. "It's so unfair, Bones. He strove so hard for so long to earn a command. He *deserved* a command, long before this. I really believed he'd get his shot eventually. Now we'll never know.

"It made me feel . . . like I got where I am through a few lucky breaks. I know, I know," he said, waving off McCoy's protest, "I earned my successes. But there are others just as capable who could've done just as well given the same opportunities. Or if they'd lived through the disasters instead of me." He paused. "It made me feel I had to prove something to myself. I was pushing myself, and I guess I pushed too far, and in the wrong direction."

McCoy put a hand on his shoulder. "You've always had a bad habit of punishing yourself for not being superhuman. Or in this case, letting others punish you for it."

Kirk groaned. "Don't remind me."

"Just try being human, Jim," the doctor went on. "It's something you're actually pretty good at—when you give yourself a chance."

Twelve

*The people . . . may be changed by the knowledge, but it's
better than exterminating them.*

—James T. Kirk

U.S.S. Sacagawea

"The microquasar Murasaki 274 has undergone a massive erup-
tion," Kirk told the assembled crew in the briefing room. "The
radiation surge is projected to endanger at least three inhabited
worlds, including two Federation colonies. The *Sacagawea* and
the *Exeter* are the closest ships to the area, so we will be assisting
Captain Tracey and his crew in providing emergency assistance,
building radiation shelters, evacuations if necessary, and so forth."

Dr. McCoy leaned forward. "Pardon me, but astrophysics was
never my best subject. A microquasar . . . that's some kind of a
black hole, correct?"

"Almost, Leonard," Rhenas Sherev replied. "It's a binary system consisting of a star and a black hole. The black hole's gravity draws in the star's atmosphere, forming an accretion disk
around it as it spirals in. The friction and compression of the
hydrogen gas make it hotter and hotter until it gives off hard
X-rays, and jets of subatomic particles spray out of its magnetic
poles at close to the speed of light. It's like a smaller version of
the quasars formed by the supermassive black holes at the cen-
ters of galaxies, hence the name."

"Sounds nasty."

"It is. Sometimes the black hole can suck in an asteroid or even a planet, creating a radiation surge massive enough to endanger life on neighboring star systems. That's what happened here."

"Unfortunately," Kirk added, "the quasar wasn't being monitored closely enough to let us predict the surge, so we were taken off guard. We just have to hope we can ensure all endangered populations are suitably shielded or evacuated before the radiation hits."

"Hold on," McCoy said. "If they're in other star systems, doesn't that mean we have years to prepare?"

"In some circumstances," Sherev said, "depending on the local subspace topology, the radiation from high-energy astronomical events like this can spontaneously tunnel into subspace and arrive at other star systems in weeks, even days. We know that happened here, because the energy we're reading from the Murasaki object through normal space is considerably less than it should be."

"Our assignment is to assist the colony on Atticus IV in constructing an emergency radiation shelter and helping the colony's twenty-three thousand citizens relocate there before the radiation surge arrives," Kirk said. "Doctor McCoy, as a precaution, you need to prepare as much hyronalin and other anti-radiation treatments as you can synthesize over the next two days, to bolster the colony's supply in case the shelter isn't completed in time."

"You mean we don't know when the surge will hit?" an alarmed McCoy asked.

"We predict four days," Sherev told him. "But occasionally the subspace topology can shift and either lengthen or shorten the radiation's travel time. So there's always a risk."

"Oh, joy," McCoy grumbled. "I hope I don't end up regretting that I ever met you two."

Atticus IV

Ling Jiang, the colony administrator, looked tired but satisfied as she stood next to Rhenas Sherev, gazing at the nearly complete emergency shelter that had been excavated at the base of a large, sturdy mountain a hundred kilometers northeast of the colony. "We never would've finished in time without your help, Commander," she said. "Nor would we have been as fully equipped to survive in there until the surge passes."

"Well, you'll also have to think about what comes after," Leonard McCoy called out, striding over from where he'd been finishing up the precautionary hyronalin injections for the last wave of evacuees. "That radiation storm's gonna kill most of your crops. And you can't rely on emergency rations for long. You'll need a plan to get fresh food growing as quickly as possible."

"Our agronomists have been working on a strategy, Doctor," Jiang said. "We faced similar problems when we first settled. This planet's fairly barren, at least on land. Most of its life is in the ocean, which is why it seemed ideal to colonize. At least that means most of the indigenous forms will survive." She fell silent, her expression growing solemn.

"Is something wrong, Administrator?" McCoy asked.

"Anything we overlooked?" added Sherev.

"No, it's not that. I just realized . . . it's probably too late for the Chenari."

The Starfleet officers frowned. "Chenari?" Sherev asked.

"They're a preindustrial society on a planet a few parsecs out. Our scientists have been monitoring their civilization for the past two decades, taking occasional orbital scans—no contact, of course. They're nonhumanoid, relatively peaceful. Mostly limited to one continent, but starting to explore beyond it." She blinked away tears. "At least, they were. They're closer to the quasar than we are. If the surge is a day away from us . . . then Chenar has surely been hit already. And its people would've had no way to predict or understand what was happening. A whole burgeoning civilization—and it's probably gone now."

McCoy and Sherev traded a look. The doctor spoke first. "We need to talk to Jim."

U.S.S. *Sacagawea*
Captain's log, supplemental

We have arrived in orbit of the planet Chenar to find its sur-face devastated by the radiation surge that passed through the system three days ago. It seems we have arrived too late—all life has been rendered extinct.

"That's what we thought at first," Kirk reported to Captain Ronald Tracey, whose saturnine visage was projected on the desk screen in Kirk's ready room. "But Commander Sherev's detailed scans have detected life signs consistent with several hundred Chenari sheltering in a deep underground cavern. We think they got lucky—they were a colony far from their home continent, so they happened to be on the far side of the planet when the worst of the surge hit. The resultant atmospheric storms must have driven them underground in time to survive the rest of the surge. There are enough of them that it would be a tight fit on the *Sac*, but if we—"

"*No*," Tracey said.

Kirk blinked. "Excuse me?"

"*You said they were preindustrial. Primitives. You know the Prime Directive as well as I do. It's up to them to survive on their own, if they can.*"

"A few hundred people? That's barely a stable population base under the best of circumstances. And with their crops and game animals dead, their atmosphere poisoned and eroded—sir, they have no chance of survival without our help."

"And you think they could survive life in the Federation?" Tracey's deep voice boomed. *"People who've barely invented sailboats? Seeing aliens and starships would probably drive them mad."*

"The colony's reports call them an intelligent, peaceful people. These are explorers, sir, curious about their world."

"Don't start identifying with them, Kirk. You aren't responsible for their lives. But you are responsible for follow-up on Atticus IV. I need you back there to clean up after the storm."

"The Atticans are fully prepared and resourceful, sir. They *can* take care of themselves for an extra day or so before we arrive. The Chenari can't."

"Then maybe they just weren't meant to survive. You have your orders, Kirk. Tracey out."

Kirk sat at his desk for some time, wrestling with himself. After a while, he reached out and activated his log recorder. "Personal log, supplemental." He'd found over the years that rehearsing his thoughts out loud helped him work through these internal debates. "Captain Tracey has issued clear orders: Obey General Order One . . . and let a civilization go extinct. And I am forced to wonder: Is it always going to come down to a war between the Prime Directive and my conscience?"

He resisted the thought. "No. I believe in the Prime Directive. It's not just an arbitrary rule, but a check on human arrogance. It reminds us to trust that other civilizations are intelligent and capable enough to solve their own problems . . . better qualified to understand their own needs than outsiders are. It's about recognizing that the Federation's superior technology does not equal superior wisdom or intellectual capacity."

He rose and began to pace. "Maybe that's why Captain Tracey's attitude toward the Chenari is sticking in my craw. He dismissed them as 'primitives.' He made it sound as if they were unintelligent—and therefore unworthy of rescue." He paused.

"No, that's unfair. Tracey's still a fellow captain, with the same training, the same values as myself. He's no doubt preoccupied with his own rescue operations, concerned with coordinating the entire effort across multiple worlds. I can't fault the man for that. Still . . . that doesn't mean the Chenari deserve to be shrugged off as an inconvenient distraction."

He thought of Daramoy, and what would have happened to her if Gary Mitchell hadn't bent the rules. He didn't need to enter that in his personal log; he'd done so often enough already.

Closing the log channel, he opened the intercom to the bridge. "Kirk to Adebayo."

"Adebayo here, Captain. Go ahead."

"Have Commander Sherev prepare a rescue party equipped for cave exploration, and have McCoy ready a medical team. We're saving the Chenari."

Chenar

Kirk watched with a mix of admiration and concern as Rhenas Sherev hopped down the forty-five-degree slope of the cavern floor with apparent ease, barely bothering to keep a hand on the safety line. He considered himself an experienced rock climber—hence his decision that he needed to accompany the rescue team personally, though delaying the inevitable chewing out from Captain Tracey was a consideration as well—but Sherev had been born and raised in one of Andoria's underground cities even before she took up archaeology, so she was basically in her native environment here. Only Kreftz, a security crewman from Denobula, was handling the descent into the cavern as easily as Sherev was, if not more so. Kirk was keeping up with them reasonably well, but the other humans on the rescue team struggled their way down the slope more slowly, with Dr. McCoy inevitably keeping up a running litany of grumbles and complaints whenever he managed to catch his breath.

Ensign Diaz stayed close to the doctor, watching him as if expecting him to collapse at any moment. Her solicitousness only made McCoy more annoyed.

Once Sherev and Kreftz made it to the bottom of the slope ahead of the others, the science officer took tricorder scans of the seemingly level ground ahead to check for potential pitfalls. The Chenari had wisely ensconced themselves deep in this cave system, well away from the hazardous conditions up above. The radiation from the quasar burst had passed by now, but it had seared away Chenar's ozone layer, allowing lethal levels of ultraviolet radiation from the system's sun to reach the surface. It had also heated much of the upper atmosphere enough to dissociate its atoms and disperse it into space, leaving the remaining air thin and dry. A gentle wind flowed steadily outward through these caverns, whose entrance was low enough for the outside pressure to remain fairly substantial for now; but over time, the air in here would grow thinner as the pressure equalized with what remained outside.

Once the captain caught up with Sherev, he told her, "I don't think you should be so casual about moving through this cave, Commander. However comfortable and familiar it may feel, it's still an alien world with unknown dangers."

"Which I'm an old hand at keeping my eyes and antennae peeled for, Jim. Trust me, it's not recklessness. I learned that lesson back at Vega." She shrugged. "I just make it look easy." Kirk was less than reassured.

Once the rest of the party had reached the bottom and McCoy had more or less caught his breath, the doctor asked, "So how much longer until we reach the Chenari? The deeper we have to go, the harder it's going to be getting them out, especially if they're suffering from radiation or malnutrition."

"We're getting very close to the life signs," Sherev said.

Kirk addressed the whole team. "We should proceed cautiously from here. Remember, these beings have never seen alien life before. According to the Attican survey reports, they're herbivores, timid by nature. If we come on too strong, we could spook them, make them afraid of us."

"Or worse, provoke an aggressive response," Sherev added. "Even herbivores can be deadly when they feel cornered."

"And if they panic and we have to stun them," Kirk finished, "it'd be impossible to drag them all to the surface."

"How *are* we going to approach them?" Diaz asked. "We've always been trained to avoid revealing ourselves to primitive cultures."

Sherev raised a finger. "First off, banish that word 'primitive' from your mind. It's easy to build a civilization when you have transtators and dilithium circuits and bulk synthesizers. It takes a lot more ingenuity, insight, and patience to do it with wood and bronze and muscle power. We're all just coasting on the hard work that our 'primitive' ancestors did in figuring out how to build civilization in the first place."

The junior science officer lowered her head. "Yes, Commander."

"The obstacle we face is that the Chenari simply have a radically different view of the world than we do. We're about to introduce them to concepts they've never encountered—ourselves included. That's going to be a hard gulf to bridge."

"And how do you suggest we go about that?" McCoy asked, his tone gentle and curious.

Sherev thought for a moment. "Best to keep it simple. We're friends, we're here to help, we can take you someplace safe. We don't want to scare them with too much new information. But we should be honest too. It's the simplest way to earn their trust."

"So . . . tell the truth, but not too much of the truth?"

"Is that so different from how you reassure a patient, Doctor?"

McCoy quirked an eyebrow. "I suppose not. But finding the

right balance is something you have to play by ear, judging each patient's mood and probable reactions. You have to read people. How do we read a species we've never met? Especially one that looks like . . . oh, how did they describe it . . . plush mini-*Triceratops* with vestigial wings?"

"We'll have to play it by ear," Kirk answered.

Once the party was sufficiently rested, the captain led them forward once more. The cavern soon narrowed into a tunnel, and Kirk spotted something that made him call the rescue party to a halt. Just in front of the tunnel entrance was a gourd and a small bundle wrapped in leaves. "Sherev?"

The science officer stepped forward and scanned them with her tricorder. "Just what it looks like, Captain. A water gourd and a small bundle of food—something akin to a rice ball, I'd say, but with dried berries and nuts mixed in."

"It looks too neatly placed to have been dropped there," Kamisha Diaz observed.

"Confirmed," said Sherev, waving her tricorder farther forward. "The heat trail and trace skin cells show a Chenari came up this passage and returned only minutes ago."

Kirk chuckled, drawing the stares of the others. "First contact protocols," he said. "We were so worried about how we'd proceed, but the Chenari beat us to it. We should've realized—they're settlers on a new continent. Of course they'd expect to encounter unfamiliar peoples and have to establish communication and trade with them."

"I see," Sherev said. "They must've heard us coming. Leaving an offering of food and water here is a way to make first contact from a distance—to let us know they're here and they're willing to be friendly, but they don't want to rush things. We have to prove ourselves friendly in return."

Diaz was peering down the tunnel as she scanned it. "It seems to widen again about twenty meters down. A natural bottleneck. Neutral ground?"

Kirk nodded. "Ensign . . . proceed to the far end and leave a ration bar and water pack there. Break them open so the Chenari don't have to figure out how. But keep alert and have your phaser ready just in case."

"Aye, sir." The ensign crept into the passageway, retrieving the items from her pack.

McCoy sidled up beside Kirk. "Why Diaz? Because she's the smallest, the least threatening?"

Kirk smiled. "Because it was her idea. Besides—I remember how I felt the first time I got to initiate a first contact. Diaz deserves to feel that too."

The doctor peered at him. "Well, that didn't take long. Youngest captain in Starfleet, yet you're already training the next generation."

"My captains did it for me," Kirk said. "I feel it's my duty to pay it forward."

Diaz soon returned, and the party waited, watching the far end of the tunnel. Soon, there was movement at the far end, a shadowed figure that appeared briefly and then retreated with Diaz's offerings. The party waited for over fifteen minutes, until the figure (or another like it) returned and left another water gourd at their end before retreating once more. "Step two," Kirk interpreted. "Inviting us to advance that far and no farther."

Kirk nodded to Diaz to go first, with himself and Sherev following single file and the rest coming behind them. They emerged from the tunnel into a large, high grotto with a steep, nearly vertical wall some thirty meters before them, rising a good fifteen meters to a plateau studded with stalagmites like trees in a forest. Stalactites filled much of the ceiling overhead like chandeliers, but there were no intact stalagmites in the basin below, just an agglomeration of boulders and scree, as if a portion of the plateau had collapsed into the basin some time in the past. The basin was empty aside from themselves, but Kirk could see a trail of footprints in the dirt and scree on the ground, leading back to the wall. He spotted a rope piled beside a stalagmite near the edge of the plateau, and there was a flickering glow of firelight somewhere behind it. "They must have climbed up there and pulled up the rope," he said.

"I could climb that easily," Crewman Kreftz said, sizing up the wall.

"No," Kirk told the Denobulan. "We want them to feel safe. Earn their trust. We'll play it their way."

Diaz picked up the offered water gourd, looking puzzled. "Okay, so what are we supposed to do next?"

An alien voice sounded from the plateau above. "Water."

Diaz peered at the shadows between the stalagmites. "Hello?"

"Water. That is water." Their communicators, preprogrammed with the Atticans' survey data, provided the translation promptly.

Kirk traded a look with Sherev. "The next step," the science officer said. "A language lesson."

"Luckily we can skip that part," Kirk said. He nodded to Diaz.

The young ensign stepped forward nervously. "It's all right," she called. "We understand your words. Please speak to us. We come in peace." She shook with excitement and whispered to the others: "I always wanted to say that!"

There was a flurry of agitated movement up above, and a chatter of voices too low and frenetic for the translators to catch. "How do you know our tongue?" one of the Chenari finally said. "Have you met our kind before?"

"Uh . . . We have a . . . tool that lets us speak to you. It can . . ." After struggling for a moment, she sighed and said, "I mean, yes. We have . . . encountered your people before." She turned to Kirk and Sherev and whispered, "That's technically true, right?"

More indecipherable discussion from above. "We do not know of your kind. We have met no people in this land, and none on our own land mass who looked as unlike us as you do. We would have thought you were animals if not for your garments and tools."

"We come from very far away," Diaz said. "Some of us have . . . visited your homeland in recent years. It's because we knew of you that we came to seek you out when the disaster struck."

After more consultation, the spokesperson said, "It is good that this is not your land, or you would have been killed. The storms are unnatural. They burn the skin, poison the blood. How did you pass through them to come here?"

"The storms have died down. They won't return any time soon, but it's no longer possible to live on this—this land. That's why we've come. To take you someplace safe, where you can live."

There was more frenzied chatter from above, yet there was no response from the spokesperson. "You may have come on too strong, Ensign," Sherev said. "They don't yet know if they can trust us."

"Would you take us back to our homeland?" the voice finally called.

Diaz threw a pleading look at Kirk, conceding that this was getting beyond her. Giving her a reassuring nod, Kirk stepped forward. "I'm afraid what you ask is not possible," he told them, though he deemed it unwise to tell them why at this point. "But there are other places we can take you that would suit your needs. Places where you could be free to live the kind of life you chose when you traveled here."

"We do not know your kind. These caverns will keep us safe for now. Make camp where you are—in the days ahead, you may tell us of yourselves. Your lands, your ways, how you know of us. Once we know you, perhaps we will join you, if that is what we choose."

"There's no time for that," Kirk told them. "Have you noticed the wind in here, the wind that never stops? Have you begun having a harder time keeping your breath, or lighting fires? The air is growing thinner. You will not be safe down here much longer, and neither will we."

"Your words are unclear," the voice said.

"Of course," Sherev muttered. "They have no concept of a vacuum or reduced air pressure."

"Let me try something," McCoy said, stepping forward. "You said the storms burned your skin, poisoned your blood. We have medicines that can help you. Let us show you we only want to help."

More discussion, then: "Leave the medicines at the base of the wall and withdraw."

"I'm afraid you wouldn't know how to use them. If you'll let me come up there—just me, no one else—I'd be happy to treat your wounded."

After additional consultation, the answer finally came. "One of us is far sicker than the rest. He is close to death, and you can do no further harm. You alone remain, healer, and we will lower him to you. Help him if you can—if only to ease his pain."

McCoy looked to Kirk. "We agree to your terms," the captain called.

At Kirk's order, the others retreated into the tunnel, leaving their hand beacons behind to light the cavern, while McCoy advanced nearer to the sheer wall. Soon, Kirk saw movement up ahead and finally got a real look at the Chenari. The *Triceratops* description was very loose at best. They were bipeds, somewhat larger than humans, but their dark blue-gray bodies were horizontal, cantilevered by stiff, heavy tails in a manner more like a raptor dinosaur. Their heads had wide frills and beaked mouths, but no horns, and their eyes and upper faces were more mammalian than saurian. Most distinctively, they had batlike wings folded up on their backs, too small for flight but still impressive. The ones who carried the dying Chenari forward had their wings somewhat spread, and Kirk remembered the Attican researchers' conjecture that they had retained the wings as a means of thermal regulation, for instance, as a way to cool blood heated by exertion.

Once the Chenari had tied a secure harness of rope around McCoy's patient, they began to belay him down using a second stalagmite right on the edge of the plateau as a pulley. Kirk heard rock crumbling and saw chunks of limestone break off the base of the stalagmite where it met the cliff face. "Bones, heads up!" he called.

As he feared, the stalagmite was unstable. McCoy darted back as it broke free, fell, and shattered on the grotto floor. The harnessed Chenari swung to the side, avoiding the falling rock, but the belayers up above were only able to slow him partially before they were forced to let go to avoid being pulled off. Kirk saw one of them spread its wings and flap them desperately to pull itself back from the crumbling edge.

Once the debris settled, McCoy darted forward to check on the fallen Chenari, taking a tricorder scan. "He's just barely alive," he called, coughing from the dust. He opened his medkit and crouched by the patient.

Kirk heard more crumbling sounds and looked around for the source. Sherev, with her cave dweller's instincts, spotted it first. "Leonard, look out!" she cried, lunging forward. As she shoved the doctor aside, Kirk saw that the first stalagmite, the one the rope was tied to, was starting to give way as well—and so was the cluster of sharp-pointed stalactites directly over Sherev's head.

Sherev could have jumped clear in time. Instead, she heaved against the unconscious Chenari and rolled him to safety as the spears of rock gave way. Sherev vanished beneath them before Kirk had a chance to react.

"Rhen!" he screamed, choking from the dust. As soon as his view cleared, he ran forward, fearing what he would see.

To his relief, Sherev was still alive and conscious, but her lower torso was pinned underneath a ton or more of shattered rock. She was wincing and moaning in agony, and blue blood trickled out from the pile of rubble.

McCoy was back on his feet, sizing up the situation. "I can't help her until you get her free," he said. He moved over to the fallen Chenari, gesturing to his medic. "Hakim, stabilize Sherev. I'll do what I can here." He was clearly worried for his friend, but his healer's instinct took precedence.

Diaz moved in beside Kirk, staring at her superior's plight in horror. "We have to do something. Can we phaser her out?"

"No," Sherev gasped. "Not until . . . scan the rock pile. It's pinning me . . . remove the wrong piece and it crushes me."

"She's right," Kirk said. "We have to be careful."

"Sir!" Kreftz called, pointing upward.

A number of spread-winged, tailed figures were gliding down from the plateau. The Chenari came down around the rescue party, several meters away. But one stepped cautiously forward and spoke in what Kirk recognized as the spokesperson's voice. "She gave her life to save Thurelor," he said in apparent puzzlement, "though he is already near death."

"Hey, I'm not . . . dead yet," Sherev gasped.

"I might still save both of them," McCoy said, "if we can get the hell out of here fast enough."

Kirk crouched to match the spokesperson's eye level. "To do that, we need your people's help, to free my friend and carry both our people's wounded to the surface. Please—will you help us?"

The spokesperson traded looks with those around him, but the answer came quickly. "Yes. We cannot turn away those in need. Not when they were hurt trying to help us." He gestured to the others. "We will bring more people down to help clear the rubble. Then we will lead you out. There is a quicker way to the surface."

Kirk met the Chenari's dewy eyes with profound gratitude. "Thank you. My name is James Kirk." He extended a hand, unsure if the Chenari would understand the gesture.

But after a moment, the spokesperson reached out and clasped the offered hand. "My name is Phelarasan."

U.S.S. Sacagawea

The Chenari's vestigial wings turned out to have another use, as a form of natural basket or knapsack, which they used to carry belongings on their backs. The largest Chenari in the group carried Sherev out of the cave on her back, her wings wrapped tightly around the Andorian's broken body to keep her immobilized as the group made swift time to the surface. But many of the others, as it turned out, carried eggs. The Chenari were an oviparous species, and according to Phelarasan, the colonists had gone through an annual spawning not long before the disaster. When the lethal storms and radiation had come, many of the settlers had been too ill or too badly burned to travel, so they had entrusted the care of their eggs to the party that had retreated to the caves. While the group consisted of only a few hundred individuals, they had more than triple that number of eggs with them, meaning that they still had a large, genetically diverse enough population base to rebuild from on a new world.

Back on the ship, while McCoy and his team struggled to save Sherev and the dying Chenari, Kirk distracted himself by supervising the evacuation of the remaining survivors of the nearly dead planet. He had feared how the Chenari would react to having starships and transporters sprung on them all at once, but as it turned out, now that the crew had earned their trust, the Chenari readily accepted everything they were shown. They were pioneers, after all, explorers of a new land, and they had seen many animals, plants, and geological formations there that they considered unprecedented wonders. Since so much of their own world was still alien to them, they were used to encountering things they did not understand, and so they took real aliens and starship technology surprisingly in stride.

Once McCoy confirmed that Sherev and Thurelor were both

stabilized, Kirk was left with one more duty to perform. Left with no choice but to face the music, he contacted the *Exeter* and filled in Captain Tracey on what he'd done.

"I'm very disappointed in you, Kirk," the senior captain intoned. *"You made it clear to me that you understood the importance of following the Prime Directive."*

"With respect, sir, I believe that's what I've done."

"By making open contact with a primitive people? Bringing them aboard your ship, showing them our technology?"

"Our obligation under the Prime Directive, sir," Kirk replied, "is to protect the natural development of alien civilizations from outside interference or disruption. As I see it, a cosmic disaster that *destroys* a civilization is the most extreme form of external disruption imaginable. By rescuing the Chenari, by finding another uninhabited world for them to settle, we can allow their culture to survive and resume its natural development."

Tracey glowered at him. *"How natural will their cultural development be now that they've learned about starships and aliens?"*

"At least they'll still have a culture to develop. These people were pioneers to begin with. They were already changing their own culture to fit a new environment. *They* were the ones who initiated contact with *us*, because they fully expected to meet new life and new civilizations. Knowing that said life exists on more than one planet won't really change their worldview that much, I think, as long as we limit their exposure to our technology and leave them to their own devices once they're resettled." He smiled slightly. "I think the young are often more adaptable than the old."

"I'll try not to take that personally," Tracey said. After a moment, the grizzled older captain sighed. *"You've got some nerve, Kirk, I'll give you that at least. Starfleet might actually buy your argument about the Directive. Now that you've gone ahead and saved an actual species from extinction—your second, if I'm not*

mistaken—they can't very well order you to undo it. Easier to ask for forgiveness than permission, right? Hell, you'll probably get a commendation for this."

"Then . . . I take it we can rely on the *Exeter* to provide logistical support for the resettlement?"

Tracey smirked. *"Like I said, you've got nerve, Jim. I may not agree with your way of seeing things, but I respect your commitment."*

"Thank you, sir."

Tracey signed off and closed the channel. Kirk stared at the blank screen, absorbing their conversation. Something about the older captain's attitude still rubbed him the wrong way. His points had all been valid, and he'd been almost complimentary toward Kirk. But he had shown no interest in the survival of the Chenari except as a matter of regulations, logistics, and politics. He'd shown no sign of the relief and gratitude Kirk felt at preventing the extinction of a civilization.

Kirk shook off his concern. Different captains just expressed themselves differently. He'd been on the wrong end of stern lectures more than a few times before, often from senior officers he admired greatly, like Stephen Garrovick and Robert Wesley. There was no reason to assume Ron Tracey was uncaring just because he'd given Kirk a rough time.

Besides, there were more immediate things to worry about. "Rhen," he muttered to the empty room. "Always rushing in headfirst. I knew it'd get you in trouble someday . . ."

———

"The Atticans have agreed to take charge of the Chenari's resettlement," Kirk told Rhenas Sherev days later as he sat by her bed in the sickbay intensive care ward. "They've decided to move their own colony to a safer planet anyway, so they're willing to help the Chenari do the same."

"Will it be the same planet, or a different one?" Sherev asked.

She was still weak, her antennae sagging, and her crushed legs and hips were encased in a support frame that was slowly knitting her bones back together, but her usual strong, optimistic spirit remained.

"They haven't decided yet," Kirk replied, "but the Chenari seem to be leaning toward going their own way, if possible. I wouldn't be surprised. They're pioneers, people who left their homeland in search of independence and the freedom to choose their own path. If anything, discovering how advanced and powerful we are in comparison makes them *less* willing to become dependent on us."

"My kind of people," Sherev said. "You think the Atticans will respect that?"

"They're pioneers too," Kirk said. "I think they understand each other well enough." He smiled. "Meanwhile, Admiral Komack tells me that Starfleet is formulating a new standing order. From now on, all vessels will be required to investigate and monitor all microquasars and quasar-like phenomena they come across, so that we'll have advance warning of any future disasters like this."

"Good. That should've been the rule from the start."

"I couldn't agree more," Kirk replied. Then he grew thoughtful. "Still . . . I'm grateful I got the chance to meet the Chenari. They're an impressive people. Gentle, cautious, but inquisitive and eager to learn. They could be great space explorers . . . in a thousand years or so."

"Then I guess Starfleet will be in good hands once we're finally gone," Sherev quipped. "Brilliant of me, wasn't it—getting myself hurt so they'd see us as the ones needing help." Then she grew quiet, her antennae taking on a solemn, thoughtful cast.

"Rhen?"

She let out a breath. "Jim . . . Bones gave me the verdict. I'll walk again, but I'll never regain full mobility. Not enough to qualify for starship duty."

Kirk took a few moments to absorb it. "Rhen, I'm sorr—"

"Don't you dare. Don't tell yourself this is somehow your fault. I was the most qualified caver—I needed to be there. Leonard would be dead if I hadn't had the experience to see the rockfall coming. And I *chose* to act on what I saw. What happened to me happened *because* of me, of who I am and what I decided. Don't make it about you."

As always, he appreciated her blunt comfort. But that was why he didn't want to lose her. "You could still be in Starfleet. Go back to Vega, or a starbase—"

She shook her head. "A desk job? I'm no more cut out for that than you are." She sighed. "I still intend to do archaeology. That's my first love. I'll just have to do it as a civilian."

He stared at her, stunned. "Resign your commission? Rhen, I . . . I . . ."

"Oh, don't react like it's such a tragedy. The rank never mattered to me. The blue uniform never worked with my skin tone anyway. All I want is to do science, Jim. Starfleet is an amazing place to do science, but it's not the only place. And it has too many other demands that distract from the science." She reached out and patted his hand. "I'll be fine, Jim. I'll be happy once I'm back on the ground, digging in the dirt."

After another moment, Kirk smiled and clasped her hand in both of his. "Then you go do what makes you happy, Rhen. But if you ever need me for anything, just call, and I'll be there."

Sherev smiled back at him warmly. "You always have been before, Jim. It's good to have someone I can rely on in my corner. So I'll hold you to that."

ENTERPRISE
2265

Thirteen

Thorwor and Kinikor looked back from their tiny raft and wept as the Beasts burned down all that was left of their island, their home, their kin. They wept until their tears raised the ocean and let them sail past the reef. "We do not know what we will face out there in the endless sea," Kinikor said, clutching her pregnant belly.

"We know it will be better than what we left," Thorwor told her. "For there will be no more Beasts to betray us, and we need never teach our children the ways of war."

—Aulacri origin myth

Karabos II

"Just call, and I'll be there."

Rhenas Sherev chuckled as she recalled Jim Kirk's words. They had turned out to be more prophetic than either of them had realized: She hadn't even called, but Kirk was here now that she needed him. *Thank Uzaveh Starfleet sent him instead of that sourpuss Captain Tracey*, she thought. *He would've probably just beamed me and my team up without stopping to ask and let all this get destroyed for the sake of a treaty.* She had joined Starfleet because of its unmatched resources for scientific study, but she had found over the years that politics, policy, and the Prime Directive sometimes forced Starfleet captains to make choices that were both scientifically and ethically unsalutary. A year and a half back in civilian life had made her grateful for the injury that had ended her career—though she still wished there had been a less agonizing way to make the transition. She still had to deal with a certain amount of pain when she exerted herself, and she relied more on the cane than she let on, but despite that, she felt freer now than she ever had in a Starfleet uniform.

Still, she didn't mind admitting that her team would never have made as much progress as it had in the past twelve hours without Starfleet's help. The team that Lieutenant Commanders Spock and Scott had brought down from the *Enterprise* had been highly skilled and efficient, aiding her own small team of fellow researchers and grad students in erecting an atmosphere dome atop the entry to the mountain crevice that allowed the closest access to the Karabosi's underground complex, pressurizing it, and then mounting and firing the phaser bores to begin the excavation. Normally they would have done that far more slowly, carefully sampling, sifting, and cataloging every cubic meter of rock they dug out in search of artifacts or geochemical traces. Under these rushed conditions, they had to settle for deep sensor scans and samples of the vaporized rock.

But Commander Spock worked with Sherev on recalibrating her team's sensor equipment and his own team's tricorders to maximize their penetration and resolution through meters of rock. The improvement in sensitivity he was able to achieve was impressive, as was his ability to compute bore power adjustments in his head to avoid overheating yet maintain a steady excavation rate. There were moments when watching the lanky young Vulcan perform his task so effortlessly gave Sherev twinges of doubt about her own adequacy as a science officer. But she quickly decided she was glad Kirk had traded up in that department as well as in starships. Surely the best captain she'd ever served with deserved the best science officer he could get.

With that in mind, Sherev took advantage of a meal break in the dome to sit opposite Spock, who was absently picking at some sort of bean and vegetable dish while reviewing scan results on a data slate. "Do you mind if we talk for a bit, Commander?"

"I am able to multitask, Doctor Sherev."

"Do I understand right that this is your first mission with Captain Kirk?"

"The second, following a medical supply run to Draxis II."

"So the first significant one. Those leg-stretching milk runs they like to start us out with hardly count."

"I believe the colonists on Draxis II would not agree."

Sherev quirked an antenna. She was still trying to adjust to Spock's dedication to Vulcan literalism. "I meant from the crew's perspective. Specifically, yours and Jim's. As his former science officer, I'm naturally curious to know how my successor is getting along with him." She thought of another tack. "As I imagine you might be curious to learn a thing or two from one of his former science officers. I just want to make sure things run smoothly between you two."

Spock nodded. "A reasonable consideration. Perhaps you might be able to offer insight on something that is unclear to me."

"Ask away."

The Vulcan set his fork down and steepled his long fingers before him. "Captain Kirk has an excellent record and a reputation as a highly disciplined commander. Indeed, his demeanor in the fifteen days we have served together has been consistent with that record. Though he does demonstrate a characteristically human tendency toward frivolity and social interaction while off duty, and is prone to idiomatic speech and wordplay, these do not in any way detract from his performance of his duties. In that respect, I have found him to be admirably focused, serious, and intellectually acute."

Sherev was tempted to make a joke about Spock thinking Kirk was acute, but given his disparaging tone when discussing wordplay, she quashed the impulse. Instead she said, "It sounds like you're hitting it off very well."

"As I understand the idiom, one would expect so." His slanted brows drew closer together. "However, I continue to get the impression that Captain Kirk is not entirely comfortable with me. It has not affected our work together as yet, so it is a minor concern. However, I find it a paradoxical reaction. Many humans and other non-Vulcans in Starfleet have responded to me in similar ways, finding my Vulcan control and precision to be a source of bemusement or irritation. Beings accustomed to emotional engagement with others often have difficulty adjusting to Vulcans' nonemotional mode of interaction."

Only Sherev's antennae showed what she thought about Vulcans' pretense of nonemotionality. She had found Spock highly expressive, and he even had a tendency to shout a bit when giving orders.

"However," Spock finished, "I had not expected an equivalent reaction from an individual as controlled and dispassionate as Captain Kirk."

This time Sherev did laugh; she couldn't help herself. Spock frowned in confusion, and she tried to catch her breath. "Jim Kirk? Dispassionate? Oh, Uzaveh." She took a few moments to calm herself. "Heed the benefit of my experience, young science officer. The thing you need to understand about James Tiberius Kirk is that he is a man of *intense* passions. Everything he does is the result of passion—the passion to explore, the passion to achieve and learn, the passion to help others and make a positive difference in the galaxy. Even that rigorous command discipline and emotional control you admire so much are the result of Jim's passion, his *need*, to be the best captain he can be."

Spock appeared skeptical. "You describe a paradox."

"Do I? Is it any more paradoxical than Vulcans suppressing

your emotions because they're so powerful that you're afraid to let them rule you? Your discipline is driven by passion too."

"That is a questionable interpretation," Spock said. "Though I have heard similar opinions expressed by my mother."

"Then I know where you got your smarts from."

Spock seemed to struggle for a moment with whether or not he should be scandalized by that. Then he wisely let it drop. "If your assessment is valid, how does it explain the captain's unease? Even if his discipline is motivated by emotion, he still values reserve and control in the performance of one's duty."

"That's just the thing, if you ask me," Sherev said.

"I *did* ask you."

"Yes, you did," she answered, rolling her eyes a little. "The point is, Jim's used to being the reserved and controlled one. He plays it straight and serious, and he relies on his more relaxed friends and crewmates to balance him out. His old exec, Commander Adebayo, was one of the kindliest, sweetest old men in Starfleet. Gary Mitchell, as you've no doubt learned already, is the resident rogue and jokester."

"Yes," Spock replied sourly. "I *have* observed as much."

"And I'm outspoken, sardonic, stubborn as hell, and prone to get carried away with my work. Jim is our pole star, the stalwart one who keeps us anchored and focused. And in turn, we keep him connected to his humanity, as he'd call it. To other people, to a life beyond duty.

"Now, that's changed. Most of the people he relied on for that are gone, except for Gary. If anything, his problem finding his balance with you is that you're too much like him. You don't give him the counterbalance he's used to."

"I see." Spock's frown deepened, no doubt an expression of his complete lack of emotion. "I am not likely to change, Doctor."

She sighed. "Well, maybe Jim will. Maybe he just needs to find a new equilibrium. Once he gets used to you being the more regimented, unemotional one, maybe he'll give himself the freedom to loosen up some. Maybe he'll finally feel free to embrace the emotional instincts that are such an important part of his success as a commander—even if he doesn't always realize it."

Before Spock could answer, a clamor of voices from the dig site deeper within the mountain crevice drew both scientists' attention. "I know that sound," Sherev said, shooting to her feet. "That's the sound of a dig team that just made a breakthrough!" She ran toward the voices, with Spock following close behind.

U.S.S. *Enterprise*

It was some time before Kirk managed to persuade Director Skovir to board the *Enterprise* and hear his counterproposals for the terraforming project. She came reluctantly, and with so little time remaining before the bombardment, Kirk had to skip any sort of banquet or entertainment and get straight to business. Mitchell and Sulu's presentation of alternative bombardment plans on the briefing room screen failed to impress her. "We have considered all these options. The thrust required to re-direct those comets would be prohibitive."

"If you let Starfleet work with you," Sulu replied, "we could provide more powerful thruster units, or even verteron beam emitters."

"Which would have a significant probability of fragmenting the comets while still in space, which would make them useless upon impact. The risk is too great."

She proved just as intractable regarding the alternative terraforming sites. "Your offer of worlds in Federation space is generous, but our goal is to increase our livable territory in *this* region. And Patavon IV's star is too cool, with too little ultraviolet. We would be dependent on vitamin supplements our whole lives."

"It seems a small inconvenience," Kirk said.

"For millions of colonists, for generations to come? Why subject them to that when there is a more ideal world available?"

"A world that had its own civilization before," Kirk said. "A civilization that left a message for others to find, a legacy of its past. We are on the verge of discovering that legacy."

"The legacy of a race of savages. Genocidal monsters."

Kirk studied Skovir. "You seem awfully sure of what they were like. I thought they'd left no evidence about themselves."

"The evidence of their destruction of their world is clear enough. That's all we need."

Her tail was twitching fiercely. *She'd make a poor poker player,* Kirk thought, now convinced that Sherev had been right that the director was hiding something.

He rose from his seat and stepped closer to where Skovir stood. "You should be aware, Director, that Doctor Sherev and an *Enterprise* science team penetrated a Karabosi vault several hours ago. The vault was designed to store records of their people's history, their scientific and technical achievements, samples of their art and literature." He paused for effect. "We now know what they looked like."

The alarm in Skovir's eyes told him what he needed. Kirk nodded to Sulu, who worked the display controls to bring up images transmitted from the vault by Spock's tricorder. "The vault contains thousands of thin platinum sheets encased in sapphire, laser-etched with millions of microdots," Sulu said. "It's an effective way to preserve vast amounts of data in a durable form that can be read by anyone who finds it." The screen showed samples of dozens of sheets slightly smaller than a Starfleet data slate, with close-ups of the microscopic engraving that put thousands of books' worth of content on each one. "The sheets contain a translation matrix starting with prime numbers and scientific constants and building from there. Our computers are working on deciphering the written languages, but we've already gleaned much from the pure mathematics."

Kirk picked up the thread, still staring intently at Skovir. "And more importantly . . . there are images."

Sulu brought up magnified medical diagrams from the sheets, followed by images of some of the artworks they had found depicting the Karabosi form. The Karabosi had been large, burly humanoids with gray skin, feline-simian features . . . and prehensile tails.

"We're still searching for detailed genetic information, Director. But the resemblance is . . . suggestive."

Skovir thought for a time, then sighed and spoke with reluctant slowness. "I could have argued that humans look almost identical to Vulcans, Makusians, and others. If only more of you out here had sharp teeth and tails.

"Yes, Captain Kirk. The Karabosi and the Aulacri are related species. My people evolved on Karabos II, in parallel with another species of our genus. I gather that it is uncommon in the galaxy for two civilized species to share a planet, that usually one such species outcompetes the others or assimilates them genetically."

"There are exceptions," Sulu said. "Xindus, Valakis . . ."

"Karabos II was another exception—for a time. The proto-Aulacri and the Karabosi evidently managed to last long enough to develop separate civilizations, perhaps because they resided on different continents. But eventually they came into direct contact—and, it seems, frequent conflict. The Karabosi would not tolerate our existence. Little knowledge survives from that era, but we know we were murdered, enslaved, raped. Possibly even consumed. We fought for our survival, but they were too powerful a foe. Too vicious. They warred with one another as well as with our ancestors. Perhaps some conflict between Karabosi gave the Aulacri enough time to develop spaceflight, to escape our world before the final, cataclysmic war.

"Eventually, four thousand years ago, a small band of survivors made their way to Aulac. They lost most of their technology, needed millennia to rebuild their population and recover to an advanced civilization." Skovir closed her eyes for a few moments. "Only legends of our origins survived. We thought they were myths. Only when we regained starflight and found our way to Karabos did we learn the truth."

"Then this vault we've found isn't the only evidence of the Karabosi after all," Kirk said.

"We found evidence of Aulacri. Remains of an early settlement on Karabos III, a world not unlike your Mars. Records revealing they had come from the second planet—and enough fragments about the Karabosi to corroborate our myths and let us reconstruct the rest."

Kirk tried to understand. "So that's why you're so determined to terraform Karabos II. You want to reclaim your original homeworld."

"We have a right to, don't we?"

"Of course," he replied. "But what I don't understand is why you've hidden the truth of your origins, your history. Why you didn't want Sherev to discover it."

"It's not about us, Captain Kirk. It's about the Karabosi. They were monsters. Creatures of pure cruelty and hate. They were too violent to survive, or to let others survive being near them. They did a service to the universe by wiping themselves out. If we remake the planet and erase the last vestiges of their existence, we will only be finishing what they started."

Skovir bared her sharp teeth at the look on Kirk's face. "This may seem vindictive to you, Captain. Perhaps, on some level, it is. But consider how it would feel to our people if they knew the world of our birth had been home to such genocide. It would taint it for all time."

She stepped forward. "Captain Kirk, I must remind you that you and Doctor Sherev's team are here as guests of the Aulacri. Karabos II is our territory, and all that you have found belongs to us. We will decide its disposition—and that includes your scans of the vault's contents as well as the actual materials. I hereby demand that you turn all your data over to us, and retrieve your team from the surface. You have no choice in the latter case, for the impacts will not be halted, and your team has only hours remaining before the first impactors hit."

Kirk wanted to argue further, but he knew it was pointless. Skovir was within her rights to make those demands. Regretfully, he told her, "We will do as you say."

"Good." Skovir strode for the door, but she paused, her tail curling down and around her legs. She turned back. "I don't blame you for your attitude toward this, Captain. Your desire for knowledge is admirable—it's one of the things that draws us to your Federation. But some knowledge does more harm than good. And some truths are better forgotten. Just let this go, and we can move forward as friends again."

Kirk traded a solemn look with Sulu once she had gone. They both knew that, for the sake of good relations, they had no choice. But Kirk knew Sherev would not accept it easily.

Karabos II

"No, Jim, we can't leave yet!" Sherev called into Spock's communicator, her voice raised over the sound of her team's digging. "We still have hours to go. And we're on the verge of a major discovery. There's a deeper section within the vault, and the records we've translated suggest there's something inside of great importance to the Karabosi, something fundamental to their identity as a people. Possibly some kind of genetic research, from what we can tell.

"But this mountain range wasn't quite as stable as they hoped. The inner vault is blocked by a cave-in, and we need a couple more hours to dig through. We need to keep the phaser bore on low power so we don't risk damaging anything inside."

"*It doesn't matter, Rhen,*" Kirk told her. "*Skovir is adamant. You wouldn't be allowed to share what you found anyway. She believes the legacy of the Karabosi needs to die, and we don't have the authority to override her.*"

"I just don't buy it," Sherev went on. "Something about her story just doesn't ring true."

"Indeed," Spock remarked. "Two closely related species sharing a planet for such a length of time, yet not interbreeding, seems unlikely. I believe Skovir and the Aulacri may have derived some inaccurate conclusions from the available evidence."

"*They're just not interested, Mister Spock. I sympathize with your curiosity, but your time's run out. I'm ordering both your teams to return to the* Enterprise *immediately.*"

"I'm not in Starfleet anymore, remember?" Sherev told him. "I'll send the rest of my team back with your people, but I intend to stay as long as possible."

"*Rhen, you're a Federation citizen on foreign soil, and the sovereign power has requested that we remove you. I'll have Mister Spock bring you back by force if I have to.*"

"Please try to understand, Jim! We're so close to solving this whole thing. Don't ask me to walk away before I absolutely have to."

"*Rhen, please—don't do this to me again.*" She was startled by the emotion in Kirk's voice. "*I've come close to losing you too many times because you didn't know when to stop chasing a discovery. Please, for my sake, come back to the ship.*"

She winced. *That's a low blow, Kirk.* "All right," she finally said through gritted teeth. "I'll come back."

The relief in Kirk's voice was palpable. "*Thank you, Rhen. Mister Spock—*"

"Captain," the first officer spoke up, surprising Sherev. "I request permission to remain and complete the excavation. I am able to perform the work myself, so no one else need be risked."

A moment of stunned silence. *"Mister Spock, surely you under-stand the risk as well as anyone."*

"Which is why I calculate that the odds of success are still high enough to justify the effort."

"The Aulacri don't want this knowledge."

"They may change their minds if they can be made aware of it. Though I am not yet certain what we will find, I have pro-jected several possibilities that could be transformative to the Aulacri's understanding of themselves and of the Karabosi. They have a right to hear that information, at least, before deciding what to do with it."

Kirk replied after another moment. *"While I admire your al-truism, Mister Spock, your sense of self-preservation leaves some-thing to be desired. I only just got you as a first officer—I don't want to lose you on our first mission together."*

The Vulcan raised a brow. "I do not consider it likely that you will, Captain Kirk. I have studied your record extensively. I have learned about your character from Doctor Sherev. And I have played thirty-four games of three-dimensional chess against you and won only nineteen. Therefore, logic tells me that I can rely upon you to devise a strategy for delaying the Aulacri's bom-bardment, or, failing that, succeed in retrieving me before I am killed.

"In human terms, Captain Kirk . . . you have my trust. What I request is that you trust me in turn when I say that I am capable of completing this work, and that it is important enough to be completed."

The silence from Kirk this time was the longest of all. At last: *"All right, Spock. I'll make sure you have the time you need. But send the others back."*

"All but me," Sherev said.

"Rhen . . ."

"Hey, if you trust Spock to take care of himself, you can trust him to drag me out at the last second too, right? And he'll work faster if I'm here to help. It's *logical* to let me stay too." Spock lifted an eyebrow at her, and she shrugged.

"*All right, Rhen,*" Kirk said through audibly clenched teeth. "*You just couldn't make this one easy for me, could you?*"

"If it were easy, Jim, they wouldn't have sent you," Sherev told her old friend. "Why do you think they gave you that ship in the first place . . . ?"

SACAGAWEA
2264

Fourteen

Excerpted from Sacagawea *captain's logs, March–September 2264:*

Stardate 1206.8: *Despite our best efforts, we have been unable to determine what force or entity eradicated every speck of organic matter aboard the Anggitay. With no trace of escape pods after a week of searching, I must reluctantly declare Captain Angelo Sabatini and the ninety-two members of his crew missing and presumed dead. Commander Mitchell has requested to lead the memorial service for his former crewmates.*

. . .

Stardate 1221.3: *With the Skorr ambassadorial party now safely delivered to the conference with their Aurelian cousins, we have remanded the pirates who abducted them to the nearby Ixion II penal colony. Despite the prison's past reputation, I am impressed by the humane conditions and advanced rehabilitation practices I observed during my tour, the result of reforms instituted in recent years by the noted penologist Dr. Tristan Adams. I am confident that the pirates will be treated better than they treated the ambassadors, and that Dr. Adams's enlightened techniques can cure them of their criminal tendencies.*

. . .

Stardate 1234.9: *Now that the xenylon-eating parasites have been identified and purged from the ship, all charges of uniform code violations and indecent conduct have been dropped. The crew's actions throughout this . . . revealing incident have proven that they are all a credit to the uniform, even in the absence of the uniform.*

First City, Ardana

Jim Kirk shielded his eyes from the light of the star Rasalas as he gazed up at the city in the clouds, a tight cluster of boxy marble towers and cylindrical turrets whose numerous windows reflected the red-orange sky in which they floated. The atmospheric condensation that formed around the city's base as a side effect of its antigravity engines' emanations created the illusion that it sat upon a cloud—hence its name, which the humans who had contacted Ardana had chosen to translate as either "Cloud City" or . . .

"Stratos," Kirk announced to Gary Mitchell, grinning in wonder. "Isn't it amazing? I can't wait to get up there." He and Gary stood in a plaza in First City, the older ground-level community positioned directly underneath the cloud city. The Ardanan City Dwellers preferred to regulate access to their skyborne capital in order to preserve its artistic and architectural treasures. If this were an official visit, Kirk could have beamed there directly, but as he was here on leave, he had chosen not to abuse his privileges. Ardana was still new to the Federation, contacted just a few years before and welcomed in with remarkable speed due to its mineral wealth and its artistic and cultural wonders, Stratos foremost among them. Normally there would have been a longer vetting period, but the continuing threat posed by the Klingons and other hostile powers made the Federation eager for new members, particularly those with strategic resources or locations such as Ardana. Both civilizations were still in the getting-acquainted phase with each other, and Kirk wanted to leave the Ardanans with a good impression of the Federation.

Beside him, Mitchell gave an affected yawn. "Yeah . . . a living museum full of classical art and architecture and learning opportunities. Just your sort of vacation spot, Jim."

"I let you drag me to Argelius and Wrigley's Pleasure Planet," Kirk countered. "You owe me this."

"Yeah, but the difference is, you actually had *fun* on those worlds."

"Give it a try, Gary. You might actually enjoy expanding your mind a little."

"Tell you what," the navigator replied as they moved into the line for the cylindrical teleport plinth that delivered tourists up to Stratos. "I'll try expanding my mind if you try expanding your social calendar. You have your fun on shore leave, sure enough, but you always close up again as soon as you get back to the ship. Not *everything* that happens on Wrigley's has to stay on Wrigley's, you know. Like that lieutenant, Helen Jorgensson."

"Johansson."

"See? She left an impression on you."

"Gary, it might be a big deal for you to remember a woman's name, but not me."

"My point is, you really clicked with her, but you refused to follow up on it. Keep this up, Jim, and you're in danger of becoming an old maid."

"You know how I feel, Gary. Command and romance just don't mix. Sooner or later, one of them has to suffer."

"I'm just worried you're getting too emotionally isolated, Jim. You can't be a great leader if you cut yourself off from basic human compassion."

Kirk frowned at him. "I think you're exaggerating. I get along well with the crew."

"These past few months, Jim? Not so much. You've gotten more distant since Rhen and Len left."

Have I? Kirk was taken aback. Certainly it had been disappointing to lose two of his three closest friends on the crew within four months of each other. First Rhenas Sherev had retired from Starfleet after her extensive injuries on Chenar. Then, Leonard McCoy's efforts assisting in the resettlement of the Chenari had imbued him with a desire to do more such work. After only fourteen months on the *Sacagawea*, McCoy had requested reassignment to a Starfleet Medical relief program providing care and assistance to other cultures that, for one reason or another, had become prematurely aware of alien life. Kirk had tried to convince him to stay, but McCoy had believed it was important to aid civilizations that lacked modern medicine, and that staying in touch with more traditional, hands-on medical techniques could be of great benefit to modern doctors. "I've always been just a country doctor, Jim," he'd said. Though Kirk knew that to be untrue, he'd respected his friend's wish and approved his transfer, promoting his assistant Liesa Wachs to CMO. He had consoled himself with the knowledge that he still had Gary Mitchell aboard, not to mention Eshu Adebayo, whose gentle wisdom and far-ranging experience he'd come to rely on greatly—though that was more an amiable professional relationship than the close friendship he had shared with the others.

Kirk believed he'd been coping well with the readjustment. His duty had always come first to him, so while there had been a definite pleasure in getting to carry it out alongside several good friends, he had been confident that he had maintained a positive attitude toward his command responsibilities even in the wake of Sherev's and McCoy's departures. He had thrown himself fully into his assignments over the past seven months, from the turbulent first contact with the neighboring Dachlyd and Gemarian species to the exploration of the Ma-aira Thenn ruins to the treatment of the Akwood's Syndrome outbreak on Kashdan IX. Throughout it all, his relations with the crew had remained productive, enabling them to function as an effective, well-coordinated unit and achieve all their mission objectives with minimal . . .

Kirk stopped when he realized where his thoughts were heading. Maybe Gary had a point about his emotional isolation.

Before he could pursue the thought any further, Kirk's communicator beeped. He drew it from his waist and flipped it open. "Kirk here."

"This is Ensign Chalan, sir. We've received an urgent hail from Commodore Wesley aboard the Lexington. *He needs to speak with you immediately."*

Kirk exchanged a look with Mitchell. They had almost made it to the teleport plinth. With a sigh, Kirk said, "I guess we'll have to come back and look around some other time."

Mitchell shrugged. "I think I can live with the disappointment."

U.S.S. *Sacagawea*

"Commodore Wesley," Kirk said in greeting as his former squadron commander appeared on the bridge viewscreen. "Belated congratulations on the promotion, sir. And on getting the *Lexington.* Both well-deserved."

"Thanks, Jim. I wish this were a social call." The commodore sighed. *"It's the Agni, Jim. They're back."*

Agni. The Vedic god of fire and sacrifice. The captain needed no reminder that Starfleet had provisionally assigned the name to the aliens who had attempted to invade the Adelphous and Bardeezi systems, once the *Enterprise*'s science officer had determined their N-Class origins. Kirk had been following every step of Starfleet's investigative and defensive efforts in response to the looming threat, ever aware of the likelihood that they would one day return and try again. He had hoped that when that day came, he would be called on to serve. Now, it seemed, he had gotten his wish.

"What's their destination, sir?"

"That's just the problem, Captain. They arrived some time ago."

Kirk sat forward, clutching the arms of his command chair. "Commodore?"

"You're aware that they had some means of slipping past our border defenses. We assumed they'd still need to drop out of warp outside a system, as they did at Bardeezi. We were wrong. They've found a way to maintain stealth all the way to their target planets."

Kirk traded an alarmed look with Adebayo, who stood behind his right shoulder. "How many?"

"Two N-Class planets that we know of have already been occupied. Their presence was first detected several days ago on the surface of Hearthside, the innermost planet of the Regulus system."

A sharp gasp sounded behind Kirk. He turned to the science station, where Kamisha Diaz was standing watch. She was wide-eyed with shock at the news that her home system had been invaded and occupied. But Adebayo was already moving toward her, talking softly to keep her focused. Kirk trusted him to handle it and turned back to the commodore. "Go on, sir."

"It was difficult to detect them on the surface, even in a system as busy as Regulus, because Hearthside's cloud layers are so dense. But once we knew what to scan for, we detected another Agni settlement on the N-Class third planet of 88 Leonis, some eight parsecs from Regulus. There's a Federation outpost on its fourth planet."

Kirk consulted his mental galaxy map. Rasalas, or Mu Leonis, was only about sixteen parsecs from Regulus, and not enormously far from Adelphous or Bardeezi. However, this system had no N-Class planets. "Do you think there may be other incursions we haven't found yet? Is this the start of a larger invasion?" He was grateful that the surface of Venus was too hot for liquid sulfuric acid. At least the Sol system would be safe.

"*The* Enterprise *and the* Sau Lan Wu *have been assigned to that search already, Captain. Starfleet's bringing in all available captains who have experience with the Agni. The* Lexington *is closest to 88 Leonis, so we're heading there. So I need you and the* Sacagawea *to handle Regulus.*"

Kirk was surprised but gratified to be given such a crucial assignment. Regulus had no native civilization, but it was heavily colonized by multiple species; it had been a Vulcan protectorate for generations before the Federation was founded, and had accumulated a large human population in the century since—including Ensign Diaz, who seemed to have recovered her discipline but still listened with intense concern to the commodore's every word. "What are our orders on arrival, sir?" Kirk asked.

"*Assess the situation and coordinate with the Regulan Defense Force. Deciding what to do about the Agni requires gathering more intelligence about their actions and intentions. With luck, maybe they'll be more talkative now that they've reached their intended destinations.*"

"At the very least," Adebayo suggested, "we can take more time to sort things out if we're not in pitched battle."

"*The situation on Hearthside is still fairly urgent, Commander. You see, the Regulans have built floating cities in the planet's clouds.*" Wesley stared at Kirk's reflexive laugh. "*Is something funny, Captain?*"

"Apologies, Commodore. It's just . . . I was literally about to visit the Cloud City of Stratos when you called. I guess I'll finally get to see a city in the sky after all."

"If I may, sir," Diaz spoke up, then continued when Kirk nodded. "Hearthside's aerial cities are very different from Stratos. They were built in the upper atmosphere, above the cloud layers, where the pressure and temperature match M-Class conditions—though still with an atmosphere of carbon dioxide and sulfur. A standard oxygen-nitrogen atmosphere mix is a lifting gas in that environment, so it's easy to build floating cities there, as long as you don't let the outside air in. There's a rich ecosystem of acidophilic bacteria floating up there, and the cities were built to study and harvest them. They have all sorts of chemical and pharmaceutical applications—they're a big part of the Regulan economy."

"Which makes this particularly urgent," Wesley said. *"The Agni bases on the surface have already fired projectile weapons near the floating cities that have come too close. The cities are maneuvering to keep their distance for now, but it looks like the Agni don't want them there, and we don't know how long they'll tolerate their presence. Some members of the Regulan leadership are pushing for a military strike, but we've convinced them not to risk an escalation until we know more."* He smirked. *"Which isn't easy. The Regulan Defense Force is older than Starfleet. You'll need to be at your most diplomatic with their people—whether or not you can find a way to open a diplomatic channel with the Agni."*

A part of Kirk rebelled at the thought of trying to talk with the beings that had murdered so many of his former crew. He reminded himself that his anger and pride did not outweigh the lives that could be saved if a peaceful resolution was found. "Understood, sir. We'll make best time to Regulus."

"Let's bring this one home at last, Jim. Wesley out."

Kirk stood. "Mister Mitchell, you heard the commodore. Set course for the Alpha Leonis system."

"Aye, aye, sir," Mitchell said. "From one cloud city to another."

Kirk smiled. "What are the odds?"

Once the course was set, Kirk ordered the helm officer to engage at warp six, then rotated his seat to face the science station. Catching Ensign Diaz's eye, he spoke softly. "I'll be in my ready room if you'd like to talk."

Even after more than three years on the *Sacagawea*, Kirk still made relatively little use of the vessel's ready room, preferring to remain in the thick of things on the bridge. But there were times when the privacy it offered was useful. Sure enough, it wasn't long before Kamisha Diaz took him up on his offer. Gesturing her to the couch, he took the seat opposite her. "It must be frightening," he said, "to learn your home system is under attack."

"Yes, sir. But it's more than my system. I've been to Hearthside. I know people there. One of my best friends from college lives on Laputa, the main aerial city."

"I know this is difficult for you, Ensign," Kirk said. "I've been in situations where friends were endangered too. More than anything else, I wanted to see them kept safe. But I learned over time that the best thing I could do for them was to stay objective, focus on my duty, and trust the rest of my team to fulfill their own duties." He let that sink in for a moment. "When we get to Regulus, I'm going to need to rely on you as part of my team, Ensign. Your knowledge of the system, particularly the aerial cities, will be of great help—if I can count on you to maintain your detachment."

The slim, dark young woman lowered her gaze. "I'll try my best, sir. I . . . I often try to follow your example."

Kirk's eyes widened. "My example?"

"Your discipline, sir. Your focus, your self-control. You never show fear or doubt. I hope I can . . . find it in me to do the same."

He smiled at her. "I'll let you in on a secret, Ensign. I often have fears and doubts, the same as everyone else. But I save them for when I'm off duty."

Diaz looked at him gratefully. "Any tips for how I can do the same?"

He thought it over. "It helps to have the faith of a superior officer, like Commodore Wesley. He knows me well enough to know I have my doubts sometimes, but he still has enough faith in me to entrust me with a mission as important as this one.

And that gives me faith in turn that I'm worthy of the responsibility."

He leaned in closer to the young science officer. "And I have faith in you, Ensign."

Diaz nodded gravely, understanding the message. "Aye, sir. Thank you, sir."

———

"I'm so glad you're finally going to visit Laputa! I've missed you so much, Meesh!" The image of H'Raal on Kamisha Diaz's comm display squeezed her golden eyes shut and gave a little purr of pleasure as she ran a brush through her luxuriant black mane. The brush had been a birthday present from Diaz years ago, and the ensign was touched that her friend had brought it with her to Hearthside.

Still, Diaz found the dainty Caitian's trademark insouciance even more inappropriate than usual. "I would've thought you'd be more worried, Harlie. I mean, there are alien invaders underneath you right now, firing potshots at the cities."

H'Raal gave a dismissive sneer, wrinkling the black-and-white felinoid features that had earned her the nickname "Harlequin" among her human friends. *"Aw, they're probably just baring their fangs. Showing your strength is the first step in a lot of relationships."* She chuckled, twitching her tail. *"You and I started out as bitter rivals, remember?"*

"Well . . . yeah." The two of them had both gotten into the University of Regulus V at an atypically early age, making both of them socially isolated and determined to prove their right to be there. They had latched on to each other as natural adversaries from the start. "At least . . . until I realized I needed your help to pass Exobiology."

"Which you knew because of all the times I'd walloped you—academically speaking, that is. It was how I showed you my worth."

"Hey, I got in a few good wallops too, Harlie-poo."

"You did. And that's how I knew you'd be a friend I could trust to have my back."

Diaz gave a brief smile, but her concern remained. "Nothing the Agni have done so far suggests they're interested in friendship."

"That just makes it a challenge. I mean, aren't you excited, Meesh? They're a whole new order of life, right under our paws! Oh, I can almost smell them! I want to chase them down and do science to them!" Her tail lashed with predatory fervor.

Diaz laughed, but she wasn't sure she'd envy the Agni if H'Raal got her way. The young Caitian, one of a band of settlers who had established a colony on the M-Class moon of Regulus VI over a decade back, had declined Diaz's offer to join her in Starfleet, insisting that the glory of Regulus was that there were so many different forms of life to study without roving far from home. Diaz had known from experience that H'Raal included her human friends among those subjects of study. The excessively inquisitive Caitian had inflicted a variety of playful "behavioral experiments" upon them over the course of their college career. Some had been irritating and embarrassing, tempting Diaz to enlighten H'Raal about what curiosity did to cats . . . but others had proven pleasurably enlightening for all concerned. Adopting some of H'Raal's disdain for boundaries had enabled Diaz to take chances she would never otherwise have dared to take, and had contributed to her eventual decision to apply to Starfleet while H'Raal had pursued graduate studies at the Regulus III Science Academy.

But as H'Raal's words sank in, they gave Diaz pause. "I guess you're right, Harl. It is our mission to find a diplomatic solution if we can. Who knows? Maybe you'll be the one who makes the scientific breakthrough that lets us do that."

"We will. You always were better with languages. You work

out how they talk, I'll work out how they think, and together we'll
make peace, so I can get on with studying them."

"You make it sound so easy."

"Things become easy when you make them that way. We just
have to show them they can have a home here at Regulus. That's
just how Regulans are. Look how welcome you made us feel when
we asked to settle your moon."

"But at least you asked first. And you didn't destroy our ships
first."

H'Raal dismissed her concerns with a flick of her ears.
"Maybe no one's ever made the Agni feel welcome before. Some-
body has to try."

Diaz stared in amused disbelief. "You haven't changed. You
always act like nothing's ever challenging enough to break a
sweat over."

"Caitians don't sweat, dear."

"Which wouldn't be so annoying if you didn't prove yourself
right so often." She sighed. "I hope this is one of those times."

"If your captain's as great as you keep telling me, it will be. Oh,
I hope I get to meet him. Is he really as sexy as they say?"

"Harlie!"

Regulus was three days from Ardana at the *Sacagawea*'s top
sustainable speed. Kirk repeatedly pressured Engineer Desai
to extract more speed from the scout vessel's single nacelle, but
despite the *Hermes* class's mythical namesake, it couldn't quite
match the speeds that the ships of the *Constitution* class could
achieve these days, after the various upgrades they had undergone in recent years. "If only Starfleet considered this class as
important to upgrade," Kirk muttered to Eshu Adebayo as they
strode toward the exit of the vessel's compact engine room following another futile meeting with Desai.

"Hey, don't let the old girl hear you say that," Adebayo said, patting the bulkhead as if to reassure the ship. "She's served us well."

"I know, I know," Kirk said, abashed at his disloyalty. "Don't get me wrong—nothing compares to your first command. I'll always cherish her. But . . ." He trailed off.

The wise old first officer missed little. "But you don't intend to stay on a scout ship forever. I thought I noticed a twinge of envy when you heard Bob Wesley had gotten the *Lexington*."

"Is it so surprising that I'd want to command a *Constitution*-class ship one day?" Kirk asked as they exited into the corridor. He spoke softly so as not to be overheard by passing crew. "It's not just their reputation, or their power—my first ship out of the Academy was one, the *Farragut*, and so were my last two ships before this one. Most of my career has been spent aboard those ships. So many of my friendships, my accomplishments, my growth as an officer and a man have been connected to those ships. I feel at home on them."

"Understandable, yes," Adebayo said. "Likely? That's another matter. There are only about a dozen *Constitution*s—all with captains who have considerably more years of experience behind them than you've gained so far."

"Believe me, Eshu, I know. And I'm willing to do the work to get there, however long it takes. It's just . . . sometimes the goal just seems so far away."

Adebayo chuckled. "Look at me. Nearly fifty years in Starfleet and I'm a first officer responsible for fewer than two hundred people. And I'm happy with that, Jim. I've experienced so much joy and wonder along the way. Much pain and loss too, but those are just as much a part of the full experience of living. I've been fulfilled in my career because I'm in it for the journey, not the destination. I've always tried to cherish each experience as it comes, rather than miss out on what's happening right in front of me because I'm racing past it toward some future goal I might never reach." He patted Kirk on the shoulder. "Look for the value in today, Jim. It's what we do today that decides our tomorrows."

Kirk appreciated his first officer's wisdom, as always. But this particular bit of advice might have gone over better if their situation hadn't called for greater speed.

Or maybe this was one piece of advice that Kirk just didn't want to take.

Fifteen

When the dying component of the Regulus A binary cast off its atmosphere, leaving a white dwarf corpse behind, its companion swallowed much of the expelled hydrogen and swelled into a much hotter blue giant, vaporizing the system's innermost planets yet warming several of the outer worlds to habitable temperatures. The resultant rapid ecological shifts created pressures that accelerated the pace of evolution on those worlds, allowing complex, diverse forms of life to emerge unusually early in the system's history. Regulans take this as a reminder that life thrives on unexpected challenges.

—Vaacith sh'Lesinas, *The Federation and Back*

Laputa, Hearthside (Regulus I)
Upon the *Sacagawea*'s arrival in the Regulus system, Kirk made contact with the Central Council on Regulus III, but the councillors requested that he head directly to Hearthside in order to coordinate with the Regulan Defense Force detachment that was already on the scene, along with Councillor T'Zeri, the administrator responsible for the system's two innermost worlds. According to the Council, the Agni had fired several more warning shots near the aerial cities in the preceding few days, but had not taken any more aggressive actions. Still, the councillors pleaded with Kirk to resolve the matter swiftly, reminding

him that lives on multiple planets and moons were potentially endangered by this quiet invasion.

The Regulans Kirk had met, including Ensign Diaz, somewhat reminded him of the inhabitants of Vega Colony—at once proud and insecure about their homeworlds, as if aware of how tenuous their existence was around such inhospitable stars. Thirty millennia ago, an advanced civilization known as the Veliki had used Regulus as a living laboratory for the genetic engineering of ultraviolet-resistant life-forms—from the pale, sluglike bloodworms that eked out a subterranean existence on the dry, scalding second planet to the iridescent, mirror-feathered birds of the lushly forested fifth planet. When a rogue Veliki faction had begun to pursue eugenics for power and conquest, much as the Augments of Earth and the Suliban Cabal would later do, their resultant assaults on neighboring star systems had discredited the Regulus experiment, and the rest of the Veliki had abandoned the system and vanished into galactic history. Other races had resettled the system since then, even before the Vulcans came and made it a protectorate of their High Command. Today, Regulus was a significant Federation member with over a billion inhabitants—primarily of UV-tolerant species like Vulcans, Chelons, and Arodi, but including a sizable human population as well, for humans had never let an environment's inhospitable conditions deter them from settling it anyway.

The aerial cities of Regulus I—Hearthside—were a case in point: delicate pockets of habitable atmosphere drifting through clouds of sulfuric acid, dozens of kilometers above a surface whose heat, pressure, and corrosive conditions would kill any humanoid in an instant and ruin a shuttlecraft within minutes. *Not so delicate*, Kirk reminded himself as he materialized in the transporter station of Laputa, the administrative capital of the planet. He knew that the cities were built with multiple safety features and redundancies, including deflector shields to supplement their acid-resistant outer shells.

The transporter station was within one of the upper spherical modules of Laputa—as Kirk could see clearly, for the station was designed so that the first thing new arrivals saw was the large window granting a panoramic view of the city outside. Dozens of spheres, each about fifty meters across, were linked together in a hex pattern, mostly in a single layer but with several scattered clusters nested above it—and probably below it as well. All in all, the city somewhat reminded Kirk of a gigantic bunch of grapes.

Beyond and below the city, the clouds of Hearthside stretched to the horizon in all directions, their sulfurous yellow-brown hue bleached by the actinic blue-white glare of the double sun looming overhead, a glare damped to tolerable levels by the window's filtering. If he looked closely, Kirk imagined he could see diffuse dark streaks in the clouds, perhaps created by the massive blooms of aerial bacteria that these cities existed to harvest. But he might just be seeing what he expected to see.

Finding that out would have to wait, though, for several Regulans were approaching the transporter pad. The *Sacagawea* captain led his party down to greet the officials. At the head of the group was a tall, bald, tan-skinned human who extended his hand. "Captain Kirk? Welcome. I'm Khalil Farouz, city administrator of Laputa. Allow me to introduce Councillor T'Zeri, who represents our part of the system on the Central Council." He gestured to a mature, slender Vulcan woman whose gray-frosted black hair was twisted into an elaborate bun. She offered a gracious nod of her head in response to Kirk's greeting.

"And this," Farouz went on, gesturing to a strongly built, ruddy-skinned woman with close-shorn silver-blond hair, "is Colonel Yelena Orloff of the Regulan Defense Force."

Orloff gave a curt greeting. "Captain."

"Pleased to meet you all," Kirk said. He gestured to the officers accompanying him. "This is my first officer, Commander Eshu Adebayo; my security chief, Lieutenant Joshua Hauraki;

and Ensign Kamisha Diaz, my science officer, who hails from Regulus V."

"Well, then, welcome home, Ensign," Farouz said. "Or nearly so. Have you had occasion to visit Hearthside before?"

"Yes, I have, Administrator," Diaz replied, "though this is my first time in Laputa."

The niceties dispensed with, Farouz turned back to Kirk. "If you'll accompany us to the conference room, please?"

As the party moved through the high, curving corridors of the city spheres and the wide, cylindrical airlocks that connected them to one another, Kirk was struck by the abundance of windows and the relative thinness of the walls that encased them. "I would have expected these cities to have sturdier construction," he remarked, "to keep out the toxic atmosphere."

"It is not necessary," Councillor T'Zeri explained in polite tones. "The exterior atmospheric pressure at this altitude is equal to the interior pressure. It is the lower density of an oxygen-nitrogen atmosphere compared to carbon dioxide that gives us buoyancy. Thus, the walls need be no stronger than standard construction, and the use of lightweight materials reduces the need for additional flotation sacs or antigravs. All that is required is to maintain an airtight seal."

The brief tour was intriguing, but once the group reached the conference room, Colonel Orloff got straight to business. "We've had no luck establishing any communication with these so-called Agni, and little luck improving our sensor scans of their surface outposts. We're facing an invading force that we have very little intelligence about. Captain, we need to know everything you can tell us about them from Starfleet's previous encounters."

"I'm afraid I can add comparatively little to what you already know," Kirk said. "They've shown no interest in communication, so their motives in occupying N-Class planets in Federation space are not yet known. But they have no concern for humanoid life or even our presence. They treat us as a nuisance, to be ignored if possible, destroyed if necessary." He turned to Diaz. "Ensign?"

"Yes, Captain." The young science officer picked up with her prepared presentation, projecting image captures and sensor schematics onto the conference room's holographic display. "Their technology is advanced, though alien in its materials and methods, since most of the metals and synthetics we use would dissolve quickly in their environment. That means their vessels, and no doubt their ground facilities, are extremely robust and hard to damage.

"Rather than using matter-antimatter, they have somehow managed to create artificial microsingularities, which generate energy when matter is injected into them and becomes super-heated in the accretion disk, creating an energetic plasma not unlike what we use in warp engines. These singularities power an advanced magnetic tractor-field system that, while not func-tioning as a deflector shield in its own right, is used in concert with a flux-pinned halo of ablative armor plates to create a point defense system that works almost as well as deflectors, and can also become a weapon by propelling the heavy armor plates at ballistic speeds, causing damage comparable to a meteoroid impact. The plates can also surround a starship and use their mutual attraction to compress around it, crushing it.

"Additionally, the singularities' plasma can be concentrated into a pinpoint beam of enormous destructive power. A single shot can overwhelm a heavy cruiser's shields and . . . punch a hole clear through the vessel." Diaz took a shaky breath, trying to maintain her detachment as sensor footage recorded by the *U.S.S. Enterprise* showed the near-destruction of the *Kongo*. Kirk forced himself to look, as he had so many times before. He would not forget Mehran Egdor's sacrifice. "The good news," Diaz went on, "is that it depletes their plasma supply and re-quires four to six minutes to recharge."

"That's terrifying," Farouz said. "But if they have that kind of weaponry . . ." He hesitated and glanced downward, as if afraid of being overheard. "Why haven't they used it on us? They've flung a few small projectiles past our cities as warnings, but they haven't tried blasting or crushing us."

"The other good news is that they probably can't use the singularity beam from the surface," Diaz said. "The superheating of the dense atmosphere down there would cause a titanic explosion, like a high-yield photon torpedo. They'd immolate themselves if they tried it."

"Thank Allah for small mercies."

T'Zeri quirked an eyebrow at the administrator. "Rather, thank the physical laws of the universe."

Farouz winked back. "Same thing."

"As for the armor plates," Diaz went on, "it's harder to say. It could be that Hearthside's atmosphere and magnetic field are too disruptive to their tractor field."

"There's another possibility," Eshu Adebayo remarked. "Maybe they don't want to destroy us if they don't have to. We've seen before that they're perfectly content to ignore us; they only retaliate when we try to stop them from getting where they're going. Now that they've gotten there, maybe they simply want to ensure that we keep our distance and leave them alone."

Yelena Orloff leaned forward, without seeming any less erect. "The cities have made no provocative moves toward them beyond simply drifting overhead. Yet they have fired their projectiles dangerously close, and getting closer day by day. The message is clear: they want us to abandon the planet altogether."

"Which is out of the question," Farouz said. "Regulus's chemical and pharmaceutical industries are too reliant on the bacteria we harvest. Not to mention that these are our homes. My family has been born and raised here for two generations. Our cities may not be moored down, but we have roots on this planet, Captain."

"Of course," Kirk said. "We may not have a good understanding of the Agni yet, but we'll do everything we can to find a way to remove them from Hearthside."

T'Zeri folded her hands before her. "Given the opportunity, my preference would be to devise a means of communication with the Agni. If there is a way to achieve peaceful coexistence with this species, it is in our interest to pursue it. The scientific and practical benefits of contact with a novel form of life with unique technology are vast. And Regulus has always benefitted from the influx of new immigrants, from humans and Chelons in the early years of the Federation to our most recent addition, the Caitians."

"The Caitians came openly, Councillor," said Orloff, her tone sharpening. "Had they attempted to sneak in and occupy the moon by stealth, had they threatened the existing outposts there with expulsion, we would have called them invaders and repelled them accordingly."

"Yet at least we could have communicated with them, so that we and they would both have been clear on one another's intentions. The ability to communicate clearly with an antagonist can be as essential in conflict as in diplomacy. Either way, devising a translation matrix should be our priority."

Kirk looked at her. "Has there been anything to translate? Have you been able to intercept any of their communications?"

"Some faint subspace signals," Orloff replied, "on a deep band, hard to detect or track. But the majority of them appear to have been aimed at 88 Leonis."

Diaz stared. "You think they're communicating with their other settlement?"

"Stands to reason. And the other signals might suggest the presence of more footholds we haven't detected yet. We've reported our findings to Commodore Wesley."

The ensign turned to Kirk. "Captain, this is our first linguistic data on the Agni. With your permission, I'd like to work with

Chalan on a translation matrix. I have a xenobiologist friend here in the city, H'Raal, who I know would be glad to work with us on this."

"A team at the Science Academy is working on interpreting the signals as well," T'Zeri said. "I am certain they would be willing to coordinate with your people, Captain Kirk."

"That seems a reasonable place to start," Kirk said. As much as the replayed image of the *Kongo* had reawakened his anger toward the Agni, he reminded himself of Wesley's orders to find a diplomatic option if at all possible. "Ensign, why don't you contact your—"

The room shuddered. An alarm sounded, and a hail came in for Farouz. *"Administrator! We're under attack from below!"*

"I'll be right there," the administrator replied. He rose, inviting the others to follow.

Laputa's control center was only a short distance from the conference room, so they arrived in mere moments. The central holographic display of the city showed several spherical modules flashing red. A lean Vulcan male turned to address Farouz and Orloff. "We have been struck by a projectile from the surface. It was swift and massive enough to overwhelm our protective shields."

"Makes sense," Diaz muttered to Kirk. "The shields are only meant to keep out clouds."

"The projectile struck at a forty-three-degree angle from horizontal," the Vulcan reported, gesturing to a red line that passed clear through the city graphic. "It penetrated entirely through an auxiliary flotation sphere and Hydroponics Sphere Three above it. Upon exit, it struck and ruptured the hull of the adjoining water processing plant."

"Thrusters," Farouz ordered. "Move us away from whatever's firing on us."

"They are not in the immediate vicinity, sir. Apparently their range of control for their projectiles is greater than we believed."

"No casualties reported," a human technician announced, "but there are several dozen people in the upper two spheres."

"We need to get them out fast," Kirk said, reaching for his communicator. "The atmosphere—"

"The equal pressure means there is relatively little external atmosphere penetration, Captain Kirk," the Vulcan technician said. "We are already increasing internal pressure to slow it further. There should be ample time to evacuate."

"If they don't strike us again," Orloff said, drawing her own communicator. "Orloff to *Venant*. Laputa is taking Agni fire from the surface. Identify the source and neutralize it."

After her crew acknowledged the order, Kirk caught her eye. "Can your phasers penetrate an atmosphere this dense?"

"We'll find out. However, if you wanted to add Starfleet phasers to the attempt . . ."

"Say no more." Kirk contacted the *Sacagawea* and ordered Mitchell to back up the Defense Force ships.

"Another projectile incoming!" a bulky Chelon technician called. Kirk barely had time to brace himself before the deck heaved. He reached for Diaz as she stumbled, but Lieutenant Hauraki caught her first, and she smiled up at the security chief in appreciation.

"That was close," Hauraki said. As if to reinforce his words, the power in the control room fluctuated, the displays flickering in and out.

Orloff scanned the intermittent hologram. "They've damaged our power plant, and nicked the edge of a manufacturing sphere. Took out another flotation sphere too. They're targeting our infrastructure, the things that keep the city afloat and functional."

Adebayo furrowed his brow as he studied the readouts. "It's a mercy their targets are relatively unpopulated. Two spheres holding only helium, several industrial facilities, and a farm."

"Probably luck rather than mercy, Commander," the colonel countered.

"Looks like these projectiles are narrower than the ones they use in space," Kirk said. "Probably more missile-shaped, to get through this dense air. That reduces the size of the holes they make, at least."

"But it lets them hit faster," Diaz said, "and penetrate clear through the city."

Kirk's communicator beeped. *"Mitchell here, sir. No luck with phasers. The atmosphere absorbs most of the energy. Desai's trying to retune them to pass through cee-oh-two, but we can't even be sure we're aiming right in that muck. Even if we are, I'd bet they have some version of that shield plate barrier."*

The captain turned to Diaz. "Are photon torpedoes an option?"

"I wouldn't recommend it, sir. In this atmosphere, the blast and EMP effects would be hugely amplified. It could endanger the cities."

"Captain," came Mitchell's voice. *"They tried lobbing a third projectile at you, but the* Venant *managed to shoot it down. We'll do what we can to run interference, but you might want to get out of there."*

Kirk turned to Farouz, who had been consulting with his technicians. "I recommend we evacuate the civilians."

"That will be difficult, Captain Kirk," the administrator said. "The damage to our power and control systems has knocked out our transporters."

Adebayo sighed. "The transporters are always the first to go."

"Besides, we don't know what other cities might come under attack from the surface," Orloff put in. "We'd have to beam them up to the ships."

Farouz frowned. "You have, what, six ships in orbit, plus the *Sacagawea*? How many evacuees could they hold? A few dozen each, a hundred?"

"It'll have to do, Administrator. I recommend prioritizing children, caregivers, the sick and elderly. We'll need able-bodied hands to assist in vacating and patching breached modules."

"Very well." Farouz turned back to Kirk. "Once that's under-way, our priority will be repairing the breaches to the power plant and hydroponics module. Even with raised pressure, the acid clouds leaking in will begin doing serious damage before long."

"My people will assist with that," Kirk said. He turned to Or-loff. "Colonel, your gunners on the *Venant* seem quite skilled, so I'd like to bring the *Sacagawea* back to assist with the evacu-ation."

Orloff appeared pleased by his praise for her crew. "That would be appreciated, Captain."

Kirk turned to Hauraki and Diaz. "You two, head to the power plant, assist however you can." Once they had acknowl-edged and left, he turned to Farouz. "I'd be happy to assist in hydroponics." He knew it would be quite different from the farm he'd grown up on, but maybe his experience could help somehow.

"Thank you, Captain. Every extra hand will help."

"Commander Adebayo will remain here to coordinate." The first officer acknowledged his implicit order with a nod. Kirk checked the map display one last time to get his bearings and headed out.

———

Kirk was given a filter mask, goggles, and gloves before enter-ing the hydroponics sphere, for a fair amount of carbon dioxide and sulfuric acid mist had begun to mix with the interior at-mosphere despite the positive pressure to limit its entry. Once inside, he saw that the interior of the stadium-sized sphere was partitioned into multiple large greenhouses with wide aisles between them. It appeared that most of the greenhouses had already sealed themselves off to protect the crops within, a built-in precaution against just this sort of crisis. But there was a gaping hole torn through the deck and canopy of one of the greenhouses, and a matching hole in the mostly clear, domed roof on the other side of the sphere, for the projectile had gone through at an angle. Debris from the damaged greenhouse and roof had breached several other greenhouses, and the hydroponics crew was already rushing to patch the holes. All the sprinklers were on and farmers were waving hoses to spray water into the air, no doubt to capture and dilute the acidic mist.

"Oh, good, you're here." The repair team with Kirk was greeted by a compact reptilian humanoid, whom Kirk recognized as one of the Arodi, a species that had settled the Regulus system millennia before the Vulcans had come. "We've almost got the lower breach in hand. We're using a fallen greenhouse wall as a temporary patch, just need to seal it. Getting to the upper breach is more of a challenge. The missile took out some of the catwalks."

"We have the means to deal with it," said Verrek, the burly, copper-haired Vulcan man who led the repair team. He took in Kirk and the others with his green-eyed gaze. "Come."

Verrek instructed the team to split into two groups, with Kirk accompanying his group as they used the overhead catwalks to approach the breach from both directions, as near as they could safely reach, for a portion of the catwalk just under the breach had been knocked out as well. Once they reached the damaged portion, one of the repair team members took a few moments to secure the loosened bolts on the damaged catwalk section, ensuring that the team could safely move out onto it. Kirk saw the other team doing the same on the far side of the breach. While he waited, he turned to examine the six-meter-wide breach in the transparent roof section, astonished to think that there was nothing between him and the atmosphere of a Venus-like world except a filter mask and goggles. Granted, it was the comparatively thin reaches of the upper atmosphere, but it was still impressive to contemplate.

Once the teams advanced onto the catwalks, they worked

together to extend a temporary bridge across the gap, allowing the tethered workers to move out beneath the breach and position flexible, acid-resistant polyvinyl sheets over the gap. Kirk assisted in rigging and securing the workers' lines, amused that his climbing experience had proven more useful than his farming experience. He quickly realized, though, that he would have to unlearn his Starfleet experience. He was used to dealing with hull breaches in the vacuum of space, where a flexible, partial patch like this would be sucked out in an instant, but anything more rigid would be held firmly in place by the internal pressure. He decided that he should think of it like patching a breach in a section already evacuated of its air, with no pressure differential to speak of. It made the patching sheets easier to move into place but required more work to seal them off at the edges. Although in this case, there was the added complication of the water mist being sprayed on everything, making it harder to adhere the patches to the roof. Once a reasonable seal was in place, though, the positive pressure was able to take hold and keep the patch secure, as Kirk could tell when his ears began to pop.

Just as the team was beginning to descend from the catwalk, an alert came in. *"Another projectile incoming!"* came the call from the control room. *"Everyone brace yourselves!"*

There was barely time for Kirk to grab the railing before Laputa heaved again. Verrek was not so lucky. The catwalk section beneath him buckled and tipped him off—and he had already detached his tether. Kirk lunged at him and grabbed his arm, catching him in the nick of time. The Vulcan's weight slammed him painfully against the catwalk and dragged him forward. The impact knocked Kirk's mask and goggles loose. Desperately, he grabbed at a stanchion with his other hand and thrust his foot out to hook around the far edge of the catwalk. Between the two, he was able to halt his descent, but Verrek's weight felt like it would wrench his shoulder from its socket.

Verrek took a deep breath and looked down and around,

assessing his situation. "I recommend you release me, Captain Kirk. I can control my fall and reduce the degree of injury I will sustain."

"Is that . . . logical?" Kirk asked. "You can . . . do more good for Laputa . . . if you're in one piece."

"And you will do more good for all of Regulus if you remain intact. Logically, the needs of the many . . ."

"Save your breath and hang on!" Kirk looked around, seeking an alternative. He spotted another level of the catwalk a few meters down and inward of them. Some team members already stood there, watching in concern. "There, behind you," Kirk said, directing Verrek's attention to it. "If I swing you, build up enough momentum, you can land safely there. Your team will catch you."

"That will materially increase the risk that you will fall, Captain."

"Risk can be managed by skill!" Kirk told him. "I know what I'm capable of as much as you do."

Verrek held his gaze for a moment. Kirk's eyes stung from some residual acid mist, but he fought to keep them open regardless. "Very well."

Making sure his feet were securely hooked, Kirk released the stanchion and took Verrek's arm in both hands. He began to swing the Vulcan, who then started to amplify his swing with his legs once he got the rhythm. "All right," Kirk said. "Counting down . . . three . . . two . . . one . . . *now!*"

He and Verrek both let go, and the Vulcan fell at an angle. He nearly missed the lower catwalk after all, but he came close enough for his team to catch him and pull him over the rail. A moment later, another team member reached Kirk and helped him to his feet.

As soon as he was back on level ground, Kirk drew his communicator. "Kirk to control room. What's the latest damage?"

"*Adebayo here, Captain. The missile struck a pair of bacte-*

rial processing spheres on the edge of the city, right where they connect. The outer one is now only attached to one other sphere, and the impact has twisted that connection. There are still over twenty people trapped in there, but the ships in orbit have already beamed up all they can hold for now. They're trying to drop off evacuees at other cities, but it'll take time."

"Understood." He closed the lid and turned to Verrek, who had gotten an equivalent report on his own comlink. "Let's go."

On her way to the power plant with Lieutenant Hauraki, Kamisha Diaz came across a very familiar, furry face. "Meesh!" H'Raal cried, pouncing on Diaz and pulling her into a tight, twirling hug. "I knew I'd find you where there was trouble!"

"Harl, you shouldn't be here," Diaz said. "You should evacuate with the rest of the nonessential personnel."

"And miss my reunion with my dear old friend? Don't be silly. And I'm going to pretend I didn't hear you call me nonessential." The black-and-white Caitian bounded off toward the power plant, her white-tufted tail swishing behind her. Diaz and Hauraki exchanged a shrug and headed off in her wake.

Once at the power plant, Diaz was roped into helping to reroute power away from one of the damaged distribution manifolds adjacent to the gaping hole that had been torn through the plant, while Hauraki and H'Raal helped evacuate the last few people who hadn't been beamed out. The influx of carbon dioxide from outside was actually beneficial here, for it helped prevent the loose, sparking power cables from setting anything on fire until they could be shut down.

No sooner had the group completed the evacuation than the city rocked from another impact. Hauraki soon found out about the damage to the bacterial processing sphere and led Diaz to assist, with H'Raal still insisting on accompanying them. "Come on, I know a shortcut!"

When the trio arrived outside the damaged sphere, they found that the entrance hatch was jammed partway open. The hatch frame was warped, as the entire sphere had twisted as a result of the impact. The interfaces between spheres were designed to be flexible to absorb the stresses of the strong high-altitude winds, but the sudden wrenching imparted by the projectile impact had been more than this one was designed to absorb. The bulkheads groaned under the torsional stresses as the loosened sphere swayed in the wind.

"Are you there?" a voice called from inside the hatch. "We need help!" Diaz ducked down to peer through the lopsided hatch opening. A bulky Chelon was on the other side, struggling to pull the door wider with no evident success. "This section's still airtight, but there are others stuck in a room back there—debris blocking the door. It's too heavy for me to move alone. Can any of you get through?"

Hauraki stepped forward and attempted to squeeze through the gap, but his large frame made it impossible. H'Raal hissed and tied her mane back into a compact bun. "All right, stand aside, Muscles. We'll handle this." She slipped through the gap and under the Chelon's arm with ease, seeming to flow through like a liquid. Diaz couldn't quite manage the same, but her slim build let her squeeze through once the Chelon gave her room.

"Go on," Hauraki said. "There are others coming—we'll get the door open from out here."

Another groan sounded, and Diaz felt the deck shift beneath her feet. "Hurry," she told her crewmate.

"You too."

Diaz ran to catch up with H'Raal, while the Chelon—who introduced herself as Chivithan—jogged after them at her best speed. H'Raal threw a glance back at Hauraki while they ran. "He's cute, for an ape. You had him yet?"

"Harlie!"

"What? I can literally smell the lust between you two. And life is short."

The deck swayed again. "I sincerely hope not."

A moment later, they arrived at the blocked doorway and got to work. Fortunately, it proved to be a matter of leverage—once Diaz and H'Raal put their full weight on one end of a heavy beam, Chivithan was just able to push its other end up and over an obstruction in the debris pile and swing it out, letting it fall to the deck. With that linchpin piece removed, the trio outside and the others trapped inside were able to move enough other chunks of debris for the room's occupants to get out.

At first, the trapped workers crowded the exit, creating a jam. But H'Raal spoke to them with her usual breezy confidence that every situation she faced was simplicity itself to overcome. "No problem, all, just make a line, one by one. There you are. See how easy that is? Now go to your left. Never mind the swaying and groaning, it's just a little wind. I sway and groan too after a long night."

Chivithan helped escort her coworkers to the exit, where Diaz could see that Hauraki and a repair team had managed to force the hatch open enough for even a Chelon to squeeze through—although the floor of their sphere was now visibly at a different angle than this one, and slightly upslope on what had been a level deck minutes before. She realized that enough outer atmosphere must have leaked in for the sphere to be losing its buoyancy. "Harlie, we'd better move."

"We're fine," H'Raal said as she helped the last worker over the debris. "See? Plenty of time. So let's go fast," she finished over the increasing groaning sounds around them.

When they were mere meters from the door, right behind the last evacuee, the module sagged sharply and the bulkhead material around the hatchway began to split open on top. Diaz stumbled, then coughed, her eyes stinging and tearing. The man in front of her was also coughing, sinking to his hands and knees. Diaz and H'Raal helped him up and into the hands of the rescuers on the other side. Diaz saw Captain Kirk standing beside Joshua Hauraki, catching her gaze, urging her forward. He and Hauraki reached out to her, and she reached back.

But just before she could take their hands, the deck tilted more sharply and she stumbled back. H'Raal caught her but was unbalanced by her weight. Both women fell to the deck, H'Raal on her back, Diaz facing her on hands and knees. H'raal's huge golden eyes locked on hers.

What happened next was almost too fast for Diaz to process. H'Raal nuzzled her quickly and gasped, "Love you, Meesh." Then she drew back her powerful legs and thrust them into Diaz's midriff, pushing her back into Kirk's and Hauraki's clutches.

The men pulled her back . . .

The bulkheads groaned and shrieked as the sphere tore free . . .

Harlie grinned up at Diaz as if she were about to go on the ride of her life . . .

And she was gone.

Sixteen

Maybe you're a soldier so often that you forget you're also trained to be a diplomat.

—Leonard McCoy

U.S.S. Sacagawea

After the processing sphere had broken loose from Laputa and sunk into the clouds, the Agni had stopped their attack. The reason for this was unclear, but it came as a relief to the city's occupants, the Regulan officials, and Kirk's crew. It gave them a chance to repair the city, offload or return evacuees, tend to the wounded . . . and mourn the dead. In addition to Kamisha Diaz's Caitian friend who had died before Kirk's eyes, a dozen other Laputans had perished, either from the direct projectile impacts, the turbulence and structural collapses they had caused, or exposure to the toxic atmosphere. Over eighty more had been injured or poisoned. Both Diaz and Hauraki had suffered minor pulmonary and optic damage from their brief exposure to the atmosphere, but Dr. Wachs had treated them as efficiently as McCoy would have, albeit with less grumbling along the way. There was little the doctor could do about Diaz's grief and guilt at the loss of her friend.

Still, there was no telling how long this lull would last without knowing what motivated it. "Maybe we did some damage to their ground facilities after all," Gary Mitchell proposed to

Kirk and Adebayo as they gathered in the briefing room with Hauraki to review the incident.

Adebayo looked unconvinced. "Or maybe the Agni simply felt their point was made. They could have easily destroyed the whole city, caused massive loss of life, but instead they did little more than infrastructure damage, with surprisingly few casualties."

"No amount of casualties is few enough," Kirk countered.

"Even we aren't always capable of avoiding casualties, no matter how surgical we try to make our strikes."

"You think this was meant to be just a warning, Commander?" Hauraki asked.

Adebayo spread his hands uncertainly. "I think it's significant that they did no more than fire warning shots until we arrived— a starship that had fought them before. Surely their sensors told them that we had beamed down to the city; even if they lack the technology themselves, they could have scanned the energy exchange and detected the increase in the city's population. After all, their sensors must be far better than ours to see through that soup of an atmosphere."

"You're saying our arrival provoked them?" Kirk asked, displeased by the suggestion.

"Ever since our first encounter, the Agni have not attacked until the situation escalated. We warn them off, they simply ignore us. We threaten them with force, and then they fight. Until now, the Agni and Regulans have been in a standoff, merely watching each other. Our arrival may have seemed like an escalation. So they made their position known. They're warning us to leave the planet."

"Us?" Mitchell asked. "As in Starfleet? Or as in the aerial cities?"

"Since they were firing warnings at the cities before we arrived, most likely the latter. They've claimed the planet and are warning us to leave."

Kirk frowned at his first officer. "On the surface or in the air, the Regulans have a prior claim to the planet. The Agni are the squatters here, the invaders. And not only here. There's no telling how many worlds they've already occupied."

"I doubt it's that many," Adebayo said. "It just strikes me that each of their incursions into Federation space has been smaller, more subtle. First nine ships came openly, and several were damaged in the fight. Then five ships tried to sneak past our defenses, and more were damaged. Now, an unknown number of ships have successfully snuck in and tried to stay hidden beneath the clouds. Only when we discovered them did they begin to threaten us." He shook his head. "This does not feel like an act of aggression or conquest to me. It feels more like need. Like they lose more and more each time, yet are compelled to keep trying."

"If they needed something from us," Kirk replied sternly, "they could have asked. Instead, they intruded on our territory and took what they wanted."

"Took something we have absolutely no use for. If we had known their intended destinations from the start, all of this could have been avoided."

"*If* they had asked. They didn't. Which means we can't be sure their intent is merely to settle the N-Class planets."

"Maybe they didn't know how to communicate with us any more than the reverse."

"Or they just didn't want to. They've ignored us, then shot at us, that's all. If we want them to talk to us, we need to make it clear to them that they have no other choice."

"You mean retaliate, Jim? Show our strength by attacking their surface outposts?"

"They have to be shown they can't get away with killing Federation citizens. To understand the value we place on sentient lives, they have to know there's a cost for taking them."

Adebayo sighed, but he could clearly tell Kirk's mind was

made up. "Even so, it won't be easy to do them damage without endangering the cities. Those people down on Hearthside are essentially the Agni's hostages. The high ground is not an advantage here."

Kirk rose. "For that, we need to bring Colonel Orloff and her people into the loop. This is their system; maybe they have ideas we haven't thought of. I'll contact the colonel and coordinate. Dismissed."

Kirk strode out, noting that Adebayo remained in his seat while the others left, seemingly lost in thought. Kirk left him to it, hoping that he would come to his senses in time.

RDF *Venant* RGC-302

Yelena Orloff was there to greet Kirk when he materialized in the transporter room of the *Venant*. "Thank you for coming, Captain," the short-haired colonel said after welcoming him aboard. "I'm grateful for the assistance your crew provided in defending against the Agni attack. I hope I can rely on you when we take the fight to them."

Kirk studied her. "We'll do whatever we must to defend the system, Colonel."

Orloff seemed satisfied by his answer. Before taking him to the conference room, she gave him a quick tour of the *Venant*, an old but well-maintained midsized cruiser named for the classical Persian designation of Regulus. In peacetime, the Regulus Defense Force had little need for its battleships, since Starfleet defended the system from outside threats; but Orloff took pride in her crew's readiness and discipline.

Kirk and Orloff were met in the vessel's compact conference room by Councillor T'Zeri. The comm display was active, linking to the main council chamber on Regulus III and to T'Zeri's fellow councillors—a Vulcan male, a human female, a Caitian male, and an Arodi (the species was monogendered). The Vulcan, Council President Sentok, asked, *"Colonel Orloff, Captain Kirk, do you believe the cities will be attacked again?"*

"It's only a matter of time, Mister President," Orloff said. "We managed to shut down their attack with a robust defense, but it's clear they want us gone from Hearthside, and the cities are under threat as long as they remain beneath us. I recommend a strike on the surface before they can regroup and devise another means of attack."

"The atmosphere creates a considerable obstacle to our attacks, Colonel," said T'Zeri. "How do you propose we damage the Agni without endangering our cities?"

"With the assistance of Captain Kirk's crew, we've had some luck retuning our phasers to penetrate deeper into the atmosphere. We also have a reserve supply of spatial torpedoes that could be equipped with conventional explosives." She set her jaw. "There is an additional option. Given that the Agni's biology is dependent on sulfuric acid just as ours depends on water, it stands to reason that alkaline compounds such as sodium hydroxide or calcium carbonate would be toxic to them."

Kirk stared. "Colonel, are you suggesting we resort to chemical warfare?"

The ruddy-faced woman smirked. "If it helps, think of it as giving the planet an antacid."

The suggestion appeared to ruffle T'Zeri's Vulcan calm. "You trivialize a drastic suggestion. At this point, the loss of life, while regrettable, is limited. It is not Federation policy to escalate a conflict preemptively."

"We have been invaded, Councillor," Orloff insisted. "Our own soil occupied by creatures seeking to expel or destroy us. We are entitled to stand our ground, whatever it takes."

"Colonel," Kirk said, "for what it's worth, we can't be certain yet of the Agni's motives. They did take care to target largely empty regions of the city. And they may have stopped of their own volition once they'd communicated their intentions."

"They targeted critical infrastructure, systems whose failure would endanger the *entire* population of the city, regardless of the immediate death toll. Their intention is to remove us from one of our own planets. If we let them do that, how long before they decide we're not welcome anywhere in the system? Or in the Federation? Who knows how many more will come if we let them get a foothold? This could just be the advance guard."

"This is their third known incursion, not the first. Each time, they've come in smaller numbers, tried harder to avoid us, as if their resources are limited and depleted by each battle." It surprised Kirk to hear himself echoing Adebayo's arguments, but Orloff's belligerence went too far in the other direction. "That means we may be dealing with them from more of a position of strength than we thought. And that creates an opportunity to offer them an alternative."

T'Zeri looked interested. "Do you propose negotiation, Captain?"

"I've already got my science and communications officers working on breaking their language, and their counterparts on the *Lexington* and *Enterprise* are doing the same."

Orloff looked bewildered. "You don't negotiate with invaders, Captain! Surely you understand the need for an aggressive defense of our sovereign territory. You've fought the Klingons multiple times, defended our borders."

"Not every enemy is the Klingons, Colonel. Conflicts have arisen from misunderstandings before, as with the Xindi or the Vertians." He sighed. "I resisted the idea myself, at first. But the fact is," he confessed, "the Agni have never initiated a move more aggressive than simply entering our territory. It was when we objected to their entry, attempted to repel them pre-emptively, that they began to fight."

"I call occupying one of our planets aggressive!" Orloff countered, her tone growing angrier.

"We didn't even know they were there for weeks after they

arrived, maybe longer. They made no moves against us until we discovered their presence. The surface is so hostile and inaccessible from the upper atmosphere that it might as well be an entirely different world. Maybe we and they just need to set some boundaries."

"They crossed our boundaries! They ignored them! What makes you think they'd start honoring them now?"

"We cannot know," T'Zeri told her, "until we talk to them. As long as they make no more aggressive moves, that should remain our priority."

On the screen, Sentok and the other councillors debated the matter for a time. The Caitian agreed strongly with Orloff, the Arodi more tentatively so, while the human favored negotiation. T'Zeri had already made it clear where she stood. That left the tiebreaker vote to Sentok. *"Councillor T'Zeri and Captain Kirk are correct,"* the president finally said. *"No conflict can be resolved until communication exists. We must attempt to negotiate."*

With the decision settled, Orloff grudgingly accepted. But as the meeting broke up and she left without a word, it was clear to Kirk that she no longer considered him an ally. He wasn't sure he could blame her, for his change in perspective still surprised him.

Now he just had to order Kamisha Diaz to redouble her efforts to make peaceful contact with the beings who had killed her best friend.

U.S.S. Sacagawea

"Of course, Captain," Ensign Diaz said when he came to her quarters and gently broke the news. Her eyes were still red from crying, but she maintained her discipline well. "I understand how important this is. It's always Starfleet's duty to look for the peaceful way first."

"I know how hard that can be in a situation like this. If you have any moral objection to this, or any concerns about your objectivity—"

"With all due respect, Captain, that won't be an issue." She cleared her throat, took a breath. "At first I didn't know if I wanted to help open a dialogue with Harlie's—H'Raal's killers. With the killers of over a dozen Regulan citizens. But then I realized . . . it's the only way the people of Regulus will ever be able to face them and demand an accounting. Whether it's for diplomacy or for seeking justice, we need to be able to make our words clear to them.

"So, no, Captain. I feel no conflict anymore. I'm committed to breaking their language."

Kirk nodded solemnly, squeezing her shoulder in support. "Thank you, Ensign. Whatever the outcome, you're doing Regulus and the Federation an important service."

Her eyes held his, fire burning in their darkness. "That's all I've ever wanted to do, sir."

Nubicuculia, Hearthside
Over the next two days, the Agni remained quiet, evidently content to wait so long as the *Sacagawea* and the Regulan ships in orbit made no moves to change the status quo. It gave Ensigns Diaz and Chalan time to work on deciphering the Agni's communications between Hearthside and 88 Leonis III—a task that required a science officer as much as a linguist (and Diaz was both) due to the need to deduce the likely structure of the Agni's brains and sensory organs and build a baseline for communication from that.

As it turned out, though, the first major breakthrough came not from Kirk's crew on the *Sacagawea*, but from the *Enterprise*'s science officer Spock and one of its junior communications officers, a xenolinguist named Uhura. After another day of subspace correspondence with them, Diaz and Chalan reported that they had constructed a partial translation matrix that should at least allow communicating the desire for negotiation. The matrix was not yet advanced enough to automate the interpretation between two such alien mentalities, so Diaz would need to be on hand for the talks to finesse the program manually and interpret between the two sides. The ensign assured Kirk that she was able and eager to perform that task.

After that, it was simply a matter of contacting the Agni and inviting them to open peace talks. Once the message had been sent, it was some time before a response came, giving Kirk some momentary doubts about the reliability of this Spock fellow's work. But when the answer did arrive, it was a terse *"Yes. Choose location and time."*

The most sensible location was one of the aerial cities. Bringing the Agni to the still-damaged Laputa would be both impractical and in poor taste, so the Regulus Council decided to hold the session on one of Hearthside's smaller cities, Nubicuculia—a choice perhaps made with a touch of humor, for the name came from the sky city in Aristophanes' comedy *The Birds* and literally meant "Cloud Cuckoo Land." Although Kirk hoped it was not an ominous choice, for in the play, the strategic position of the city had allowed the mortals dwelling below to conquer the Olympian gods above.

Nubicuculia also had extensive laboratories for studying the microbial life of Hearthside—not merely the life that existed in the more comfortable conditions of the upper atmosphere, but the hyperthermophilic forms that had adapted to the hotter, denser atmosphere below. Thus, it already had facilities that could replicate and endure the planet's surface conditions. Rather than asking the Agni to entrust their survival to an environment controlled by their enemies, the chosen lab's external airlock was rigged to be compatible with the shuttle specs the Agni transmitted, so that they could dock with it and modify its atmospheric and thermal conditions using their own craft's environmental systems, or retreat readily into their shuttle if they felt threatened.

Of course, it was Kirk's job to ensure they did not feel threatened, unless they initiated an open threat. Councillor T'Zeri had agreed that he, as a Starfleet captain experienced at diplomatic and military dealings with alien species, should take the lead in the negotiations, though she would be alongside him the entire time. Kirk requested that Adebayo join him as an advisor. A table was set up for the three of them in the lab's observation room, facing the thick, acid-proof window into the atmosphere chamber. Diaz would sit at a side console adjacent to the window, one she had programmed with the Agni translation protocol, with a direct link to the *Sacagawea*'s main computer for extra processing power.

The Agni shuttle arrived early, visible on the lab screen as a shell-like oval craft emerging from the clouds below, appearing to be made of the same yellow-brown material as the armor plates of their cylinder ships. However, the shuttle merely hovered in the air beyond Nubicuculia, conducting repeated scans of the converted lab and the city overall, before finally moving in to dock with the airlock precisely on time. Kirk and the others took their places and waited, but it took a number of minutes more for the Agni to adjust the chamber conditions to their liking. Soon the chamber interior began to redden and ripple as the carbon dioxide atmosphere within grew dense enough to absorb and distort light. Even the heavily reinforced transparent aluminum partition began to creak and groan as it adjusted to the increasing pressure and temperature. Soon a fine mist of sulfuric acid droplets billowed into the chamber, making the air hazy.

"The Agni don't seem to rely on vision as a primary sense," Diaz commented to occupy the time, "seeing as how their atmosphere is opaque over a distance to nearly everything but radio, microwaves, and near infrared. We think their main long-range senses are thermal and acoustic. That's part of why it was so hard to crack their language—the lack of direct sensory analogies."

Kirk gave Adebayo a wry look. "I was hoping I'd finally be able to look them in the eyes. Now I don't know if I'll even be able to see them clearly."

The older officer chuckled. "How well do you think they can see beings who give off as little heat as we do, or hear us through air as thin as ours? To them, this might be like talking to ghosts."

Is that why they ignored us? Kirk wondered. *Are we even fully real to them?*

At last, he saw movement through the mist—the Agni representatives were emerging from their airlock. They moved tentatively through the dusky haze, edging slowly closer to the window. Mindful of Adebayo's words, Kirk led the others to rise and come around the table to greet the Agni, moving closer to the window and standing well apart to maximize their visibility.

Finally, Kirk could discern three figures, large, wide, and low. Each one gave him the impression of a pair of large, spherical lobes crawling forward on thick tentacles, with a lancelike horn extending forward from the top. As he discerned more features through the murk, he realized that they resembled mollusks or cephalopods to a degree. The spherical lobes were flexible, but they rested underneath a pair of rigid hemispherical shells, with the "horn" being a forward extension of the shell structure, emerging from the hinge where the halves met. As he studied one Agni's unicorn-like horn, some sort of translucent sac emerged from its hollow tip and inflated like a miniature party balloon, then quickly retreated. The same was happening periodically with the other two. Kirk had the impression that the sac was some sort of sensory organ, but he had no idea how it might work.

The lead Agni suddenly slapped two of its forward tentacles against the window, making Kirk and Diaz jump. Their startlement induced an even more startled reaction in the Agni, with the two in the rear withdrawing their entire bodies and most of their tentacles into their shells, which folded nearly shut like fat clamshells. Kirk began to understand why their starship defenses were based so heavily on solid armor instead of the pliable skin of energy fields.

But he knew better than to assume their invertebrate bodies made them vulnerable or weak. Their tentacles seemed as densely covered in suckers as those of the Earthly octopus, a species capable of extraordinarily fine manipulation. Controlling such complex, adaptable limbs required a very sophisticated brain.

Understanding the ideas and intentions within those brains would take some time, though. Before negotiations could begin, it required over an hour and a half for Diaz to conduct a language lesson to calibrate the translation program and ensure its accuracy. This was challenging due to the massive differences between the two species; one could not simply point to an eye or a hand and ask for the equivalent word.

Once Diaz declared the translator suitably calibrated, the talks could finally begin. Mutual introductions had been part of the calibration process, but Diaz had been unable to extract anything meaningful or pronounceable from the Agni's personal names; instead, she had decided to designate them by the titles or positions they had ascribed to themselves, which translated roughly as Speaker, Observer, and Protector. "Or Warrior?" Kirk asked when Diaz proposed the third title.

"It's hard to say, sir. I do get the sense that Protector is more than just a security guard. Maybe a military advisor of some sort."

Kirk moved forward, reminding himself not to jump to conclusions. His job was to be as objective as possible until the facts could be established. He took a moment to formulate his words before addressing the Agni. "The first thing we should establish," he said, "for the sake of our understanding, is the nature of your intentions in Federation space. Why have you made repeated attempts to enter our space and establish occupancy on worlds within it? Why did you not attempt to communicate with us, its prior inhabitants, before doing so?"

The Agni debated the question among themselves for some time before Speaker answered. Diaz studied the translator results, then interpreted them as best she could. "'You speak without meaning. We occupy our hot realm'—our environment, our worlds, perhaps—'and you occupy your cold realm. They are separate. Yet cold beings fight us when we attempt to occupy our realm. You interfere with our existence when it does not affect you. We do not understand *your* intentions.'"

Kirk pursed his lips, considering. "We do not begrudge your right to live in your own territories. Had you approached us ahead of time, we would have been open to negotiating your settlement in our territory, provided your intentions were peaceful. It was only when you intruded on our territory, and did not wait to establish communication, that we found it necessary to defend ourselves."

Diaz looked confused by Speaker's reply, but she did her best. "'You speak like other cold beings. When we attempt to occupy our realm, they attack us. When we can understand them, they say we have attempted to take something that is theirs. We have nothing of theirs. We have little left that is ours. But still they say we have taken, and they strike and kill, so we must defend ourselves.'"

Kirk's initial reflex was to protest that Starfleet had never escalated to lethal force until the Agni had done so first. What gave him pause was Speaker's previous sentence. Apparently T'Zeri noted the same thing, for she asked, "Why is it that you have little left that is yours? What has caused its depletion?"

"'Change came to our first realm. We could not live there anymore. We found the way to leave it, but few of us escaped in time. We have sought new realms . . . but wherever we have gone, cold beings have stopped us in the middle.' En route, I guess. 'You have fought us where there is nothing to fight over. We have not known why. We wonder if you are . . .' I think it's 'damaged' or 'mentally ill.'" Diaz looked apologetic. "'We have tried to flee you, to reach our . . . our new realm, but you fight harder. You damage us. We cannot repair our ships fully without a place to rest them. We only want to occupy our realm and tend our wounds. We do not know why you kill us for it.'"

The Agni's words were sobering. T'Zeri leaned over and murmured to Kirk, "I believe the Agni do not share our conception of territory, Captain. They do not understand the concept of claiming empty space."

"Or perhaps," said Adebayo, "they don't understand why we'd begrudge them the right to travel to planets we have no use for."

Kirk found it hard to believe they could be so oblivious to the concept of territorial borders. He tried to think of a way to put it in terms the Agni would understand. "We have seen that you have formidable weapons and combat tactics. So you must have had conflict between rival populations on your own world. Surely it was necessary to secure the borders of your lands, to observe who came and went. To protect yourselves against those who would do you harm, you would need to communicate with those who approached your lands, to determine their intentions before they came too close to where your people lived. If they resisted communication, the security of your people would require reacting as if they were a threat." How could they not know this?

The Agni had a lengthy discussion, and then Observer slithered forward and spoke. "'To clarify: Do you speak of realms as property?'"

Kirk blinked. "That is correct. We consider our territory, on planets and in space, to belong to us. To be our responsibility to protect."

Now Protector spoke up. "'You speak without meaning. A place belongs to itself. It lives its own life. You may live upon it, but only until it changes . . . or you do.'"

Diaz broke character and turned to Kirk. "Captain . . . It makes sense. In their native N-Class environment, even solid rock would be partially molten and subject to heavy corrosion. Geological features would be impermanent. Judging from their anatomy, I'd bet they live largely in sulfuric-acid seas and lakes. They seem quite comfortable on land, but to them it would be as mutable as the sea, just somewhat more slowly. They couldn't have the same concept of fixed territories and borders that we have."

The captain shook his head. "That still doesn't explain why they didn't *ask*. Why they didn't try to talk to us first. We could've explained our reasons for challenging them, if they'd just asked instead of opening fire. Tell them that, Ensign."

Diaz processed the translation, presumably rephrasing it as a question, and transmitted it into the Agni's chamber. It was Protector who answered. "'We have searched for new realms for a long time. Many cold beings have interrupted us. At first, we tried to speak with them. When we did, they spoke without meaning, as you do, and then they fought us. We lost many Agni, many ships. We have lost more with each battle. So . . .'" Diaz swallowed, cleared her throat. "'So we stopped trying to speak. It cost us too much. Cold beings only seem to understand force. We learned to respond in kind.'"

"They were refugees." Kirk paced the confines of the meeting room to which the negotiating party had withdrawn to discuss the Agni's revelations. "All this time, we've been shooting at refugees."

"We couldn't have known that," Eshu Adebayo reminded him. "We gave them the chance to respond peacefully."

"But we assumed they understood our concepts of borders.

'This far and no farther.' We assumed that pushing forward past our imaginary walls in empty space meant they had hostile intent. Instead they assumed *we* were the hostile ones, attacking them in the middle of nowhere over nothing."

"They gave us no way to determine otherwise."

"Because they'd given up hope that 'cold beings' could be reasoned with." He gazed outward. "Imagine what it must have been like for them. The survivors of a dead world, looking for a new home—yet everywhere they go, they find beings incomprehensibly alien to them, attacking them for reasons they can't understand. We know they fought the Klingons before us . . . how many other territories did they pass through? How many others met them with the same violence?

"We like to tell ourselves we're enlightened. That we're more peaceful, more open-minded than the other civilizations out there." Kirk shook his head. "What gets me is that, to the Agni, we acted just like all the others. Is that what we've become? So overprotective of what we have that we've become fearful of outsiders? In defending the physical borders of the Federation, have we forgotten what we were really fighting to protect?"

T'Zeri stepped forward. "It is futile to dwell on past events that we cannot change. We should focus on the opportunity we have to begin changing things now. The fact that the Agni have accepted our offer of communication is itself a promising indicator of change. This is our opportunity to create understanding and avoid further conflict."

"Is it?" Ensign Diaz spoke up. "Pardon me, Councillor . . . Captain . . . but can we be so sure we can find a settlement both sides will agree to? If they don't respect territory, why should they accept our claim to Hearthside and let us stay?"

"Why should they forbid us to stay, if they have no concept of exclusive territorial claims?" T'Zeri asked her. "They wish us to leave because they perceive us as a threat. What we must do is establish that we pose no threat."

"And what if the only way to prove that to them is to leave? To abandon the cities?"

"Ensign," Kirk said. Diaz immediately fell silent, looking abashed. "Let us worry about the larger questions when the time comes. Your responsibility is to make sure we have clear communication with the Agni so we can address those questions." He stepped closer, briefly squeezing her shoulder. "Your job is the most important part of this whole process. But that's why you need to keep your eyes on that job alone and leave the rest to us. All right, Ensign?"

Diaz smiled up at him, though it was tinged with the grief he could still see in her eyes. "Yes, Captain. I understand."

———————

When negotiations resumed, T'Zeri began by saying, "We deeply regret the loss of life on both sides of our encounters to date. Those lives were lost due to a lack of communication and understanding between our peoples. With that in mind, we wish to show you the history of the Regulus system, which you now occupy, and of the United Federation of Planets, the larger union of peoples to which it belongs."

T'Zeri went on to offer a lesson in the history of the modern Regulan civilization, from the earliest remaining settlers such as the Arodi to the era of the Vulcan protectorate, its settlement by new species including Chelons and humans, and its eventual admission as a full member of the Federation. With assistance from Kirk and Adebayo, she segued into a history of the Federation as a whole, again stressing how different, initially mistrustful species had learned to coexist in peace and partnership. Records from the Federation database were offered as proof, but it required some work on Diaz's part to process the audiovisual recordings into a form that would be meaningful to the Agni's thermal and echolocation senses.

"Regulus has welcomed newcomers on numerous past occasions," T'Zeri finished, "and we are willing to do so again, provided that we can be assured of the peace and safety of all the peoples of Regulus, and of the Federation. However, we suggest that it might be simpler to relocate your complement here to your existing outpost on 88 Leonis III. Unlike us, the Federation colonists there have no use for that planet, so there would be no need for territorial conflict."

Observer came forward to answer. "'That world offers less than we need. It has useful resources, but is not ideal for our life. It can sustain far fewer of us than this world can. This world is much like the one we lost. It has everything we need, and more.'"

"I understand. In that case, we are willing to negotiate an agreement whereby you may remain on this planet, providing we can establish mutual assurances of nonhostility."

The three Agni discussed the matter for some time among themselves before responding. Diaz audibly struggled to control her tone as she translated Speaker's words. "'You request assurances of our nonhostility, but it has always been cold beings who attacked us first. You must give *us* assurance. We wish only a place to live. But you are above us. You surround us. To give us assurance that you will not attack . . . you must withdraw. Leave us . . . leave us this planet. You have many other places you can go, many ships to take you there. We have few of either. Leave us this planet, and there will be peace.'"

The humanoid negotiators exchanged a concerned look. "That will not be feasible," T'Zeri said. "The chemicals and medicines extracted from the microbial life of Hearthside's atmosphere are of considerable importance to Regulus's economy. Millions of lives would be negatively affected, and thousands could be lost, if we abandoned the aerial cities. There must be some other way to show you we are not a threat. What you ask would be a threat to us."

Again, the Agni took time to discuss the matter. Finally Speaker made a counteroffer. "'Leave us the cities. We will harvest the substances you need. We will provide them to you, in exchange for being left alone.' "

Adebayo blinked. "They're offering to work off their rent."

"What you suggest would be difficult to achieve," T'Zeri told the Agni. "The aerial cities and the harvesting equipment are designed for humanoid use. Adapting them to your environmental and sensory needs would take time. You would need to be instructed in their operation. It would be difficult to ensure that there was no loss of productivity."

" 'We have lost many lives, ships, and resources to the attacks of cold beings. We are alone. You are part of a vast Federation that can compensate for any losses. The risk for you is far less than for us.' " Diaz paused to translate Speaker's next statement. " 'In time, if you assure us we can trust you, we may allow you to return. We have been without homes for far longer.' "

Kirk studied Speaker throughout this exchange, intrigued. It was hard to say whether he could read anything into such an alien creature's body language, or through their speech filtered through both machine and human translation. But somehow, he sensed a kindred spirit—a leader dedicated to the protection of their people, alert to threats from outside, but still committed to finding a path to peace if one was possible.

He tried to put himself in the Agni's position, to imagine being a refugee hounded across the galaxy, then finally being on the verge of finding a safe haven. He could understand the fear and mistrust that such a life could inure one to . . . but he believed that it would be tempered by hope, by a genuine desire to believe that someone, at last, would give them the welcome and security they had craved for so long. That was what drove refugees all over the galaxy—that hope of finding a welcoming community, a place to belong. And yet, so often, they were seen as a threat and a burden by those who took their own belonging for granted. So often, they were hounded and ostracized. And yet they kept looking, kept hoping.

All the Agni were asking for was space, enough to give them a feeling of security. They even offered to do a service for those they feared—and allowed for the possibility that, once mutual trust was earned, they would seek closer engagement with them. It was not so different from the journeys of many immigrants and refugees throughout history.

Surely, he thought, the Regulans would recognize that.

RDF *Venant*

"Abandon our cities?" Colonel Orloff exclaimed. "These creatures squat in our system, attack a planetary capital, kill over a dozen Regulans, and now they demand that we retreat and accept their conquest? Never!"

"We are still early in the negotiations," T'Zeri told her. "Perhaps some compromise position can be reached."

"Compromise with invaders? No. They had their chance to request entry peacefully. Having bad experiences with others in the past, assuming that's even true, is no excuse for the things they've done. They are the aggressors here, not the victims."

Kirk caught her eye across the meeting table. "With all due respect, Colonel, things aren't always that clear-cut when dealing with alien civilizations, alien mindsets. Believe me, I understand how you feel. My initial reaction was much the same. But we can't ignore what we've learned about the Agni and their different way of looking at things."

"Can't we? We only have their word that any part of this sob story of theirs is true."

"We know they were driven out of Klingon space. We know they've faced us with fewer ships each time."

"Ships with devastating weapons. Ships with stealth capability so that we don't see them coming."

"As a matter of fact, Colonel," Kirk told her, "their account explains some of our questions about their weapons. They're powerful, yes, but they also have major deficiencies. Using their armor plates as projectiles is potent but inefficient, and leaves them increasingly vulnerable the more they use them. Their plasma beams have a limited range of fire, are cumbersome to aim and relatively easy to avoid, and can only fire once every several minutes. We saw these drawbacks all along, but we shrugged and attributed them to the Agni's alien way of thinking. We didn't consider that they made the most sense if the systems weren't originally designed to function as weapons, but were adapted to that purpose out of necessity. They throw their defensive armor at us, redirect the plasma meant for warp power into a weapon, because it's all they've got to fight with."

"They adapted the tech to atmospheric missiles well enough."

"But in limited quantity. Their attack on Laputa was much more tentative than their battle tactics in space. It suggests they had fewer projectiles to work with."

"Or that they believe they can bide their time with the atmosphere protecting them from our weapons." Orloff leaned forward intently. "I recommend we show them how wrong they are about that, now that the necessary modifications have been made. They need to be made aware that if they want to live in our system, it'll be on our terms. They can't be allowed to just steal one of our planets."

"The concept of permanent possession of territory," T'Zeri told her, "is not one they will readily understand. Any such attack would merely be interpreted as further proof that 'cold beings' are intrinsically violent and irrational, and incline them to abandon efforts at negotiation. That would most likely escalate the violence of their response."

"Not if we overwhelm them quickly, before they have a chance to fight back."

Kirk stared. "You're not suggesting we just kill them all?"

"I'm suggesting we do what it takes to neutralize a threat

to Regulan citizens and Regulan territory. They're welcome to leave if it gets too hot—sorry, too *cold* for them."

Shaking his head, Kirk told her, "No. I respect your commitment to protecting the Regulan people, Colonel, but there's more at stake here. What happens here may also affect the outpost on 88 Leonis, and there may still be other undiscovered Agni settlements in Federation space."

"My responsibility is to the worlds of Regulus."

"And Regulus is a member of the Federation, which means Starfleet's authority supersedes yours in matters of interstellar defense. T'Zeri is right—we're still negotiating. We may yet be able to talk them into a compromise. It's too early to consider extreme responses. For now, Colonel, we keep talking. Understood?"

Orloff seethed, but grudgingly answered, "Understood."

Kirk nodded, offering a bit of a smile in hopes of softening his order. He didn't like being in the position of the outsider coming in to tell her how to do her job on her home turf. That was part of why he preferred being a deep-space explorer—it let him avoid that kind of hierarchical clash most of the time, from both directions.

But he had to consider the security of the whole Federation—and the integrity of its principles when it came to dealing with refugees. He just had to hope that Yelena Orloff would recognize that what was good for the Federation was good for Regulus.

U.S.S. *Sacagawea*

H'Raal reached out for Kamisha Diaz's hand, begging for her help as the module broke away into the toxic air. But Diaz refused to reach back and catch her, for she was too busy working her console, translating the Agni's demands. A tentacle stroked her shoulder appreciatively, and the pleading in Harlie's golden eyes hardened into betrayal as she fell away slowly, beginning to choke in the air as more tentacles embraced Diaz, claiming her . . .

"Harlie!" Diaz woke up sobbing, terrified. On realizing that she was safe in her bed aboard the ship, she slowed her breathing until her panic subsided. She was still crying, but she was resigned to that. These nightmares had been a painfully regular occurrence these past few nights. At first, she had only relived her guilt at being unable to save H'Raal; tonight's dream had added a new layer. She shuddered at the memory of the tentacles slithering across her.

Diaz shed her nightclothes and took a sonic shower to try to wash away that sensation, along with the panic sweat from her nightmare. She closed her eyes, breathed deeply, and tried to lose herself in the steady whir of the sonic waves, grateful that she and her roommate were on staggered shifts so she could have peace and quiet. Well, at least quiet. Peace would be a long time coming. How ironic that it was her assistance in Captain Kirk's efforts to make peace that filled her with such turmoil. She had always tried to fulfill her duties to Starfleet diligently, to set aside personal needs and considerations for the sake of a career she believed in passionately. But it was hard to believe in a system that commanded her to cooperate with the beings who had killed her best friend—and who now sought to take away another piece of her home.

Realizing that her attempt at relaxation was having the opposite effect, Diaz got a glass of water, hoping that her dark thoughts were a symptom of unbalanced electrolytes and lack of sleep. She sat at the desk and set to work refining the translator algorithms, hoping that poring over lines of code long enough would help her with the sleep issue.

After a while, she was interrupted by a hail from the night-shift communications officer on the bridge. *"Ensign? You have a call from Colonel Yelena Orloff aboard the* Venant. *Shall I put it through?"*

Startled, Diaz took a moment to put on a robe and run her fingers through her hair a couple of times. "Yes, okay, put her through."

Orloff's pale, stern features appeared on the desktop monitor, flanked by the flags of Regulus and the Defense Force. *"Ensign Diaz. I hope I didn't catch you at a bad time."*

"No, no, I was up. What can I do for you, Colonel?"

"I've been reviewing your work on the Agni translations, Ensign. I understand that you're almost single-handedly responsible for enabling us to communicate with them."

"Well . . . thank you, Colonel, but that's an exaggeration. It was the *Enterprise* crew that made the first breakthrough, and our comms officer Chalan has helped me a lot."

"But you're the one taking the lead. And that comes with the responsibility for the success of the entire operation. A responsibility you've taken to well." Orloff paused. *"Which is particularly impressive . . . given what the Agni took from you."*

Diaz almost gasped. She quashed her immediate surprise that Orloff seemed to know what she had just been thinking about; after all, she thought of little else when she didn't have her duties to occupy her. "I . . . I understand what's at stake, Colonel. For the good of Regulus, and the Federation, I have to put my duty above my personal feelings."

Orloff smiled. *"I'm glad to hear you put Regulus first."*

The comment made Diaz uneasy. "It . . . it shouldn't make a difference. We're all part of the Federation."

"Still, there's nothing wrong with feeling a special responsibility to your home, your own people. After all, the Federation and Starfleet leaders back at Earth are eighty light-years away. There are times when we Regulans understand our needs better than they do."

"Do you . . . do you think this is one of those times?"

"Do you, Ensign? Do you think they understand what we'd be sacrificing if we bent to the Agni's demand and abandoned our

Hearthside cities? What it would mean to our sense of ourselves if we gave in to that kind of intimidation? How it would make us look to the rest of the galaxy?"

Diaz bristled. "How would it make us look if we fired on refugees, people who came here for asylum? My friend . . . the one they killed . . . she was proud of Regulus's tradition of welcoming newcomers. She was grateful for our welcome of her people."

"And we are *welcoming—to those who truly mean no harm. That doesn't mean we're required to bend over for those who come with hostile intent. Who claim need and desperation as a diversion from their true aggressive intentions."*

The ensign shook her head. "I'm sorry, Colonel, but I'm just not convinced that's a valid reading of the Agni's motives."

"Ah, but that's the thing. The reading of their words and actions is subject to interpretation. It depends on the perspective . . . the priorities . . . of the one doing the translation. They could *have malicious intent. They* could *be lying to us, negotiating in bad faith to distract us while they plan an attack. It all depends, Ensign, on how you decide to interpret the evidence."* Orloff leaned closer to the sensor pickup. *"And whether that interpretation is in the best interests of Regulus. Do you understand what I'm suggesting, Ensign?"*

Diaz believed she did. It made her too nervous to have any hope of getting back to sleep. But the more she thought about it, the more she considered that it might be a way to banish the tentacles from her dreams. "What . . . what sort of interpretation did you have in mind, Colonel?"

ENTERPRISE
2265

Seventeen

Not chess, Mister Spock—poker. Do you know the game?
—James T. Kirk

U.S.S. Enterprise

"You had no right to allow your people to remain on the planet, Captain Kirk!" Director Skovir declared over the bridge's main viewscreen. *"Or to attempt this . . . this pointless blockade action with your ship."* Kirk had taken the *Enterprise* out of orbit to face down the Aulacri fleet shepherding the incoming comets. If he intended to take a stand on Sherev and Spock's behalf, he figured he should commit to it fully.

"This is not a Federation operation," Skovir went on. *"You are not entitled to dictate to us or interfere with our affairs."*

"Doctor Sherev and Commander Spock made their own choice to remain, Director," Kirk said, trying to personify them in the director's mind. "They are aware that they're risking their lives by doing so, but they chose to take that risk for the sake of knowledge—knowledge that they believe will benefit the Aulacri people. They're acting in accordance with Starfleet's primary mission, as they interpret it. I plead with you for understanding, Director. If my officers have erred, it is only on the side of curiosity and discovery."

"It was not their place to make that decision on our behalf!" the small, fierce-featured terraformer insisted. *"That is supposed*

to be the point of your directive of noninterference, is it not? To respect the cultural autonomy and choice of others? But your people are defying the will of the Aulacri, taking our choice away from us!"

Kirk couldn't help himself. "Isn't that what you're doing, Director?" he replied with some heat. "Hiding the truth from your people, trying to destroy information that they have a right to know?"

"That is our choice to make."

Rising from the command chair, Kirk stepped forward. "You're right—our highest principle as Starfleet officers is to respect the right and responsibility of others to make their own choices. But making responsible choices requires being informed and aware of the facts. Concealing the truth from the Aulacri denies them that right. Are you really willing to take that choice away from the rest of your people?"

He extended his hands, palms up. "Please, Director. Give Sherev and Spock the time they need to finish their work. They're determined to stay, no matter what. At least let that decision have meaning."

Skovir remained unmoved. *"Their decision was foolish, Captain! There is nothing of value they or we can learn from monsters like the Karabosi, the species that almost exterminated our kind. And I cannot abandon twenty years of work and expense on the part of thousands of Aulacri for the sake of two fools who lack the sense to get out of an impact zone!"*

Kirk made one last try. "If you decide that any lives are worth sacrificing for the convenience of your people, how does that make you better than the Karabosi?"

Skovir did wrestle with that for a moment. But she finally said, *"I gave your people every chance to get away, Captain. I asked Starfleet to send a ship to retrieve them. I demanded that you complete that assignment. I have done all I was obligated to do and more.*

"I'm sorry, but their fate now is on their own heads—and yours."

Skovir's image disappeared from the screen, replaced by a tactical display of the comets that were now just hours away from impact. Lieutenant Kelso spoke up from behind Kirk, and the captain turned to face him. "Sir? There's still time to retrieve Commander Spock and Doctor Sherev if we head back now."

Kirk thought it over. *Why are you so set on this?* he asked himself. Throughout his career, he had striven to follow the rules, to be a good, disciplined officer. True, he had learned to be flexible, to apply his best judgment in cases where exceptions needed to be made. The Chenari were alive today because of that flexibility. He had earned command of the *Enterprise* by proving he had the judgment to adapt and interpret the rules, not just blindly enforce them.

But arbitrarily violating regulations, let alone the Prime Directive, was no better. Kirk was no maverick ready to throw out the rule book at a whim. Why, then, was he so bent on this action when the rule book, his direct orders from Starfleet, and General Order One all told him it was the wrong play?

Part of it was what he had said to Skovir. If the Prime Directive was about respecting a people's self-determination, then it felt wrong to use it to justify a lie, a cover-up that would deny them the right to make informed choices. Skovir may have represented her government, but she was just a terraforming director; her superiors on Aulac might have overruled her if they knew what Sherev and Spock had found. But there was no time left to notify them, and it would be best to present them with the complete picture, the full set of answers that his past and present science officers were certain lay just out of reach. If they were right, the Aulacri authorities might agree after the fact that Kirk's intervention had been justified.

But what if Spock and Sherev were wrong? What if the contents of that inner vault had been destroyed in the rockfall, or were of no benefit to the Aulacri after all? Sherev had always been a gambler, taking excessive risks. And Spock, for all his sterling reputation, was still an unknown commodity.

Even as he had the thought, Kirk regretted it. Sherev took risks, yes, and they didn't always pay off—but not because her judgment of the potential reward had been wrong. When she took the most extreme risks, whether at the poker table or in the field, it had always been justified by the potential gain. When she had lost, when she had suffered or nearly died, it had been due to the vagaries of fate, not because there had been nothing of value to pursue.

As for Spock . . . He may not have been a poker player, but Kirk knew from their chess games that he was meticulous, rational, a master of prediction and calculation. He saw the whole board and projected permutations dozens of moves ahead. If he took a risk, it was because he had calculated a high probability of success.

More importantly, Spock was his first officer now. Trust between a captain and exec was intrinsic to the relationship. It was Spock's job to be someone the captain could rely on—and it was the captain's job to be someone the whole crew could rely on. This was the nature and the discipline of the service, intrinsic to the oaths the officers took to Starfleet and to one another. By trusting his captain, Spock had shown that he accepted that bond. How could Kirk do any less in return, least of all at the very start of their partnership?

All this went through Kirk's head in mere seconds. Once his resolve was settled, he returned to his command chair and took his place in it. "Negative, Mister Kelso. We will remain here and make sure that Spock and Sherev have the time they need to complete their work."

Mitchell turned to stare at Kirk. "Even if it means diverting the comets by force?"

"Unless we get a call from the surface very soon, that's going to be our only option." The captain turned to the science station, which Kirk had ordered Lieutenant Sulu to operate in Spock's absence, just in case matters came to this. "Mister Sulu, begin calculations for diverting the comets' courses with tractor beams and phasers. I trust we don't have to displace them too far."

The young, dark-haired physicist shook his head. "Negative, sir. It's only the four largest ones intended to make it to the surface that we have to worry about, and even those are coming in on a shallow trajectory so that most of their volatiles will vaporize in the atmosphere before they hit. That means we only have to nudge them a little bit out of the way to miss the atmosphere completely." He frowned. "Even so, that just means it's possible, not easy. Diverting masses of that size this close to the planet . . . well, it'd be a lot easier if we'd done this days ago. But I'll do my best, Captain."

"Very good." Kirk swung the chair forward again. "Mister Kelso, arm phasers and initialize the tractor beam. Stand by for trajectory data from Sulu."

After an uneasy moment, Kelso rose from his seat and faced Kirk stiffly. "I'm sorry, Captain. I can't do that."

Kirk stared. "Explain yourself, mister."

"With all due respect, Captain . . . I do not believe your orders are in keeping with our mission for Starfleet or our duties under the Prime Directive. I'm concerned that you're acting out of personal loyalty to Doctor Sherev and failing to consider how this could damage our diplomatic relations with the Aulacri."

In the adjacent seat, Mitchell grew furious as Kelso spoke. "You're way out of line, Lee!"

"The captain ordered me to explain myself, sir!"

Kirk held out a hand to Mitchell. "Yes, I did, Mister Kelso. But I am not obligated to explain my orders to you."

"No, sir, you are not. But I am obligated to refuse orders that I believe are illegal or unethical. Firing on the Aulacri comets could trigger a diplomatic crisis or even a war, and I cannot in good conscience be a part of that. Sir."

Kirk held Kelso's gaze for a moment. He'd known the man was having difficulty adjusting to his new captain, but he hadn't believed it would come to this. Still, it was a problem he had to deal with immediately.

"Very well, Lieutenant Kelso. In that case, you are relieved of duty. Return to your quarters. We'll discuss this later."

After a moment's hesitation, Kelso threw brief, apologetic glances toward Mitchell and Sulu, but could not meet his captain's eyes as he strode to the turbolift.

Sulu rose from his seat at the science station. "Captain? My primary training is in flight control. I could complete my computations at the helm."

Kirk nodded. He was already aware of Sulu's record as a pilot. "Man the helm, Mister Sulu."

Karabos II

"How much time do we have left?"

Spock's voice betrayed a hint of annoyance at the increasing frequency with which Rhenas Sherev asked that question, but he managed to avoid calling attention to it. "Approximately one hour, twenty-seven minutes until the first surface impact event."

Sherev cocked her antennae thoughtfully as she turned back to examine the door before them. "Then we'd better solve this puzzle fast."

"Puzzle" was an accurate characterization of the locking mechanism the Karabosi had built into the door to the inner vault. It seemed the Karabosi had wanted to ensure that access to its contents would only be granted to beings intelligent and scientifically advanced enough to understand them—and they'd devised an ingenious mechanism, one simple and durable enough to remain functional over geologic time. "To review, then," Spock said. He pointed to a small, glinting square of corrosion-proof metal in the door. "When power is fed into this electrical contact, it activates an electroluminescent diamond semiconductor within the door. The light shines through these three horizontal slots below, which are the correct size to contain the platinum data sheets in the outer library. Underneath the slots is a converse piezoelectric crystal sheathed in photoelectric material; when exposed to light, the crystal undergoes mechanical deformation that should release the inner locking mechanism."

"But just shining the light through the empty slots doesn't do it," Sherev said. "The photoelectric sheath is microstructured to respond only to the right pattern of light hitting its surface."

"Clearly we are meant to insert the three correct data sheets so that their microdots will align in such a way as to transmit the correct pattern of light. Our challenge is to determine which three out of two thousand, seven hundred and thirty data sheets are the correct ones. And our only clues are the symbols carved alongside the slots."

"Which seem to relate to Karabosi life sciences and genetic notation," Sherev said. "That narrows it down."

"To seventy-nine data sheets. The number of distinct permutations of seventy-nine items taken three at a time is four hundred seventy-four thousand, four hundred seventy-four."

Sherev stared, amazed that he could do the computation in his head, though the number sounded so contrived that she almost wondered if he was making it up. "Well, some cultures think symmetrical numbers are good luck."

"Luck is an erroneous belief, particularly in this case. We would need to test ninety-two of the data sheets per second to complete them all in eighty-six minutes. We cannot rely on trial and error; we must select the correct sheets based on their contents. We are meant to deduce which sheets are indicated by which symbols."

"Then we'd better get to it."

They returned to the outer vault, clambering over the remains of the rockfall they had cleared through the application of the phaser bore and combined Vulcan and Andorian strength, then made their way to the section of the data-sheet archive indexed for life sciences. As they began withdrawing the sheets and laying them out for comparison, Sherev took advantage of the drudge work to ask a question that she'd been too busy to ask up to now. "Tell me something, Mister Spock. Just why did you, of all people, choose to stay behind? Why is it so important to you to find out what this mysterious link is between the Karabosi and the Aulacri?"

He cocked a brow at her. "As a fellow scientist, you should understand the importance of the pursuit of knowledge."

She cocked an antenna right back. "And as a fellow scientist, I'm asking you to level with me about why this is personal for you. And don't just say it's logical. Logic is a method for solving problems, not the thing that sets the problems in the first place. Why is this a problem that you need to solve?"

Spock continued to retrieve data sheets from their slotted rack and lay them out on the adjacent slab. For a moment, Sherev thought he was ignoring her question. Finally, he spoke. "I concede that my personal experience gives me insight into why this information could be vital to the Aulacri. It is an experience that I alone possess, for I am only half-Vulcan."

She studied him. Once it was pointed out, she could recognize the subtle variations from the Vulcan norm in his appearance, his scent, his electrical field. "The other half . . . human?"

His eyes betrayed momentary surprise at her perceptiveness. "Correct."

"How is that even possible? The blood chemistry differences alone . . ."

"Let us simply say that it required extensive medical intervention."

"We're not so different, then." She pointed a thumb at herself. "Four parents. Arranging a *shelthreth*—our reproductive ceremony—is a complicated thing, both finding four compatible people and, well, going through the actual mechanics of conception. It's not something that happens easily, or by accident." She smiled. "It's a comforting feeling, I've always thought. To know that my parents went through such effort to have me—it proves they really wanted me. I guess you must feel the same."

Spock looked away. "I . . . do not indulge in sentiment. In answer to your original question . . . As a half-human raised on Vulcan, and later as a half-Vulcan serving in a predominantly human Starfleet, I have been faced throughout my life with questions of identity. I have had to make difficult choices about what heritage I would define myself by."

"You can't just be both?"

His eyes met hers again. "If I were to attempt that, it would not 'just' happen. It would be its own complex choice, requiring a full understanding of both heritages. All such choices require an understanding of who we are, what our origins and context are. They cannot be made well in the absence of true knowledge of our identity and history."

Sherev looked deeper into his eyes. "I understand. You believe the Aulacri deserve that true knowledge of their own history, so they can find their own answers to those questions."

"I believe it is every being's right. I admit, there have been times, given the . . . complicated composition of my family, when I have found the barrage of conflicting messages about what it means to be Vulcan, or human, or some combination of the two, somewhat overwhelming. But at least I have been aware of my range of options. I believe it is better to have an excess of information to select from than a deficit. Imagine if we had only one of the data sheets we needed, rather than seventy-nine. At least this way, we have all the information we need to succeed; we must simply make our choices wisely."

Sherev looked at the multiple stacks of data sheets laid out before them on the slab. "'Simply.' Sure. Well, let's get to it."

At first, they attempted to scan the microtext on the data sheets for symbol strings matching the symbols on the slots. But none had an exact match, and many contained all of the depicted symbols in different configurations. "It was unlikely to be that simple," Spock said. "This is a test for our comprehension of the principles discussed in these sheets. We must deduce which sheets contain the formulas or operations that would result in the expressions carved beside the wall slots."

Sherev shook her head. "I'm afraid I'm a little rusty on the life sciences. Too used to studying what's already dead. I'm also better at games of chance than logic puzzles."

"You have the training of a Starfleet science officer, Doctor, just as I do. Given the time pressure, it is counterproductive to underestimate yourself."

Sherev stared, trying to parse whether that had been a compliment or a chastisement. *Oh, this one's going to be a handful for Jim.*

But Spock was right—once she applied herself to the problem, her life-sciences training came back to her, and she was able to assist in spotting the necessary patterns. Between them, the two science officers deduced that each of the three sheets they needed contained several equations that could implicitly be combined in a certain way—a way hinted at by discussion on the other two sheets—that would produce a derived equation matching the pattern of the symbols by one of the wall slots. The exact expression could be obtained by plugging the sheet's unique index number in as the undefined variable, a further confirmation that they had the right sheets.

"Fascinating," Spock said. "The three sheets we need pertain to the topics of genetics and cellular biology . . . reproduction and childhood development . . ." He turned to meet Sherev's eyes. "And cloning,"

Her antennae stiffened as the ramifications sank in. "We have to get those doors open right now."

U.S.S. *Enterprise*

Deflecting the comets had been a real test of the *Enterprise* and her crew. Given more time, Kirk knew, it would have been easy for even a much smaller ship to nudge bodies of their mass away from their impact trajectories through the prolonged, gentle application of a tractor beam. But with barely an hour to spare, it was far more challenging. The ship needed to exert considerably greater force upon the comets to change their course so quickly, yet do so gently enough not to shatter them, which would make it far harder to divert the multiple smaller pieces. Even if not all the fragments reached the surface intact, the total amount of kinetic energy and heat they would separately impart to Karabos II's atmosphere as they burned up within it would be the same, just spread out over a larger atmospheric volume—which could potentially be even more dangerous for Spock and Sherev on the surface.

Lieutenant Sulu's deflection strategy entailed a combination of wide-focus tractor beams, to spread out the acceleration evenly across the comets and minimize the fragmentation risk, and pinpoint-targeted phasers to bore into the comets' surface, with the vaporized ice and rock erupting out of the bore holes like exhaust blasting out of rocket nozzles, imparting an extra degree of thrust. It was an impressive demonstration of the *Enterprise*'s power and precision, and of Sulu's skill at wielding them. If Kirk couldn't get things sorted out with Lee Kelso, he thought, then Sulu would make a fine replacement.

As for Skovir and the Aulacri terraformers, it was fortunate that they only had a few small, unarmed ships, unable to put up any real resistance. They had made some brief attempts to place themselves in the *Enterprise*'s path, but space was big and open and the *Enterprise* was remarkably maneuverable for a ship of its mass, so Sulu had simply veered around them. Since then, they had merely kept pace with the comets and watched as they closed on Karabos II. Kirk had advised them to focus on tracking the smaller comets and ensuring they burned up in the upper atmosphere as planned. He hoped the water and nitrogen they restored to the planet would make a substantial difference to its habitability even without the impact winter.

But as the operation continued and the comets drew inexorably closer to impact, Sulu's normally cheerful manner grew increasingly solemn. Eventually he turned to Kirk and said, "Captain, we've managed to deflect the first three comets sufficiently, but I'm afraid there's no time to complete deflection of the largest one. And the Karabosi vault is still within its projected impact zone."

Kirk threw a glance at the large comet on the main viewer, staring it down like an enemy ship. The irregular ovoid was wreathed in a wispy cloud of water and nitrogen vapor, trailing off into a tail as it was blown away by Karabos's stellar wind, but being replenished by geysers that periodically burst from the surface as pockets of ice sublimated in the star's heat. "Options?"

Sulu spoke hesitantly. "There are still Aulacri thruster pods installed on the surface, sir. I didn't propose using them before because I don't know if they have enough fuel left, and because the surface conditions would be dangerously unstable this close to the star—even more so now, thanks to our phasers and tractors. It would be extremely risky, sir, but if we sent a team to the main thruster assembly and were able to reactivate it, we could operate the thrusters from there and gain the extra acceleration we needed to miss the atmosphere. But we'd have to do it within the next eighteen minutes."

Kirk turned to his chief engineer. "Mister Scott? Any other options?"

The burly Scotsman replied with a grim, alarmed look on

his face. "I'm afraid I can't give you any, sir. Mister Sulu's plan is dangerous, but it's all we've got."

The captain turned to Mitchell, who shrugged. "A crazy, life-threatening gambit at the last minute? Of course I'm in."

"I can lead the team myself, sir," Sulu said.

"No, I need you where you are, Lieutenant. I'll lead the team."

Mitchell stared at Kirk. "Jim, you're needed here too."

"It's settled, Mister Mitchell." Kirk had been through this debate with him enough times over the years. He didn't like ordering others to take risks he wasn't willing to take himself. Especially in this case, when the mission was legally questionable to begin with. The responsibility, and the risk, had to fall on him. "I'm going."

"Okay—then so am I. You need someone backing you up, and we don't need a navigator to tell us we're heading straight for a planet."

Their eyes locked, but after a brief moment, Kirk nodded. "All right, Gary."

"You'll need an engineer too, sir," Scott said. "I volunteer."

"That's not necessary, Mister Scott."

The other man tilted his head to the side. "With all due respect, sir, I'm not about to let my captain get himself killed in my second week aboard. I'd never live it down."

Kirk studied the man. Despite the humor in his words, Kirk realized that Scott was driven by a sense of personal responsibility not unlike his own. A chief engineer was as much a leader in his way as a captain, and even in their short time together, Kirk had already seen that Scott was the most hands-on chief engineer he'd ever served with. He smiled. "Very well, Mister Scott. You're with us."

"Captain!" It was Lieutenant Alden at communications. "Message from the surface!"

Kirk moved over to the rail by Alden's station while Mitchell and Scott moved to wait by the turbolift. "Mister Spock?"

"Yes, sir . . . but it's hard to clear it up. The first comets are entering the atmosphere . . . there's interference."

Alden did his best, and finally Spock's voice came through. *"Spock to . . . prise, do . . . ead me?"*

Kirk spoke up. "Spock, this is the captain. We read you. Are you ready to beam up? Repeat, are you ready to beam up?"

". . . gative, Captain. You must not . . . this vault to . . . destroyed. Repeat: You must not allow this vault to be destroyed." Alden had finally cleaned up the channel.

"Spock, what did you find?"

Spock told him in a few terse sentences—and Kirk realized that the stakes had just gotten far higher.

SACAGAWEA
2264

Eighteen

Computer translation creates the illusion of pure objectivity, but the software can all too easily reflect and even amplify the unconscious biases of its programmers. It's a delicate balance—we want to interpret other languages into terms we understand, yet not let our preconceptions distort their real meaning. It helps if translator programming teams are multicultural and multispecies, but the programmers still have a responsibility to remove themselves from the equation as much as possible.

—Hoshi Sato

U.S.S. Sacagawea

"*The situation is getting more serious, Jim,*" said Commodore Wesley.

Seated at his ready room desk for a change, Kirk furrowed his brow at the image of his mentor on the screen. "Has the *Enterprise* or the *Sau Lan Wu* found another Agni colony?"

"*No, not yet. And no Federation worlds have detected any Agni presence on N-Class planets in their systems. But we've improved our scans enough to make a concerning discovery about the nature of the Agni's facility here on 88 Leonis.*" He paused for emphasis. "*Jim—it's a shipyard.*"

Kirk took a moment to absorb that. "How many ships?"

"Seven of the cylinder types we've fought before. At least eleven smaller craft, roughly destroyer or frigate size."

"Can you tell if they're building them on site?"

"It seems unlikely that they could have, given the time frame, and there's insufficient evidence of large-scale mining to suggest they were made from local materials. It's more likely they've brought part of their existing fleet here for repairs and refitting— perhaps as a reserve force to support whatever they plan to do at Regulus."

"Sir . . . The Agni negotiators say they only want a new home to settle. They specifically mentioned needing a place to set down their ships in order to repair them fully after the damage they sustained in battle. If they are a refugee fleet, those ships, plus the few that settled here on Regulus I, may be all they have. 88 Leonis may be the first safe haven they've found to let them repair them all. It would explain why they've come with less force in each encounter."

"Until and unless you can secure a peace agreement, Jim, we can't afford to presume that. Even if it's true, that makes them desperate, willing to fight. These ships at 88 Leo could do a lot of damage to the Federation settlement in the system. Or they could be sent to reinforce the Agni there at Regulus. Our working theory is that they've modified their warp drive to dive deep into subspace, into a deeper domain than our sensors can reach. If we can't track them, we can't stop them before they get to Regulus. And that many ships invading the system at once could be devastating.

"Jim, the success of your negotiations could be the only thing that will prevent a war against an enemy that could strike from anywhere without warning."

Once Wesley signed off, Kirk found himself reflecting on the part the commodore hadn't mentioned. If hostilities did break out, it could cost many Regulan lives—but unless the Agni were far more numerous than they appeared, the numbers would inevitably favor the Federation. In the long term, Regulus would not be lost—but saving it might require driving the Agni to the brink of extinction. And that would cost the Federation something more intangible, but just as precious.

"Only if the negotiations fail," Kirk said to his reflection in the darkened screen. He held his own gaze emphatically. "So don't fail."

Nubicuculia, Hearthside

"We are concerned about the discovery of your shipyard at 88 Leonis," Kirk said to the three Agni negotiators. The diplomatic parties on both sides of the window had reconvened, though the Regulan group had been joined by Colonel Orloff, who had insisted on sitting in as an observer upon hearing of the shipyard. For her benefit as much as Starfleet's, Kirk had chosen to address that issue right off the bat. "As you are aware, that system also holds a Federation settlement, and while its inhabitants have no use for the third planet, its proximity to their world requires us to seek assurances as to the intentions of the facility. You said before that you only wanted a place to rest and repair your ships. If that is the only purpose of the shipyard facility, we are willing to allow you to remain there at least long enough to complete repairs and resupply, and to negotiate a longer stay if you desire. As a condition, we would require your cooperation in allowing automated probes to inspect your shipyard and confirm that its purpose is nonmilitary."

Diaz got to work on processing Kirk's words through the translator. This time, she had brought a portable computer with her to enhance the translation console's processing power, saying it was faster than relying on the subspace link with the *Sacagawea*'s computers in orbit. She frowned as she worked the controls on the boxy gray unit. "Anything wrong, Ensign?" Adebayo asked.

Diaz cleared her throat. "Just . . . perfecting the calibrations, sir. We can't afford any mistakes, after all."

Regardless of her extra caution, the request did not appear to go over well with the Agni, if Kirk was any judge of their body language. The response came from Protector, also not a good sign. "'Again cold beings attempt to claim control of our realm. You are not welcome in our places. Our terms are that you leave this world, not that you enter our other world.'"

Kirk was puzzled. "You said yourselves that a place could not belong to anyone. There is no need for impenetrable barriers between our peoples. We wish merely to establish trust—but that has to go both ways. If we can be allowed to inspect your shipyard, to verify its intentions, it will help us build that trust."

"'Observing our ships would give you an advantage over us. We will no longer allow cold beings to dictate what we do. We will control our own realm, and we will defend against cold beings who intrude on it—just as you have against us. It is all you understand.'"

Kirk sighed, exchanging looks with his fellow negotiators. "It feels like we're suddenly going backward."

"That is often the case in negotiations," T'Zeri told him. "Allow me."

The mature Vulcan woman stepped forward to address the Agni. "As we have discussed before, the people of Regulus have a tradition of welcoming newcomers. We are not averse to your colonization of Hearthside. But your demand that we vacate it is difficult to honor.

"I would like to propose an alternative. Rather than abandoning the aerial cities, we could move them to latitudes well removed from your ground facilities, so that they will not pass near enough overhead to pose an immediate threat. This will limit our access to many of the richest bacterial blooms, but in return, we suggest that you could harvest the bacteria at those latitudes and deliver them to our cities for processing. You have already expressed a willingness to perform the collection, processing, and interplanetary delivery for us in exchange for our departure. This proposal would require you to be involved only in collection, which would make it a smaller concession for you.

"If you accept this proposition, we could then negotiate a gradual withdrawal of our population over time, if that continues to be your preference. However, it is our hope that through our cooperation, we may learn to trust one another and be mutually content to remain on the same planet."

Beside Kirk, Colonel Orloff crossed her arms, shaking her head in wordless disapproval. She began to pace, pausing by Diaz's station and watching idly as the ensign completed encoding the translation. Her icy blue eyes then went to the Agni, who were reacting to T'Zeri's proposal with renewed agitation. "I don't think they liked that," Orloff murmured.

Diaz glanced up at the colonel, who gave her a tight, apologetic smile and moved away to let her concentrate on translating Speaker's response. The ensign spoke hesitantly, uncomfortable with the words. "'We have already made our terms clear. We will not live with cold beings. You cannot be trusted. You will leave this planet. If you leave voluntarily, we will provide the chemicals you need. If you do not, we will remove you by force, and you will get no more chemicals.'"

Orloff caught Kirk's gaze, a vindicated look in her eyes. But the captain's puzzlement remained. He stood and moved toward Speaker, hoping to make some sort of connection with a fellow leader across the barriers of biology and environment. "You must realize that if you force us to fight for the resources we need, you will inevitably lose. You may cost us a great deal in the fight, but we can bring reinforcements from many other worlds, and you will lose far more in the long term. Your species may not even survive. That's not what we want, and I can't believe it's what you want.

"I understand why you mistrust us. The fear of the unknown

is a universal trait. It helps keep us alive. And your experience has taught you that there is often good reason for that fear.

"But equally important for our survival is *fascination* with the unknown—the willingness to see its possibilities and embrace them. My species, humanity, has always had an inborn drive to explore the unknown, to find ways to live in realms that were alien, even hostile to us—from deserts and mountains on our own world to the emptiness of space. It was that need to move beyond our starting point that let us thrive when our environments changed and less adaptable species went extinct. Your people have had the same experience—you survived the death of your homeworld by moving out into the unknown, the hostile cold of space. You must see, as I do, that the unknown, for all its very real dangers, contains hope and opportunity as well.

"Your people and mine face a new frontier now. We face each other. And we can both survive that entry into the unknown if we're willing to look for the opportunities instead of just the dangers. If we listen to our hopes instead of our fears."

Kirk could see in the window's reflections that Adebayo was smiling broadly, and even T'Zeri looked impressed by his speech. Orloff merely crossed her arms, a dismissive sneer on her face. As for Diaz, Kirk realized she was blinking away tears. He tried not to let it go to his head.

The Agni, however, did not seem to react positively. They continued to gesticulate intensely, puffing out and retracting the sacs at the ends of their horns with increasing speed. It seemed as if Protector was arguing with Speaker and Observer . . . and Speaker looked subdued, perhaps even dejected, upon finally ceding the floor to Protector.

Diaz cleared her throat, wiped her eyes, and after throwing nervous glances toward Kirk and Orloff, spoke with difficulty as she interpreted Protector's words. "'You say . . . we cannot survive a fight. We do not agree. We have ships you cannot see coming. We have weapons you cannot defend against.'" She hesitated. "'Do not think you understand the Agni, or that you think the way we do. We have seen the madness of cold life too often. It would be a mercy to destroy you.'"

Orloff stepped forward. "You heard the captain. You don't have enough ships or weapons to hold us off forever."

"Colonel, please," T'Zeri said.

The human woman took a deep breath. "My apologies, Councillor."

But Diaz had already translated Orloff's words, and now she could barely be heard as she interpreted Protector's reply. "'You . . . do not know how many ships we have. But you will.'"

"That does it," said Orloff. "Captain, I think we can officially declare these talks a failure. There could be Agni ships warping toward us even now. I suggest we return to orbit and prepare our defense."

"Wait, wait," Kirk said. "Something isn't right about this." He still couldn't believe a leader like Speaker would so cavalierly ignore the safety of their people. Speaker's body language still struck him as conveying resignation, possibly even disappointment, rather than hostility. He couldn't know for certain, but after hours of observing the Agni through these negotiations, his intuition was telling him that something was off.

He strode over to Diaz. "Ensign, run a diagnostic on the portable computer, the workstation, everything. Are you sure our words are being translated correctly?"

As Diaz ran the check, she avoided meeting Kirk's eyes. *Why?* he wondered. It was unlike her to fear being chastised for an error. She had never lacked for confidence, and she had always welcomed his advice, even his criticism, in the past, much as he had valued the guidance of captains like Garrovick and Wesley.

She did finally look up at him as she answered, "Confirmed, sir. The equipment, the protocols . . . it all checks out."

"So they heard everything we said."

"Yes, sir." But her eyes darted away as she said it.

They darted toward Orloff. Why Orloff?

"It's settled, then," the colonel said. "Time we put an end to this farce."

"No, wait," Kirk insisted, his voice growing firmer. "We need a recess. Ensign, ask them to wait. Let's all take some time to process this."

"An excellent suggestion, Captain," said T'Zeri. "The interval might allow emotions to cool and reason to return."

"I can't afford to waste any more time," Orloff insisted. "I'm going back up to my fleet. They may be needed at any moment."

"You do that, Colonel," Kirk said, holding her steadily in his gaze. "I don't think you can do anything more down here."

Once the Agni grudgingly agreed to stand by a while longer, Kirk led Kamisha Diaz into a small observation lounge nearby for a private conversation. The city had drifted into the planet's night side by now, so all that could be seen were the lights of Nubicuculia's other spherical modules and the halos they formed in the cloud bank that engulfed them. "Too bad," Diaz said. "At the right times, when there's a break in the clouds and haze, the night sky is really beautiful. So many stars."

"For me, it was the sky above my parents' farm in Iowa," Kirk told her. "As soon as I learned that other stars had people living around them, looking back toward me, I felt an irresistible desire to go and meet them. To visit every single star I could see."

She gave him a knowing smile. "How many have you crossed off your list so far?"

"Not enough. Never enough." He studied her. "Ensign, what's really going on in there? Why did Colonel Orloff come today?"

Diaz turned to look out at the empty haze, as if suddenly fascinated by it. "I wouldn't presume to say, sir. I . . . I serve Starfleet, not the Defense Force."

He moved around to see her face. "But you feel loyal to Regulus. Just as she does."

She thought for a long moment. "This is my home. We have to protect it."

"At any cost?"

"Sir, are you accusing me of something?"

He was surprised at the suddenness of it—and heartened. "I think, Ensign . . . that you're accusing yourself of something. That you're not sure where your loyalties lie, or what the right choice is . . . and you're afraid you've made the wrong one."

Another loaded silence. "And what if I have?"

He put a hand on her shoulder. "Then there's still time to make it right."

Sobbing, Diaz fell into a seat. Kirk sat down beside her, a hand on her shoulder, as she confessed. "The colonel convinced me . . . to distort the translations. Make both sides think the other was being belligerent and unreasonable."

"Sabotage the peace talks so we'd believe the only path left was war."

"She believes it's the only way to protect Regulus, sir. And . . . she's not wrong that they were the aggressors. We have grounds for our grievances."

"Yes, you do," Kirk said with deep sympathy. "But do you really think starting a war will heal that pain?"

She winced. "No. No, it would only make things worse," she confessed. "And Harlie would be ashamed of me for doing this in her name. She cherished how welcoming we were. I should've listened to the things she said in life, not just how I felt about her death."

Kirk smiled. "Sounds like you've already worked through most of this on your own."

"By about halfway through the session in there, sir, I knew I'd made the biggest mistake of my career. But I was too deep to pull out, and the colonel was right there . . ." She looked up at him. "I guess I've blown my whole Starfleet career now, huh? Just as well I'm already back home."

He patted her shoulder. "Don't hand in your communicator yet, Ensign. You can still help us resolve this, if we go back in there and let the Agni know what we *really* said."

The only thing to do was to come clean entirely—to confess to the Agni that Colonel Orloff had corrupted the translation process and that the two sides had not heard each other's actual words. "We were both fooled," Kirk told the Agni, "and the one responsible will be held accountable. But we have a chance to repair the situation before it's too late."

Luckily, Diaz's computers had recorded the original statements, enabling them to be replayed with a correct translation. The Agni had, in fact, confirmed that the ships on 88 Leonis were the bulk of their surviving fleet, with no other settlements in Federation space. They had been receptive to allowing an inspection to confirm this, in exchange for permission to remain. Upon finally hearing T'Zeri's genuine compromise proposal, followed by Kirk's exhortation for understanding, Protector showed resistance, but was overruled by Speaker and Observer.

"'We understand your protector's actions,'" Speaker said through Diaz. "'Some of our protectors also object to these talks. But most of them are with our fleet. If they had been here, these talks might not have happened at all.'"

Diaz paused to interpret Speaker's next statement. "'There are those who only see fear in the unknown. They have their role in new places. But . . . those of us who see opportunity in the unknown are the ones who take our people to those places. We cannot let fear deafen us to opportunity.'"

Kirk smiled. His instinct about Speaker had been correct. Even across the most profound gulfs of biology and culture, one leader could recognize another.

The other humans in the room looked hopeful now, and even T'Zeri seemed to relax. "A promising statement," the councillor said. "I believe we have achieved—"

Kirk's communicator beeped, and a moment later T'Zeri's comlink signaled as well. Kirk moved aside and lifted the lid. "Kirk here."

"Mitchell here, Captain. You're gonna want to get back up here fast."

The sound of distant thunder resonated through the walls of the city. But as it slowly died down, Kirk realized it did not sound like thunder. "What's going on, Gary?"

"It's the Venant, *sir. It's just started bombarding the Agni settlements. And the rest of Orloff's ships are moving to join in."*

Nineteen

We've been trained to think in other terms than war. We've been trained to fight its causes, if necessary.

—James T. Kirk

U.S.S. Sacagawea

When Kirk, Adebayo, and Diaz reached the bridge, Mitchell hopped out of the command chair and faced the captain. "The Regulan fleet has moved into low forced orbits above the Agni settlements, sir. They've opened fire with retuned phasers and spatial torpedoes."

"Alkaline bombs?" Kirk asked. "Any sign of chemical attack?"

"Not yet. Maybe Orloff wants to break through their defenses first."

"Then we need to stop this quickly," Kirk said as he took his seat. He noted that Mitchell had already assigned Lieutenant Hauraki to take the helm station in anticipation of combat. "Mister Mitchell, set an intercept course for the nearest RDF ship. Hauraki, engage when ready."

"Captain," Chalan said, "Colonel Orloff began broadcasting a speech to her fleet while you were on the way to the bridge. I have it cued up for playback."

Kirk nodded to the Cygnian ensign. "Go ahead."

He turned back to the main viewscreen, where Orloff's visage appeared, the compact but well-equipped bridge of the *Venant* behind her. She was framed beneath the Regulan flag on the rear wall, a flattened blue oval with a darker blue band across it and a white dot to its upper right, representing Regulus A and its white dwarf companion. *"My fellow Regulans. We are in a time of crisis. The peace talks with the Agni have broken down irreparably. As you can see in the transcript attached to this transmission, they have delivered an ultimatum that we must vacate Hearthside or be forced to leave. Starfleet has confirmed that they have a fleet of powerful warships standing by at 88 Leonis, capable of moving through warp undetected and striking without warning.*

"Astonishingly, the inexperienced young captain that Starfleet has assigned to this crisis refuses to acknowledge the threat." Kirk blinked. That was a characterization he hadn't heard in a while. *"He uncritically accepts these aggressors' rationalization of their invasion as the act of desperate refugees, ignoring the hundreds of Federation lives they have taken over the past three years and the direct threats they have made against the population of Regulus. A complaint has been filed with Starfleet, but there is no hope of relief in time to prevent the Agni attack that is clearly imminent."*

Orloff straightened her shoulders. *"We Regulans have long prided ourselves on the welcoming hand we offer to immigrants. But pride can easily become fatal overconfidence. We can become so welcoming that we let down our guard—that we forget that, for every outsider who comes in peace, there are others who come to do us harm. Invaders and brutalizers like the Klingons. Pirates and slave traders like the Orions and their Syndicate. Criminal thugs like the Nausicaans and Acamarians, and even some of our fellow humans, Rigelians, and others, freeloaders who come to take advantage of our openness rather than serving the good of the community."*

Mitchell turned to Kirk with a bewildered expression. "She's starting to lose the plot a bit there."

"No," Adebayo said, crossing his arms. "I think she's finally getting to the true point, as she sees it."

"*Our own leaders, such as Councillor T'Zeri and even President Sentok, pride themselves so much on our welcoming reputation that it has left them vulnerable to the Agni's lies and manipulations—and has left Regulus vulnerable to an ongoing invasion by a species of profoundly alien nature, lacking our concepts of territorial rights and dismissive of our very existence. We cannot extend welcome to a species that does not recognize our own right to be here and has declared its overt intention to sweep us away by force.*

"*Therefore, the defense of Regulus falls to those of us who remain strong and vigilant, trained and ready to fight for our homeland. The Regulan Defense Force has been protecting this system since long before Starfleet or the Federation existed. Now that those institutions have failed us, now that our own Council refuses to defy the Federation even to protect its own people, it falls to the RDF to do so once again.*

"*Our impending actions may seem excessive, even cruel. But the cruelty and contempt of the Agni leave us no alternative. To halt their imminent assault on our system, we must strike first and strike hard. We must drive them from Hearthside quickly and ruthlessly, deprive them of their foothold in our system before they can solidify it, and demonstrate decisively that the cost of invading our system is too great for them to endure. Only by staying strong, determined, and united against foreign foes can we preserve our Regulan homeland . . . our Regulan identity . . . our Regulan greatness.*"

The transmission went out, and Mitchell shook his head and gave a low whistle. "And *sieg* freakin' *heil* while she's at it."

"Ensign Chalan," Kirk said, "open a general hail to the RDF fleet."

"I'm sorry, sir, the *Venant* is jamming transmissions," Chalan replied. "Councillor T'Zeri already contacted them as soon as you beamed aboard. She announced that Colonel Orloff was engaging in a deception, but she was cut off before she could elaborate."

"Damn." She must have been attempting the same thing Kirk had planned, to broadcast the record of the corrected translations, and thereby tipped off the colonel to the discovery of her deceit.

"Coming up on the nearest Regulan ship, sir," Lieutenant Hauraki announced. "The *RDF Lionheart*. Destroyer type, crew complement ninety. Its torpedo tubes are open, targeting the Agni settlement below."

"Take us in beneath them," Kirk said. "Don't let those torpedoes reach the surface."

Hauraki managed to shoot down one of the spatial torpedoes with phasers, but the second—fortunately still a conventional charge—slipped past him. He then maneuvered the *Sacagawea* to block the *Lionheart*'s firing solution for the settlement below, forcing them to reposition and recalibrate.

"Sir," Chalan said, "message from the *Lexington*. Commodore Wesley reports that five Agni ships have launched from 88 Leonis III and gone into warp. Course, bound for Regulus. *Lexington* unable to track or intercept."

"If we don't stop Orloff before they get here," Adebayo said, "she'll get her war."

The bridge shook. "Sorry, sir," Hauraki said. "Only way to block that one was to take the hit ourselves. Shields down to eighty-four percent."

Kirk gave his next order reluctantly. "Target the *Lionheart*. Attempt to disable their weapons ports. Minimum necessary force."

Ensign Diaz had been watching quietly, but she stepped forward now. "It won't work, Captain. Their shields are too good."

The viewscreen showed two phaser strikes bouncing off the *Lionheart*'s deflectors just above their firing ports. "She's right, sir," Hauraki said. "Their shields are holding. To hit them hard enough to have effect would virtually guarantee significant casualties."

Am I willing to kill Federation citizens to save the Agni? Kirk asked himself. But he refused to accept that there was no alternative. That was *Kobayashi Maru* thinking.

"Chalan," Kirk said, "any luck piercing *Venant*'s jamming? We have to let the RDF crews know that Orloff has deceived them."

"I've been trying, sir," the Cygnian said, "but they know Federation comm systems too well. They have countermeasures for everything I've tried."

After a moment's thought, Kirk turned to Diaz. "That can go both ways, can't it, Ensign Diaz? Those ships use Regulan equipment, Regulan protocols. Their crews studied the same texts you did, passed the same exams."

The concern in the young science officer's eyes turned to surprise, and a moment later into hope. "I get it! I mean, understood, Captain! Just let me think . . ."

"Reports from Hearthside, Captain," Chalan said. "*Venant*'s bombardment is intensifying. The blast effects in the atmosphere are causing turbulence on the nearest city. They're trying to divert course, but the air currents are moving them toward the impact zone."

"Now she's endangering her own people," Adebayo rumbled. "How many more will die once those Agni ships get here?"

"Of course!" Diaz cried. "The weather band!"

Kirk turned to her. "Ensign?"

"Sorry, sir—I meant stellar weather. Regulus A spins so fast that it tosses off a lot of its atmosphere. Like low-level ion storms, potentially disruptive to ships and orbital facilities. Every vessel in the system gets constant activity updates from the monitor satellites around the star—we think of them as space weather reports. They're on a dedicated band not used in regular communications, and the update process is so routine we rarely even think about it. I'd bet *Venant*'s jamming doesn't include the weather band."

"You think we can get a signal through to them that way?"

"To their computers, yes. Which would let us fake an emergency alert, like for a major stellar storm, which the computer would automatically relay to every ship's bridge. We could transmit the real session transcript as a data burst through that relay."

Kirk beamed at her. "Very good, Ensign! Proceed."

The ship rocked under a phaser hit from the *Lionheart*. "Sir, our shields are weakening faster than theirs," Hauraki cautioned, his tone wavering between *Please let me take the gloves off* and *Please don't make me kill our own people.*

Adebayo was covering the science station while Diaz worked with Chalan. "The *Venant* has nearly brought down the defensive barrier around its target settlement. It won't be long before they can deploy a chemical warhead."

"The relay's ready, sir," Diaz reported, to Kirk's relief. "The transcript is going through now."

"It'll take too much time for them to review it," Adebayo said.

"Then we have to get them to stop and take that time," Kirk said. "Diaz, is the back channel open for voice transmission?"

"Yes, sir. You can get a message through."

Kirk stepped toward her. "Not me, Ensign. You."

Her eyes widened. "Me, sir? But . . . I betrayed you."

"You acted out of loyalty to the colonel, and to Regulus. And you changed your mind. Who better to convince your fellow Regulans to do the same?" He smiled. "Besides . . . I already got to make my big speech today. I don't want to hog the spotlight."

Diaz gave a nervous, grateful laugh. "Yes, sir."

With Kirk's prompting, she stepped to the front of the bridge, facing the visual pickup. Taking a deep breath, she cued Chalan with a gesture, and the Cygnian opened the transmission.

"My fellow Regulans," she said, looking embarrassed about it a moment later. "Crews of the Defense Force ships. My name is Ensign Kamisha Diaz, and I was born on Regulus V. I grew up here, as one of you. I made a dear and wonderful friend named H'Raal, who . . . who died the other day, in the Agni attack on Laputa.

"Because of that, because of my patriotism, my grief, and my anger, I allowed Colonel Yelena Orloff to convince me to betray my oath to Starfleet and my principles as a scientist. Tasked with operating the translation program that would permit the Regulan people to resolve our unnecessary conflict with the Agni and ensure that no one else would have to die, I . . . I instead worked under Colonel Orloff's instruction to sabotage the translation and convince both sides that the other intended imminent hostility, in order to give the colonel the excuse to launch the attack currently underway.

"The truth is that the Agni are refugees, homeless survivors who came to Regulus in search of safe haven. Our difficulty in understanding each other kept us from seeing that they were exactly the kind of people we have always welcomed into our community and taken pride in assisting.

"Yes, they killed my friend. Yes, that made me angry and afraid. But that anger, that fear, kept me from understanding what H'Raal's death really meant. She wasn't a helpless victim of aggression. She didn't have to die that day. She could've lived if she'd just thought of her own survival, her own fear, and ignored the needs of others.

"But that wasn't H'Raal's way, because she believed in what Regulus stands for. What the Federation stands for. She chose to take a risk, to look beyond her fear for her own safety, and selflessly help others in need. She saved lives because of that. She saved *my* life. In her final moment, she chose to save me instead of herself. Because she knew that we, as a people, are not driven by fear and selfishness. We don't sacrifice the lives of others because we fear for our own.

"This is what Colonel Orloff has forgotten, what she wants you to forget. We have so much that it's easy to get defensive about it, afraid that it will be taken from us. But when we have so much more wealth and security and comfort than others like the Agni, it is absurd to say that we are the ones being threatened or deprived if they ask to share in our plenty. That claim is a direct inversion of reality, and it depends on a lie—a lie I helped Colonel Orloff sell to you. Because I was hurt and afraid, I let her convince me of the lie that Regulans were weak and endangered.

"But we are *not* weak. We are a strong, healthy, and prosperous civilization, and that means we have it within us to be generous and forgiving, to face others without fear and take a chance on connecting with them, no matter how alien they seem.

"So I implore you, officers of the Defense Force—halt your attack on the surface. Refuse Colonel Orloff's orders. At least stop long enough to investigate what I'm telling you, to review the evidence we've transmitted. It's our last hope to preserve the essence of who we are as Regulans, instead of just the place where we live."

After a few moments, Diaz glanced back at Kirk, her eyes asking, *Is that enough?*

"The *Lionheart* has stopped firing," Hauraki added, offering a partial answer.

"The rest of the fleet?" Kirk asked.

"The *Venant* is still jamming, Captain," Adebayo said. "Still in position to open fire on the Agni settlement, though holding fire for now."

"Move us to intercept," Kirk ordered Hauraki.

"Some of the RDF ships are doing the same already," said the first officer.

"It seems you convinced most of them, Ensign," Kirk told Diaz. "At least enough to give us a chance."

Diaz did not look satisfied. "I doubt the colonel will be that easy to convince."

An alert sounded on Hauraki's panel. "*Venant* has fired a torpedo toward the surface! It's . . . it's the chemical warhead, sir!"

"Full speed! Intercept that warhead!"

"We'll never make it in time!" Mitchell cried.

But Hauraki clutched his targeting scope tightly, peering harder at its readouts. "Sir . . . The *Venant* has just fired phasers on its own torpedo! Detonation well short of the atmosphere."

Chalan spoke up. "The jamming field has fallen, sir. Hail coming in from the *Venant*."

Kirk gestured to Chalan to open the channel. *Venant*'s bridge appeared on the screen, but Orloff was no longer in sight. *"This is Lieutenant Colonel Mandip Krishnamurti, first officer of the* Venant," said the serious-featured woman who stood in her place. *"Colonel Orloff . . . has been relieved of command. I hereby order the fleet to stand down from battle stations. For further instructions, Captain Kirk of Starfleet has the rightful command authority."*

Kirk rose and moved forward to stand by Diaz. "Congratulations, Ensign. You just prevented a war." He smiled. "And gave me a run for my money at public speaking."

Once Kirk and Diaz returned to Nubicuculia and convinced Speaker and the others that their attackers had withdrawn, the Agni leaders agreed to halt the advance of their fleet—though it would remain in deep space near the Regulus system until a formal treaty could be established. As for the RDF ships, they returned to their home ports, while the *Venant* under Lieutenant Colonel Krishnamurti delivered Yelena Orloff to Regulus III's capital for arraignment. Apparently, Orloff had attempted to forbid her bridge crew from listening to the *Sacagawea*'s broadcast, and when Krishnamurti had insisted on being allowed to hear it, Orloff had drawn her weapon and commandeered the tactical controls to fire the alkaline torpedo. She had been subdued and dragged off the bridge, insisting to the end that she was acting in defense of Regulus against all outsiders who threatened its sovereignty, Starfleet included. It was a sobering reminder, Kirk thought, of how easily protectiveness could transform into intolerance. He hoped the Regulan penal system—itself a beneficiary of Tristan Adams's rehabilitative reform program—could help Orloff understand where she had gone wrong.

Once more urgent matters were settled, it was time to deal with Kamisha Diaz. She may have done remarkable work making amends for her sabotage of the peace talks, but the sabotage itself had been a serious offense, one that could have cost thousands of lives or even brought a species to the brink of extinction. Kirk couldn't just let it go.

"I understand, sir," Diaz told him when he came to visit her under confinement in her quarters. "I won't make any excuses for what I did. It was a major crime. I deserve to be drummed out of Starfleet."

Kirk studied her sadly. Even after all this, he saw great potential in her. He wasn't prepared to throw that away. Maybe this was how Commander Cheng had felt about young Lieutenant Kirk back on the *Farragut*, seeing him racked with guilt about his failure to prevent Captain Garrovick's death, but refusing to let him hang himself for it.

"Kamisha . . . What you did was at the bidding of Colonel Orloff. You may not have officially been in her chain of command, but she was effectively a superior officer. You don't have to take the blame for what she pressured you to do."

"My responsibility is to you, Captain. I should've contacted you or Commander Adebayo immediately. But I chose to go along with her."

"You made a mistake. And you corrected it before any great damage could be done. I can't say there won't be consequences. There will have to be a hearing, and at the very least, there will be a serious reprimand on your record."

She lowered her head and gave a dejected sigh. "So much for trying to beat your 'youngest captain' record, sir. I'll be lucky to make it to lieutenant. I don't see Starfleet trusting me again any time soon."

Kirk took a step closer. "You still have people who trust you, Ensign. You're the only person in the Federation that the Agni really trust right now. And the Regulan Council trusts you too." He smiled. "That's why both parties have requested that I assign you to detached duty as their official translator and diplomatic liaison."

She jerked her head back up, staring at him openmouthed. "I—you mean—really, sir?"

He chuckled. "That's right. It won't be easy work, and it will probably be very slow going. Worst of all, you'll have to deal with politicians on a regular basis."

She echoed his chuckle with a feebler one. "Well, I did say I deserve to be punished."

"Call it 'rehabilitated,' Ensign. This is a chance to make a real difference. To learn about a new, truly alien species, and to build a lasting peace between former enemies. I can't think of a worthier achievement for a Starfleet officer."

Diaz smiled wistfully. "The worthiest achievement would be to keep exploring the galaxy under your command, Captain. And one day to follow in your footsteps. But . . . this will do nearly as well."

ENTERPRISE
2265

Twenty

When all you have are your memories, let no one take them from you—least of all yourself.

—Aulacri proverb

Comet surface, Karabos system

Kirk had tried to contact Skovir and tell her what Spock and Sherev had learned from the vault on Karabos II's surface, but the terraforming director refused to accept his hails. With little time remaining, Kirk proceeded with the plan to beam over to the largest comet and activate its thruster pods manually. He just hoped that Skovir and the Aulacri government would understand his actions once they learned the whole truth.

Kirk, Mitchell, and Scott beamed over to the comet in thruster suits, necessary since its surface gravity was a fraction of a percent of Earth's. A forceful step could send them into orbit. They also carried harpoon guns to anchor themselves to the surface, which should make it easier to open and operate the Aulacri thruster unit's manual controls.

The cometary surface around them was made mostly of water ice intermixed with coal-black carbon compounds, but Kirk was struck by how familiar it looked. The towering crags and scarps surrounding the level plain where they stood reminded him uncannily of the desert terrain of the American Southwest, if viewed in monochrome—and through a fisheye lens, for the horizon, where he could see it, was startlingly close and curved vertiginously down and away. A faint haze of ice crystals and rock dust filled the air, a new-formed atmosphere spit out by the erupting geysers as the comet warmed in Karabos's ever-nearer light. The ground beneath Kirk's feet was covered in fine scree, and the visible rock—or rather, ice—underneath it was cracked and crazed like the top of a fresh pan of brownies. The brittle, friable appearance of the surface made Kirk grateful that he was featherlight in this gravity.

The primary thruster unit was anchored before them in the middle of the plain, one of the few relatively level and solid surfaces on the comet. It was a hexagonal pyramid about six meters high, with a rosette of thrust control vanes surrounding the opening at the apex. From each face extended a leg that had bored into the surface to secure it here.

But once the trio circled around to the control panel under Scott's guidance, Kirk saw that the surface had not been as solid as it seemed. A large pit gaped in the ground, and from it a crack extended clear to one of the thruster's anchor legs, which had been torn loose. *"A geyser must've erupted here,"* Mitchell said. *"Right by the thruster. We're lucky it's still attached."*

"Not so lucky, Commander," Scott said, shaking his head as he examined the control panel. *"Look."*

The panel was torn open and pitted, its controls and inner circuitry wrecked. *"Shrapnel from the geyser must've done it,"* Scott said.

"Can you bypass the controls?" Kirk asked.

"Not in the available time, sir. We need to get to one of the other thrusters. This was the master unit, but I can still access the control network from one of the auxiliaries. The thruster's still good to fire, it's just a matter of startin' it."

"How much time do we have?"

"Less than ten minutes for minimum safe deflection," Mitchell said.

"Lead the way, Mister Scott," Kirk said, grateful for the comet's relatively small size.

Despite the shortness of the journey, it was not without its hazards. The comet's surface was cracking and shifting beneath their feet as they coasted above it using their suit thrusters. Puffs of vapor spat out of cracks in the surface, and at one point, a geyser erupted from a spot they'd passed over no more than ten seconds earlier. Any closer, and the icy shrapnel might have done to their EV suits what it had done to the main thruster's controls.

As they neared the auxiliary thruster, another obstacle presented itself. Five Aulacri, immediately recognizable through the tail sheaths extending back from their thruster suits, blocked the humans' path. "Watch yourselves," Kirk said to the others. He remembered how lithe, quick, and acrobatic they had been in the entertainment they had put on the other day, even though they were scientists by profession. He wasn't about to underestimate their fighting prowess.

"Turn back now!" Skovir's voice came over the comm channel. *"This is your final warning! Please, Captain Kirk, abandon this insane risk in the name of an unwanted past!"*

"Skovir, listen to me," Kirk said. "You've been wrong about the Karabosi this whole time."

"The Karabosi are dead! They deserve to stay that way!"

Before Kirk could answer, she lunged at him, kicking off the large thruster unit with her strong legs and using her suit jets to accelerate toward him. It happened too quickly for Kirk to react; before he could reach his own thrust controls, she slammed into him feetfirst. The impact brought her to a near halt while sending Kirk sailing backward on a tangent to the surface, which quickly began curving down away from him. He tumbled, drifting farther and farther into the hazy sky.

Finally, he recovered enough to reach the thruster control panel on his suit. Once he stabilized himself, he began thrusting back toward the surface. He raised his harpoon gun and fired a tether line into the ice, using it to reel himself in faster.

As he neared the thruster site, he saw Mitchell and Scott fending off their own attackers; unlike Kirk, they'd had the presence of mind to anchor themselves with their harpoon tethers ahead of time. The Aulacri moved fluidly and swiftly in the minimal gravity, using their tails to reorient their bodies in midair like falling cats, relying on their suit jets only for thrust rather than direction changes.

Scott had managed to wrap his tether around one of the Aulacri like a lasso, binding his arms to his sides, but another was thrusting toward him. Mitchell was struggling in the grip of the remaining two; Kirk drew his phaser and stunned one, who drifted slowly off and down toward the surface while Mitchell continued to vie with the other. Kirk aimed at the second attacker . . .

And his harpoon tore free from the crumbling surface. The line lost tension and snaked toward him, tangling his arms and legs. He scrambled free, having to detach the harpoon gun from his belt to do so. But the surface was now rising rapidly toward him. He fired his jets, but still hit hard and bounced at a shallow angle.

Kirk caught himself on a craggy outcropping, bringing himself to a halt. He looked around until he spotted the others: Mitchell was holding his own against the terraformer whose arms, legs, and tail were wrapped around him, but Scott had been overpowered by his two attackers, who were binding his arms behind him.

"*Captain!*" Seeing a shadow on the ground before him, he looked up to see Skovir crouching atop the outcropping, her own harpoon gun leveled at his helmet visor. "*Your time is almost up. Another few minutes and it'll be too late to divert the comet. You've lost!*"

"You have no idea how much *you'll* lose if you let this comet hit, Skovir!"

"*I'll lose everything I've worked toward for twenty years if I don't!*"

Kirk felt a faint, building rumble in the ground beneath his feet, saw pebbles begin to break away from the outcropping on which Skovir stood. "Director, we need to move now!"

"*You're staying right where you—*"

Kirk lunged upward, taking her by surprise. He slammed into her and knocked them both into the sky . . . and as they tumbled, they caught glimpses of the massive geyser that erupted right where they had been standing moments before. A burst of sublimating water vapor and fragments of ice slammed into their suits, but they were far enough away that it did minimal damage.

As he fired his thrusters to stabilize them several hundred meters above the comet's surface, Skovir met his eyes in bewilderment. "Maybe now you'll listen to me," he said, gripping her upper arms firmly as he let gravity draw them slowly back down. But it seemed the fight had gone out of her.

"Skovir, you were wrong. The Karabosi didn't try to destroy the Aulacri."

"*W-what? What are you saying?*"

"What Spock and Sherev found down there in the vault—it's a gene bank. It contains preserved genetic samples of thousands of different forms of Karabosian life—including the Karabosi themselves."

Skovir snarled. "*Of course they preserved themselves and not us!*"

"That's where your history got it wrong, Skovir. My people scanned the genetic code of the Karabosi samples. It's essentially identical to Aulacri genes. Skovir, there weren't two different species on Karabos II. There was only one—your ancestors."

The terraformer was stunned. She shook her head in disbelief. "*No. No, they got it wrong. You saw the images! The Karabosi were larger than us, more hirsute, more gray-skinned.*"

"Only a surface difference—the result of four millennia of genetic drift in the new environment of Aulac. But no greater than the difference between the ethnic groups of my species. Skovir—the Karabosi were not your enemies. They were *you*."

"No. It can't be true! We're nothing like those genocidal monsters!"

He gripped her arms again, but this time to support her rather than restrain her. "No, you're not—not anymore. Because your people learned from their mistakes. The survivors who made their way to Aulac—they must have been ashamed of the savagery that led them to destroy their homeworld. They must have resolved to become better, to get it right the second time and leave that dark side of themselves behind."

They touched down lightly on the surface, and Kirk saw that the fighting had stopped; the other Aulacri were listening raptly to their dialogue. Skovir looked up at him searchingly. *"If that is what our ancestors wanted, then why not let us finish what they started? Let us wipe away the last vestiges of our ancestors' crimes and give our people a new, purified beginning on Karabos II?"*

"Because that's not how it works, Skovir," Kirk said. "You can't move forward by forgetting your past. You have to learn from all of it, the good and the bad.

"Many of us have similar atrocities in our ancestry. My own ancestral culture on Earth, in a land called America, was founded on one of the greatest genocides in my planet's history, the theft of an entire continent from its native peoples . . . and on the brutal enslavement of humans from yet another continent. Yet at the same time, America pioneered representative democracy, social justice, diplomacy, and innovation, laying the foundation for the guiding principles of the Federation. Both extremes coexisted in the same culture, as they do in so many. It's a paradox of history we struggle with to this day."

"And . . . how do you resolve it, Captain?"

"For myself . . . by having faith in humans' ability to learn from our mistakes. It's only by admitting our wrongs and our failures, by confronting them honestly, that we can ever transcend them. The greatest evils are committed by those who assume they can do no wrong. It's our acceptance of our capacity to do evil that drives us to be better.

"Your ancestors, Director, built the peaceful, benevolent society you so prize out of guilt and regret toward what they did to their own homeworld. If you erase the knowledge of their misdeeds, then your descendants will lose that incentive to keep striving to improve."

Skovir shook her head. "I still can't believe anything good could come from reviving the knowledge of that violent, hateful culture, even if they were our forebears."

"Director, your forebears were the same as mine. For every cruel, violent faction driven by greed and hate, there were others striving for the greater good. The people who built that vault were determined to preserve as much as they could of the world that others of their race—your race—were about to destroy. In addition to art and literature from every major culture on Karabos II, they preserved genetic samples from every ethnic group. Viable samples that can be cloned. So that, one day, the Karabosi people—all their peoples—might live again.

"You wanted to remake a world from scratch, Skovir. Wouldn't it be better to restore one?"

Skovir gasped as the weight of his words finally sank in. "By the Seed! We only have minutes left! We have to get these thrusters up and running immediately!"

U.S.S. Enterprise

It was as close as Kirk ever wanted to cut it. Half an hour later, he, Skovir, and the others stood on the Enterprise bridge together, clenching their fists as the comet streaked through the upper atmosphere. The thrusters and the Enterprise's tractor beam had been nudging its trajectory outward arcsecond by arcsecond that entire time, and the simulations gave a reasonably high probability of success. But they were only just now coming back into orbit, with no time to evacuate Spock and Sherev before the moment of truth, so Kirk couldn't bring himself to relax until the comet had completed its passage through the edge of the atmosphere and flown back on into the depths of space, depositing a fraction of its water and ammonia vapor and leaving the planet surface unharmed.

Skovir turned to him. "You stopped us from making a terrible mistake, Captain Kirk. And you have given us the chance to reclaim hundreds of Karabosian species we had thought to be long extinct—and to allow many of our own ancestors to live again, after a fashion." The clones, of course, would not have the memories of their originals, but they would be the Karabosi's direct inheritors, and they could be raised with the culture their forebears had left for them in the archive's data sheets. They would add a whole new subculture to the Aulacri's diversity, and though Kirk expected that had the potential for conflict, he had faith that both cultures—the one preserved by the ancients in defiance of the others' violence and the one built by the Aulacri to ensure it was never repeated—would find their way through it and be better for it.

Watching the last wisps of cometary vapors diffuse into Karabos II's atmosphere, Gary Mitchell sidled over to Kirk. "That's, what, three peoples saved from extinction now? This is starting to be a habit with you."

Kirk shook his head. "No. I'd say Mister Spock deserves the credit for this one."

His old friend looked at him askance. "Don't let Rhen hear you say that."

"I think Rhen would agree with me. If Spock hadn't insisted on staying behind, if he hadn't solved that puzzle as quickly as he did, the Karabosi civilization would've been destroyed all over again, and we'd never even have known it." Kirk shook his head. "I still don't know what made that logical, scientific mind so driven to fight on their behalf, but I'm glad he did."

Mitchell grinned. "Sounds like you've finally accepted your new first officer."

Kirk thought it over. "I think we still have a lot to learn about our Mister Spock. But I look forward to finding it out."

ENTERPRISE
2264

Twenty-One

For the past quarter-century, the Agni have remained on peaceful but distant terms with the Federation and have resisted a closer relationship, needing nothing from it besides acceptance of their parallel existence within its space. Since neither order of life can exist in each other's worlds, since they can barely even perceive one another and can communicate only indirectly and imperfectly, the Agni are in many ways more remote from the Federation than the most distant M-Class civilizations yet discovered. Yet their coexistence within Federation systems is proof that even the most extreme divides can be bridged.

—Dr. Monali Bhasin
Ministers of Sacrifice

U.S.S. Enterprise
"Negotiations with the Agni are going well," the image of Robert Wesley said to Christopher Pike as the latter sat at the desk in his quarters, arms folded in thought. *"Provisionally, the surface of Regulus I is being set aside as a territorial enclave for the Agni, along with the entirety of 88 Leonis III. It's possible that the Federation outpost in that system will be relocated or scaled back. It's not like we don't have plenty of other suitable worlds to choose from."*

Pike shook his head. "Imagine how it must be for them. Coming out into the galaxy and finding that worlds you can live on are few and far between, and that most of the life out here is almost inconceivably alien. We got incredibly lucky to find a universe whose worlds and peoples are so close a match to our own."

"*There are days when I still find that damned hard to believe, no matter how often I see the proof,*" Wesley said. "*The best explanation I can come up with? The Great Bird of the Galaxy really likes hairless apes.*"

"Don't tell the Agni that," Pike said. "Refugees or not, I gather they're not the sort of people you want to piss off."

"*Yeah, about that. Now that we've gotten a better look at their technologies, it looks like there's little that's worth adapting for Federation use. According to Captain Kirk and his science crew, the singularity drives are an impressive technological achievement, but hard to contain and repair, and inefficient to create in the first place. You could power both our ships for a year with the energy it takes to create even one microsingularity. We're better off with the power systems we have. And without the singularity, there's no plasma beam.*"

"Fine with me," Pike said. "We're not out here to build bigger and better weapons."

"*You know how I feel about that, Chris. There's a need for military readiness. However, this particular weapon is only bigger, not better. The drawbacks outweigh the benefits. Same with the armor plate system. It's no better than deflectors, and it traps too much waste heat inside the ship—not a problem for the Agni, but definitely for us 'cold beings.'*"

"*As for their stealth warp drive,*" Wesley went on, "*according to Kirk's people, the Agni say it only works for relatively short hops— and even so, it exposes the crew to intense subspace radiation that's harmless to the Agni but fatal for water-based life like us.*"

"That tracks with what Commander Spock theorized," Pike replied.

Wesley chuckled. "*Sometimes it seems like that Vulcan has all the answers ahead of time. I don't know how he does it, but the fleet could use fifty like him."*

"Sorry—he's one of a kind." Pike tilted his head, contemplating his longtime colleague. "You know, you should save some of that praise for Captain Kirk. He achieved something remarkable at Regulus. The Federation owes him a great debt."

Wesley shrugged. *"Don't get me wrong, I'm proud of him. I've already recommended him for the Preantares Ribbon for this. But let's keep things in perspective. The Agni threat didn't turn out to be the invasion we feared it was."*

"There are more intangible threats, Bob. Sometimes from ourselves. Kirk held on to Starfleet's ideals when they were tested, and in so doing, he saved us from doing real harm to what we stand for. That's a valuable thing—especially out on the frontier."

The commodore peered at Pike. *"You look even more brooding than usual. What are you thinking, Chris?"*

"I'm thinking that Preantares Ribbon will jump James Kirk to the top of the list for promotion to a senior captaincy. Maybe for a ship like the *Enterprise*."

Wesley took that in. *"You're thinking of doing it, aren't you? Accepting Command's offer. Taking the fleet captain post."*

Pike was slow to respond. "Fleet captain" was an impressive-sounding title for what was basically a bureaucratic position, the chief of staff to a starbase commander. It would be a promotion, giving Pike responsibility for the deployment and operations of all the ships under the starbase's authority, even still allowing him to lead the occasional diplomatic or scientific mission if the need arose. But it would also mean giving up the independence that came with being a captain on the frontier. In many ways, after all these years, Pike would welcome the chance to rest. That independence, that sole responsibility for hundreds of lives on his ship and countless millions beyond, was a heavy burden for any person to bear for a decade straight. There had been times in the past when he had believed himself to be over-whelmed by that burden and considered retreating from it, but he'd always changed his mind, largely with the encouragement of his crew. But now his stalwart Number One was captain of the *Yorktown*, Dr. Boyce had retired, and only Spock remained from the command crew Pike had led for so long. So maybe it was finally time for him to seek out new horizons as well.

For Wesley's benefit, Pike distilled his thoughts to a simple "I have been considering it, yes." He sighed. "But I've been reluc-tant to leave the *Enterprise*, since I wanted to be sure she'd be in good hands. If I could have that assurance . . ."

"Well, if you did take the promotion, I daresay Jim Kirk would be a leading candidate to replace you." He smiled. *"And I'd be happy to add my recommendation to yours."*

"I appreciate that, Bob."

After signing off, Pike continued to contemplate his future, and that of the *Enterprise* without him. It would still be a few more months before their current tour was over—not to men-tion Kirk's, for the *Sacagawea* had been assigned to seek out the remainder of the scattered Agni refugee ships in deep space and escort them safely to their new homeworlds. But that would give Pike plenty of time to research Kirk and other candidates and set-tle on his final recommendation. Ultimately it would be Starfleet's decision, of course, but Pike had been with the *Enterprise* for the majority of her time in service. He was sure Starfleet Command would give his recommendation the appropriate weight.

The harder part, Pike realized, might be convincing Com-mander Spock to accept a new captain. Spock was loyal to a fault, a stalwart presence at Pike's side, but Pike knew his bril-liance would be wasted as the right-hand man of a fleet captain sitting behind a desk at a starbase. Starfleet needed him out here on the frontier, and he needed to be out here too, to face the challenges that would shape him into the leader Pike knew he could become.

But Pike suspected that if anyone could win Spock's acceptance, it would be James Kirk. In many ways, the man reminded Pike of his own younger self, the captain that Spock had met when he came aboard the *Enterprise* more than a decade ago. He hoped that Spock would see the resemblance as well—and that it would help him accept Kirk long enough to discover and appreciate the things that would make him unique as a commanding officer.

Christopher Pike paced his quarters, trying to imagine what he would say to Kirk, or to whoever ended up replacing him as captain of the *Enterprise*. He still had months to figure it out, but he knew it would be important to get it right.

ENTERPRISE
2265

Twenty-Two

Commanding a starship is your first, best destiny.

—Spock

U.S.S. *Enterprise*
When Lee Kelso saw Kirk standing outside his quarters, he stiffened to attention. "Captain! Sir." He stared at Kirk uneasily.

"May I come in, Lieutenant?"

Kelso started. "Of course, sir! Come right in." He stepped back awkwardly.

Once the door had closed, Kelso turned to face him. "Permission to speak, Captain?"

Kirk looked him over. "Granted."

"Captain . . . I can't tell you how sorry I am that I defied you. I heard what happened . . . I can't believe I was so wrong. I thought your judgment was compromised by your feelings for—I mean, your friendship with Doctor Sherev. But I was the one who lacked judgment. I didn't see the things you saw. I should've trusted that, as the captain, you'd be able to, well, do that." He trailed off, interlacing his fingers nervously.

"I accept your apology, Lieutenant," Kirk said. "I'm just curious to know what made it difficult for you to trust me."

"Well . . . to be honest, sir . . . I'm just not used to having a captain who's barely older than I am. And, well, I was at the Academy when those rumors about the *Kobayashi Maru* started and, well, I guess I assumed the worst. Again, I apologize deeply for that."

Kirk offered him a small smile. "It's not the first time I've been judged for my youth, Mister Kelso, and I doubt it'll be the last. I understand it must be a difficult adjustment after serving for a veteran like Captain Pike. Frankly, Lee, I envy you for having had that opportunity."

"Only for a few months, sir. I'd hoped it would be longer. And I took that out on you." He sighed. "The fact is, Captain Pike wasn't above bending the rules when he had to. In his case, I trusted that he had his reasons. I had no right to think otherwise of you, sir."

"I appreciate it, Lieutenant."

Kelso fidgeted. "I suppose . . . if you want me to apply for a transfer . . ."

Kirk held out a hand. "Stop right there, Lieutenant. That won't be necessary."

The fair-haired helmsman stared. "But after what I did . . ."

"You made a mistake. It happens to the best of us. And as I recently pointed out to Director Skovir, it's by confronting and learning from our mistakes that we better ourselves. I think you deserve that same chance.

"After all—as misguided as you were, I respect that you had the courage to stand up to authority when you believed it was necessary. The ironic thing is, you were standing up to me for doing the same. So I really have no business judging you for it, do I?"

"Um . . . if you say so, sir."

"I need officers who can serve as checks on my judgment, who can tell me when they think I'm wrong. I won't always agree with them, but I always want to hear what they have to say—as long as they accept my orders without question once they're issued."

Kelso nodded. "Yes, sir. I understand, sir." Though it was

only after those words that full understanding seemed to dawn. "Then—I can stay aboard?"

"Yes, Lieutenant. The helm is still yours." Kirk felt a twinge of regret that Sulu would have to remain in astrophysics, but Kelso deserved his post. Sulu's turn would come again in time.

Kelso brightened. "Yes, sir! Thank you, sir! I promise I won't let you down again."

Kirk shook Kelso's hand, having a good feeling about the young man's future.

———

"It would appear," Spock said, "that the impact of our actions upon the Aulacri's terraforming plan was smaller than expected."

He stood beside his science station on the bridge, flanked by Sherev and Sulu. Kirk stood in the command well a few steps below them, leaning slightly against his command chair as he listened. "Go on, Mister Spock."

"The quantity of cometary volatiles released into the atmosphere was reduced by the deflection of the four large impactors. However, the lack of surface impacts means that even the small expected amount of volatile ejection into space did not occur, which partially offsets the deficit."

"Of course, the impact winter won't happen now," Sulu said, "so a lot of the water might still be lost to space over time. But with Federation help, there might be other ways to cool the planet. There were various geoengineering methods developed on Earth in the early twenty-first century, for instance, to offset the effects of global warming—before we had our own nuclear winter to cancel it out."

Sherev shook her head. "You humans got lucky. Imagine if you'd perfected antimatter bombs before that war. You might've ended up like the Karabosi. Or . . . the ancient Aulacri. I'm not sure what to call them now."

"In fact," Spock said, "I have been reviewing the biological samples discovered in the vault and running biospheric simulations. There is a breed of indigenous vegetation that grows well in arid, hot conditions and has bright foliage that reflects a fair percentage of the light that strikes it—an adaptation that prevents it from photosynthesizing its limited water and carbohydrate reserves too quickly, perhaps. If it were planted across a large portion of the planet's surface—with no competing flora and no fauna to feed upon it—it could spread to cover a fair amount of the surface area and reflect much of the star's light and heat into space, helping to bring the planet's temperature back toward a livable range for the Aulacri and Karabosi. It might achieve as much as fifty-three percent of the expected cooling effect of the impact winter, with fewer negative side effects to the planetary environment."

Kirk lifted his brows. "That's an amazing stroke of luck, Mister Spock."

"I do not believe in luck, Captain, unless you mean the stochastic operation of chance and coincidence. In this case, however, I believe there was more than chance involved. It seems likely to me that the vault builders extrapolated the effects of a global antimatter war and made sure to preserve species that could assist in bioremediation afterward. It is possible that further study of the archives might reveal more preserved species that could assist in the process."

Sherev sighed. "I guess that's my cue, Jim. That vault isn't going to study itself. I need to get back to my team on the surface."

Kirk smiled at her wistfully. "I'm glad the Aulacri asked you to stay . . . but it's a shame to see you go so soon."

"It's been fun, but we both have work to get back to. For my part, I can't wait."

"You never could."

Sherev said her goodbyes to Spock and Sulu and let Kirk lead her into the turbolift. Once they were en route to the transporter room, she said, "You know, the reason I'm okay leaving you behind with this bunch is because I can see how well you've meshed already. It may not have seemed like it, but you really came together as a unit and pulled off a difficult save very effectively." She smiled. "And that's because your team had a terrific leader pulling them together. You've grown into a very impressive captain in just a few short years, Jim."

Kirk clasped her shoulder. "I never would have without your example, and your friendship. You, Gary, Bones, Eshu, all of you helped make me the officer I am today. Even if we're not in the same crew anymore . . . I'll always carry you with me."

She put her hand atop his. "I know you will, Jim. But you know what? The same is true of Spock, Sulu, Kelso, and the rest. They will help make you the officer you'll be five years from now, and ten, and beyond. And I look forward to getting to meet that officer and see what he's achieved . . . with his crewmates and his friends at his side."

Starfleet Medical Center, San Francisco

"Bones, he needs you."

Leonard McCoy chuckled at the words from the dark-skinned Andorian *shen* on his desk screen. "Are you and Jim ganging up on me, Rhen? He told me the same thing."

"Then you know it's true," Sherev told him.

"He looked fine to me when we spoke the other week. Like he was finally where he belonged. He doesn't need me hanging around complaining all the time."

His old friend smiled. *"I think he really might be where he belongs, Leonard. He just seems to* fit *in command of the* Enterprise. *But you know how driven Jim can be, how easily he can get too caught up in his work. Obsessed, even."*

McCoy snorted. "Says the *shen* who refused to leave her work even when a comet was heading right for her."

"And when I've gone too far, I've had Jim there to bring me back. Who'll be there to bring him back?"

"Gary Mitchell's still there, right?"

Sherev scoffed. *"Gary? You expect* him *to be a tempering influence on Jim? I'm amazed he hasn't been court-martialed yet."*

"Hmm, and I suppose that Vulcan first officer wouldn't be much help. Probably incredible at his job, but with no clue about the human heart."

"You'd be surprised. I think he and Jim will work well together. But Jim needs more in his life than work. He needs friends around him, people to anchor him emotionally, like you and I did. Like Eshu did. We were a family there for a while. I miss it, Leonard. I can't get that back. But you can."

McCoy peered at her. "Are you trying to talk me into this for Jim's benefit, or for mine?"

"You tell me."

He sat back, absorbing her words. He'd left the *Sacagawea* because he'd thought he could do more good with the relief program. He'd spent the past fourteen months convincing himself that was true. But at times, it was very lonely work. Sherev's words reminded him of the sense of community, even of family, that he'd felt aboard the *Sac*, something he'd never quite felt aboard any of the past ships he'd served on. He'd thought that was a fluke, the result of serving alongside Kirk and Sherev, continuing the friendship they'd forged on Vega IX. Without Sherev around anymore, he had felt that exceptional state of affairs was over.

But now Sherev was telling him it could happen again, even without her. That he and Kirk, and Gary Mitchell and maybe others in the *Enterprise* crew, could build a community much like the one he'd known before. She had no guarantees, but she believed it was worth the attempt.

His thoughts returned to Vega, three years ago when he and Kirk had first met. He hadn't believed then that he and the cocky young captain could be friends, and neither had Kirk. They didn't share a lot in common, in background or outlook. But once the connection had been formed, Kirk had stuck with it and made it work, forging it into a fast friendship. And over the following two years, on Vega and on the *Sac*, that circle of unlikely friends had expanded and strengthened, thanks to the man at the center of it. Maybe the qualities that made him such a capable and determined leader made him a good and stalwart friend as well.

And if Kirk had done it once, maybe he could do it again.

"Okay, Rhen," McCoy said. "You talked me into it. I'll contact Jim, let him know I'll accept the CMO posting."

"That's great, Bones! I know you won't regret it."

McCoy shook his head. "Heaven knows, with bad influences like Gary and that Vulcan fellow around, Jim's gonna need *somebody* on that ship with a lick of common sense."

U.S.S. *Enterprise*

Kirk stared sourly at the three-dimensional chessboard, disturbed by how quickly Spock had positioned his bishops and queen to gain control of the center board. He would have his work cut out for him if he wanted to regain the advantage. "I've been meaning to ask, Mister Spock. Now that Karabos II is behind us, how would you assess your new commanding officer?"

Spock rested his elbows before him on the rec room table and steepled his fingers. "You are . . . more unorthodox than your reputation would suggest, Captain."

Kirk smiled. "So are you, Mister Spock. There's more to you than cold calculation. You were willing to fight for the Aulacri's benefit, to take a risk for them, even when they didn't want you to. Even after I ordered you to leave, you stood your ground and talked me out of it. That's real dedication, and I find it admirable."

Spock seemed uneasy with the praise. "I merely examined the

evidence and calculated a high probability that the information contained in the Karabosi vault would be of value to the Aulacri. The chance that it contained resources or data that would assist in their terraforming efforts was high. Therefore, it would have been counterproductive to those efforts to allow its destruction."

"You didn't mention that possibility at the time."

"I did not have sufficient evidence yet to verify it. I can see how that omission might give the impression that I acted out of intuition or emotion, but it was purely a logical calculation of probabilities."

Kirk studied him. "You're quite sure of that."

"It is still your move, Captain."

Kirk had spotted a way to clear a path from his queen's current level to an attack board that Spock seemed to have overlooked. It might well have been a trap on Spock's part, but risk was part of the game. He moved a pawn up a level to start the maneuver.

Spock promptly captured the piece with a knight to strengthen his control of the center. "If I may, Captain, I have noted a tendency in your game to sacrifice pawns too easily. It seems uncharacteristically reckless."

"A calculated risk, Mister Spock. They're only chess pieces." His ploy to focus Spock on the center while he built a path along the periphery seemed to be working. He moved his king's rook off its attack board, ostensibly to align it with Spock's king to pin his queen in place protecting it, but actually to free the movable attack board for inversion. Changing the configuration of the board in an unexpected way could create new possibilities. Taking advantage of that relative unpredictability had been the key to several of his past victories over Spock. "I assure you I don't apply the same thinking to my crew."

"Given the lengths to which you went to ensure Doctor Sherev's and my safety, I would not have thought you would."

Kirk met the Vulcan's hooded eyes. Was that a *thank you*

he sensed beneath the surface? Spock gave little away. It was quite an adjustment after a first officer as outspoken as Mehran Egdor or as open and supportive as Eshu Adebayo. But after having that thought, Kirk recalled how prickly things had been between him and Egdor at first. It hadn't been until Kirk had reached out and made an effort to bridge the gulf between them that they had started to become an effective team, and friends as well. After recent events, Kirk was already confident that he and Spock would be an effective team. As for the rest, maybe Kirk just needed to keep trying to reach out. The challenge of befriending a Vulcan was intimidating . . . but how much harder could it be than beating one at chess?

Either way, it was probably best to approach it subtly, to probe Spock's defenses before making his move. So far, they had bonded over their mutual devotion to duty, so it was best to build on that for now. "Anyway," Kirk said, "just because I respect your convictions in this case, that doesn't mean you should make a habit of putting me in spots like that. When I give an order, I expect it to be followed."

"Of course, sir. The circumstance was exceptional."

Kirk tilted his head. "One thing I've learned, Spock—out here, the exceptional can happen with surprising frequency."

Spock raised an eyebrow. "Several years ago, Captain Pike told me I should 'expect the unexpected.' When I replied that this was a contradiction in terms, he agreed, then informed me that it was nonetheless part of my job." Spock casually moved a rook in a way that served no obvious, immediate purpose, but that effectively blocked the surprise maneuver Kirk had been planning to make after moving the attack board. "Captain Pike was an excellent teacher."

Kirk stared at the board, disheartened.

Never mind, he told himself a moment later. *You've surmounted worse odds. No matter the challenge . . . there's always a way to win.*

THREE WEEKS EARLIER

Twenty-Three

Excerpted from orders to Captain James T. Kirk:

III: *You are therefore posted, effective immediately, to command the following: The U.S.S. Enterprise.*

> *Constitution-class Cruiser—Gross 190,000 tonnes*
> *Crew complement—430 persons*
> *Drive—Warp 8 class*
> *Range—18 years at standard warp factor*
> *Registry—Earth, United Starship NCC-1701*

IV: *Nature and minimum duration of assignment:*
> *Galaxy exploration and investigation; 5 years . . .*

VII: *You will conduct this patrol to accomplish primarily:*

> (a) *Federation security, via exploration of intelligence and social systems capable of a galactic threat;*
>
> (b) *Scientific investigation to add to the Federation's body of knowledge of other life-forms and social systems;*
>
> (c) *Any required assistance to the several Earth and Federation colonies in this patrol zone, and the enforcement of appropriate statutes affecting such Federated commerce vessels and traders as you may contact in the course of your mission. . . .*

> *By order of*
> *Robert L. Comsol*
> *Commanding Officer, Starfleet Command*

U.S.S. *Sacagawea*

On the one hand, the orders from Admiral Comsol had come as no surprise to Kirk. After all, he had spent nearly four years aboard the *Sacagawea* on and off, an unusual duration for a first captaincy—perhaps justified in Starfleet's eyes by the fact that it had been broken into two distinct phases with largely different crews and distinct mission profiles, thus giving him a range of experience effectively equivalent to two separate commands. But at the same time, spending so long in command of one ship had led him to form a strong attachment. It would be difficult to let her go.

Yet the fact that he was trading up to a *Constitution*-class vessel—an achievement he hadn't dreamed of experiencing for several years more at least—did much to mitigate that sense of loss. The fact that it was the *Enterprise*, one of the first and most accomplished ships of the class, was a particular honor. The opportunity to work alongside Commander Spock, who had been of such value in the Agni crisis, was also welcome, though Kirk was unsure how he felt about the prospect of Spock as his first officer. Adebayo had declined to transfer with him, insisting that it was time for Kirk to leave the nest while the elder officer shepherded some other young captain. Kirk had then requested that Starfleet transfer Gary Mitchell along with him and promote him to first officer. If he were to take on such an imposing assignment as the captaincy of the *Enterprise*, he wanted a second-in-command he knew and trusted by his side, and he hoped that the greater responsibility would give Gary some much-needed tempering. But Captain Pike had insisted that Spock remain as first officer and Starfleet had agreed, so Mitchell had only been approved as Kirk's second officer. Kirk had already summoned him back from his extended leave, and he would be joining Kirk on the *Enterprise* in a few days.

For now, Kirk had only Eshu Adebayo to see him off in the transporter room, along with Engineer Desai and Dr. Wachs, neither of whom he'd ever developed more than a professional relationship with. The two junior officers said their formal goodbyes, and then it came down to Adebayo, who pulled Kirk into a fatherly embrace. "I'll miss your guidance, Eshu," Kirk told him. "I've learned so much aboard this ship. We've achieved so many great things together."

"And you will achieve even greater things aboard the *Enterprise*," the older man said. "And beyond, in all your future commands. I have no doubt of it. One day, people will look back on the career of James Kirk, and the *Sacagawea* will be a mere footnote that hardly anyone remembers."

"I refuse to believe that. This has been the finest crew I've ever served with."

"A crew is shaped by its captain. Your responsibility on the *Enterprise* will be to shape one even finer."

Kirk took one final look around the transporter room and drew in a deep breath. "Then I guess I'd better get to it." He shook Adebayo's hand one last time before climbing onto the platform. "Thank you, Commander. It's been a great honor."

"And a great joy. Good luck, Jim. And may the wind be at your back."

U.S.S. *Enterprise*

Kirk had never met Christopher Pike before, but the captain's reputation preceded him. The man himself was far less imposing, a serious but relaxed individual with graying hair and an accessible, unassuming manner. Kirk took to him instantly and regretted that their paths were crossing so briefly.

Commander Spock, who stood stiffly behind Pike when the outgoing captain met the incoming one in the *Enterprise* transporter room, was another matter. His greeting to Kirk was perfunctory. "Welcome aboard, Captain Kirk. Your service record is impressive. I shall have a full report on vessel personnel and operations available for your perusal within the hour. I was not anticipating your early arrival."

"That's . . . fine, Commander Spock," Kirk said before Pike dismissed the other man. Once Spock departed, Kirk gazed after him and said, "That was . . . brief."

Pike clapped him on the back. "Not every first meeting is one for the books. But for Spock, that was a downright friendly greeting. He's trying to do something useful for you, to provide information. For a Vulcan, that's basically like sending flowers. And Spock is as Vulcan as they come."

Kirk frowned. "His service record said he's half-human."

Pike smirked. "Which is why he tries so hard to be all Vulcan."

The older captain took Kirk on a tour of the *Enterprise*—as much to give himself one last loving look as to familiarize his replacement, judging from the expression on his face and the wistful tone in his voice. Once they finally reached the observation lounge to share a drink, Kirk felt compelled to say, "Captain Pike—"

"Call me Chris."

Kirk smiled. "And I'm Jim. Chris, if it's all right to ask . . . how can you stand to give up starship command? It's all I've ever aspired to. And I can tell it isn't easy for you to walk away."

Pike was slow to answer, nursing his drink. "Let's just say I realized I needed a break from the responsibility. Maybe someday you'll feel the same. Or who knows—maybe you'll handle the burden better than I could."

"I'm sorry. I didn't mean to pry."

"No, I'm sorry. I have this maudlin side that comes out sometimes. This shouldn't be the time for it. We're both moving up in the galaxy. Moving on to new challenges, new horizons. We should be happy."

"I am. But I understand how hard it is to leave the old horizons behind."

Pike chuckled. "I think I've had a few more of those than you." He went on more seriously. "So I hope you'll take some advice from an old soldier."

Kirk leaned closer. "Of course. I welcome any insight you have to offer."

The outgoing captain gathered his thoughts. "Spock was right—your service record is very impressive. It shows a serious, dedicated officer who has great respect for rules and regulations."

"Thank you, sir," Kirk said, straightening by reflex.

"But that's not why I recommended you to replace me, Jim. What got my attention was that you know how to look beyond the rules. In the Agni encounter, your training told you to think like a soldier, to defend against a threat—but you had the imagination, and the compassion, to look beyond your training and take a chance on peace. Before that, with the Chenari, you looked beyond the strict letter of the Prime Directive and recognized that its spirit was about respecting other species' right to survive on their own terms, not about us deciding their fate for them."

Kirk lowered his head. "Those were hard-won lessons, Chris. I almost didn't see those options."

"But you did, when it counted. And you're going to face a lot more challenges like that out on the frontier." Pike shook his head. "A lot of people back home, they look at us captains out in deep space and call us mavericks, cowboys who play fast and loose with the rules. They don't understand that it's a captain's *job* to interpret the rules. Out on the frontier, days or weeks from contact with Starfleet Command, captains are often the highest or only Federation authorities on the scene. So we have a responsibility to interpret and adapt the regulations to fit the unpredictable situations we face."

Kirk nodded. "I'm aware of that responsibility, sir."

Pike softened. "I know you are, Jim. Your actions proved that. Not only the fact that you bent the rules when you had to, but the fact that you were slow to do so. True, I've seen captains and other officers fail by being too inflexible in dealing with the unknown and unprecedented. But I've also seen them go too far astray, even become a danger to their crews and others. It's a narrow tightrope we walk out there. I believe you have the judgment to walk it—to adjust your footing when you need to without stepping too far and overbalancing." He shrugged. "Or however tightrope walking works. That metaphor drew me in deeper than I intended." The two men shared a laugh.

"The point is, that judgment only works if you believe in it. Of course it's healthy to stop and question your decisions before you act on them. That's what keeps us honest. It's what laws like the Prime Directive are for—to remind us of our fallibility, to make us stop and think before we act. It's when those other captains stopped questioning their own rightness that they started to go wrong.

"But you have to make sure you keep perspective. Question yourself, yes. Be honest about your failures—and you will have failures, that's a given—and keep trying to do better. But don't wallow in it. Don't indulge your doubts and recriminations to the point where they eat you alive. That's always been my own greatest weakness. My old doctor used to say I set standards for myself that no human could meet, then beat myself up for falling short of them."

Kirk stared. "I have a doctor friend who said the same thing about me."

"I'm not surprised," Pike said. "We're a lot alike, I think. Maybe that's why I feel the *Enterprise* is in such good hands with you." He leaned forward and put a hand on Kirk's wrist. "And that's why I hope you take my advice. Cut yourself a break. Keep that discipline and that flexibility, but *trust* yourself to know which to use when.

"More importantly—trust your crew. Let them into your life, your decisions. There's a temptation for men like us to isolate ourselves. To be so dedicated to our careers that we close ourselves off socially. I note that you're single—so am I," he went on before Kirk could formulate an answer or protest. "It's not an uncommon affliction in our profession. But that doesn't mean we have to be alone. We have our crews, and they can be more than just subordinates if we let them. It's valuable to have friends by your side that you can lean on, because there will be times when you're too weak or too tired to stand on your own."

Kirk nodded gravely. "I've always valued having friends by my side. My incoming second officer, Lieutenant Commander Mitchell, has been with me on and off since the Academy. We're practically inseparable by now."

"That's good—but be open to the new friendships you could make among the *Enterprise* crew. I admit, many of the ones I was closest to have moved on, but you're inheriting a good bunch of people. Be open to the possibility that they could be more than just your crew."

The younger captain chuckled. "I'm not sure there's much chance of Mister Spock and I becoming bosom pals."

Pike gave a gentle smile. "You'd be surprised. Just give him a chance. Do you play three-dimensional chess?"

Kirk perked up. "At a master level."

Pike's smile widened. "Then I think you and Spock will hit it off just fine."

TWO MONTHS LATER

Epilogue

U.S.S. *Enterprise*

"The edge of the galaxy?"

Kirk repeated Admiral Komack's words in disbelief, staring at the gray-haired senior officer on the desk screen in his quarters. When Komack had ordered him to divert the *Enterprise* to the Aldebaran Colony to pick up new personnel and sensor equipment for a special scientific mission, he had been momentarily distracted by the destination, aware that Janet Miller—no, Janet Wallace now—was still stationed there. He had promptly filed the data away as irrelevant; after all, it had been Janet who had taught him that a starship captain's life had no room for romance. But in his distraction, he wasn't sure he'd heard the admiral correctly. "With all due respect, sir," he said, "are you making some sort of joke? We both know the galaxy has no definable edge."

Komack nodded. *"Just a gradual thinning out with distance, of course. That's true of the stellar disk, and we* thought *it was true of the interstellar medium as well."*

"You mean it isn't, sir?"

"Not entirely, at least. A deep-space survey conducted by the Delta Vega Mining Consortium discovered a subspace lane last year that gave them a significantly reduced travel time to the southern face of the galactic inner disk, several hundred parsecs away." Kirk nodded in realization. Of course the actual *rim* of the

galaxy, the first thing he'd thought of, was decades away at top warp, so naturally it had to be one of the much nearer faces of the Milky Way's flat disk. It embarrassed him that after so many years in space, he was still subject to two-dimensional thinking. *"They kept it proprietary at first,"* Komack went on, *"but the astrometric data their long-range probes gathered was significant enough that they brought it to the Federation Science Council.*

"Apparently, there's a discontinuity in the interstellar medium running roughly parallel to the face of the disk, a plane beyond which the gas density drops off abruptly. Almost as if there's some sort of filter or barrier there, something that stars can pass through but interstellar gas and dust have a harder time with. Or maybe it's some sort of soliton wave in the medium, a resonance of some kind that causes the discontinuity. We don't know how far it spreads, whether it's a local anomaly of the region within sensor range or a property of the whole disk. The Consortium's long-range probes can't detect anything that could be causing it. Maybe a starship observing the phenomenon at point-blank range—or even crossing the boundary and looking back from the outside— could have better luck."

Kirk furrowed his brow. "That's . . . an interesting astrophysical mystery, sir. But it hardly seems sufficient reason to send a starship. I'd expected that we'd be assigned to proceed with the five-year general survey tour as planned."

"And you will be, once this mission is concluded. Believe me, Command is more than satisfied with your work so far. Your recent efforts at Mestiko may not have been as successful as we'd hoped, but you helped prevent a much worse outcome. And your work at Karabos II was exceptional. The Aulacri have already submitted their formal application for Federation membership and invited Federation medical and archaeological teams to work with them on restoring the Karabosi population. Which suggests they expect our relationship to last a very long time.

"But there are other potential benefits to this mission to the

edge. This is a rare opportunity to get 'above' the mass of the galaxy's stars and dust clouds and get a more unobstructed look at the core and the far half of the Milky Way—like climbing to the top of a tree to get a peek above the canopy, see the lay of the land. The benefits to our galactic mapping program could be enormous. And observing intergalactic space without the interstellar medium in the way could reveal . . . well, think of x-ray astronomy, all the discoveries that were impossible until we were able to observe space from beyond the Earth's atmosphere. This could be a comparable breakthrough, if we're lucky.

"At the very least," Komack went on, "the subspace lane will be exploited in the decades ahead. Ships will travel to the edge out of curiosity, if nothing else. Eventually there will be trade outposts and colonies along the lane. The Delta Vega Consortium has already set up one of their deep-space automated mining outposts to supply future expeditions. Which might come in handy for the Enterprise while you're out there."

"I understand, Admiral," Kirk said. "It will be a long trip both ways, but it should be worth it."

He must have sounded unconvinced, for Komack grew wry. "Take my advice, Captain. Learn to appreciate the slow, boring missions when you get them. Out there on the frontier, they can be all too rare. Take the opportunity to get to know your ship and crew better," the admiral suggested. "You'll be spending the next five years with them, after all."

Kirk gave a thought to the new crewmates he'd seen in action over the past weeks—Spock, Kelso, Scott, Sulu, Alden, Uhura. They measured up well to the likes of Mitchell, Egdor, Khorasani, Sherev, McCoy, Adebayo, Diaz, and all the others he'd commanded on the Sacagawea. Kirk had learned a great deal from his crew over his years on that ship, and the accomplishments that had earned him the captaincy of the Enterprise would never have been possible without them. He would always remember his first crew, but he looked forward to finding out what his new crew could teach him, and what they would achieve together over the years to come.

Once Komack had signed off and transmitted the formal orders packet, Kirk loaded the course information onto a data card and headed up to the bridge. Emerging into the domed, circular command center, he took a moment to watch his crew at their work—Scott at engineering, Alden at communications performing a systems check alongside Uhura, Kelso and Mitchell side by side at flight control, Sulu filling in at sciences while Spock sat in the command chair, examining a report that had been handed to him by Yeoman Maynard—and looked forward to getting to know them better on the long trip ahead. (Well, all except Maynard, who had been granted a hardship transfer to care for a dying relative and would be leaving the ship at their next port of call. Kirk had barely gotten used to having a yeoman, and now he'd have to adjust to a new one.)

After signing the report and handing it back to Maynard, Spock turned to face Kirk. "Captain."

"I relieve you," Kirk said, stepping down in the command well as Spock vacated the chair.

"I stand relieved."

"Ship's status?"

"All systems functioning normally. The deflector grid recalibrations are performing well within expected parameters, and Commander Scott has already proposed several enhancements. Ship's stores are fully restocked, and all personnel stand ready."

"Very good, Mister Spock. Because we have our next assignment—and it's a doozy."

The Vulcan furrowed his brows. "I am not familiar with that mission designation, sir."

Kirk smiled. "Don't worry, you'll have plenty of time to figure it out." He stepped over to Gary Mitchell, putting a hand on the back of his seat. "Navigator, set course for Aldebaran III. Mister Kelso, engage at warp factor four when ready."

Mitchell looked up at him. "Aldebaran? That doesn't sound like a doozy."

"That's just our starting point. We'll be picking up personnel and equipment there. Once that's done, you're to enter this course." He handed Mitchell the data card and winked. "Trust me, Gary, you're gonna love it."

"Captain," Spock asked, "what is the purpose of the new personnel and equipment?"

"They're to assist us in a scientific survey, Mister Spock."

"What manner of survey, Captain?" Spock asked, trying but failing to avoid sounding intrigued.

Kirk smiled. "The kind this ship was made for, Commander. We're going to fulfill Starfleet's motto quite literally."

"Starfleet's motto, sir?"

"You know the one, Spock. 'To boldly go . . .'"

THE BEGINNING

Acknowledgments

My goal in this book was to show the events that shaped Captain Kirk into the man we met in the first season of *Star Trek: The Original Series*, a Kirk who was more disciplined, serious, and emotionally detached than he became later on (as, for instance, in "Mudd's Women," where Kirk was the only human male on the ship unaffected by the title characters' allure). My portrait of Kirk may challenge some readers' expectations about the character, but that was essentially my intent—to refute the popular myths and perceptions that have grown up around James T. Kirk and paint a portrait more closely rooted in the textual evidence from TOS. This is my homage to the Kirk I met forty-five years ago, before most of the mythology had formed around the character, and my attempt to fill in the largely unexplored gap in his pre-*Enterprise* biography, much as I did for Jean-Luc Picard in *Star Trek: The Next Generation—The Buried Age* a dozen years ago.

As a result, I've drawn on information from numerous canonical and related sources, particularly *The Making of Star Trek* by Stephen E. Whitfield and Gene Roddenberry, the only source we have about Kirk's first command (described therein as the equivalent of a destroyer-sized vessel) besides a throwaway line in the second pilot. For once, I'll try to keep my acknowledgments brief; I'll no doubt provide more detail in my online annotations. The screenwriters whose characters and concepts I've utilized in this book include Stanley Adams, Margaret Armen, Harve Bennett, Rick Berman, Kenneth Biller, Robert Bloch, Brannon Braga, Steven W. Carabatsos, Lawrence V. Conley, Gene L. Coon, Oliver Crawford, James Crocker, Robert Doherty, D.C. Fontana, David Gerrold, Robert Hamner, David P. Harmon, Maurice Hurley, Don Ingalls, Robert Lewin, David Loughery, Don M. Mankiewicz, Joe Menosky, Samuel L. Peeples, Gene Roddenberry, Sam Rolfe, Paul Schneider, George F. Slavin, Jack B. Sowards, Jeri Taylor, Art Wallace, Shimon Wincelberg, and Laurence N. Wolfe. Novel and comics authors whose works I've done my best to stay consistent with include Margaret Wander Bonanno, Keith R.A. DeCandido, Kevin Dilmore, Julia Ecklar, David R. George III, David Mack, Steve Mollmann, S.D. Perry, Michael Schuster, Scott & David Tipton, Dayton Ward, Howard Weinstein, and Phaedra M. Weldon. Other authors and artists whose fiction, reference works, or other creations I've borrowed from, homaged, or paraphrased include Mike W. Barr, John Byrne, Paula Crist, Doug Drexler, Lora Johnson, Geoffrey Mandel, Masao Okazaki, Michael Okuda, Eileen Palestine, Franz Joseph Schnaubelt, and the unknown author of the "Captain James T. Kirk: Psycho-File" featurette in Gold Key Comics' 1976 *Star Trek: The Enterprise Logs, Volume 1*. The poem "Sea-Fever" was published by John Masefield in 1902. The "Earth poet" Kirk paraphrases in Chapter Seven is Stephen Crane, specifically his 1899 poem "A Man Said to the Universe."

Thanks are due to Jim Johnson for recruiting me to write for the *Star Trek Adventures* role-playing game, since several of this novel's major story threads started out as potential game ideas. The frame storyline was also inspired by the article "In Sudan, Rediscovering Ancient Nubia Before It's Too Late" by Amy Maxmen, *Undark* 2/19/2018. A couple of other ideas herein were sparked by discussions with Keith R.A. DeCandido and the commenters in his *Star Trek* rewatch threads at Tor.com. A suggestion from "jayrath" on the TrekBBS helped me figure out why the *Enterprise* has no ready room.

My initial inspiration for the idea of life using a sulfuric acid solvent came from *Science Fiction Writing Series: World-Building* by Stephen L. Gillett (Writer's Digest Books, 1996); however, that book suggests it in the context of silicon-based life, which Starfleet does not encounter until a couple of years after this novel. The alternative of carbon-carbon covalent bonds in sulfuric acid comes from Chapter 6 of National Research Council 2007, *The Limits of Organic Life in Planetary Systems*, Washington, DC: The National Academies Press, https://doi.org/10.17226/11919. Information on the potential for bacterial life in the upper atmosphere of a Venus-type world comes from "Could Dark Streaks in Venus' Clouds Be Microbial Life?" by Keith Cooper, *Astrobiology at NASA*, Feb. 1, 2017, and from the web page "Life on Venus?" at http://www.solstation.com/life/ven-life.htm.

Finally, a particular thanks to the fans who came through for me with their generous donations at a point when my financial situation was desperate. My deep gratitude to Vasilios Arabatzis II, Byron Bailey, Matthew Buck, Scott Crick, Adam Czarnecki, Michael Evans, Shawn Fox, David Gian-Cursio, Justin Hilyard, Mari Johnson, Ronald Mallory, Cody Lee Martin, Daniel Nicholls, Bernd Perplies, Troy Rodgers, Johanna Schliemann, Clive Viagas, Christian Zenker, Mark Zieba, and everyone else who helped.

About the Author

Christopher L. Bennett is a lifelong resident of Cincinnati, Ohio, with bachelor's degrees in physics and history from the University of Cincinnati. He has written such critically acclaimed *Star Trek* novels as *Ex Machina* and *The Buried Age*; the *Star Trek: Titan* novels *Orion's Hounds* and *Over a Torrent Sea*; the *Department of Temporal Investigations* series, including the novels *Watching the Clock* and *Forgotten History*; and the *Star Trek: Enterprise— Rise of the Federation* series. His shorter works include stories in the anniversary anthologies *Constellations*, *The Sky's the Limit*, *Prophecy and Change*, and *Distant Shores*. Beyond Star Trek, he has penned the novels *X-Men: Watchers on the Walls* and *Spider-Man: Drowned in Thunder*. His original work includes the hard science fiction superhero novel *Only Superhuman* and various works of short fiction in *Analog* and other magazines, most of which have been collected in the volumes *Among the Wild Cybers: Tales Beyond the Superhuman*, *Hub Space: Tales from the Greater Galaxy*, and *Crimes of the Hub*. More information, ordering links, annotations, and the author's blog can be found at christopherlbennett.wordpress.com.